THE CLASSIC FAVOURITE
FAIRY TALES OF
ANDERSEN &
GRIMM

The Snow Queen. (Edmund Dulac)

THE CLASSIC FAVOURITE
FAIRY TALES OF
ANDERSEN
& GRIMM

WORTH
PRESS

Concept, design, introduction text and treatment
© Worth Press Ltd 2012.
Introductions © 2012 Charles Mosley and Peter Harness.

First published 2012 by Worth Press Limited, Cambridge, UK
www.worthpress.co.uk

British Library Publication Data
A catalogue record for this book is available from the British Library.

ISBN 978-1-84931-064-2

10 9 8 7 6 5 4 3 2 1

Designed, edited and typeset by Bookcraft Limited, Stroud, Gloucestershire, UK
Printed and bound in China by Imago

CONTENTS

HANS CHRISTIAN ANDERSEN'S FAIRY TALES

THE BROTHERS GRIMM'S FAIRY TALES

ANDERSEN'S FAIRY TALES

HANS CHRISTIAN ANDERSEN'S FAIRY TALES
INTRODUCTION BY CHARLES MOSLEY

What is a fairy tale? Before Hans Christian Andersen, it was a kind of moral fable set in a parallel world, though not necessarily a world populated by fairies. It might or might not concern a fairy-tale romance, and there was no guarantee of a happy outcome – the proverbial fairy-tale ending. But what all fairy tales did have in common before Andersen was that they were from the oral tradition, passed on from generation to generation, from long, long ago, disseminated by wandering storytellers from region to region, culture to culture. Before Andersen there were no authors of fairy tales. There were only collectors of fairy tales.

The term 'fairy tale' itself is quite recent, invented, probably, by a racy French writer called Marie-Catherine d'Aulnoy, who published a volume of traditional folk tales in 1697 with the title *Les Contes des Fées* ('Stories of the Fairies'), among them a version of Cinderella. But these were distinctly adult stories of the kind declaimed in the fashionable salons of the day. They were not for children.

By curious coincidence in the same year, another French writer, Charles Perrault, a retired civil servant from the court of King Louis XIV, also produced a book of old tales he had collected under a title that translates as *Stories of the Past with Morals*. These were intended for children – in particular his own children – and for their benefit he subtitled the book *Tales of Mother Goose*. Included were stories we know today as Little Red Riding Hood, Sleeping Beauty, and a version of Cinderella quite different from the one rendered by Madame d'Aulnoy.

Perrault's was in effect the first collection of children's fairy tales, and established this sort of story as a genre in literature. The next major collection was to appear a century later, when the German folklorists Jacob and Wilhelm Grimm added their fairy tales to the published canon between 1812 and 1815.

At this time, Hans Christian Andersen was in his childhood. He was born on 2nd April 1805 in Odense, a rural town on Denmark's island of Funen, now the country's third city, and named, suitably enough, after the mythic Norse god Odin. The Andersens were ordinary folk, his father struggling as a shoemaker, intelligent but unschooled and prone to depression, but always gratefully remembered by his son, who liked to recall that his father read to him from the *Arabian Nights*, and encouraged his early interest in theatre. Andersen died in 1816, but by then might have had an inkling of his son's potential. Hans had a fine soprano voice, read voraciously, and was already attempting to write plays to enact on the toy stage he and his father had built together, complete with cut-out paper characters or dolls, for which the lad took pleasure in sewing tiny costumes – a predilection that aroused unkind comment among his peers.

He was a lonely boy, gangly and unprepossessing. His family, even among the poorest of Odense, were looked down on. His mother had had an illegitimate child before Hans, a daughter who turned to prostitution (and later attempted to blackmail her half-brother). It did not help that the boy's paternal grandfather was confined to an insane asylum, and that his aunt kept a brothel.

For five hard years after his father's death, he seems to have experienced little other than poverty and alienation in what was then an out-of-the-way region of pre-industrial Denmark. He tried and failed, among other brief endeavours, to be apprenticed to a tailor, but did acquire the beginnings of an education, and through the harsh experiences of his young life, the genesis of many stories. Equally important, he discovered his own courage. He carefully saved up the small sums of money he earned from singing at private recitals and municipal events and obtained a passport (then compulsory for inter-regional travel) for Copenhagen. In September of 1819, aged 14, he set out for the capital, resolved on making his name as a playwright, or at the very least an actor in metropolitan theatre. It might now all sound the stuff of fairy tales, but in Andersen's case his childhood and this brave escape from it were an all-too prosaic reality, including the unhappy ending to the two-day journey by coach to the great city. He could not afford the whole fare, and had to walk the last ten miles to Copenhagen's gates.

He did find work on the stage, more by way of persistence than talent, and largely thanks to his singing voice, and managed, barely, to subsist. In 1822 he came across the piece of luck that, in the proper story-book tradition, transforms so many great lives. In a dancing role in a production at Copenhagen's Royal Theatre, he caught the attention of a senior public servant and director of the theatre, Jonas Collin, who fortuitously was also a leading philanthropist and patron of the arts. Collin may have heard a rumour, never substantiated, that the decidedly odd-looking boy might have been distantly related to the royal family, but for whatever reason Collin saw something in Andersen and introduced him to the king, Frederick VI. The monarch was duly impressed and Hans was dispatched on a full bursary to the country's foremost grammar school at Slagelse, 60 miles south of Copenhagen. So backward was the 17-year-old in the traditional curriculum that he was enrolled in a class of boys aged 11, which he found deeply humiliating. He remained at school, miserable and abused according to his own account, for five more years before Collin considered him sufficiently versed (though he never learned to spell well, and might have been dyslexic) to take up the career in literature his patron believed him fitted for.

The faith Collin, who was to remain a lifelong friend, had shown in his protégé was gradually warranted. Back in Copenhagen in 1827, where he was put up at the Collin family home, Andersen produced an extraordinary extended article with the title *A Journey on Foot from Holman's Canal to the East Point of Amager*. A whimsical, autobiographical fantasy that included a graphic prediction of routine air travel, the little volume was published in German as well as Danish, and provided its author with his first measurable literary earnings. A book of poetry followed, and a comic play.

Now in his mid-twenties, Andersen also embarked on the first of his several unhappy love affairs, with the sister of one of his friends. It came to nothing, and he turned for sympathy to Louise Collin, daughter of his patron. She indulged him, but he mistook her kindness for something more, and thought himself in love with her too. She had other plans. It might have been no coincidence that her father at this time obtained for Andersen a modest royal grant, to enable him to spend the next two years travelling in Europe.

This was the turning point. He went through 29 different countries, met fellow writers and folklorists along the way, read avidly, and accumulated vast quantities of notes. Returning to Copenhagen in 1835, he published a novel based in Italy, *The Improvisatore*, which became an immediate success. And he produced, too, his debut booklet of *Eventyr fortalte for Børn*, fairy tales told for children. He recorded a conversation about the stories in March 1835 with a scientist friend: 'Ørsted says of them that if *The Improvisatore* makes me famous, these tales will make me immortal, as they are the most perfect things I have ever written – even if I don't think so myself.'

These first stories, including *The Princess and the Pea* and *The Tinder Box* (both in this edition), astounded Denmark's literary establishment. Although ostensibly targeted at younger readers, Andersen had adopted a realism hitherto unknown in the genre, along with a plainness of language, a clarity of moral, and an openly satirical humour, all shockingly new. With what could legitimately be called a child-like directness, Andersen brought a new kind of wonder into his writing, animating humble objects and every kind of creature with a powerful verve, championing the oppressed, and daring to ridicule the entrenched order. He admitted he had taken adult readers into consideration: 'I take an idea for the grown-ups then tell the story for the little ones always remembering that Father and Mother are quite likely to be listening. They too must be given something for their minds.'

It took two more years for Andersen to complete the first volume of his *Fairy Tales*, including *The Little Mermaid* in 1836 and *The Emperor's New Clothes* in 1837. The second series, completed in the following year, included *The Galoshes of Good Fortune*, *The Steadfast Tin Soldier* and *The Wild Swans*. There were many other works to follow, such as the novel *O.T.* and a popular romance *Only a Fiddler*, a number of little-remembered plays, and the hugely successful miscellanies *The Picture-Book without Pictures* and *Poet's Bazaar* of 1840–42. These adult works probably earned more for

Andersen than his fairy tales in these early days, particularly in Denmark, where his radically new approach to children's writing caught on but slowly. But by 1845, when the third volume of fairy tales (*The Nightingale*, *The Red Shoes*, *The Snow Queen* and *The Ugly Duckling* among them) was published, the author's renown had crossed many boundaries, largely thanks to the continual tours he took in Europe to give talks, meet other writers and promote his own work. Everything he wrote was translated at once into German and a fast-growing number of other languages. He was taken up in English by translator and periodical publisher Mary Howitt, who worked from German translations (Danish speakers were few in England) and thus produced rather distanced versions of the originals. But the Andersen magic got through, and he became so popular that he decided on a visit in 1847.

He was fêted wherever he went, entertained at the home of the Foreign Secretary Lord Palmerston, where he reported that 'English ladies overwhelmed me with their praise for *The Ugly Duckling*' and he met 'the highest of the nobility'. The newspapers, according to Andersen's own version, dubbed him 'one of the most remarkable and interesting men of his day'. The poet and publisher Leigh Hunt, who met Andersen at the home of statesman Lord Stanley, enthused equivocally that 'he looks like a large child, a sort of half-angel,' but added 'There were many people of rank present, yet no one in the room looked more *distingué* than Andersen, the shoemaker's son'.

The zenith for Andersen came near the end of his visit at another grand reception. As he recalled it, he was signing a book when 'a man entered the room, just like the portrait we have all seen, someone who had come to town for my sake and had written "I *must* see Andersen!" We seized both each other's hands, gazed into each other's eyes and laughed with joy. We knew each other so well, though it was our first meeting. It was Charles Dickens.' On his last day, departing from Ramsgate, Andersen was thrilled to find Dickens standing on the wharf. 'He had walked from Broadstairs to wish me goodbye, wearing a green Scots dress coat and colourful shirt – so very, elegantly English. His was the last hand I shook in England.'

Andersen did return to Kent a decade later to visit Dickens and his family at their home, notoriously overstaying his welcome ('we are suffering a good deal from Andersen,' Dickens wrote in the fifth week), but this sort of gaucheness did not diminish the Dane's influence in English writing. Andersen was midwife to children's literature in the century in which childhood was invented. Victorian Britain's brutal exploitation of child labour and the new, if sentimental, compassion for children that grew from it found poignant expression in Andersen's stories. They were the first that animated the fantasies of children, and that spoke in their voices. The fairy tales were to inspire Lewis Carroll and those many who followed. Looking back from the early twentieth century, G.K. Chesterton shrewdly observed that 'When the English romantics wanted to find the folk-tale spirit still alive … they found a whole fairyland under one head and under one nineteenth-century top hat. Those of the English who were then children owe to Hans Andersen more than to any of their own writers, the essential educational emotion which feels that domesticity is not dull but rather fantastic; that sense of the fairyland of the furniture, and the travel and adventure of the farmyard.'

The unique conviction Andersen brought to his writing – *The Ugly Duckling* is more piquantly personal than any reference Dickens made in his fiction to his own troubled childhood – is as significant as his inventiveness in keeping his stories so fresh and so in demand for so long. The tales have been translated into more than one hundred languages, and have been endlessly adapted for the theatre and cinema, ballet and opera. The biographical movie of 1952 starring American actor Danny Kaye extended Andersen's work to a huge worldwide audience, and Kaye's renderings into unforgettable songs of The Ugly Duckling and The Emperor's New Clothes continue to resonate for post-war generations.

Andersen wrote and travelled extensively all his life, including several distinguished travel books, further novels, plays and books of verse. He continued to produce the *Fairy Tales*, in instalments, until 1872. In the spring of that year he injured himself in an accident falling out of bed and never fully recovered. He died aged seventy in 1875. Denmark's great storyteller is commemorated in a museum at Odense which includes a restoration of the Andersen family's one-room home, and there is an impressive statue of him in front of the town hall in Copenhagen. A further tribute stands on the Langeline Quay in the city's harbour, a fine bronze of The Little Mermaid, seated on a rock, unveiled in 1913. The figure is no larger than that of a child, and is among the most-visited monuments in the world.

The Little Mermaid. (Margaret Tarrant)

Hans Christian Andersen's Fairy Tales

The Tinder Box

THERE CAME A soldier marching down the high road – one, two! one, two! He had his knapsack on his back and his sword at his side as he came home from the wars. On the road he met a witch, an ugly old witch, a witch whose lower lip dangled right down on her chest.

"Good evening, soldier," she said. "What a fine sword you've got there, and what a big knapsack. Aren't you every inch a soldier! And now you shall have money, as much as you please."

"That's very kind, you old witch," said the soldier.

"See that big tree." The witch pointed to one near by them. "It's hollow to the roots. Climb to the top of the trunk and you'll find a hole through which you can let yourself down deep under the tree. I'll tie a rope around your middle, so that when you call me I can pull you up again."

"What would I do deep down under that tree?" the soldier wanted to know.

"Fetch money," the witch said. "Listen. When you touch bottom you'll find yourself in a great hall. It is very bright there, because more than a hundred lamps are burning. By their light you will see three doors. Each door has a key in it, so you can open them all.

"If you walk into the first room, you'll see a large chest in the middle of the floor. On it sits a dog, and his eyes are as big as saucers. But don't worry about that. I'll give you my blue checked apron to spread out on the floor. Snatch up that dog and set him on my apron. Then you can open the chest and take out as many pieces of money as you please. They are all copper.

"But if silver suits you better, then go into the next room. There sits a dog and his eyes are as big as mill wheels. But don't you care about that. Set the dog on my apron while you line your pockets with silver.

"Maybe you'd rather have gold. You can, you know. You can have all the gold you can carry if you go into the third room. The only hitch is that there on the money-chest sits a dog, and each of his eyes is as big as the Round Tower of Copenhagen. That's the sort of dog he is. But never you mind how fierce he looks. Just set him on my apron and he'll do you no harm as you help yourself from the chest to all the gold you want."

"That suits me," said the soldier. "But what do you get out of all this, you old witch? I suppose that you want your share."

"No indeed," said the witch. "I don't want a penny of it. All I ask is for you to fetch me

"Good evening, soldier," she said. "What a fine sword you've got there, and what a big knapsack."
(Lucy Mabel Attwell)

an old tinder box that my grandmother forgot the last time she was down there."

"Good," said the soldier. "Tie the rope around me."

"Here it is," said the witch, "and here's my blue checked apron."

The soldier climbed up to the hole in the tree and let himself slide through it, feet foremost down into the great hall where the hundreds of lamps were burning, just as the witch had said. Now he threw open the first door he came to. Ugh! There sat a dog glaring at him with eyes as big as saucers.

"You're a nice fellow," the soldier said, as he shifted him to the witch's apron and took all the coppers that his pockets would hold. He shut up the chest, set the dog back on it, and made for the second room. Alas and alack! There sat the dog with eyes as big as mill wheels.

"Don't you look at me like that." The soldier set him on the witch's apron. "You're apt to

strain your eyesight." When he saw the chest brimful of silver, he threw away all his coppers and filled both his pockets and knapsack with silver alone. Then he went into the third room. Oh, what a horrible sight to see! The dog in there really did have eyes as big as the Round Tower, and when he rolled them they spun like wheels.

"Good evening," the soldier said, and saluted, for such a dog he had never seen before. But on second glance he thought to himself, "This won't do." So he lifted the dog down to the floor, and threw open the chest. What a sight! Here was gold and to spare. He could buy out all Copenhagen with it. He could buy all the cake-woman's sugar pigs, and all the tin soldiers, whips, and rocking horses there are in the world. Yes, *there* was really money!

In short order the soldier got rid of all the silver coins he had stuffed in his pockets and knapsack, to put gold in their place. Yes sir, he crammed all his pockets, his knapsack, his cap, and his boots so full that he scarcely could walk. Now he made of money. Putting the dog back on the chest he banged out the door and called up through the hollow tree:

"Pull me up now, you old witch."

"Have you got the tinder box?" asked the witch.

"Confound the tinder box," the soldier shouted. "I clean forgot it."

When he fetched it, the witch hauled him up. There he stood on the highroad again, with his pockets, boots, knapsack and cap full of gold.

"What do you want with the tinder box?" he asked the old witch.

"None of your business," she told him. "You've had your money, so hand over my tinder box."

"Nonsense," said the soldier. "I'll take out my sword and I'll cut your head off if you don't tell me at once what you want with it."

There sat a dog glaring at him with eyes as big as saucers. (Harry Clark)

13

"I won't," the witch screamed at him.

So he cut her head off. There she lay! But he tied all his money in her apron, slung it over his shoulder, stuck the tinder box in his pocket, and struck out for town.

It was a splendid town. He took the best rooms at the best inn, and ordered all the good things he liked to eat, for he was a rich man now because he had so much money. The servant who cleaned his boots may have thought them remarkably well worn for a man of such means, but that was before he went shopping. Next morning he bought boots worthy of him, and the best clothes. Now that he had turned out to be such a fashionable gentleman, people told him all about the splendors of their town – all about their King, and what a pretty Princess he had for a daughter.

"Where can I see her?" the soldier inquired.

"You can't see her at all," everyone said. "She lives in a great copper castle inside all sorts of walls and towers. Only the King can come in or go out of it, for it's been foretold that the Princess will marry a common soldier. The King would much rather she didn't."

"I'd like to see her just the same," the soldier thought. But there was no way to manage it.

Now he lived a merry life. He went to the theater, drove about in the King's garden, and gave away money to poor people. This was to his credit, for he remembered from the old days what it feels like to go without a penny in your pocket. Now that he was wealthy and well dressed, he had all too many who called him their friend and a genuine gentleman. That pleased him

But he spent money every day without making any, and wound up with only two coppers to his name. He had to quit his fine quarters to live in a garret, clean his own boots, and mend them himself with a darning needle. None of his friends came to see him, because there were too many stairs to climb.

It was the one with eyes as big as saucers.
(Arthur Scheiner)

One evening when he sat in the dark without even enough money to buy a candle, he suddenly remembered there was a candle end in the tinder box that he had picked up when the witch sent him down the hollow tree. He got out the tinder box, and the moment he struck sparks from the flint of it his door burst open and there stood a dog from down under the tree. It was the one with eyes as big as saucers.

"What," said the dog, "is my lord's command?"

"What's this?" said the soldier. "Have I got the sort of tinder box that will get me whatever I want? Go get me some money," he ordered the dog. *Zip*! The dog was gone. *Zip*! He was back again, with a bag full of copper in his mouth.

Now the soldier knew what a remarkable tinder box he had. Strike it once and there was the dog from the chest of copper coins. Strike it twice and here came the dog who had the silver. Three times brought the dog who guarded gold.

Back went the soldier to his comfortable quarters. Out strode the soldier in fashionable clothes. Immediately his friends knew him again, because they liked him so much.

Then the thought occurred to him, "Isn't it odd that no one ever gets to see the Princess? They say she's very pretty, but what's the good of it as long as she stays locked up in that large copper castle with so many towers? Why can't I see her? Where's my tinder box?" He struck a light and, *zip!* came the dog with eyes as big as saucers.

"It certainly is late," said the soldier. "Practically midnight. But I do want a glimpse of the Princess, if only for a moment."

Out the door went the dog, and before the soldier could believe it, here came the dog with the Princess on his back. She was sound asleep, and so pretty that everyone could see she was a Princess. The soldier couldn't keep from kissing her, because he was every inch a soldier. Then the dog took the Princess home.

Next morning when the King and Queen were drinking their tea, the Princess told them about the strange dream she'd had – all about a dog and a soldier. She'd ridden on the dog's back, and the soldier had kissed her.

"Now that was a fine story," said the Queen. The next night one of the old ladies of the court was under orders to sit by the Princess's bed, and see whether this was a dream or something else altogether. The soldier was longing to see the pretty Princess again, so the dog came by night to take her up and away as fast as he could run. But the old lady pulled on her storm boots and ran right after them. When she saw them disappear into a large house she thought, "Now I know where it is," and drew a big cross on the door with a piece of chalk. Then she went home to bed, and before long the dog brought the Princess home too. But when the dog saw that cross marked on

the soldier's front door, he got himself a piece of chalk and cross-marked every door in the town. This was a clever thing to do, because now the old lady couldn't tell the right door from all the wrong doors he had marked.

Early in the morning along came the King and the Queen, the old lady, and all the officers, to see where the Princess had been.

"Here it is," said the King when he saw the first cross mark.

"No, my dear. There it is," said the Queen who was looking next door.

"Here's one, there's one, and yonder's another one!" said they all. Wherever they looked they saw chalk marks, so they gave up searching.

The Queen, though, was an uncommonly clever woman, who could do more than ride in a coach. She took her big gold scissors, cut out a piece of silk, and made a neat little bag. She filled it with fine buckwheat flour and tied it on to the Princess's back. Then she pricked a little hole in it so that the flour would sift out along the way, wherever the Princess might go.

Again the dog came in the night, took the Princess on his back, and ran with her to the soldier, who loved her so much that he would have been glad to be a Prince just so he could make his wife.

The dog didn't notice how the flour made a trail from the castle right up to the soldier's window, where he ran up the wall with the Princess. So in the morning it was all too plain to the King and Queen just where their daughter had been.

They took the soldier and they put him in prison. There he sat. It was dark, and it was dismal, and they told him, "Tomorrow is the day for you to hang." That didn't cheer him up any, and as for his tinder box he'd left it behind at the inn. In the morning he could see through his narrow little window how the people all hurried out of town to see him hanged. He heard the drums beat and he saw the soldiers march. In the crowd of running people he saw a shoemaker's boy in a leather apron and slippers. The boy galloped so fast that off flew one slipper, which hit the wall right where the soldier pressed his face to the iron bars.

"Hey there, you shoemaker's boy, there's no hurry," the soldier shouted. "Nothing can happen till I get there. But if you run to where I live and bring me my tinder box, I'll give you four coppers. Put your best foot foremost."

The shoemaker's boy could use four coppers, so he rushed the tinder box to the soldier, and – well, now we shall hear what happened!

Outside the town a high gallows had been built. Around it stood soldiers and many hundred thousand people. The King and Queen sat on a splendid throne, opposite the judge and the whole council. The soldier already stood upon the ladder, but just as they were about to put the rope around his neck he said the custom was to grant a poor criminal one last small favor. He wanted to smoke a pipe of tobacco – the last he'd be smoking in this world.

The King couldn't refuse him, so the soldier struck fire from his tinder box, once – twice – and a third time. *Zip*! There stood all the dogs, one with eyes as big as saucers, one with eyes as big as mill wheels, one with eyes as big as the Round Tower of Copenhagen.

"Help me. Save me from hanging!" said the soldier. Those dogs took the judges and all the council, some by the leg and some by the nose, and tossed them so high that they came down broken to bits.

"Don't!" cried the King, but the biggest dog took him and the Queen too, and tossed them up after the others. Then the soldiers trembled and the people shouted, "Soldier, be our King and marry the pretty Princess."

So they put the soldier in the King's carriage. All three of his dogs danced in front of it, and shouted "Hurrah!" The boys whistled through their fingers, and the soldiers saluted. The Princess came out of the copper castle to be Queen, and that suited her exactly. The wedding lasted all of a week, and the three dogs sat at the table, with their eyes opened wider than ever before.

LITTLE CLAUS AND BIG CLAUS

IN A VILLAGE there lived two men who had the self-same name. Both were named Claus. But one of them owned four horses, and the other owned only one horse; so to distinguish between them people called the man who had four horses Big Claus, and the man who had only one horse Little Claus. Now I'll tell you what happened to these two, for this is a true story.

The whole week through, Little Claus had to plow for Big Claus and lend him his only horse. In return, Big Claus lent him all four of his horses, but only for one day a week and that had to be Sunday.

Each Sunday how proudly Little Claus cracked his whip over all the five horses, which were as good as his own on that day. How brightly the sun shone. How merry were the church bells that rang in the steeple. How well dressed were all the people who passed him with hymn books tucked under their arms. And as they went their way to church, to hear the parson preach, how the people did stare to see Little Claus plowing with all five horses. This made him feel so proud that he would crack his whip and hollo, "Get up, all my horses."

"You must not say that," Big Claus told him. "You know as well as I do that only one of those horses is yours." But no sooner did another bevy of churchgoers come by than

Little Claus and Big Claus.
(Harry Clark)

Little Claus forgot he mustn't say it, and holloed, "Get up, all my horses."

"Don't you say that again," Big Claus told him. "If you do, I'll knock your horse down dead in his traces, and that will be the end of him."

"You won't catch me saying it again," Little Claus promised. But as soon as people came by, nodding to him and wishing him "Good morning," he was so pleased and so proud of how grand it looked to have five horses plowing his field, that he holloed again, "Get up, all my horses!"

"I'll get up your horse for you," Big Claus said, and he snatched up a tethering mallet, and he knocked Little Claus's one and only horse on the head so hard that it fell down dead.

"Now I haven't any horse at all," said Little Claus, and he began to cry. But by and by he skinned his dead horse and hung the hide to dry in the wind. Then he crammed the dry skin in a sack, slung it up over his shoulder, and set out to sell it in the nearest town.

It was a long way to go, and he had to pass through a dark, dismal forest. Suddenly a terrible storm came up, and he lost his way. Before he could find it again, evening overtook him. The town was still a long way off, and he had come too far to get back home before night.

Not far from the road he saw a large farmhouse. The shutters were closed, but light showed through a crack at the top of the windows. "Maybe they'll let me spend the night here," Little Claus thought, as he went to the door and knocked.

The farmer's wife opened it, but when she heard what he wanted she told him to go away. She said her husband wasn't home, and she wouldn't have any strangers in the house.

"Then I'll have to sleep outside," Little Claus decided, as she slammed the door in his face.

Near the farmhouse stood a large haystack, leading up to the thatched roof of a shed which lay between it and the house. "That's where I'll sleep," said Little Claus when he noticed the thatch. "It will make a wonderful bed. All I hope is that the stork doesn't fly down and bite my legs." For a stork was actually standing guard on the roof where it had a nest.

So Little Claus climbed to the roof of the shed. As he turned over to make himself comfortable, he discovered that the farmhouse shutters didn't come quite to the top of the windows, and he could see over them. He could see into a room where a big table was spread with wine and roast meat and a delicious fish. The farmer's wife and the sexton were sitting there at the table, all by themselves. She kept helping him to wine, and he kept helping himself to fish. He must have loved fish.

"Oh, if only I could have some too," thought Little Claus. By craning his neck toward the window he caught sight of a great, appetizing cake. Why, they were feasting in there!

Just then he heard someone riding down the road to the house. It was the farmer coming home. He was an excellent man except for just one thing. He could not stand the sight of a sexton. If he so much as caught a glimpse of one, he would fly into a furious rage, which was the reason why the sexton had gone to see the farmer's wife while her husband was away from home, and the good woman could do no less than set before him all the good things to eat that she had in the house. When she heard the farmer coming, she trembled for the sexton, and begged him to creep into a big empty chest which stood in one corner of the room. He lost no time about it, because he knew full well that her poor husband couldn't stand the sight of a sexton. The woman quickly set aside the wine and hid the good food in her oven, because if her husband had seen the feast he would have asked questions hard to answer.

"Oh dear!" Up on the shed Little Claus sighed to see all the good food disappearing.

"Who's up there?" the farmer peered at Little Claus. "Whatever are you doing up there? Come into the house with me." So Little Claus came down. He told the farmer how he had lost his way, and asked if he could have shelter for the night.

"Of course," said the farmer, "but first let's have something to eat."

The farmer's wife received them well, laid the whole table, and set before them a big bowl of porridge. The farmer was hungry and ate it with a good appetite, but Little Claus was thinking about the good roast meat, that fish, and that cake in the oven. Beside his feet under the table lay his sack with the horsehide, for as we know he was on his way to sell it in the town. Not liking the porridge at all, Little Claus trod on the sack, and the dry hide gave a loud squeak.

"Sh!" Little Claus said to his sack, at the same time that he trod on it so hard that it squeaked even louder.

"What on earth have you got in there?" said the farmer.

"Oh, just a conjuror," said Little Claus. "He tells me we don't have to eat porridge, because he has conjured up a whole oven-full of roast meat, fish, and cake for us."

"What do you say?" said the farmer. He made haste to open the oven, where he found all the good dishes. His wife had hidden them there, but he quite believed that they had been conjured up by the wizard in the sack. His wife didn't dare open her mouth as she helped them to their fill of meat, fish, and cake.

Then Little Claus trod upon the sack to make it squeak again.

"What does he say now?" asked the farmer.

"He says," Little Claus answered, "that there are three bottles of wine for us in the corner by the oven."

So the woman had to bring out the wine she had hidden. The farmer drank it till he grew merry, and wanted to get himself a conjuror just like the one Little Claus carried in his sack.

"Can he conjure up the devil?" the farmer wondered. "I'm in just the mood to meet him."

"Oh, yes," said Little Claus. "My conjuror can do anything I tell him. Can't you?" he asked and trod upon the sack till it squeaked. "Did you hear him answer? He said 'Yes.' He can conjure up the devil, but he's afraid we won't like the look of him."

"Oh, I'm not afraid. What's he like?"

"Well, he looks an awful lot like a sexton."

"Ho," said the farmer, "as ugly as that? I can't bear the sight of a sexton. But don't let that stop us. Now that I know it's just the devil I shan't mind it so much. I'll face him, provided he doesn't come near me."

"Wait, while I talk with my conjuror." Little Claus trod on the sack and stooped down to listen.

"What does he say?"

"He says for you to go and open that big chest in the corner, and there you'll find the devil doubled up inside it. But you must hold fast to the lid, so he doesn't pop out."

"Will you help me hold it?" said the farmer. He went to the chest in which his wife had hidden the sexton – once frightened, now terrified. The farmer lifted the lid a little, and peeped in.

"Ho!" he sprang back. "I saw him, and he's the image of our sexton, a horrible sight!" After that they needed another drink, and sat there drinking far into the night.

"You must sell me your conjuror," said the farmer. "You can fix your own price. I'd pay you a bushel of money right away."

"Oh, I couldn't do that," Little Claus said. "Just think how useful my conjuror is."

"But I'd so like to have him." The farmer kept begging to buy it.

"Well," said Little Claus at last, "you've been kind enough to give me a night's lodging, so I can't say no. You shall have my sack for a bushel of money, but it must be full to the brim."

"You shall have it", said the farmer. "But you must take that chest along with you too. I won't have it in the house another hour. He might still be inside it. You never can tell."

So Little Claus sold his sack with the dried horsehide in it, and was paid a bushel of money, measured up to the brim. The farmer gave him a wheelbarrow too, in which to wheel away the money and the chest.

"Fare you well," said Little Claus, and off he went with his money and his chest with the sexton in it. On the further side of the forest was a deep, wide river, where the current ran so strong that it was almost impossible to swim against it. A big new bridge had been built across the river, and when Little Claus came to the middle of it he said, very loud so the sexton could hear him:

"Now what would I be doing with this silly chest? It's as heavy as stone, and I'm too tired to wheel it any further. So I'll throw it in the

"Now what would I be doing with this silly chest?"
(Fritz Kredel)

river, and if it drifts down to my house, well and good, but if it sinks I haven't lost much." Then he tilted the chest a little, as if he were about to tip it into the river.

"Stop! Don't!" the sexton shouted inside. "Let me get out first."

"Oh," said Little Claus pretending to be frightened, "is he still there? Then I'd better throw him into the river and drown him."

"Oh no, don't do that to me!" the sexton shouted. "I'd give a bushel of money to get out of this."

"Why, that's altogether different," said Little Claus, opening the chest. The sexton popped out at once, pushed the empty chest into the water and hurried home to give Little Claus a bushel of money. What with the farmer's bushel and the sexton's bushel, Little Claus had his wheelbarrow quite full.

"I got a good price for my horse," he said when he got home and emptied all the money in a heap on the floor of his room. "How Big Claus will fret when he finds out that my one horse has made me so rich, but I won't tell him how I managed it." Then he sent a boy to borrow a bushel measure from Big Claus.

"Whatever would he want with it?" Big Claus wondered, and smeared pitch on the bottom of the bushel so that a little of what he

19

measured would stick to it. And so it happened that when he got his measure back he found three newly minted pieces of silver stuck to it.

"What's this?" Big Claus ran to see Little Claus. "Where did you get so much money?"

"Oh, that's what I got for the horsehide I sold last night."

"Heavens above! How the price of hides must have gone up." Big Claus ran home, took an ax, and knocked all four of his horses on the head. Then he ripped their hides off, and set out to town with them.

"Hides, hides! Who'll buy hides?" he bawled, up and down the streets. All the shoemakers and tanners came running to ask what their price was. "A bushel of money apiece," he told them.

"Are you crazy?" they asked. "Do you think we spend money by the bushel?"

"Hides, hides! Who'll buy hides?" he kept on shouting, and to those who asked how much, he said, "A bushel of money."

"He takes us for fools," they said. The shoemakers took their straps, and the tanners their leather aprons, and they beat Big Claus through the town.

"Hides, hides!" they mocked him. "We'll tan your hide for you if you don't get out of town." Big Claus had to run as fast as he could. He had never been beaten so badly.

"Little Claus will pay for this," he said when he got back home. "I'll kill him for it."

Now it so happened that Little Claus's old grandmother had just died. She had been as cross as could be – never a kind word did she have for him – but he was sorry to see her die. He put the dead woman in his own warm bed, just in case she came to life again, and let her lie there all night while he napped in a chair in the corner, as he had done so often before.

As he sat there in the night, the door opened and in came Big Claus with an ax. He knew exactly where Little Claus's bed was, so he went straight to it and knocked the dead grand-mother on the head, under the impression that she was Little Claus.

"There," he said, "You won't fool me again." Then he went home.

"What a wicked man," said Little Claus. "Why, he would have killed me. It's lucky for my grandmother that she was already dead, or he'd have been the death of her."

He dressed up his old grandmother in her Sunday best, borrowed a neighbor's horse, and hitched up his cart. On the back seat he propped up his grandmother, wedged in so that the jolts would not topple her over, and away they went through the forest.

When the sun came up they drew abreast of a large inn, where Little Claus halted and went in to get him some breakfast. The innkeeper was a wealthy man, and a good enough fellow in his way, but his temper was as fiery as if he were made of pepper and snuff.

"Good morning," he said to Little Claus. "You're up and dressed mighty early."

"Yes," said Little Claus. "I am bound for the town with my old grandmother, who is sitting out there in the cart. I can't get her to come in, but you might take her a glass of mead. You'll have to shout to make her hear you, for she's deaf as a post."

"I'll take it right out." The innkeeper poured a glass full of mead and took it to the dead grandmother, who sat stiffly on the cart.

"Your grandson sent you a glass of mead," said the innkeeper, but the dead woman said never a word. She just sat there.

"Don't you hear me?" the innkeeper shouted his loudest. "Here's a glass of mead from your grandson."

Time after time he shouted it, she didn't budge. He flew into such a rage that he threw the glass in her face. The mead splashed all over her as she fell over backward, for she was just propped up, not tied in place.

"Confound it!" Little Claus rushed out the door and took the innkeeper by the throat.

"You've gone and killed my grandmother. Look! There's a big hole in her forehead."

"Oh, what a calamity!" The innkeeper wrung his hands. "And all because of my fiery temper. Dear Little Claus, I'll give you a bushel of money, and I'll bury your grandmother as if she were my very own. But you must hush this thing up for me, or they'll chop off my head – how I'd hate it."

So it came about that Little Claus got another bushel of money, and the landlord buried the old grandmother as if she'd been his own.

Just as soon as Little Claus got home, he sent a boy to borrow a bushel measure from Big Claus.

"Little Claus wants to borrow it?" Big Claus asked. "Didn't I kill him? I'll go and see about that." So he himself took the measure over to Little Claus.

"Where did you get all that money?" he asked when he saw the height of the money pile.

"When you killed my grandmother instead of me," Little Claus told him, "I sold her for a bushel of money."

"Heavens above! That was indeed a good price," said Big Claus. He hurried home, took an ax, and knocked his old grandmother on the head. Then he put her in a cart, drove off to town, and asked the apothecary if he wanted to buy a dead body.

"Whose dead body?" asked the apothecary. "Where'd you get it?"

"It's my grandmother's dead body. I killed her for a bushel of money," Big Claus told him.

"Lord," said the apothecary. "Man, you must be crazy. Don't talk like that or they'll chop off your head." Then he told him straight he had done a wicked deed, that he was a terrible fellow, and that the worst of punishments was much too good for him. Big Claus got frightened. He jumped in his cart, whipped up the horses, and drove home as fast as they would take him. The apothecary and everyone else thought he must be a madman, so they didn't stand in his way.

"I'll see that you pay for this," said Big Claus when he reached the highroad. "Oh, won't I make you pay for this, Little Claus!" The moment he got home he took the biggest sack he could find, went to see Little Claus, and said:

"You've deceived me again. First I killed my four horses. Then I killed my old grandmother, and it's all your fault. But I'll make sure you don't make a fool of me again." Then he caught Little Claus and put him in the sack, slung it up over his back and told him, "Now I shall take you and drown you."

It was a long way to the river, and Little Claus was no light load. The road went by the church, and as they passed they could hear the organ playing and the people singing very beautifully. Big Claus set down his sack just outside the church door. He thought the best thing for him to do was to go in to hear a hymn before he went any further. Little Claus was securely tied in the sack, and all the people were inside the church. So Big Claus went in too.

"Oh dear, oh dear!" Little Claus sighed in the sack. Twist and turn as he might, he could not loosen the knot. Then a white-haired old cattle drover came by, leaning heavily on his staff. The herd of bulls and cows he was driving bumped against the sack Little Claus was in, and overturned it.

"Oh dear," Little Claus sighed, "I'm so young to be going to Heaven."

"While I," said the cattle drover, "am too old for this earth, yet Heaven will not send for me."

"Open the sack!" Little Claus shouted. "Get in and take my place. You'll go straight to Heaven."

"That's where I want to be," said the drover, as he undid the sack. Little Claus jumped out at once. "You must look after my cattle," the

21

old man said as he crawled in. As soon as Little Claus fastened the sack, he walked away from there with all the bulls and cows.

Presently Big Claus came out of church. He took the sack on his back and found it light, for the old drover was no more than half as heavy as Little Claus.

"How light my burden is, all because I've been listening to a hymn," said Big Claus. He went on to the deep wide river, and threw the sack with the old cattle drover into the water.

"You'll never trick me again," Big Claus said, for he thought he had seen the last splash of Little Claus.

He started home, but when he came to the crossroads he met Little Claus and all his cattle.

"Where did you come from?" Big Claus exclaimed. "Didn't I just drown you?"

"Yes," said Little Claus. "You threw me in the river half an hour ago."

"Then how did you come by such a fine herd of cattle?" Big Claus wanted to know.

"Oh, they're sea cattle," said Little Claus. "I'll tell you how I got them, because I'm obliged to you for drowning me. I'm a made man now. I can't begin to tell you how rich I am.

"But when I was in the sack, with the wind whistling in my ears as you dropped me off the bridge into the cold water, I was frightened enough. I went straight to the bottom, but it didn't hurt me because of all the fine soft grass down there. Someone opened the sack and a beautiful maiden took my hand. Her clothes were white as snow, and she had a green wreath in her floating hair. She said, 'So you've come, Little Claus. Here's a herd of cattle for you, but they are just the beginning of my presents. A mile further up the road another herd awaits you.'

"Then I saw that the river is a great highway for the people who live in the sea. Down on the bottom of the river they walked and drove their cattle straight in from the sea to the land where the rivers end. The flowers down there

"But when I was in the sack, with the wind whistling in my ears as you dropped me off the bridge into the cold water, I was frightened enough." (Fritz Kredel)

are fragrant. The grass is fresh, and fish flit by as birds do up here. The people are fine, and so are the cattle that come grazing along the roadside."

"Then why are you back so soon?" Big Claus asked. "If it's all so beautiful, I'd have stayed there."

"Well," said Little Claus, "I'm being particularly clever. You remember I said the sea maiden told me to go one mile up the road and I'd find another herd of cattle. By 'road' she meant the river, for that's the only way she travels. But I know how the river turns and twists, and it seemed too roundabout a way of getting there. By coming up on land I took a short cut that saves me half a mile. So I get my cattle that much sooner."

"You *are* a lucky man," said Big Claus, "Do you think I would get me some cattle too if I went down to the bottom of the river?"

"Oh, I'm sure you would," said Little Claus. "Don't expect me to carry you there in a sack, because you're too heavy for me, but if you walk to the river and crawl into the sack, I'll throw you in with the greatest of pleasure."

"Thank you," said Big Claus, "but remember, if I don't get a herd of sea cattle down there, I'll give you a thrashing, believe me."

"Would you really?" said Little Claus.

As they came to the river, the thirsty cattle saw the water and rushed to drink it. Little Claus said, "See what a hurry they are in to get back to the bottom of the river."

"Help me get there first," Big Claus commanded, "or I'll give you that beating right now." He struggled into the big sack,

which had been lying across the back of one of the cattle. "Put a stone in, or I'm afraid I shan't sink," said Big Claus.

"No fear of that," said Little Claus, but he put a big stone in the sack, tied it tightly, and pushed it into the river.

Splash! Up flew the water and down to the bottom sank Big Claus.

"I'm afraid he won't find what I found!" said Little Claus as he herded all his cattle home.

THE PRINCESS ON THE PEA

ONCE THERE WAS a Prince who wanted to marry a Princess. Only a real one would do. So he traveled through all the world to find her, and everywhere things went wrong. There were Princesses aplenty, but how was he to know whether they were real Princesses? There was something not quite right about them all. So he came home again and was unhappy, because he did so want to have a real Princess.

One evening a terrible storm blew up. It lightened and thundered and rained. It was really frightful! In the midst of it all came a knocking at the town gate. The old King went to open it.

Who should be standing outside but a Princess, and what a sight she was in all that rain and wind. Water streamed from her hair down her clothes into her shoes, and ran out at the heels. Yet she claimed to be a real Princess.

"We'll soon find that out," the old Queen thought to herself. Without saying a word about it she went to the bedchamber, stripped back the bedclothes, and put just one pea in the bottom of the bed. Then she took twenty mattresses and piled them on the pea. Then she took twenty eiderdown feather beds and piled them on the mattresses. Up on top of all these the Princess was to spend the night.

Then she took twenty eiderdown feather beds and piled them on the mattresses. Up on top of all these the Princess was to spend the night.
(Edmund Dulac)

In the morning they asked her, "Did you sleep well?"

"Oh!" said the Princess. "No. I scarcely slept at all. Heaven knows what's in that bed.

I lay on something so hard that I'm black and blue all over. It was simply terrible."

They could see she was a real Princess and no question about it, now that she had felt one pea all the way through twenty mattresses and twenty more feather beds. Nobody but a Princess could be so delicate. So the Prince made haste to marry her, because he knew he had found a real Princess.

As for the pea, they put it in the museum. There it's still to be seen, unless somebody has taken it.

THUMBELINA

THERE ONCE WAS a woman who wanted so very much to have a tiny little child, but she did not know where to find one. So she went to an old witch, and she said:

"I have set my heart upon having a tiny little child. Please could you tell me where I can find one?"

"Why, that's easily done," said the witch. "Here's a grain of barley for you, but it isn't at all the sort of barley that farmers grow in their fields or that the chickens get to eat. Put it in a flower pot and you'll see what you shall see."

"Oh thank you!" the woman said. She gave the witch twelve pennies, and planted the barley seed as soon as she got home. It quickly grew into a fine large flower, which looked very much like a tulip. But the petals were folded tight, as though it were still a bud.

"This is such a pretty flower," said the woman. She kissed its lovely red and yellow petals, and just as she kissed it the flower gave a loud *pop*! and flew open. It was a tulip, right enough, but on the green cushion in the middle of it sat a tiny girl. She was dainty and fair to see, but she was no taller than your thumb. So she was called Thumbelina.

A nicely polished walnut shell served as her cradle. Her mattress was made of the blue petals of violets, and a rose petal was pulled up to cover her. That was how she slept at night. In the daytime she played on a table where the woman put a plate surrounded with a wreath of flowers. Their stems lay in the water, on which there floated a large tulip petal.

She was no taller than your thumb. So she was called Thumbelina. (Margaret Tarrant)

Thumbelina used the petal as a boat, and with a pair of white horsehairs for oars she could row clear across the plate – a charming sight. She could sing, too. Her voice was the softest and sweetest that anyone ever has heard.

One night as she lay in her cradle, a horrible toad hopped in through the window – one of the panes was broken. This big, ugly, slimy toad jumped right down on the table where Thumbelina was asleep under the red rose petal.

"Here's a perfect wife for my son!" the toad exclaimed. She seized upon the walnut shell in which Thumbelina lay asleep, and hopped off with it, out the window and into the garden. A big broad stream ran through it, with a muddy marsh along its banks, and here the toad lived with her son. Ugh! he was just like his mother, slimy and horrible. "Co–ax, co–ax, brek–ek–eke–kex," was all that he could say when he saw the graceful little girl in the walnut shell.

"Don't speak so loud, or you will wake her up," the old toad told him. "She might get away from us yet, for she is as light as a puff of swan's-down. We must put her on one of the broad water lily leaves out in the stream. She is so small and light that it will be just like an island to her, and she can't run away from us while we are making our best room under the mud ready for you two to live in."

Many water lilies with broad green leaves grew in the stream, and it looked as if they were floating on the surface. The leaf which lay furthest from the bank was the largest of them all, and it was to this leaf that the old toad swam with the walnut shell which held Thumbelina.

The poor little thing woke up early next morning, and when she saw where she was she began to cry bitterly. There was water all around the big green leaf and there was no way at all for her to reach the shore. The old toad sat in the mud, decorating a room with green rushes and yellow water lilies, to have it looking its best for her new daughter-in-law. Then she and her ugly son swam out to the leaf on which Thumbelina was standing. They came for her pretty little bed, which they wanted to carry to the bridal chamber before they took her there.

The old toad curtsied deep in the water before her, and said:

"Meet my son. He is to be your husband, and you will share a delightful home in the mud."

"Here's a perfect wife for my son!"
(Margaret Tarrant)

"Co–ax, co–ax, brek–ek–eke–kex," was all that her son could say.

Then they took the pretty little bed and swam away with it. Left all alone on the green leaf, Thumbelina sat down and cried. She did not want to live in the slimy toad's house, and she didn't want to have the toad's horrible son for her husband. The little fishes who swam in the water beneath her had seen the toad and heard what she had said. So up popped their heads to have a look at the little girl. No sooner had they seen her than they felt very sorry that anyone so pretty should have to go down to live with that hideous toad. No, that should never be! They gathered around the green stem which held the leaf where she was, and gnawed it in two with their teeth. Away went the leaf down the stream, and away went Thumbelina, far away where the toad could not catch her.

Thumbelina sailed past many a place, and when the little birds in the bushes saw her they sang, "What a darling little girl." The leaf drifted further and further away with her, and so it was that Thumbelina became a traveler.

A lovely white butterfly kept fluttering around her, and at last alighted on the leaf, because he admired Thumbelina. She was a happy little girl again, now that the toad could not catch her. It was all very lovely as she floated along, and where the sun struck the water it looked like shining gold. Thumbelina undid her sash, tied one end of it to the butterfly, and made the other end fast to the leaf. It went much faster now, and Thumbelina went much faster too, for of course she was standing on it.

Just then, a big May-bug flew by and caught sight of her. Immediately he fastened his claws around her slender waist and flew with her up into a tree. Away went the green leaf down the stream, and away went the butterfly with it, for he was tied to the leaf and could not get loose.

My goodness! How frightened little Thumbelina was when the May-bug carried her up in the tree. But she was even more sorry for the nice white butterfly she had fastened to the leaf, because if he couldn't free himself he would have to starve to death. But the May-bug wasn't one to care about that. He sat her down on the largest green leaf of the tree, fed her honey from the flowers, and told her how pretty she was, considering that she didn't look the least like a May-bug. After a while, all the other May-bugs who lived in the tree came to pay them a call. As they stared at Thumbelina, the lady May-bugs threw up their feelers and said:

"Why, she has only two legs – what a miserable sight!"

"She hasn't any feelers," one cried.

"She is pinched in at the waist – how shameful! She looks like a human being – how ugly she is!" said all of the female May-bugs.

Yet Thumbelina was as pretty as ever. Even the May-bug who had flown away with her knew that, but as every last one of them kept calling her ugly, he at length came to agree

with them and would have nothing to do with her – she could go wherever she chose. They flew down out of the tree with her and left her on a daisy, where she sat and cried because she was so ugly that the May-bugs wouldn't have anything to do with her.

Nevertheless, she was the loveliest little girl you can imagine, and as frail and fine as the petal of a rose.

All summer long, poor Thumbelina lived all alone in the woods. She wove herself a hammock of grass, and hung it under a big burdock leaf to keep off the rain. She took honey from the flowers for food, and drank the dew which she found on the leaves every morning. In this way the summer and fall went by. Then came the winter, the long, cold winter. All the birds who had sung so sweetly for her flew away. The trees and the flowers withered. The big burdock leaf under which she had lived shriveled up until nothing was left of it but a dry, yellow stalk. She was terribly cold, for her clothes had worn threadbare and she herself was so slender and frail. Poor Thumbelina, she would freeze to death! Snow began to fall, and every time a snowflake struck her it was as if she had been hit by a whole shovelful, for we are quite tall while she measured only an inch. She wrapped a withered leaf about her, but there was no warmth in it. She shivered with cold.

Near the edge of the woods where she now had arrived, was a large grain field, but the grain had been harvested long ago. Only the dry, bare stubble stuck out of the frozen ground. It was just as if she were lost in a vast forest, and oh how she shivered with cold! Then she came to the door of a field mouse, who had a little hole amidst the stubble. There this mouse lived, warm and cozy, with a whole store-room of grain, and a magnificent kitchen and pantry. Poor Thumbelina stood at the door, just like a beggar child, and pled for a little bit of barley, because she hadn't had anything to eat for two days past.

"Why, you poor little thing," said the field mouse, who turned out to be a kind-hearted old creature. "You must come into my warm room and share my dinner." She took such a fancy to Thumbelina that she said, "If you care to, you may stay with me all winter, but you must keep my room tidy, and tell me stories, for I am very fond of them." Thumbelina did as the kind old field mouse asked and she had a very good time of it.

"Soon we shall have a visitor," the field mouse said. "Once every week my neighbor comes to see me, and he is even better off than I am. His rooms are large, and he wears such a beautiful black velvet coat. If you could only get him for a husband you would be well taken care of, but he can't see anything. You must tell him the very best stories you know."

Thumbelina did not like this suggestion. She would not even consider the neighbor, because he was a mole. He paid them a visit in his black velvet coat. The field mouse talked about how wealthy and wise he was, and how his home was more than twenty times larger than hers. But for all of his knowledge he cared nothing at all for the sun and the flowers. He had nothing good to say for them, and had never laid eyes on them. As Thumbelina had to sing for him, she sang, "May-bug, May-bug, fly away home," and "The Monk goes afield." The mole fell in love with her sweet voice, but he didn't say anything about it yet, for he was a most discreet fellow.

He had just dug a long tunnel through the ground from his house to theirs, and the field mouse and Thumbelina were invited to use it whenever they pleased, though he warned them not to be alarmed by the dead bird which lay in this passage. It was a complete bird, with feather and beak. It must have died quite recently, when winter set in, and it was buried right in the middle of the tunnel.

The mole took in his mouth a torch of decayed wood. In the darkness it glimmered

The mole fell in love with her sweet voice.
(Margaret Tarrant)

like fire. He went ahead of them to light the way through the long, dark passage. When they came to where the dead bird lay, the mole put his broad nose to the ceiling and made a large hole through which daylight could fall. In the middle of the floor lay a dead swallow, with his lovely wings folded at his sides and his head tucked under his feathers. The poor bird must certainly have died of the cold. Thumbelina felt so sorry for him. She loved all the little birds who had sung and sweetly twittered to her all through the summer. But the mole gave the body a kick with his short stumps, and said, "Now he won't be chirping any more. What a wretched thing it is to be born a little bird. Thank goodness none of my children can be a bird, who has nothing but his 'chirp, chirp,' and must starve to death when winter comes along."

"Yes, you are so right, you sensible man," the field mouse agreed. "What good is all his chirp-chirping to a bird in the winter time, when he starves and freezes? But that's considered very grand, I imagine."

Thumbelina kept silent, but when the others turned their back on the bird she bent over, smoothed aside the feathers that hid the bird's head, and kissed his closed eyes.

"Maybe it was he who sang so sweetly to me in the summertime," she thought to herself. "What pleasure he gave me, the dear, pretty bird."

The mole closed up the hole that let in the daylight, and then he took the ladies home. That night Thumbelina could not sleep a wink, so she got up and wove a fine large coverlet out of hay. She took it to the dead bird and spread it over him, so that he would lie warm in the cold earth. She tucked him in with some soft thistledown that she had found in the field mouse's room.

"Good-by, you pretty little bird," she said. "Good-by, and thank you for your sweet songs last summer, when the trees were all green and the sun shone so warmly upon us." She laid her head on his breast, and it startled her to feel a soft thump, as if something were beating inside. This was the bird's heart. He was not dead – he was only numb with cold, and now that he had been warmed he came to life again.

In the fall, all swallows fly off to warm countries, but if one of them starts too late he gets so cold that he drops down as if he were dead, and lies where he fell. And then the cold snow covers him.

Thumbelina was so frightened that she trembled, for the bird was so big, so enormous compared to her own inch of height. But she mustered her courage, tucked the cotton wool down closer around the poor bird, brought the mint leaf that covered her own bed, and spread it over the bird's head.

The following night she tiptoed out to him again. He was alive now, but so weak that he could barely open his eyes for a moment to

"Thank you, pretty little child," the sick swallow said. (Margaret Tarrant)

look at Thumbelina, who stood beside him with the piece of touchwood that was her only lantern.

"Thank you, pretty little child," the sick swallow said. "I have been wonderfully warmed. Soon I shall get strong once more, and be able to fly again in the warm sunshine."

"Oh," she said, "It's cold outside, it's snowing, and freezing. You just stay in your warm bed and I'll nurse you."

Then she brought him some water in the petal of a flower. The swallow drank, and told her how he had hurt one of his wings in a thorn bush, and for that reason couldn't fly as fast as the other swallows when they flew far, far away to the warm countries. Finally he had dropped to the ground. That was all he remembered, and he had no idea how he came to be where she found him.

The swallow stayed there all through the winter, and Thumbelina was kind to him and tended him with loving care. She didn't say anything about this to the field mouse or to the mole, because they did not like the poor unfortunate swallow.

As soon as spring came and the sun warmed the earth, the swallow told Thumbelina it was time to say good-by. She reopened the hole that the mole had made in the ceiling, and the sun shone in splendor upon them. The swallow asked Thumbelina to go with him. She could sit on his back as they flew away through the green woods. But Thumbelina knew that it would make the old field mouse feel badly if she left like that, so she said:

"No, I cannot go."

"Fare you well, fare you well, my good and pretty girl," said the swallow, as he flew into the sunshine. Tears came into Thumbelina's eyes as she watched him go, for she was so fond of the poor swallow.

"Chirp, chirp!" sang the bird, at he flew into the green woods.

Thumbelina felt very downcast. She was not permitted to go out in the warm sunshine. Moreover, the grain that was sown in the field above the field mouse's house grew so tall that, to a poor little girl who was only an inch high, it was like a dense forest.

"You must work on your trousseau this summer," the field mouse said, for their neighbor, that loathsome mole in his black velvet coat, had proposed to her. "You must have both woolens and linens, both bedding and wardrobe, when you become the mole's wife."

Thumbelina had to turn the spindle, and the field mouse hired four spiders to spin and weave for her day and night. The mole came to call every evening, and his favorite remark was that the sun, which now baked the earth as hard as a rock, would not be nearly so hot when summer was over. Yes, as soon as summer was past he would be marrying Thumbelina. But she was not at all happy about it, because she didn't like the tedious mole the least bit. Every morning at sunrise and every evening at sunset, she would steal out the door. When the breeze blew the ears of grain apart she could catch glimpses of the blue sky. She could dream about how bright and fair it was out of doors, and how she wished she would see her dear swallow again. But he did not come back, for doubtless he was far away, flying about in the lovely green woods.

When fall arrived, Thumbelina's whole trousseau was ready.

"Your wedding day is four weeks off," the field mouse told her. But Thumbelina cried and declared that she would not have the tedious mole for a husband.

"Fiddlesticks," said the field mouse. "Don't you be obstinate, or I'll bite you with my white teeth. Why, you're getting a superb husband. The queen herself hasn't a black velvet coat as fine as his. Both his kitchen and his cellar are well supplied. You ought to thank goodness that you are getting him."

Then came the wedding day. The mole had come to take Thumbelina home with him, where she would have to live deep underground and never go out in the warm sunshine again, because he disliked it so. The poor little girl felt very sad that she had to say good-by to the glorious sun, which the field mouse had at least let her look out at through the doorway.

"Farewell, bright sun!" she said. With her arm stretched toward it she walked a little way from the field mouse's home. The grain had been harvested, and only the dry stubble was left in the field. "Farewell, farewell!" she cried again, and flung her little arms around a small red flower that was still in bloom. "If you see my dear swallow, please give him my love."

"Chirp, chirp! Chirp, chirp!" She suddenly heard a twittering over her head. She looked up and there was the swallow, just passing by. He was so glad to see Thumbelina although, when she told him how she hated to marry the mole and live deep underground where the sun never shone, she could not hold back her tears.

"Now that the cold winter is coming," the swallow told her, "I shall fly far, far away to the warm countries. Won't you come along with me? You can ride on my back. Just tie yourself on with your sash, and away we'll fly, far from the ugly mole and his dark hole – far, far away, over the mountains to the warm countries where the sun shines so much fairer than here, to where it is always summer and there are always flowers. Please fly away with me, dear little Thumbelina, you who saved my life when I lay frozen in a dark hole in the earth."

"Yes, I will go with you!" said Thumbelina. She sat on his back, put her feet on his outstretched wings, and fastened her sash to one of his strongest feathers. Then the swallow soared into the air over forests and over lakes, high up over the great mountains that are always capped with snow. When Thumbelina felt cold in the chill air, she crept under the bird's warm feathers, with only her little head stuck out to watch all the wonderful sights below.

At length they came to the warm countries. There the sun shone far more brightly than it ever does here, and the sky seemed twice as high. Along the ditches and hedgerows grew marvelous green and blue grapes. Lemons and oranges hung in the woods. The air smelled sweetly of myrtle and thyme. By the wayside, the loveliest children ran hither and thither, playing with the brightly colored butterflies.

But the swallow flew on still farther, and it became more and more beautiful. Under magnificent green trees, on the shore of a blue lake there stood an ancient palace of dazzling white marble. The lofty pillars were wreathed with vines, and at the top of them many swallows had made their nests. One nest belonged to the swallow who carried Thumbelina.

"This is my home," the swallow told her. "If you will choose one of those glorious flowers in bloom down below, I shall place you in it, and you will have all that your heart desires."

"That will be lovely," she cried, and clapped her tiny hands.

A great white marble pillar had fallen to the ground, where it lay in three broken pieces. Between these pieces grew the loveliest large white flowers. The swallow flew down with Thumbelina and put her on one of the large petals. How surprised she was to find in the center of the flower a little man, as shining and transparent as if he had been made of glass. On his head was the daintiest of little gold crowns, on his shoulders were the brightest shining wings, and he was not a bit bigger than Thumbelina. He was the spirit of the flower. In every flower there lived a small man or woman just like him, but he was the king over all of them.

"Oh, isn't he handsome?" Thumbelina said softly to the swallow. The king was somewhat afraid of the swallow, which seemed a very giant of a bird to anyone as small as he. But when he saw Thumbelina he rejoiced, for she was the prettiest little girl he had ever laid eyes on. So he took off his golden crown and put it on her head. He asked if he might know her name, and he asked her to be his wife, which would make her queen over all the flowers.

Here indeed was a different sort of husband from the toad's son and the mole with his black velvet coat. So she said "Yes" to this charming king. From all the flowers trooped little ladies and gentlemen delightful to behold. Every one of them brought Thumbelina a present, but the best gift of all was a pair of wings that had belonged to a large silver fly. When these were made fast to her back, she too could flit from flower to flower. Everyone rejoiced, as the swallow perched above them in his nest and sang his very best songs for them. He was sad though, deep down in his heart, for he liked Thumbelina so much that he wanted never to part with her.

"You shall no longer be called Thumbelina," the flower spirit told her. " That name is too ugly for anyone as pretty as you are. We shall call you Maia."

"Good-by, good-by," said the swallow. He flew away again from the warm countries, back to far-away Denmark, where he had a little nest over the window of the man who can tell you fairy tales. To him the bird sang, "Chirp, chirp! Chirp, chirp!" and that's how we heard the whole story.

THE LITTLE MERMAID

FAR OUT IN the ocean the water is as blue as the petals of the loveliest cornflower, and as clear as the purest glass. But it is very deep too. It goes down deeper than any anchor rope will go, and many, many steeples would have to be stacked one on top of another to reach from the bottom to the surface of the sea. It is down there that the sea folk live.

Now don't suppose that there are only bare white sands at the bottom of the sea. No indeed! The most marvelous trees and flowers grow down there, with such pliant stalks and leaves that the least stir in the water makes them move about as though they were alive. All sorts of fish, large and small, dart among the branches, just as birds flit through the trees up here. From the deepest spot in the ocean rises the palace of the sea king. Its walls are made of coral and its high pointed windows of the clearest amber, but the roof is made of mussel shells that open and shut with the tide. This is a wonderful sight to see, for every shell holds glistening pearls, any one of which would be the pride of a queen's crown.

The sea king down there had been a widower for years, and his old mother kept house for him. She was a clever woman, but very proud of her noble birth. Therefore she flaunted twelve oysters on her tail while the other ladies of the court were only allowed to wear six. Except for this she was an altogether praiseworthy person, particularly so because she was extremely fond of her granddaughters, the little sea princesses. They were six lovely girls, but the youngest was the most beautiful of them all. Her skin was as soft and tender as a rose petal, and her eyes were as blue as the deep sea, but like all the others she had no feet. Her body ended in a fish tail.

The whole day long they used to play in the palace, down in the great halls where live flowers grew on the walls. Whenever the high amber windows were thrown open the fish would swim in, just as swallows dart into our rooms when we open the windows. But these fish, now, would swim right up to the little princesses to eat out of their hands and let themselves be petted.

Outside the palace was a big garden, with flaming red and deep-blue trees. Their fruit glittered like gold, and their blossoms flamed like fire on their constantly waving stalks. The soil was very fine sand indeed, but as blue as burning brimstone. A strange blue veil lay over everything down there. You would have thought yourself aloft in the air with only the blue sky above and beneath you, rather than down at the bottom of the sea. When there was a dead calm, you could just see the sun, like a scarlet flower with light streaming from its calyx.

Each little princess had her own small garden plot, where she could dig and plant whatever she liked. One of them made her little flower bed in the shape of a whale, another thought it neater to shape hers like a little mermaid, but the youngest of them made hers as round as the sun, and there she grew only flowers which were as red as the sun itself. She was an unusual child, quiet and wistful, and when her sisters decorated their gardens with all kinds of odd things they had found in sunken ships, she would allow nothing in hers except flowers as red as the sun, and a pretty marble statue. This figure of a handsome boy, carved in pure white marble, had sunk down to the bottom of the sea from some ship that was wrecked. Beside the statue she planted a rose-colored weeping willow tree, which thrived so well that its graceful branches shaded the statue and hung down to the blue sand, where their shadows took on a violet tint, and swayed as the branches swayed. It looked as if the roots

This figure of a handsome boy, carved in pure white marble, had sunk down to the bottom of the sea from some ship that was wrecked.
(W. Heath Robinson)

and the tips of the branches were kissing each other in play.

Nothing gave the youngest princess such pleasure as to hear about the world of human beings up above them. Her old grandmother had to tell her all she knew about ships and cities, and of people and animals. What seemed nicest of all to her was that up on land the flowers were fragrant, for those at the bottom of the sea had no scent. And she thought it was nice that the woods were green, and that the fish you saw among their branches could sing so loud and sweet that it was delightful to hear them. Her grandmother had to call the little birds "fish," or the princess would not have known what she was talking about, for she had never seen a bird.

"When you get to be fifteen," her grandmother said, "you will be allowed to rise up out of the ocean and sit on the rocks in the moonlight, to watch the great ships sailing by. You will see woods and towns, too."

Next year one of her sisters would be fifteen, but the others – well, since each was a whole year older than the next the youngest still had five long years to wait until she could rise up from the water and see what our world was like. But each sister promised to tell the others about all that she saw, and what she found most marvelous on her first day. Their grandmother had not told them half enough, and there were so many things that they longed to know about.

The most eager of them all was the youngest, the very one who was so quiet and wistful. Many a night she stood by her open window and looked up through the dark blue water where the fish waved their fins and tails. She could just see the moon and stars. To be sure, their light was quite dim, but looked at through the water they seemed much bigger than they appear to us. Whenever a cloud-like shadow swept across them, she knew that it was either a whale swimming overhead, or a ship with many human beings aboard it. Little did they dream that a pretty young mermaid was down below, stretching her white arms up toward the keel of their ship.

The eldest princess had her fifteenth birthday, so now she received permission to rise up out of the water. When she got back she had a hundred things to tell her sisters about, but the most marvelous thing of all, she said, was to lie on a sand bar in the moonlight, when the sea was calm, and to gaze at the large city on the shore, where the lights twinkled like hundreds of stars; to listen to music; to hear the chatter and clamor of carriages and people; to see so many church towers and spires; and to hear the ringing bells. Because she could not enter the city, that was just what she most dearly longed to do.

Oh, how intently the youngest sister listened. After this, whenever she stood at her open window at night and looked up through the dark blue waters, she thought of that great city with all of its clatter and clamor, and even fancied that in these depths she could hear the church bells ring.

The next year, her second sister had permission to rise up to the surface and swim wherever she pleased. She came up just at sunset, and she said that this spectacle was the most marvelous sight she had ever seen. The heavens had a golden glow, and as for the clouds – she could not find words to describe their beauty. Splashed with red and tinted with violet, they sailed over her head. But much faster than the sailing clouds were wild swans in a flock. Like a long white veil trailing above the sea, they flew toward the setting sun. She too swam toward it, but down it went, and all the rose-colored glow faded from the sea and sky.

The following year, her third sister ascended, and as she was the boldest of them all she swam up a broad river that flowed into the ocean. She saw gloriously green, vine-colored hills. Palaces and manor houses could be glimpsed through the splendid woods. She heard all the birds sing, and the sun shone so brightly that often she had to dive under the water to cool her burning face. In a small cove she found a whole school of mortal children, paddling about in the water quite naked. She wanted to play with them, but they took fright and ran away. Then along came a little black animal – it was a dog, but she had never seen a dog before. It barked at her so ferociously that she took fright herself, and fled to the open sea. But never could she forget the splendid woods, the green hills, and the nice children who could swim in the water although they didn't wear fish tails.

The fourth sister was not so venturesome. She stayed far out among the rough waves, which she said was a marvelous place. You could see all around you for miles and miles, and the heavens up above you were like a vast dome of glass. She had seen ships, but they were so far away that they looked like sea gulls. Playful dolphins had turned somersaults, and monstrous whales had spouted water through their nostrils so that it looked as if hundreds of fountains were playing all around them.

Now the fifth sister had her turn. Her birthday came in the wintertime, so she saw things that none of the others had seen. The sea was a deep green color, and enormous icebergs drifted about. Each one glistened like a pearl, she said, but they were more lofty than any church steeple built by man. They assumed the most fantastic shapes, and sparkled like diamonds. She had seated herself on the largest one, and all the ships that came sailing by sped away as soon as the frightened sailors saw her there with her long hair blowing in the wind.

In the late evening clouds filled the sky. Thunder cracked and lightning darted across the heavens. Black waves lifted those great bergs of ice on high, where they flashed when the lightning struck.

On all the ships the sails were reefed and there was fear and trembling. But quietly she sat there, upon her drifting iceberg, and watched the blue forked lightning strike the sea.

Each of the sisters took delight in the lovely new sights when she first rose up to the surface of the sea. But when they became grown-up girls, who were allowed to go wherever they liked, they became indifferent to it. They would become homesick, and in a month they said that there was no place like the bottom of the sea, where they felt so completely at home.

On many an evening the older sisters would rise to the surface, arm in arm, all five in a row. They had beautiful voices, more charming than those of any mortal beings. When a storm was brewing, and they anticipated a shipwreck, they would swim before the ship and sing most seductively of how beautiful it was at the bottom of the ocean, trying to overcome the prejudice that the sailors had against coming down to them. But people could not understand their song, and mistook it for the voice of the storm. Nor was it for them to see the glories of the deep. When their ship went down they were drowned, and it was as dead men that they reached the sea king's palace.

On the evenings when the mermaids rose through the water like this, arm in arm, their youngest sister stayed behind all alone, looking after them and wanting to weep. But a mermaid has no tears, and therefore she suffers so much more.

"Oh, how I do wish I were fifteen!" she said. "I know I shall love that world up there and all the people who live in it."

And at last she too came to be fifteen.

"Now I'll have you off my hands," said her grandmother, the old queen dowager. "Come, let me adorn you like your sisters." In the little maid's hair she put a wreath of white lilies, each petal of which was formed from half of a pearl. And the old queen let eight big oysters fasten themselves to the princess's tail, as a sign of her high rank.

"But that hurts!" said the little mermaid.

"You must put up with a good deal to keep up appearances," her grandmother told her.

Oh, how gladly she would have shaken off all these decorations, and laid aside the cumbersome wreath! The red flowers in her garden were much more becoming to her, but she didn't dare to make any changes. "Good-by," she said, and up she went through the water, as light and as sparkling as a bubble.

The sun had just gone down when her head rose above the surface, but the clouds still shone like gold and roses, and in the delicately tinted sky sparkled the clear gleam of the evening star. The air was mild and fresh and the sea unruffled. A great three-master lay in view with only one of all its sails set, for there was not even the whisper of a breeze,

A great three-master lay in view.
(Honor Appleton)

and the sailors idled about in the rigging and on the yards. There was music and singing on the ship, and as night came on they lighted hundreds of such brightly colored lanterns that one might have thought the flags of all nations were swinging in the air.

The little mermaid swam right up to the window of the main cabin, and each time she rose with the swell she could peep in through the clear glass panes at the crowd of brilliantly dressed people within. The handsomest of them all was a young Prince with big dark eyes. He could not be more than sixteen years old. It was his birthday and that was the reason for all the celebration. Up on deck the sailors were dancing, and when the Prince appeared among them a hundred or more rockets flew through the air, making it as bright as day. These startled the little mermaid so badly that she ducked under the water. But she soon peeped up

again, and then it seemed as if all the stars in the sky were falling around her. Never had she seen such fireworks. Great suns spun around, splendid fire-fish floated through the blue air, and all these things were mirrored in the crystal clear sea. It was so brilliantly bright that you could see every little rope of the ship, and the people could be seen distinctly. Oh, how handsome the young Prince was! He laughed, and he smiled and shook people by the hand, while the music rang out in the perfect evening.

It got very late, but the little mermaid could not take her eyes off the ship and the handsome Prince. The brightly colored lanterns were put out, no more rockets flew through the air, and no more cannon boomed. But there was a mutter and rumble deep down in the sea, and the swell kept bouncing her up so high that she could look into the cabin.

Now the ship began to sail. Canvas after canvas was spread in the wind, the waves rose high, great clouds gathered, and lightning flashed in the distance. Ah, they were in for a terrible storm, and the mariners made haste to reef the sails. The tall ship pitched and rolled as it sped through the angry sea. The waves rose up like towering black mountains, as if they would break over the masthead, but the swan-like ship plunged into the valleys between such waves, and emerged to ride their lofty heights. To the little mermaid this seemed good sport, but to the sailors it was nothing of the sort. The ship creaked and labored, thick timbers gave way under the heavy blows, waves broke over the ship, the mainmast snapped in two like a reed, the ship listed over on its side, and water burst into the hold.

Now the little mermaid saw that people were in peril, and that she herself must take care to avoid the beams and wreckage tossed about by the sea. One moment it would be black as pitch, and she couldn't see a thing. Next moment the lightning would flash so brightly that she could distinguish every soul on board. Everyone was looking out for himself as best he could. She watched closely for the young Prince, and when the ship split in two she saw him sink down in the sea. At first she was overjoyed that he would be with her, but then she recalled that human people could not live under the water, and he could only visit her father's palace as a dead man. No, he should not die! So she swam in among all the floating planks and beams, completely forgetting that they might crush her. She dived through the waves and rode their crests, until at length she reached the young Prince, who was no longer able to swim in that raging sea. His arms and legs were exhausted, his beautiful eyes were closing, and he would have died if the little mermaid had not come to help him. She held his head above water, and let the waves take them wherever the waves went.

She held his head above water, and let the waves take them wherever the waves went.
(Gennady Spinn)

At daybreak, when the storm was over, not a trace of the ship was in view. The sun rose out of the waters, red and bright, and its beams seemed to bring the glow of life back to the cheeks of the Prince, but his eyes remained closed. The mermaid kissed his high and shapely forehead. As she stroked his wet hair in place, it seemed to her that he looked like that marble statue in her little garden. She kissed him again and hoped that he would live.

She saw dry land rise before her in high blue mountains, topped with snow as glistening white as if a flock of swans were resting there. Down by the shore were splendid green woods, and in the foreground stood a church, or perhaps a convent; she didn't know which, but anyway it was a building. Orange and lemon trees grew in its garden, and tall palm trees grew beside the gateway. Here the sea formed a little harbor, quite calm and very deep. Fine white sand had been washed up below the cliffs. She swam there with the handsome Prince, and stretched him out on the sand, taking special care to pillow his head up high in the warm sunlight.

The bells began to ring in the great white building, and a number of young girls came out into the garden. The little mermaid swam away behind some tall rocks that stuck out of the water. She covered her hair and her shoulders with foam so that no one could see her tiny face, and then she watched to see who would find the poor Prince.

In a little while one of the young girls came upon him. She seemed frightened, but only for a minute; then she called more people. The mermaid watched the Prince regain consciousness, and smile at everyone around him. But he did not smile at her, for he did not even know that she had saved him. She felt very unhappy, and when they led him away to the big building she dived sadly down into the water and returned to her father's palace.

She had always been quiet and wistful, and now she became much more so. Her sisters asked her what she had seen on her first visit up to the surface, but she would not tell them a thing.

Many evenings and many mornings she revisited the spot where she had left the Prince. She saw the fruit in the garden ripened and harvested, and she saw the snow on the high mountain melted away, but she did not see the Prince, so each time she came home sadder than she had left. It was her one consolation to sit in her little garden and throw her arms about the beautiful marble statue that looked so much like the Prince. But she took no care of her flowers now. They overgrew the paths until the place was a wilderness, and their long stalks and leaves became so entangled in the branches of the tree that it cast a gloomy shade.

Finally she couldn't bear it any longer. She told her secret to one of her sisters. Immediately all the other sisters heard about it. No one else knew, except a few more mermaids who told no one – except their most intimate friends. One of these friends knew who the Prince was. She too had seen the birthday celebration on the ship. She knew where he came from and where his kingdom was.

"Come, little sister!" said the other princesses. Arm in arm, they rose from the water in a long row, right in front of where they knew the Prince's palace stood. It was built of pale, glistening, golden stone with great marble staircases, one of which led down to the sea. Magnificent gilt domes rose above the roof, and between the pillars all around the building were marble statues that looked most lifelike. Through the clear glass of the lofty windows one could see into the splendid halls, with their costly silk hangings and tapestries, and walls covered with paintings that were delightful to behold. In the center of the main hall a large fountain played its columns of spray up to the glass-domed roof, through which the sun shone down on the water and upon the lovely plants that grew in the big basin.

Now that she knew where he lived, many an evening and many a night she spent there in the sea. She swam much closer to shore than any of her sisters would dare venture, and she even went far up a narrow stream, under the splendid marble balcony that cast its long shadow in the water. Here she used to sit and watch the young Prince when he thought himself quite alone in the bright moonlight.

On many evenings she saw him sail out in his fine boat, with music playing and flags a-flutter. She would peep out through the green rushes, and if the wind blew her long silver veil, anyone who saw it mistook it for a swan spreading its wings.

On many nights she saw the fishermen come out to sea with their torches, and heard them tell about how kind the young Prince was. This made her proud to think that it was she who had saved his life when he was buffeted about, half dead among the waves. And she thought of how softly his head had rested on her breast, and how tenderly she had kissed him, though he knew nothing of all this nor could he even dream of it.

Increasingly she grew to like human beings, and more and more she longed to live among them. Their world seemed so much wider than her own, for they could skim over the sea in ships, and mount up into the lofty peaks high over the clouds, and their lands stretched out in woods and fields farther than the eye could see. There was so much she wanted to know. Her sisters could not answer all her questions, so she asked her old grandmother, who knew about the "upper world," which was what she said was the right name for the countries above the sea.

"If men aren't drowned," the little mermaid asked, "do they live on forever? Don't they die, as we do down here in the sea?"

"Yes," the old lady said, "they too must die, and their lifetimes are even shorter than ours. We can live to be three hundred years old, but when we perish we turn into mere foam on the sea, and haven't even a grave down here among our dear ones. We have no immortal soul, no life hereafter. We are like the green seaweed – once cut down, it never grows again. Human beings, on the contrary, have a soul which lives forever, long after their bodies have turned to clay. It rises through thin air, up to the shining stars. Just as we rise through the water to see the lands on earth, so men rise up to beautiful places unknown, which we shall never see."

"Why weren't we given an immortal soul?" the little mermaid sadly asked. "I would gladly give up my three hundred years if I could be a human being only for a day, and later share in that heavenly realm."

"You must not think about that," said the old lady. "We fare much more happily and are much better off than the folk up there."

"Then I must also die and float as foam upon the sea, not hearing the music of the waves, and seeing neither the beautiful flowers nor the red sun! Can't I do anything at all to win an immortal soul?"

"No," her grandmother answered, "not unless a human being loved you so much that you meant more to him than his father and mother. If his every thought and his whole heart cleaved to you so that he would let a priest join his right hand to yours and would promise to be faithful here and throughout all eternity, then his soul would dwell in your body, and you would share in the happiness of mankind. He would give you a soul and yet keep his own. But that can never come to pass. The very thing that is your greatest beauty here in the sea – your fish tail – would be considered ugly on land. They have such poor taste that to be thought beautiful there you have to have two awkward props which they call legs."

The little mermaid sighed and looked unhappily at her fish tail.

"Come, let us be gay!" the old lady said. "Let us leap and bound throughout the three hundred years that we have to live. Surely that is time and to spare, and afterwards we shall be glad enough to rest in our graves. – We are holding a court ball this evening."

This was a much more glorious affair than is ever to be seen on earth. The walls and the ceiling of the great ballroom were made of massive but transparent glass. Many hundreds of huge rose-red and grass-green shells stood on each side in rows, with the blue flames that burned in each shell illuminating the whole room and shining through the walls so clearly that it was quite bright in the sea outside. You could see the countless fish, great and small, swimming toward the glass walls. On some of them the scales gleamed purplish-red, while others were silver and gold. Across the floor of the hall ran a wide stream of water, and upon this the mermaids and mermen danced to their own entrancing songs. Such beautiful voices are not to be heard among the people who live on land. The little mermaid sang more sweetly than anyone else, and everyone applauded her. For a moment her heart was happy, because she knew she had the loveliest voice of all, in the sea or on the land. But her thoughts soon strayed to the world up above. She could not forget the charming Prince, nor her sorrow that she did not have an immortal soul like his. Therefore she stole out of her father's palace and, while everything there was song and gladness, she sat sadly in her own little garden.

Then she heard a bugle call through the water, and she thought, "That must mean he is sailing up there, he whom I love more than my father or mother, he of whom I am always thinking, and in whose hands I would so willingly trust my lifelong happiness. I dare do anything to win him and to gain an immortal soul. While my sisters are dancing here, in my father's palace, I shall visit the sea witch of whom I have always been so afraid. Perhaps she will be able to advise me and help me."

The little mermaid set out from her garden toward the whirlpools that raged in front of the witch's dwelling. She had never gone that way before. No flowers grew there, nor any seaweed. Bare and gray, the sands extended to the whirlpools, where like roaring mill wheels the waters whirled and snatched everything within their reach down to the bottom of the sea. Between these tumultuous whirlpools she had to thread her way to reach the witch's waters, and then for a long stretch the only trail lay through a hot seething mire, which the witch called her peat marsh. Beyond it her house lay in the middle of a weird forest, where all the trees and shrubs were polyps, half animal and half plant. They looked like hundred-headed snakes growing out of the soil. All their branches were long, slimy arms, with fingers like wriggling worms. They squirmed, joint by joint, from their roots to their outermost tentacles, and whatever they could lay hold of they twined around and never let go. The little mermaid was terrified, and stopped at the edge of the forest. Her heart thumped with fear and she nearly turned back, but then she remembered the Prince and the souls that men have, and she summoned her courage. She bound her long flowing locks closely about her head so that the polyps could not catch hold of them, folded her arms across her breast, and darted through the water like a fish, in among the slimy polyps that stretched out their writhing arms and fingers to seize her. She saw that every one of them held something that it had caught with its hundreds of little tentacles, and to which it clung as with strong hoops of steel. The white bones of men who had perished at sea and sunk to these depths could be seen in the polyps' arms. Ships' rudders, and seamen's chests, and the skeletons of land animals had

also fallen into their clutches, but the most ghastly sight of all was a little mermaid whom they had caught and strangled.

She reached a large muddy clearing in the forest, where big fat water snakes slithered about, showing their foul yellowish bellies. In the middle of this clearing was a house built of the bones of shipwrecked men, and there sat the sea witch, letting a toad eat out of her mouth just as we might feed sugar to a little canary bird. She called the ugly fat water snakes her little chickabiddies, and let them crawl and sprawl about on her spongy bosom.

"I know exactly what you want," said the sea witch. "It is very foolish of you, but just the same you shall have your way, for it will bring you to grief, my proud princess. You want to get rid of your fish tail and have two props instead, so that you can walk about like a human creature, and have the young Prince fall in love with you, and win him and an immortal soul besides." At this, the witch gave such a loud cackling laugh that the toad and the snakes were shaken to the ground, where they lay writhing.

"You are just in time," said the witch. "After the sun comes up tomorrow, a whole year would have to go by before I could be of any help to you. I shall compound you a draft, and before sunrise you must swim to the shore with it, seat yourself on dry land, and drink the draft down. Then your tail will divide and shrink until it becomes what the people on earth call a pair of shapely legs. But it will hurt; it will feel as if a sharp sword slashed through you. Everyone who sees you will say that you are the most graceful human being they have ever laid eyes on, for you will keep your gliding movement and no dancer will be able to tread as lightly as you. But every step you take will feel as if you were treading upon knife blades so sharp that blood must flow. I am willing to help you, but are you willing to suffer all this?"

"Yes," the little mermaid said in a trembling voice, as she thought of the Prince and of gaining a human soul.

"Remember!" said the witch. "Once you have taken a human form, you can never be a mermaid again. You can never come back through the waters to your sisters, or to your father's palace. And if you do not win the love of the Prince so completely that for your sake he forgets his father and mother, cleaves to you with his every thought and his whole heart, and lets the priest join your hands in marriage, then you will win no immortal soul. If he marries someone else, your heart will break on the very next morning, and you will become foam of the sea."

"I shall take that risk," said the little mermaid, but she turned as pale as death.

"Also, you will have to pay me," said the witch, "and it is no trifling price that I'm asking. You have the sweetest voice of anyone down here at the bottom of the sea, and while I don't doubt that you would like to captivate the Prince with it, you must give this voice to me. I will take the very best thing that you have, in return for my sovereign draft. I must pour my own blood in it to make the drink as sharp as a two-edged sword."

"But if you take my voice," said the little mermaid, "what will be left to me?"

"Your lovely form," the witch told her, "your gliding movements, and your eloquent eyes. With these you can easily enchant a human heart. Well, have you lost your courage? Stick out your little tongue and I shall cut it off. I'll have my price, and you shall have the potent draft."

"Go ahead," said the little mermaid.

The witch hung her caldron over the flames, to brew the draft. "Cleanliness is a good thing," she said, as she tied her snakes in a knot and scoured out the pot with them. Then she pricked herself in the chest and let her black blood splash into the caldron. Steam swirled up from it, in such ghastly shapes that anyone would have been terrified by them. The witch constantly threw new ingredients into the caldron, and it started to boil with a sound like that of a crocodile shedding tears. When the draft was ready at last, it looked as clear as the purest water.

"There's your draft," said the witch. And she cut off the tongue of the little mermaid, who now was dumb and could neither sing nor talk.

"If the polyps should pounce on you when you walk back through my wood," the witch said, "just spill a drop of this brew upon them and their tentacles will break in a thousand pieces." But there was no need of that, for the polyps curled up in terror as soon as they saw the bright draft. It glittered in the little mermaid's hand as if it were a shining star. So she soon traversed the forest, the marsh, and the place of raging whirlpools.

She could see her father's palace. The lights had been snuffed out in the great ballroom, and doubtless everyone in the palace was asleep, but she dared not go near them, now that she was stricken dumb and was leaving her home forever. Her heart felt as if it would break with grief. She tip-toed into the garden, took one flower from each of her sisters' little plots, blew a thousand kisses toward the palace, and then mounted up through the dark blue sea.

The sun had not yet risen when she saw the Prince's palace. As she climbed his splendid marble staircase, the moon was shining clear. The little mermaid swallowed the bitter, fiery draut, and it was as if a two-edged sword struck through her frail body. She swooned away, and lay there as if she were dead. When the sun rose over the sea she awoke and felt a flash of pain, but directly in front of her stood the handsome young Prince, gazing at her with his coal-black eyes. Lowering her gaze, she saw that her fish tail was gone, and that she had the loveliest pair of white legs any young maid could hope to have. But she was naked, so she clothed herself in her own long hair.

The Prince asked who she was, and how she came to be there. Her deep blue eyes looked at him tenderly but very sadly, for she could not speak. Then he took her hand and led her into his palace. Every footstep felt as if she were walking on the blades and points of sharp knives, just as the witch had foretold, but she gladly endured it. She moved as lightly as a bubble as she walked beside the Prince. He and all who saw her marveled at the grace of her gliding walk.

Once clad in the rich silk and muslin garments that were provided for her, she was the loveliest person in all the palace, though she was dumb and could neither sing nor speak. Beautiful slaves, attired in silk and cloth of gold, came to sing before the Prince and his royal parents. One of them sang more sweetly than all the others, and when the Prince smiled at her and clapped his hands, the little mermaid felt very unhappy, for she knew that she herself used to sing much more sweetly.

"Oh," she thought, "if he only knew that I parted with my voice forever so that I could be near him."

Graceful slaves now began to dance to the most wonderful music. Then the little mermaid lifted her shapely white arms, rose up on the tips of her toes, and skimmed over the floor. No one had ever danced so well. Each movement set off her beauty to better and better advantage, and her eyes spoke more directly to the heart than any of the singing slaves could do.

She charmed everyone, and especially the Prince, who called her his dear little foundling. She danced time and again, though every time she touched the floor she felt as if she were treading on sharp-edged steel. The Prince said he would keep her with him always, and that she was to have a velvet pillow to sleep on outside his door.

He had a page's suit made for her, so that she could go with him on horseback. They would ride through the sweet scented woods, where the green boughs brushed her shoulders, and where the little birds sang among the fluttering leaves.

She climbed up high mountains with the Prince, and though her tender feet bled so that all could see it, she only laughed and followed him on until they could see the clouds driving far below, like a flock of birds in flight to distant lands.

At home in the Prince's palace, while the others slept at night, she would go down the broad marble steps to cool her burning feet in the cold sea water, and then she would recall those who lived beneath the sea. One night her sisters came by, arm in arm, singing sadly as they breasted the waves. When she held out her hands toward them, they knew who she was, and told her how unhappy she had made them all. They came to see her every night after that, and once far, far out to sea, she saw her old grandmother, who had not been up to the surface this many a year. With her was the sea king, with his crown upon his head. They stretched out their hands to her, but they did not venture so near the land as her sisters had.

Day after day she became more dear to the Prince, who loved her as one would love a good little child, but he never thought of making her his Queen. Yet she had to be his wife or she would never have an immortal soul, and on the morning after his wedding she would turn into foam on the waves.

"Don't you love me best of all?" the little mermaid's eyes seemed to question him, when he took her in his arms and kissed her lovely forehead.

"Yes, you are most dear to me," said the Prince, "for you have the kindest heart. You love me more than anyone else does, and you look so much like a young girl I once saw but never shall find again. I was on a ship that was wrecked, and the waves cast me ashore near a holy temple, where many young girls performed the rituals. The youngest of them found me beside the sea and saved my life. Though I saw her no more than twice, she is the only person in all the world whom I could love. But you are so much like her that you almost replace the memory of her in my heart. She belongs to that holy temple, therefore it is my good fortune that I have you. We shall never part."

"Alas, he doesn't know it was I who saved his life," the little mermaid thought. "I carried him over the sea to the garden where the temple stands. I hid behind the foam and watched to see if anyone would come. I saw the pretty maid he loves better than me." A sigh was the only sign of her deep distress, for a mermaid cannot cry. "He says that the other maid belongs to the holy temple. She will never come out into the world, so they will never see each other again. It is I who will care for him, love him, and give all my life to him."

Now rumors arose that the Prince was to wed the beautiful daughter of a neighboring King, and that it was for this reason he was having such a superb ship made ready to sail. The rumor ran that the Prince's real interest in visiting the neighboring kingdom was to see the King's daughter, and that he was to travel with a lordly retinue. The little mermaid shook her head and smiled, for she knew the Prince's thoughts far better than anyone else did.

"I am forced to make this journey," he told her. "I must visit the beautiful Princess, for this is my parents' wish, but they would not have me bring her home as my bride against my own will, and I can never love her. She does not resemble the lovely maiden in the temple, as you do, and if I were to choose a bride, I would sooner choose you, my dear mute foundling with those telling eyes of yours."

And he kissed her on the mouth, fingered her long hair, and laid his head against her heart so that she came to dream of mortal happiness and an immortal soul.

"I trust you aren't afraid of the sea, my silent child," he said, as they went on board the magnificent vessel that was to carry them to the land of the neighboring King. And he told her stories of storms, of ships becalmed, of strange deep-sea fish, and of the wonders that divers have seen. She smiled at such stories, for no one knew about the bottom of the sea as well as she did.

In the clear moonlight, when everyone except the man at the helm was asleep, she sat on the side of the ship gazing down through the transparent water, and fancied she could catch glimpses of her father's palace. On the topmost tower stood her old grandmother, wearing her silver crown and looking up at the keel of the ship through the rushing waves. Then her sisters rose to the surface, looked at her sadly, and wrung their white hands. She smiled and waved, trying to let them know that all went well and that she was happy. But along came the cabin boy, and her sisters dived out of sight so quickly that the boy supposed the flash of white he had seen was merely foam on the sea.

Next morning the ship came in to the harbor of the neighboring King's glorious city. All the church bells chimed, and trumpets were sounded from all the high towers, while the soldiers lined up with flying banners and glittering bayonets. Every day had a new festivity, as one ball or levee followed another, but the Princess was still to appear. They said she was being brought up in some far-away sacred temple, where she was learning every royal virtue. But she came at last.

The little mermaid was curious to see how beautiful this Princess was, and she had to grant that a more exquisite figure she had never seen. The Princess's skin was clear and fair, and behind the long, dark lashes her deep blue eyes were smiling and devoted.

"It was you!" the Prince cried. "You are the one who saved me when I lay like a dead man beside the sea." He clasped the blushing bride of his choice in his arms. "Oh, I am happier than a man should be!" he told his little mermaid. "My fondest dream – that which I never dared to hope – has come true. You will share in my great joy, for you love me more than anyone does."

The little mermaid kissed his hand and felt that her heart was beginning to break. For the morning after his wedding day would see her dead and turned to watery foam.

All the church bells rang out, and heralds rode through the streets to announce the wedding. Upon every altar sweet-scented oils were burned in costly silver lamps. The priests swung their censers, the bride and the bridegroom joined their hands, and the bishop blessed their marriage. The little mermaid, clothed in silk and cloth of gold, held the bride's train, but she was deaf to the wedding march and blind to the holy ritual. Her thought turned on her last night upon earth, and on all she had lost in this world.

That same evening, the bride and bridegroom went aboard the ship. Cannon thundered and banners waved. On the deck of the ship a royal pavilion of purple and gold was set up, and furnished with luxurious cushions. Here the wedded couple were to sleep on that calm, clear night. The sails swelled in the breeze, and the ship glided so lightly that it scarcely seemed to move over the quiet sea. All nightfall brightly colored lanterns were lighted, and the mariners merrily danced on the deck. The little mermaid could not forget that first time she rose from the depths of the sea and looked on at such pomp and happiness. Light as a swallow pursued by his enemies, she joined in the whirling dance. Everyone cheered her, for never had she danced so wonderfully.

Her tender feet felt as if they were pierced by daggers, but she did not feel it. Her heart suffered far greater pain. She knew that this was the last evening that she ever would see him for whom she had forsaken her home and family, for whom she had sacrificed her lovely voice and suffered such constant torment, while he knew nothing of all these things. It was the last night that she would breathe the same air with him, or look upon deep waters or the star fields of the blue sky. A never-ending night, without thought and without dreams, awaited her who had no soul and could not get one. The merrymaking lasted long after midnight, yet she laughed and danced on despite the thought of death she carried in her heart. The Prince kissed his beautiful bride and she toyed with his coal-black hair. Hand in hand, they went to rest in the magnificent pavilion.

A hush came over the ship. Only the helmsman remained on deck as the little mermaid leaned her white arms on the bulwarks and looked to the east to see the first red hint of daybreak, for she knew that the first flash of the sun would strike her dead. Then she saw her sisters rise up among the waves. They were as pale as she, and there was no sign of their lovely long hair that the breezes used to blow. It had all been cut off.

"We have given our hair to the witch," they said, "so that she would send you help, and save you from death tonight. She gave us a knife. Here it is. See the sharp blade! Before the sun rises, you must strike it into the Prince's heart, and when his warm blood bathes your feet they will grow together and become a fish tail. Then you will be a mermaid again, able to come back to us in the sea, and live out your three hundred years before you die and turn into dead salt sea foam. Make haste! He or you must die before sunrise. Our old grandmother is so grief-stricken that her white hair is falling fast, just as ours did under the witch's scissors. Kill the Prince and come back to us. Hurry!

"We are the daughters of the air," they answered. (W. Heath Robinson)

Hurry! See that red glow in the heavens! In a few minutes the sun will rise and you must die." So saying, they gave a strange deep sigh and sank beneath the waves.

The little mermaid parted the purple curtains of the tent and saw the beautiful bride asleep with her head on the Prince's breast. The mermaid bent down and kissed his shapely forehead. She looked at the sky, fast reddening for the break of day. She looked at the sharp knife and again turned her eyes toward the Prince, who in his sleep murmured the name of his bride. His thoughts were all for her, and the knife blade trembled in the mermaid's hand. But then she flung it from her, far out over the waves. Where it fell the waves were red, as if bubbles of blood seethed in the water. With eyes already glazing she looked once more at the Prince, hurled herself over the bulwarks into the sea, and felt her body dissolve in foam.

The sun rose up from the waters. Its beams fell, warm and kindly, upon the chill sea foam, and the little mermaid did not feel the hand of death. In the bright sunlight overhead, she saw hundreds of fair ethereal beings. They were so transparent that through them she could see the ship's white sails and the red clouds in the sky. Their voices were sheer music, but so spirit-like that no human ear could detect the sound, just as no eye on earth could see their forms. Without wings, they floated as light as the air itself. The little mermaid discovered that she was shaped like them, and that she was gradually rising up out of the foam.

"Who are you, toward whom I rise?" she asked, and her voice sounded like those above her, so spiritual that no music on earth could match it.

"We are the daughters of the air," they answered. "A mermaid has no immortal soul, and can never get one unless she wins the love of a human being. Her eternal life must depend upon a power outside herself. The daughters of the air do not have an immortal soul either, but they can earn one by their good deeds. We fly to the south, where the hot poisonous air kills human beings unless we bring cool breezes. We carry the scent of flowers through the air, bringing freshness and healing balm wherever we go. When for three hundred years we have tried to do all the good that we can, we are given an immortal soul and a share in mankind's eternal bliss. You, poor little mermaid, have tried with your whole heart to do this too. Your suffering and your loyalty have raised you up into the realm of airy spirits, and now in the course of three hundred years you may earn by your good deeds a soul that will never die."

The little mermaid lifted her clear bright eyes toward God's sun, and for the first time her eyes were wet with tears.

On board the ship all was astir and lively again. She saw the Prince and his fair bride in search of her. Then they gazed sadly into the seething foam, as if they knew she had hurled herself into the waves. Unseen by them, she kissed the bride's forehead, smiled upon the Prince, and rose up with the other daughters of the air to the rose-red clouds that sailed on high.

"This is the way that we shall rise to the kingdom of God, after three hundred years have passed."

"We may get there even sooner," one spirit whispered. "Unseen, we fly into the homes of men, where there are children, and for every day on which we find a good child who pleases his parents and deserves their love, God shortens our days of trial. The child does not know when we float through his room, but when we smile at him in approval one year is taken from our three hundred. But if we see a naughty, mischievous child we must shed tears of sorrow, and each tear adds a day to the time of our trial."

THE EMPEROR'S NEW CLOTHES

MANY YEARS AGO there was an Emperor so exceedingly fond of new clothes that he spent all his money on being well dressed. He cared nothing about reviewing his soldiers, going to the theater, or going for a ride in his carriage, except to show off his new clothes. He had a coat for every hour of the day, and instead of saying, as one might, about any other ruler, "The King's in council," here they always said. "The Emperor's in his dressing room."

In the great city where he lived, life was always gay. Every day many strangers came to town, and among them one day came two swindlers. They let it be known they were weavers, and they said they could weave the most magnificent fabrics imaginable. Not only were their colors and patterns uncommonly fine, but clothes made of this cloth had a wonderful way of becoming invisible to anyone who was unfit for his office, or who was unusually stupid.

"Those would be just the clothes for me," thought the Emperor. "If I wore them I would be able to discover which men in my empire are unfit for their posts. And I could tell the wise men from the fools. Yes, I certainly must get some of the stuff woven for me right away." He paid the two swindlers a large sum of money to start work at once.

They set up two looms and pretended to weave, though there was nothing on the looms. All the finest silk and the purest gold thread which they demanded went into their traveling bags, while they worked the empty looms far into the night.

"I'd like to know how those weavers are getting on with the cloth," the Emperor thought, but he felt slightly uncomfortable when he remembered that those who were unfit for their position would not be able to see the fabric. It couldn't have been that he doubted himself, yet he thought he'd rather send someone else to see how things were going. The whole town knew about the cloth's peculiar power, and all were impatient to find out how stupid their neighbors were.

"I'll send my honest old minister to the weavers," the Emperor decided. "He'll be the best one to tell me how the material looks, for he's a sensible man and no one does his duty better."

So the honest old minister went to the room where the two swindlers sat working away at their empty looms.

"Heaven help me," he thought as his eyes flew wide open, "I can't see anything at all". But he did not say so.

Both the swindlers begged him to be so kind as to come near to approve the excellent pattern, the beautiful colors. They pointed to the empty looms, and the poor old minister stared as hard as he dared. He couldn't see anything, because there was nothing to see. "Heaven have mercy," he thought. "Can it be that I'm a fool? I'd have never guessed it, and not a soul must know. Am I unfit to be the minister? It would never do to let on that I can't see the cloth."

"Don't hesitate to tell us what you think of it," said one of the weavers.

"Oh, it's beautiful – it's enchanting." The old minister peered through his spectacles. "Such a pattern, what colors! I'll be sure to tell the Emperor how delighted I am with it."

"We're pleased to hear that," the swindlers said. They proceeded to name all the colors and to explain the intricate pattern. The old minister paid the closest attention, so that he could tell it all to the Emperor. And so he did.

The swindlers at once asked for more money, more silk and gold thread, to get on with the weaving. But it all went into their pockets.

Not a thread went into the looms, though they worked at their weaving as hard as ever.

The Emperor presently sent another trustworthy official to see how the work progressed and how soon it would be ready. The same thing happened to him that had happened to the minister. He looked and he looked, but as there was nothing to see in the looms he couldn't see anything.

"Isn't it a beautiful piece of goods?" the swindlers asked him, as they displayed and described their imaginary pattern.

"I know I'm not stupid," the man thought, "so it must be that I'm unworthy of my good office. That's strange. I mustn't let anyone find it out, though." So he praised the material he did not see. He declared he was delighted with the beautiful colors and the exquisite pattern. To the Emperor he said, "It held me spellbound."

All the town was talking of this splendid cloth, and the Emperor wanted to see it for himself while it was still in the looms. Attended by a band of chosen men, among whom were his two old trusted officials – the ones who had been to the weavers – he set out to see the two swindlers. He found them weaving with might and main, but without a thread in their looms.

"Magnificent," said the two officials already duped. "Just look, Your Majesty, what colors! What a design!" They pointed to the empty looms, each supposing that the others could see the stuff.

"What's this?" thought the Emperor. "I can't see anything. This is terrible! Am I a fool? Am I unfit to be the Emperor? What a thing to happen to me of all people! – Oh! It's *very* pretty," he said. "It has my highest approval." And he nodded approbation at the empty loom. Nothing could make him say that he couldn't see anything.

His whole retinue stared and stared. One saw no more than another, but they all joined the

So off went the Emperor in procession.
(Paul Hey)

Emperor in exclaiming, "Oh! It's *very* pretty," and they advised him to wear clothes made of this wonderful cloth especially for the great procession he was soon to lead. "Magnificent! Excellent! Unsurpassed!" were bandied from mouth to mouth, and everyone did his best to seem well pleased. The Emperor gave each of the swindlers a cross to wear in his buttonhole, and the title of "Sir Weaver."

Before the procession the swindlers sat up all night and burned more than six candles, to show how busy they were finishing the Emperor's new clothes. They pretended to take the cloth off the loom. They made cuts in the air with huge scissors. And at last they said, "Now the Emperor's new clothes are ready for him."

Then the Emperor himself came with his noblest noblemen, and the swindlers each raised an arm as if they were holding something. They said, "These are the trousers, here's the coat, and this is the mantle," naming each garment. "All of them are as light as a spider web. One would almost think he had nothing on, but that's what makes them so fine."

"Exactly," all the noblemen agreed, though they could see nothing, for there was nothing to see.

"If Your Imperial Majesty will condescend to take your clothes off," said the swindlers, "we will help you on with your new ones here in front of the long mirror."

The Emperor undressed, and the swindlers pretended to put his new clothes on him, one garment after another. They took him around the waist and seemed to be fastening something – that was his train – as the Emperor turned round and round before the looking glass.

"How well Your Majesty's new clothes look. Aren't they becoming!" He heard on all sides, "That pattern, so perfect! Those colors, so suitable! It is a magnificent outfit."

Then the minister of public processions announced: "Your Majesty's canopy is waiting outside."

"Well, I'm supposed to be ready," the Emperor said, and turned again for one last look in the mirror. "It is a remarkable fit, isn't it?" He seemed to regard his costume with the greatest interest.

The noblemen who were to carry his train stooped low and reached for the floor as if they were picking up his mantle. Then they pretended to lift and hold it high. They didn't dare admit they had nothing to hold.

So off went the Emperor in procession under his splendid canopy. Everyone in the streets and the windows said, "Oh, how fine are the Emperor's new clothes! Don't they fit him to perfection? And see his long train!" Nobody would confess that he couldn't see anything,

for that would prove him either unfit for his position, or a fool. No costume the Emperor had worn before was ever such a complete success.

"But he hasn't got anything on," a little child said.

"But he hasn't got anything on," a little child said. (Arthur Rackham)

"Did you ever hear such innocent prattle?" said its father. And one person whispered to another what the child had said, "He hasn't anything on. A child says he hasn't anything on."

"But he hasn't got anything on!" the whole town cried out at last.

The Emperor shivered, for he suspected they were right. But he thought, "This procession has got to go on." So he walked more proudly than ever, as his noblemen held high the train that wasn't there at all.

THE GALOSHES OF FORTUNE

1

A BEGINNING

IT WAS IN Copenhagen, in one of the houses on East Street, not far from King's Newmarket, that someone was giving a large party. For one must give a party once in a while, if one expects to be invited in return. Half of the guests were already at the card tables, and the rest were waiting to see what would come of their hostess's query:

"What can we think up now?"

Up to this point, their conversation had gotten along as best it might. Among other things, they had spoken of the Middle Ages. Some held that it was a time far better than our own. Indeed Councilor of Justice Knap defended this opinion with such spirit that his hostess sided with him at once, and both of them loudly took exception to Oersted's article in the Almanac, which contrasted old times and new, and which favored our own period. The Councilor of Justice, however, held that the time of King Hans, about 1500 A.D., was the noblest and happiest age.

While the conversation ran pro and con, interrupted only for a moment by the arrival of a newspaper, in which there was nothing worth reading, let us adjourn to the cloak room, where all the wraps, canes, umbrellas, and galoshes were collected together. Here sat two maids, a young one and an old one. You might have thought they had come in attendance upon some spinster or widow, and were waiting to see their mistress home. However, a closer inspection would reveal that these were no ordinary serving women. Their hands were too well kept for that, their bearing and movements too graceful, and their clothes had a certain daring cut.

They were two fairies. The younger one, though not Dame Fortune herself, was an assistant to one of her ladies-in-waiting, and was used to deliver the more trifling gifts of Fortune. The older one looked quite grave. She was Dame Care, who always goes in her own sublime person to see to her errands herself, for then she knows that they are well done.

They were telling each other about where they had been that day. The assistant of Fortune had only attended to a few minor affairs, she said, such as saving a new bonnet from the rain, getting a civil greeting for an honest man from an exalted nincompoop, and such like matters. But her remaining errand was an extraordinary one.

"I must also tell you," she said, "that today is my birthday, and in honor of this I have been entrusted to bring a pair of galoshes to mankind. These galoshes have this peculiarity, that whoever puts them on will immediately find himself in whatever time, place, and condition of life that he prefers. His every wish in regard to time and place will instantly be granted, so for once a man can find perfect happiness here below."

"Take my word for it," said Dame Care, "he will be most unhappy, and will bless the moment when he can rid himself of those galoshes."

"How can you say such a thing?" the other woman exclaimed. "I shall leave them here beside the door, where someone will put them on by mistake and immediately be the happy one."

That ended their conversation.

II

WHAT HAPPENED TO THE COUNCILOR OF JUSTICE

It was getting late when Councilor Knap decided to go home. Lost in thought about the good old days of King Hans, as fate would have it, he put on the galoshes of Fortune instead of his own, and wore them out into East Street. But the power that lay in the galoshes took him back into the reign of King Hans, and as the streets were not paved in those days his feet sank deep into the mud and the mire.

"Why, how deplorable!" the Councilor of Justice said. "The whole sidewalk is gone and all the street lights are out."

As the moon had not yet risen high enough, and the air was somewhat foggy, everything around him was dark and blurred. At the next corner a lantern hung before an image of the Madonna, but for all the light it afforded him it might as well not have been there. Only when he stood directly under it did he make out that painting of the mother and child.

"It's probably an art museum," he thought, "and they have forgotten to take in the sign."

Two people in medieval costumes passed by.

"How strange they looked!" he said. "They must have been to a masquerade."

Just then the sound of drums and fifes came his way, and bright torches flared. The Councilor of Justice stopped and was startled to see an odd procession go past, led by a whole band of drummers who were dexterously drubbing away. These were followed by soldiers armed with long bows and crossbows. The chief personage of the procession was a churchman of rank. The astounded Councilor asked what all this meant, and who the man might be.

"That is the Bishop of Seeland," he was told.

"What in the name of heaven can have come over the Bishop?" the Councilor of Justice wondered. He sighed and shook his head. "The Bishop? Impossible."

Still pondering about it, without glancing to right or to left, he kept on down East Street and across Highbridge Square. The bridge that led from there to Palace Square was not to be found at all; at last on the bank of the shallow stream he saw a boat with two men in it.

"Would the gentleman want to be ferried over to the Holm?" they asked him.

"To the Holm?" blurted the Councilor, who had not the faintest notion that he was living in another age. "I want to go to Christian's Harbor on Little Market Street."

The men gaped at him.

"Kindly tell me where the bridge is," he said. "It's disgraceful that all the street lamps are out, and besides, it's as muddy to walk here as in a swamp." But the more he talked with the boatmen, the less they understood each other. "I can't understand your jabbering Bornholm accent," he finally said, and angrily turned his back on them. But no bridge could he find. Even the fence was gone.

"What a scandalous state of affairs! What a way for things to look!" he said. Never had he been so disgruntled with his own age as he was this evening. "I think I'd better take a cab." But where were the cabs? There were none in sight. "I'll have to go back to King's Newmarket, where there is a cab stand, or I shall never reach Christian's Harbor."

So back he trudged to East Street, and had nearly walked the length of it when the moon rose.

"Good Heavens, what have they been building here?" he cried as he beheld the East Gate, which in the old days stood at the end of East Street. In time, however, he found a gate through which he passed into what is now Newmarket. But all he saw there was a large meadow. A few bushes rose here and there and the meadow was divided by a wide canal or

"Kindly tell me where the bridge is," he said.
(Fritz Kredel)

stream. The few wretched wooden huts on the far shore belonged to Dutch sailors, so at that time the place was called Dutch Meadow.

"Either I'm seeing what is called Fata Morgana, or I'm drunk," the Councilor of Justice moaned. "What sort of place is this? Where am I?" He turned back, convinced that he must be a very ill man. As he walked through the street again he paid more attention to the houses. Most of them were of wood, and many were thatched with straw.

"No, I don't feel myself at all," he complained. "I only took one glass of punch, but it doesn't agree with me. The idea of serving punch with hot salmon! I'll speak about it severely to our hostess – that agent's wife. Should I march straight back and tell her how I feel? No, that would be in bad taste, and besides I doubt whether her household is still awake." He searched for the house, but wasn't able to find it.

"This is terrible!" he cried. "I don't even recognize East Street. There's not a shop to be seen; wretched old ramshackle huts are all I see, as if I were in Roskilde or Ringstedt. Oh, but I'm ill! There's no point in standing on ceremony, but where on earth is the agent's house? This hut doesn't look remotely like it,

but I can hear that the people inside are still awake. Ah, I'm indeed a very sick man."

He reached a half-open door, where light flickered through the crack. It was a tavern of that period – a sort of alehouse. The room had the look of a farmer's clay-floored kitchen in Holstein, and the people who sat there were sailors, citizens of Copenhagen, and a couple of scholars. Deep in conversation over their mugs, they paid little attention to the newcomer.

"Pardon me," the Councilor of Justice said to the landlady who came toward him, "but I am far from well. Would you send someone for a cab to take me to Christian's Harbor?"

The woman stared at him, shook her head, and addressed him in German. As the Councilor of Justice supposed that she could not speak Danish, he repeated his remarks in German. This, and the cut of his clothes, convinced the woman that he was a foreigner. She soon understood that he felt unwell, and fetched him a mug of water, decidedly brackish, for she drew it directly from the sea-level well outside. The Councilor put his head in his hands, took a deep breath, and thought over all of the queer things that surrounded him.

"Is that tonight's number of *The Day*?" he remarked from force of habit, as he saw the woman putting away a large folded sheet. Without quite understanding him, she handed him the paper. It was a woodcut, representing a meteor seen in the skies over Cologne.

"This is very old," said the Councilor, who became quite enthusiastic about his discovery. "Where did you get this rare old print? It's most interesting, although of course the whole matter is a myth. In this day and age, such meteors are explained away as a manifestation of the Northern Lights, probably caused by electricity."

Those who sat near him heard the remark and looked at him in astonishment. One of them rose, respectfully doffed his hat, and said with the utmost gravity:

"Sir, you must be a great scholar."

"Not at all," replied the Councilor. "I merely have a word or two to say about things that everyone should know."

"*Modestia* is an admirable virtue," the man declared. "In regard to your statement, I must say, *mihi secus videtur*, though I shall be happy to suspend my *judicium*."

"May I ask whom I have the pleasure of addressing?" the Councilor of Justice inquired.

"I am a Bachelor of Theology," the man told him in Latin.

This answer satisfied the Councilor of Justice, for the degree was in harmony with the fellow's way of dressing. "Obviously," he thought, "this is some old village schoolmaster, an odd character such as one still comes across now and then, up in Jutland."

"This is scarcely a *locus docendi*," the man continued, "but I entreat you to favor us with your conversation. You, of course, are well read in the classics?"

"Oh, more or less," the Councilor agreed. "I like to read the standard old books, and the new ones too, except for those 'Every Day Stories' of which we have enough in reality."

" 'Every Day Stories'?" our bachelor asked.

"Yes, I mean these modern novels."

"Oh," the man said with a smile. "Still they are very clever, and are popular with the court. King Hans is particularly fond of the 'Romance of Iwain and Jawain,' which deals with King Arthur and his Knights of the Round Table. The king has been known to jest with his lords about it."

"Well," said the Councilor, "one can't keep up with all the new books. I suppose it has just been published by Heiberg."

"No," the man said, "not by Heiberg, but by Gotfred von Ghemen."

"Indeed! What a fine old name for a literary man. Why Gotfred von Ghemen was the first printer in Denmark."

"Yes," the man agreed, "he is our first and foremost printer."

Thus far, their conversation had flowed quite smoothly. Now one of the townsmen began to talk about the pestilence which had raged some years back, meaning the plague of 1484. The Councilor understood him to mean the last epidemic of cholera, so they agreed well enough.

The Freebooters' War of 1490 was so recent that it could not be passed over. The English raiders had taken ships from our harbor, they said, and the Councilor of Justice, who was well posted on the affair of 1801, manfully helped them to abuse the English.

After that, however, the talk floundered from one contradiction to another. The worthy bachelor was so completely unenlightened that the Councilor's most commonplace remarks struck him as being too daring and too fantastic. They stared at each other, and when they reached an impasse the bachelor broke into Latin, in the hope that he would be better understood, but that didn't help.

The landlady plucked at the Councilor's sleeve and asked him, "How do you feel now?" This forcibly recalled to him all of those things which he had happily forgotten in the heat of his conversation.

"Merciful heaven, where am I?" he wondered, and the thought made him dizzy.

"We will drink claret wine, and mead, and Bremen beer," one of the guests cried out, "and you shall drink with us." Two girls came in, and one of them wore a cap of two colors. They filled the glasses and made curtsies. The Councilor felt cold shivers up and down his spine. "What is all this? What is all this?" he groaned, but drink with them he must. They overwhelmed him with their kind intentions until he despaired, and when one man pronounced him drunk he didn't doubt it in the least. All he asked was that they get him a *droschke*. Then they thought he was speaking in Russian.

Never before had he been in such low and vulgar company! "One would think that the country had lapsed back into barbarism," he told himself. "This is the most dreadful moment of my life."

Then it occurred to him to slip down under the table, crawl to the door, and try to sneak out, but just as he neared the threshold his companions discovered him and tried to pull him out by his feet. However, by great good luck they pulled off his galoshes, and – with them – the whole enchantment.

The Councilor of Justice now distinctly saw a street lamp burning in front of a large building. He knew the building and the other buildings nearby. It was East Street as we all know it today. He lay on the pavement with his legs against a gate, and across the way a night watchman sat fast asleep.

"Merciful heavens! Have I been lying here in the street dreaming?" the Councilor of Justice said. "To be sure, this is East Street. How blessedly bright and how colorful it looks. But what dreadful effect that one glass of punch must have had on me."

Two minutes later he was seated in a cab, and well on his way to Christian's Harbor. As he recalled all the past terror and distress to which he had been subjected, he whole-heartedly approved of the present, our own happy age. With all its shortcomings it was far preferable to that age into which he had recently stumbled. And that, thought the Councilor of Justice, was good common sense.

III

THE WATCHMAN'S ADVENTURE

"Why, I declare! There's a pair of galoshes," said the watchman. "They must belong to the lieutenant who lives up there on the top floor, for they are lying in front of the door." A light still burned upstairs, and the honest fellow was perfectly willing to ring the bell and return the overshoes. But he didn't want to disturb the other tenants in the house, so he didn't do it.

"It must be quite comfortable to wear a pair of such things," he said. "How soft the leather feels." They fitted his feet perfectly. "What a strange world we live in. The lieutenant might be resting easy in his soft bed, yet there he goes, pacing to and fro past his window. There's a happy man for you! He has no wife, and he has no child, and every night he goes to a party. Oh, if I were only in his place, what a happy man I would be."

Just as he expressed his wish, the galoshes transformed him into the lieutenant, body and soul, and there he stood in the room upstairs. Between his fingers he held a sheet of pink paper on which the lieutenant had just written a poem. Who is there that has not at some time in his life felt poetic? If he writes down

A light still burned upstairs.
(Edmund Dulac)

his thoughts while this mood is on him, poetry is apt to come of it. On the paper was written:

IF ONLY I WERE RICH

"If only I were rich;" I often said in prayer
"When I was but a tiny lad without much
    care
If only I were rich, a soldier I would be
With uniform and sword, most handsomely;
At last an officer I was, my wish I got
But to be rich was not my lot;
But You, oh Lord, would always help.

"I sat one eve, so happy, young and proud;
A darling child of seven kissed my mouth
For I was rich with fairy tales, you see
With money I was poor as poor can be,
But she was fond of tales I told
That made me rich, but – alas – not with
    gold;
But You, oh Lord, You know!

"If only I were rich, is still my heavenly
    prayer.
My little girl of seven is now a lady fair;
She is so sweet, so clever and so good;
My heart's fair tale she never understood.
If only, as of yore, she still for me would care,
But I am poor and silent; I confess I do not
    dare.
It is Your will, oh Lord!

"If only I were rich, in peace and comfort
    rest,
I would my sorrow to this paper never trust.
You, whom I love, if still you understand
Then read this poem from my youth's far
    land,
Though best it be you never know my pain.
I am still poor, my future dark and vain,
But may, O Lord, You bless her!"

Yes, a man in love writes many a poem that a man in his right mind does not print. A lieutenant, his love and his lack of money – there's an eternal triangle for you, a broken life that can never be squared. The lieutenant knew this all too well. He leaned his head against the window, and sighed, and said:

"The poor watchman down there in the street is a far happier man than I. He does not know what I call want. He has a home. He has a wife and children who weep with him in his sorrows and share in his joy. Ah, I would be happier if I could trade places with him, for he is much more fortunate than I am."

Instantly, the watchman was himself again. The galoshes had transformed him into the lieutenant, as we have seen. He was far less contented up there, and preferred to be just what he had been. So the watchman turned back into a watchman.

"I had a bad dream," he said. "Strangely enough, I fancied I was the lieutenant, and I didn't like it a bit. I missed my wife and our youngsters, who almost smother me with their kisses."

He sat down and fell to nodding again, unable to get the dream out of his head. The galoshes were still on his feet when he watched a star fall in the sky.

"There goes one," he muttered. "But there are so many it will never be missed. I'd like to have a look at those trinkets at close range. I'd especially like to see the moon, which is not the sort of thing to get lost in one's hands. The student for whom my wife washes, says that when we die we fly about from star to star. There's not a word of truth in it. But it would be nice, just the same, if I could take a little jaunt through the skies. My body could stay here on the steps for all that I'd care."

Now there are certain things in the world that we ought to think about before we put them into words, and if we are wearing the galoshes of Fortune it behooves us to think twice. Just listen to what happened to that watchman.

All of us know how fast steam can take us. We've either rushed along in a train or sped

Now there are certain things in the world that we ought to think about before we put them into words. (Fritz Kredel)

by steamship across the ocean. But all this is like the gait of a sloth, or the pace of a snail, in comparison with the speed of light, which travels nineteen million times faster than the fastest race horse. Yet electricity moves even faster. Death is an electric shock to the heart, and the soul set free travels on electric wings. The sunlight takes eight minutes and some odd seconds to travel nearly one hundred million miles. On the wings of electricity, the soul can make the same journey in a few moments, and to a soul set free the heavenly bodies are as close together as the houses of friends who live in the same town with us, or even in the same neighborhood. However, this electric shock strips us of our bodies forever, unless, like the watchman, we happen to be wearing the galoshes of Fortune.

In a few seconds the watchman took in his stride the two hundred and sixty thousand miles to the moon. As we know, this satellite is made of much lighter material than the earth, and is as soft as freshly fallen snow. The watchman landed in one of the numerous mountain rings which we all know from Doctor Maedler's large map of the moon. Within the ring was a great bowl, fully four miles deep. At the bottom of this bowl lay a town. We may get some idea of what it looked like by pouring the white of an egg into a glass of water. The town was made of stuff as soft as the egg albumen, and its form was similar, with translucent towers, cupolas, and terraces, all floating in thin air.

Over the watchman's head hung our earth, like a huge dull red ball. Around him he noticed crowds of beings who doubtless corresponded to men and women of the earth, but their appearance was quite different from ours. They also had their own way of speaking, but no one could expect that the soul of a watchman would understand them. Nevertheless he did understand the language of the people in the moon very well. They were disputing about our earth, and doubting whether it could be inhabited. The air on the earth, they contended, must be too thick for any intelligent moon-man to live there. Only the moon was inhabited, they agreed, for it was the original sphere on which the people of the Old World lived.

Now let us go back down to East Street, to see how the watchman's body was making out. Lifeless it lay, there on the steps. His morning star, that spiked club which watchmen carry, had fallen from his hands, and his eyes were turned toward the moon that his honest soul was exploring.

"What's the hour, watchman?" asked a passer-by. But never an answer did he get. He gave the watchman a very slight tweak of the nose, and over he toppled. There lay the body at full length, stretched on the pavement. The man was dead. It gave the one who had tweaked him a terrible fright, for the watchman was dead, and dead he remained. His death was reported, and investigated. As day broke, his body was taken to the hospital.

It would be a pretty pass if the soul should come back and in all probability look for its body in East Street, and fail to find it. Perhaps it would rush to the police station first, next to the Directory Office where it could advertise for lost articles, and last of all to the hospital. But we needn't worry. The soul by itself is clever enough. It's the body that makes it stupid.

As we said before, the watchman's body was taken to the hospital. They put it in a room to be washed, and naturally the galoshes were pulled off first of all. That brought the soul dashing back posthaste, and in a flash

the watchman came back to life. He swore it had been the most terrible night he had ever experienced, and he would never go through it again, no, not for two pennies. But it was over and done with. He was allowed to leave that same day, but the galoshes were left at the hospital.

IV

A GREAT MOMENT, AND A MOST EXTRAORDINARY JOURNEY

Everyone in Copenhagen knows what the entrance to Frederic's Hospital looks like, but as some of the people who read this story may not have been to Copenhagen, we must describe the building – briefly.

The hospital is fenced off from the street by a rather high railing of heavy iron bars, which are spaced far enough apart – at least so the story goes – for very thin internes to squeeze between them and pay little visits to the world outside. The part of the body they had most difficulty in squeezing through was the head. In this, as often happens in the world, small heads were the most successful. So much for our description.

One of the young internes, of whom it could be said that he had a great head only in a physical sense, had the night watch that evening. Outside the rain poured down. But in spite of these difficulties he was bent upon getting out for a quarter of an hour. There was no need for the doorman to know about it, he thought, if he could just manage to slip through the fence. There lay the galoshes that the watchman had forgotten, and while the interne had no idea that they were the galoshes of Fortune, he did know that they would stand him in good stead out in the rain. So he pulled them on. Now the question was whether he could squeeze between the bars, a trick that he had never tried before. There he stood, facing the fence.

"I wish to goodness I had my head through," he said, and though his head was much too large and thick for the space, it immediately slipped through quickly and with the greatest of ease.

The galoshes saw to that. All he had to do now was to squeeze his body through after his head, but it wouldn't go. "Uff!" he panted, "I'm too fat. I thought my head would be the worst difficulty. No, I shall never get through."

He quickly attempted to pull his head back again, but it couldn't be done. He could move his neck easily, but that was all. First his anger flared up. Then his spirits dropped down to zero. The galoshes of Fortune had gotten him in a terrible fix, and unluckily it did not occur to him to wish his way out of it. No, instead of wishing he struggled and strove, but he could not budge from the spot. The rain poured down; not a soul could be seen in the street; and he could not reach the bell by the gate. How could he ever get free? He was certain he would have to stay there till morning, and that they would have to send for a blacksmith to file through the iron bars. It would take time. All the boys in the school across the way would be up and shout, and the entire population of "Nyboder," where all the sailors lived, would turn out for the fun of seeing the man in a pillory. Why, he would draw a bigger crowd than the one that went to see the championship wrestling matches last year.

"Huff!" he panted, "the blood's rushing to my head. I'm going mad! Yes, I'm going mad! Oh, if I were only free again, and out of this fix, then I would be all right again."

This was what he ought to have said in the first place. No sooner had he said it than his head came free, and he dashed indoors, still bewildered by the fright that the galoshes of Fortune had given him. But don't think that this was the end of it. No! The worst was yet to come.

The night went by, and the next day passed, but nobody came for the galoshes. That evening there was to be a performance at the little theater in Kannike Street. The house was packed and in the audience was our friend, the interne, apparently none the worse for his adventure of the night before. He had again put on the galoshes. After all, no one had claimed them, and the streets were so muddy that he thought they would stand him in good stead.

At the theater a new sketch was presented. It was called "My Grandmother's Spectacles" and had to do with a pair of eyeglasses which enabled anyone who wore them to read the future from people's faces, just as a fortune teller reads it from cards.

The idea occupied his mind very much. He would like to own such a pair of spectacles. Properly used, they might enable one to see into people's hearts. This, he thought, would be far more interesting than to foresee what would happen next year. Future events would be known in due time, but no one would ever know the secrets that lie in people's hearts.

"Look at those ladies and gentlemen in the front row," he said to himself. "If I could see straight into their hearts what stores of things – what great shops full of goods would I behold. And how my eyes would rove about those shops. In every feminine heart, no doubt I should find a complete millinery establishment. There sits one whose shop is empty, but a good cleaning would do it no harm. And of course some of the shops would be well stocked. Ah me," he sighed, "I know of one where all the goods are of the very best quality, and it would just suit me, but – alas and alack – there's a shopkeeper there already, and he's the only bad article in the whole shop. Many a one would say, 'Won't you walk in?'

and I wish I could. I would pass like a nice little thought through their hearts."

The galoshes took him at his word. The interne shrank to almost nothing, and set out on a most extraordinary journey through the hearts of all the spectators in the first row. The first heart he entered was that of a lady, but at first he mistook it for a room in the Orthopaedic Institute, or Hospital, where the plaster casts of deformed limbs are hung upon the walls. The only difference was that at the hospital those casts were made when the patients came in, while these casts that were kept in the heart were made as the good people departed. For every physical or mental fault of the friends she had lost had been carefully stored away.

He quickly passed on to another woman's heart, which seemed like a great holy cathedral. Over the high altar fluttered the white dove of innocence, and the interne would have gone down on his knees except that he had to hurry on to the next heart. However, he still heard the organ roll. And he felt that it had made a new and better man of him – a man not too unworthy to enter the next sanctuary. This was a poor garret where a mother lay ill, but through the windows the sun shone, warm and bright. Lovely roses bloomed in the little wooden flower box on the roof, and two bluebirds sang of happy childhood, while the sick woman prayed for a blessing on her daughter.

Next the interne crawled on his hands and knees through an overcrowded butcher shop. There was meat, more meat, and meat alone, wherever he looked in this heart of a wealthy, respectable man, whose name you can find in the directory.

Next he entered the heart of this man's wife, and an old tumble-down dove-cot he found it. Her husband's portrait served as a mere weathervane, which was connected with the doors in such a way that they opened and closed as her husband turned round.

Then he found his way into a cabinet of mirrors such as is to be seen at Rosenborg Castle, though in this heart the mirrors had the power of magnifying objects enormously. Like the Grand Lama of Tibet, the owner's insignificant ego sat in the middle of the floor, in admiring contemplation of his own greatness.

After this he seemed to be crammed into a narrow case full of sharp needles. "This," he thought, "must certainly be an old maid's heart," but it was nothing of the sort. It was the heart of a very young officer who had been awarded several medals, and of whom everyone said, "Now there's a man of both intellect and heart."

Quite befuddled was the poor interne when he popped out of the heart of the last person in the front row. He could not get his thoughts in order, and he supposed that his strong imagination must have run away with him.

"Merciful heavens," he groaned, "I must be well on the road to the madhouse. And it's so outrageously hot in here that the blood is rushing to my head." Suddenly he recalled what had happened the night before, when he had jammed his head between the bars of the hospital fence. "That must be what caused it," he decided. "I must do something before it is too late. A Russian bath might be the very thing. I wish I were on the top shelf right now."

No sooner said, than there he lay on the top shelf of the steam bath. But he was fully dressed, down to his shoes and galoshes. He felt the hot drops of condensed steam fall upon him from the ceiling.

"Hey!" he cried, and jumped down to take a shower. The attendant cried out too when he caught sight of a fully dressed man in the steam room. However, the interne had enough sense to pull himself together and whisper, "I'm just doing this because of a bet."

But the first thing he did when he got back to his room was to put hot plasters on his neck and his back, to draw out the madness.

Next morning he had a blistered back and that was all he got out of the galoshes of Fortune.

V

THE TRANSFORMATION OF THE COPYING CLERK

The watchman – you remember him – happened to remember those galoshes he had found, and that he must have been wearing them when they took his body to the hospital. He came by for them, and as neither the lieutenant nor anyone else in East Street laid claim to them, he turned them in at the police station.

"They look exactly like my own galoshes," one of the copying clerks at the police station said, as he set the ownerless galoshes down beside his own. "Not even a shoemaker could tell one pair from the other."

"Mr. Copying Clerk!" said a policeman, who brought him some papers.

The clerk turned around to talk with the policeman, and when he came back to the galoshes he was uncertain whether the pair on the right or the pair on the left belonged to him.

"The wet ones must be mine," he thought, but he was mistaken, for they were the galoshes of Fortune. The police make their little mistakes too.

So he pulled them on, pocketed some papers, and tucked some manuscripts under his arm to read and abstract when he got home. But as this happened to be Sunday morning, and the weather was fine, he thought, "A walk to Frederiksberg will be good for me." And off he went.

A quieter, more dependable fellow than this young man you seldom see. Let him take his little walk, by all means. It will do him a world of good after so much sitting. At first he strode along without a wish in his head, so

"They look exactly like my own galoshes," one of the copying clerks at the police station said, as he set the ownerless galoshes down beside his own.
(Fritz Kredel)

there was no occasion for the galoshes to show their magic power. On the avenue he met an acquaintance of his, a young poet, who said he was setting out tomorrow on a summer excursion.

"What, off again so soon?" said the clerk. "What a free and happy fellow you are! You can fly away wherever you like, while the rest of us are chained by the leg."

"Chained only to a breadfruit tree," the poet reminded him. "You don't have to worry along from day to day, and when you get old they will give you a pension."

"You are better off, just the same," the clerk said. "How agreeable it must be to sit and write poetry. Everyone pays you compliments, and you are your own master. Ah, you should see what it's like to devote your life to the trivial details of the courts."

The poet shook his head, and the clerk shook his too. Each held to his own conviction, and they parted company.

"They are a queer race, these poets," thought the clerk. "I should like to try my hand at their trade – to turn poet myself. I'm sure I would

never write such melancholy stuff as most of them do. What a splendid spring day this is, a day fit for a poet. The air is so unusually clear, the clouds so lovely, and the green grass so fragrant. For many a year I have not felt as I feel just now."

Already, you could tell that he had turned poet. Not that there was anything you could put your finger on, for it is foolish to suppose that a poet differs greatly from other people, some of whom are far more poetic by nature than many a great and accepted poet. The chief difference is that a poet has a better memory for things of the spirit. He can hold fast to an emotion and an idea until they are firmly and clearly embodied in words, which is something that others cannot do. But for a matter-of-fact person to think in terms of poetry is noticeable enough, and it is this transformation that we can see in the clerk.

"What a glorious fragrance there is in the air!" he said. "It reminds me of Aunt Lone's violets. Ah me, I haven't thought of them since I was a little boy. The dear old girl! She used to live over there, behind the Exchange. She always had a spray or a few green shoots in water, no matter how severe the winter was. I'd smell those violets even when I was putting hot pennies against the frozen window pane to make peep holes. What a view that was – ships frozen tight in the canal, deserted by their crew, and a shrieking crow the only living creature aboard them. But when the springtime breezes blew the scene turned lively again. There were shouts and laughter as the ice was sawed away. Freshly tarred and rigged, the ships sailed off for distant lands. I stayed here, and I must forever stay here, sitting in the police office where others come for their passports to foreign countries. Yes, that's my lot! Oh, yes!" he said, and heaved a sigh. Then he stopped abruptly. "Great heavens! What's come over me. I never thought or felt like this before. It must be the spring air! It is as frightening as it is pleasant." He fumbled among the papers in his pockets.

"These will give me something else to think about," he said, as he glanced at the first page. "*Lady Sigbrith, An Original Tragedy in Five Acts*," he read. "Why, what's this? It's in my own handwriting too. Have I written a tragedy? *The Intrigue on the Ramparts, or The Great Fast Day – a Vaudeville*. Where did that come from? Someone must have slipped it in my pocket. And here's a letter." It was from the board of directors of the theater, who rejected his plays, and the letter was anything but politely phrased.

"Hem, hem!" said the copying clerk as he sat down on a bench. His thoughts were lively and his heart sensitive. He plucked a flower at random, an ordinary little daisy. What the professor of botany requires several lectures to explain to us, this flower told in a moment. It told of the mystery birth, and of the power of the sunlight which opened those delicate leaves and gave them their fragrance. This made him think of the battle of life, which arouses emotions within us in similar fashion. Air and light are the flowers' lovers, but light is her favorite. Toward it the flower is ever turning, and only when the light is gone does she fold her petals and sleep in the air's embrace.

"It is the light that makes me lovely," the flower said.

"But," the poet's voice whispered, "the air enables you to breathe."

Not far away, a boy was splashing in a muddy ditch with his stick. As the water flew up among the green branches, the clerk thought of the innumerable microscopic creatures in the splashing drops. For them to be splashed so high, was as if we were to be tossed up into the clouds. As the clerk thought of these things, and of the great change that had come over him, he smiled and said:

"I must be asleep and dreaming. It's marvelous to be able to dream so naturally, and yet to know all along that this is a dream. I hope I can recall every bit of it tomorrow, when I wake up. I seem to feel unusually exhilarated. How clearly I understand things, and how wide awake I feel! But I know that if I recall my dream it will only be a lot of nonsense, as has happened to me so often before. All those brilliant and clever remarks one makes and one hears in his dreams, are like the gold pieces that goblins store underground. When one gets them they are rich and shining, but seen in the daylight they are nothing but rocks and dry leaves. Ah me," he sighed, as he sadly watched the singing birds flit merrily from branch to branch. "They are so much better off than I. Flying is a noble art, and lucky is he who is born with wings. Yes, if I could change into anything I liked, I would turn into a little lark."

In a trice his coat-tails and sleeves grew together as wings, his clothes turned into feathers, and his galoshes became claws. He noticed the change clearly, and laughed to himself.

"Now," he said, "I know I am dreaming, but I never had a dream as silly as this one."

Up he flew, and sang among the branches, but there was no poetry in his song, for he was no longer a poet. Like anyone who does a thoroughgoing job of it, the galoshes could only do one thing at a time. When he wishes to be a poet, a poet he became. Then he wanted to be a little bird, and in becoming one he lost his previous character.

"This is most amusing," he said. "In the daytime I sit in the police office, surrounded by the most matter-of-fact legal papers, but by night I can dream that I'm a lark flying about in the Frederiksberg Garden. What fine material this would make for a popular comedy."

He flew down on the grass, twisting and turning his head, and pecking at the waving grass blades. In proportion to his own size, they seemed as large as the palm branches in

North Africa. But this lasted only a moment. Then everything turned black, and it seemed as if some huge object had dropped over him. This was a big cap that a boy from Nyboder had thrown over the bird. A hand was thrust in. It laid hold of the copying clerk by his back and wing so tightly that it made him shriek. In his terror he called out, "You impudent scoundrel! I am the copying clerk at the police office!" But this sounded like "Peep! peep!" to the boy, who thumped the bird on its beak and walked off with it.

On the avenue this boy met with two other schoolboys. Socially, they were of the upper classes, though, properly ranked according to their merit, they were in the lowest class at school. They bought the bird for eight pennies, and in their hands the clerk came back to Copenhagen, to a family who lived in Gothers Street.

"It's a good thing I'm only dreaming this," said the clerk, "or I'd be furious. First I was a poet, and now I'm a lark. It must have been my poetic temperament which turned me into this little creature. It is a very sad state of affairs, especially when one falls into the hands of a couple of boys. But I wonder how it will all turn out."

The boys carried him into a luxuriously appointed room, where a stout, affable lady received them. She was not at all pleased with their common little field bird, as she called the lark, but she said that, for one day only, they could keep it in the empty cage near the window.

"Perhaps Polly will like it," she said, and smiled at the large parrot that swung proudly to and fro on the ring in his ornate brass cage. "It's Polly's birthday," she said, like a simpleton. "The little field bird wants to congratulate him."

Polly did not say a word, as proudly he swung back and forth. But a pretty canary bird who had been brought here last summer from his warm, sweet-scented homeland, began to sing at the top of his voice.

"Bawler!" the lady said, and threw a white handkerchief over his cage.

"Peep, peep. What a terrible snowstorm," the canary sighed, and with that sigh he kept quiet.

The clerk, or as the lady called him, the field bird, was put in a cage next to the canary's and not far from the parrot's. The only human words that the parrot could say, and which at times sounded quite comical, were "Come now, let us be men." All the rest of his chatter made as little sense as the twittering of the canary. However, the clerk, who was now a bird himself, understood his companions perfectly.

"I used to fly beneath green palms and flowering almond trees," the canary bird sang. "With my brothers and sisters, I flew above beautiful flowers, and over the smooth sea where the plants that grow under water waved up at us. We used to meet many brilliant parrots, who told us the funniest stories – long ones and so many."

"Those were wild parrots!" said Polly. "Birds without any education. Come now, let us be men. Why don't you laugh? If the lady and all her guests laugh at my remark, so should you. To lack a sense of humor is a very bad thing. Come now, let us be men."

"Do you remember the pretty girls who danced in the tents spread beneath those flowering trees?" the canary sang. "Do you remember those delicious sweet fruits, and the cool juice of the wild plants?"

"Why yes," said the parrot, "but I am much better off here, where I get the best of food and intimate treatment. I know that I am a clever bird, and that's enough for me. Come now, let us be men. You have the soul of a poet, as they call it, and I have sound knowledge and wit. You have genius, but no discretion. You burst into that shrill, spontaneous song of yours. That's why people cover you up. They don't ever treat me like that. No, I have cost them a lot and, what is more imposing, my beak and my wits are sharp. Come now, let us be men."

"Oh, my warm flowery homeland!" said the canary. "I shall sing of your deep green trees and your quiet inlets, where the down-hanging branches kiss the clear mirror of the waters. I shall sing of my resplendent brothers and sisters, who rejoice as they hover over the cups of water in the cactus plants that thrive in the desert."

"Kindly stop your whimpering tunes," the parrot said. "Sing something to make us laugh. Laughter is a sign of the loftiest intellectual development. Can a dog or a horse laugh? No! They can cry, but as for laughter – that is given to mankind alone. Ho, ho, ho!" the parrot chuckled, and added his, "Come now, let us be men."

"You little grey bird of Denmark," the canary said to the lark, "have they made you a prisoner too? Although it must be very cold in your woods, you have your freedom there. Fly away! They have forgotten to close your cage. The door of the top is open. Fly! fly!"

Without pausing to think, the clerk did as he was told. In a jiffy he was out of the cage. But just as he escaped from his prison, the half-open door leading into the next room began to creak. Stealthily, with green shining eyes, the house cat pounced in and gave chase to him. The canary fluttered in his cage. The parrot flapped his wings and called out, "Come now, let us be men." The dreadfully frightened clerk flew out of the window and away over the streets and houses, until at last he had to stop to rest.

That house across the street looked familiar. He flew in through one of its open windows. As he perched on the table he found that he was in his own room.

"Come now, let us be men," he blurted out, in spontaneous mockery of the parrot. Instantly he resumed the body of the copying clerk, who sat there, perched on the table.

"How in the name of heaven," he said, "do I happen to be sleeping here? And what a disturbing dream I've had – all nonsense from beginning to end."

VI

THE BEST THAT THE GALOSHES BROUGHT

Early the next morning, before the clerk was out of bed, someone tapped on his door. In walked his neighbor, a young theological student who lived on the same floor.

"Lend me your galoshes," he requested. "It is very wet in the garden, but the sun is shining so gloriously that I'd like to smoke a pipeful down there."

He pulled on the galoshes and went out into the garden, where there was one plum tree and a pear tree. But even a little garden like this one is a precious thing in Copenhagen.

It was only six o'clock. As the student walked up and down the path, he heard the horn of a stagecoach in the street.

"Oh, to travel, to travel!" he exclaimed, "that's the most pleasant thing in the world.

It's the great goal of all my dreams. If only I could travel, I'm sure that this restlessness within me would be stilled. But it must be far, far away. How I should like to see beautiful Switzerland, to tour Italy, and—"

Fortunately the galoshes began to function at once, or he might have traveled entirely too much to suit him or to please us. Travel he did. He was high up in Switzerland, tightly packed in a diligence with eight other travelers. He had a pain in his head, his neck felt tired, and the blood had ceased to circulate in his legs. His feet were swollen and his heavy boots hurt him. He was half awake and half asleep. In his right-hand pocket he had his letter of credit, in his left-hand pocket he had his passport, and sewn into a little bag inside his breast pocket he had a few gold

"Oh, to travel, to travel!"
(Fritz Kredel)

pieces. Every time he dozed off he dreamed that he had lost one or another of these things. Starting feverishly awake, his first movement would be to trace with his hand a triangle from right to left, and up to his breast, to feel whether his treasures were still there.

Umbrellas, hats, and walking sticks swung in the net above him and almost spoiled the magnificent view. As he glanced out the window his heart sang, as at least one poet has sung in Switzerland, these as yet unpublished words:

"This view is as fine as a view can be.
Mount Blanc is sublime beyond a doubt,
And the traveler's life is the life for me –
But only as long as my money holds out."

Vast, severe, and somber was the whole landscape around him. The pine woods looked like patches of heather on the high cliffs, whose summits were lost in fog and cloud. Snow began to fall, and the cold wind blew.

"Ah," he sighed, "if only we were on the other side of the Alps, then it would be summer weather and I could get some money on my letter of credit. Worrying about my finances spoils all my enjoyment of Switzerland. Oh, if only I were on the other side."

And there he was on the other side, in the middle of Italy, between Florence and Rome. Before him lay Lake Thrasymene. In the evening light it looked like a sheet of flaming gold among the dark blue hills. Here, where Hannibal beat Flaminius, the grape vines clung peacefully to each other with their green tendrils. Pretty little half-clothed children tended a herd of coal-black pigs under a fragrant clump of laurels by the roadside, and if we could paint the scene in its true colors all would exclaim, "Glorious Italy!" But neither the student nor his companions in the stage-coach made any such exclamation.

Poisonous flies and gnats swarmed into the coach by the thousands. In vain the travelers tried to beat them off with myrtle branches. The flies stung just the same. There was not a passenger whose face was not puffed and spotted with bites. The poor horses looked like carcasses. The flies made life miserable for them, and it only brought them a momentary relief when the coachman got down and scraped off swarms of the insects that settled upon them.

Once the sun went down, an icy chill fell upon everything. It wasn't at all pleasant. However, the hills and clouds took on that wonderful green tint, so clear and so shining. Yes, go and see for yourself. That is far better than to read about it. It was a lovely sight, and the travelers thought so too, but their stomachs were empty, their bodies exhausted, and every thought in their heads was directed toward a lodging for the night. But where would they lodge? They watched the road ahead far more attentively than they did the splendid view.

Their road ran through an olive grove, and the student could fancy that he was at home, passing through a wood of gnarled willow trees. And there stood a lonely inn. A band of crippled beggars were camping outside and the liveliest among them looked like the eldest son of Famine who had just come of age. The rest either were blind, or so lame that they crawled about on their hands, or had withered arms and hands without any fingers. Here really was misery in rags.

"*Eccelenza, miserabili!*" they groaned, and stretched forth their crippled limbs. The hostess herself went barefoot. With uncombed hair and an unwashed blouse, she received her guests. The doors were hinged with string; half of the bricks of the floors had been put to other use; bats flew about the ceiling; and the smell—

"It were better to have supper in the stable," one traveler maintained. "There one at least knows what he is breathing."

The windows were opened to let a little fresh air come inside, but swifter than the air came those withered arms and that perpetual whine, "*Miserabili, eccellenza.*" On the walls were many inscriptions, and half of them had little good to say for *la bella Italia*.

Supper was served. Supper was a watery soup flavored with pepper and rancid oil. This same oil was the better part of the salad. Dubious eggs and roasted cockscombs were the best dishes, and even the wine was distasteful. It was a frightful collation.

That night the trunks were piled against the door, and one of the travelers mounted guard while the others slept. The student stood the first guard mount. How close it was in there! The heat was overpowering, the gnats droned and stabbed, and outside, the *miserabili* whined in their dreams.

"Traveling," said the student, "would be all very well if one had no body. Oh, if only the body could rest while the spirit flies on without it. Wherever I go, there is some lack that I feel in my heart. There is always something better than the present that I desire. Yes, something better – the best of all, but what is it, and where shall I find it? Down deep in my heart, I know what I want. I want to reach a happy goal, the happiest goal of all."

As soon as the words were said, he found himself back in his home. Long white curtains draped the windows, and in the middle of the floor a black coffin stood. In this he lay, sleeping the quiet sleep of death. His wish was fulfilled – his body was at rest, and his spirit was free to travel. "Call no man happy until he rests in his grave," said Solon, and here his words proved true again.

Every corpse is a sphinx of immortality. The sphinx in this black casket that confronts us could say no more than the living man had written two days before:

"*Stern Death, your silence has aroused my
    fears.
Shall not my soul up Jacob's ladder pass,
Or shall your stone weight me throughout
    the years,
And I rise only in the graveyard grass?
"Our deepest grief escapes the world's sad
    eye!
You who are lonely to the very last,
A heavier burden on your heart must lie
Than all the earth upon your coffin cast!*"

Two figures moved about the room. We know them both. Those two who bent over the dead man were Dame Care and Fortune's minion.

"Now," said Care, "you can see what happiness your galoshes have brought mankind."

"They have at least brought everlasting rest to him who here lies sleeping," said Fortune's minion.

"Oh, no!" said Care. "He went of his own free will. He was not called away. His spiritual power was not strong enough to undertake the glorious tasks for which he is destined. I shall do him a favor."

She took the galoshes from his feet. Then the sleep of death was ended, and the student awakened to life again. Care vanished, and she took the galoshes along with her, for she probably regarded them as her own property.

THE STEADFAST TIN SOLDIER

THERE WERE ONCE five-and-twenty tin soldiers. They were all brothers, born of the same old tin spoon. They shouldered their muskets and looked straight ahead of them, splendid in their uniforms, all red and blue.

The very first thing in the world that they heard was, "Tin soldiers!" A small boy shouted it and clapped his hands as the lid was lifted off their box on his birthday. He immediately set them up on the table.

All the soldiers looked exactly alike except one. He looked a little different as he had been cast last of all. The tin was short, so he had only one leg. But there he stood, as steady on one leg as any of the other soldiers on their two. But just you see, he'll be the remarkable one.

On the table with the soldiers were many other playthings, and one that no eye could miss was a marvelous castle of cardboard. It had little windows through which you could look right inside it. And in front of the castle were miniature trees around a little mirror supposed to represent a lake. The wax swans that swam on its surface were reflected in the mirror. All this was very pretty but prettiest of all was the little lady who stood in the open doorway of the castle. Though she was a paper doll, she wore a dress of the fluffiest gauze. A tiny blue ribbon went over her shoulder for a scarf, and in the middle of it shone a spangle that was as big as her face. The little lady held out both her arms, as a ballet dancer does, and one leg was lifted so high behind her that the tin soldier couldn't see it at all, and he supposed she must have only one leg, as he did.

"That would be a wife for me," he thought. "But maybe she's too grand. She lives in a castle. I have only a box, with four-and-twenty roommates to share it. That's no place for her.

Where he could admire the dainty little dancer who kept standing on one leg without ever losing her balance. (Kay Neilsen)

But I must try to make her acquaintance." Still as stiff as when he stood at attention, he lay down on the table behind a snuffbox, where he could admire the dainty little dancer who kept standing on one leg without ever losing her balance.

When the evening came the other tin soldiers were put away in their box, and the people of the house went to bed. Now the toys began to play among themselves at visits, and battles, and at giving balls. The tin soldiers rattled about in their box, for they wanted to play too, but they could not get the lid open. The nutcracker turned somersaults, and the slate pencil squeaked out jokes on the slate. The toys made such a noise that they woke up the canary bird, who made them a speech, all in verse. The only two who stayed still were the tin soldier and the little dancer. Without ever swerving from the tip of one toe, she held out her arms to him, and the tin soldier was just as steadfast on his one leg. Not once did he take his eyes off her.

Then the clock struck twelve and – *clack!* – up popped the lid of the snuffbox. But there was no snuff in it, no – out bounced a little black bogey, a jack-in-the-box.

"Tin soldier," he said. "Will you please keep your eyes to yourself?" The tin soldier pretended not to hear.

The bogey said, "Just you wait till tomorrow."

But when morning came, and the children got up, the soldier was set on the window ledge. And whether the bogey did it, or there was a gust of wind, all of a sudden the window flew open and the soldier pitched out headlong from the third floor. He fell at breathtaking speed and landed cap first, with his bayonet buried between the paving stones and his one leg stuck straight in the air.

They made a boat out of newspaper, and put the tin soldier in the middle of it. (Fritz Kredel)

The housemaid and the little boy ran down to look for him and, though they nearly stepped on the tin soldier, they walked right past without seeing him. If the soldier had called, "Here I am!" they would surely have found him, but he thought it contemptible to raise an uproar while he was wearing his uniform.

Soon it began to rain. The drops fell faster and faster, until they came down by the bucketful. As soon as the rain let up, along came two young rapscallions.

"Hi, look!" one of them said, "there's a tin soldier. Let's send him sailing."

They made a boat out of newspaper, put the tin soldier in the middle of it, and away he went down the gutter with the two young rapscallions running beside him and clapping their hands. High heavens! How the waves splashed, and how fast the water ran down the gutter. Don't forget that it had just been raining by the bucketful. The paper boat pitched, and tossed, and sometimes it whirled about so rapidly that it made the soldier's head spin. But he stood as steady as ever. Never once flinching, he kept his eyes front, and carried his gun shoulder-high. Suddenly the boat rushed under a long plank where the gutter was boarded over. It was as dark as the soldier's own box.

"Where can I be going?" the soldier wondered. "This must be that black bogey's revenge. Ah! if only I had the little lady with me, it could be twice as dark here for all that I would care."

Out popped a great water rat who lived under the gutter plank.

"Have you a passport?" said the rat. "Hand it over."

The soldier kept quiet and held his musket tighter. On rushed the boat, and the rat came right after it, gnashing his teeth as he called to the sticks and straws:

"Halt him! Stop him! He didn't pay his toll. He hasn't shown his passport." But the current ran stronger and stronger. The soldier could see daylight ahead where the board ended, but he also heard a roar that would frighten the bravest of us. Hold on! Right at the end of that gutter plank the water poured into the great canal. It was as dangerous to him as a waterfall would be to us.

He was so near it he could not possibly stop. The boat plunged into the whirlpool. The poor tin soldier stood as staunch as he could, and no one can say that he so much as blinked an eye. Thrice and again the boat spun around. It filled to the top – and was bound to sink. The water was up to his neck and still the boat went down, deeper, deeper, deeper, and the paper got soft and limp. Then the water rushed over his head. He thought of the pretty little dancer whom he'd never see again, and in his ears rang an old, old song:

"Farewell, farewell, O warrior brave,
Nobody can from Death thee save."

And now the paper boat broke beneath him, and the soldier sank right through. And just at that moment he was swallowed by a most enormous fish.

My! how dark it was inside that fish. It was darker than under the gutter plank and it was so cramped, but the tin soldier still was staunch. He lay there full length, soldier fashion, with musket to shoulder.

Then the fish flopped and floundered in a most unaccountable way. Finally it was perfectly still, and after a while something struck through him like a flash of lightning. The tin soldier saw daylight again, and he heard a voice say, "The Tin Soldier!" The fish had been caught, carried to market, bought, and brought to a kitchen where the cook cut him open with her big knife.

She picked the soldier up bodily between her two fingers, and carried him off upstairs. Everyone wanted to see this remarkable traveler who had traveled about in a fish's stomach, but the tin soldier took no pride in it. They put him on the table and – lo and behold, what curious things can happen in this world – there he was, back in the same room as before. He saw the same children, the same toys were on the table, and there was the same fine castle with the pretty little dancer. She still balanced on one leg, with the other raised high. She too was steadfast. That touched the soldier so deeply that he would have cried tin tears, only soldiers never cry. He looked at her, and she looked at him, and never a word was said. Just as things were going so nicely for them, one of the little boys snatched up the tin soldier and threw him into the stove. He did it for no reason at all. That black bogey in the snuffbox must have put him up to it.

The tin soldier stood there dressed in flames. He felt a terrible heat, but whether it came from the flames or from his love he didn't know. He'd lost his splendid colors, maybe from his hard journey, maybe from grief, nobody can say.

He looked at the little lady, and she looked at him, and he felt himself melting. But still he stood steadfast, with his musket held trim on his shoulder.

Then the door blew open. A puff of wind struck the dancer. She flew like a sylph, straight into the fire with the soldier, blazed up in a flash, and was gone. The tin soldier melted, all in a lump. The next day, when a servant took up the ashes she found him in the shape of a little tin heart. But of the pretty dancer nothing was left except her spangle, and it was burned as black as a coal.

THE WILD SWANS

FAR, FAR AWAY where the swallows fly when we have winter, there lived a King who had eleven sons and one daughter, Elisa. The eleven brothers, Princes all, each went to school with a star at his breast and a sword at his side. They wrote with pencils of diamond upon golden slates, and could say their lesson by heart just as easily as they could read it from the book. You could tell at a glance how princely they were. Their sister, Elisa, sat on a little footstool of flawless glass. She had a picture book that had cost half a kingdom. Oh, the children had a very fine time, but it did not last forever.

Their father, who was King over the whole country, married a wicked Queen, who did not treat his poor children at all well. They found that out the very first day. There was feasting throughout the palace, and the children played at entertaining guests. But instead of letting them have all the cakes and baked apples that they used to get, their new stepmother gave them only some sand in a teacup, and told them to make believe that it was a special treat.

The following week the Queen sent little Elisa to live in the country with some peasants. And before long she had made the King believe so many falsehoods about the poor Princes that he took no further interest in them.

"Fly out into the world and make your own living," the wicked Queen told them. "Fly away like big birds without a voice."

But she did not harm the Princes as much as she meant to, for they turned into eleven magnificent white swans. With a weird cry, they flew out of the palace window, across the park into the woods.

It was so early in the morning that their sister, Elisa, was still asleep when they flew over the peasant hut where she was staying. They hovered over the roofs, craning and twisting

Poor little Elisa stayed in the peasant hut, and played boo with a green leaf, for she had no other toy. (W. Heath Robinson)

their long necks and flapping their wings, but nobody saw them or heard them. They were forced to fly on, high up near the clouds and far away into the wide world. They came down in a vast, dark forest that stretched down to the shores of the sea.

Poor little Elisa stayed in the peasant hut, and played boo with a green leaf, for she had no other toy. She made a little hole in the leaf and looked through it at the sun. Through it she seemed to see her brothers' bright eyes, and whenever the warm sunlight touched her cheek it reminded her of all their kisses.

One day passed like all the others. When the wind stirred the hedge roses outside the hut, it whispered to them, "What could be prettier than you?" But the roses shook their heads and answered, "Elisa!" And on Sunday, when the old woman sat in the doorway reading the psalms, the wind fluttered through the pages and said to the book, "Who could be more saintly than you?" "Elisa," the book testified. What it and the roses said was perfectly true.

Elisa was to go back home when she became fifteen but, as soon as the Queen saw what a beautiful Princess she was, the Queen felt spiteful and full of hatred toward her. She would not have hesitated to turn her into a wild swan, like her brothers, but she did not dare to do it just yet, because the King wanted to see his daughter.

In the early morning, the Queen went to the bathing place, which was made of white marble, furnished with soft cushions and carpeted with the most splendid rugs. She took three toads, kissed them, and said to the first:

"Squat on Elisa's head, when she bathes, so that she will become as torpid as you are." To the second she said, "Squat on her forehead, so that she will become as ugly as you are, and her father won't recognize her." And to the third, she whispered, "Lie against her heart, so that she will be cursed and tormented by evil desires."

Thereupon the Queen dropped the three toads into the clear water, which at once turned a greenish color. She called Elisa, made her undress, and told her to enter the bath. When Elisa went down into the water, one toad fastened himself to her hair, another to her forehead, and the third against her heart. But she did not seem to be aware of them, and when she stood up three red poppies floated on the water. If the toads had not been poisonous, and had not been kissed by the witch, they would have been turned into red roses. But at least they had been turned into flowers, by the mere touch of her head and heart. She was too innocent and good for witchcraft to have power over her.

When the evil Queen realized this, she rubbed Elisa with walnut stain that turned her dark brown, smeared her beautiful face with a vile ointment, and tousled her lovely hair. No one could have recognized the beautiful Elisa, and when her father saw her he was shocked. He said that this could not be his daughter. No one knew her except the watchdog and the swallows, and they were humble creatures who had nothing to say.

Poor Elisa cried and thought of her eleven brothers, who were all away. Heavy-hearted, she stole away from the palace and wandered all day long over fields and marshes, till she came to the vast forest. She had no idea where to turn. All she felt was her sorrow and her longing to be with her brothers. Like herself, they must have been driven out into the world, and she set her heart upon finding them. She had been in the forest only a little while when night came on, and as she had strayed from any sign of a path she said her prayers and lay down on the soft moss, with her head pillowed against a stump. All was quiet, the air was so mild, and hundreds of fireflies glittered like a green fire in the grass and moss. When she lightly brushed against a single branch, the shining insects showered about her like falling stars.

She dreamed of her brothers all night long. They were children again, playing together, writing with their diamond pencils on their golden slates, and looking at her wonderful picture book that had cost half a kingdom. But they no longer scribbled sums and exercises as they used to do. No, they set down their bold deeds and all that they had seen or heard. Everything in the picture book came alive. The birds sang, and the people strolled out of the book to talk with Elisa and her brothers, but whenever she turned a page they immediately jumped back into place, to keep the pictures in order.

When she awoke, the sun was already high. She could not see it plainly, for the tall trees spread their tangled branches above her, but the rays played above like a shimmering golden gauze. There was a delightful fragrance of green foliage, and the birds came near enough to have perched on her shoulder. She heard the water splashing from many large springs, which all flowed into a pool with the most beautiful sandy bottom. Although it was hemmed in by a wall of thick bushes, there was one place where the deer had made a path wide enough for Elisa to reach the water. The pool was so clear that, if the wind had not stirred the limbs and bushes, she might have supposed they were painted on the bottom of the pool. For each leaf was clearly reflected, whether the sun shone upon it or whether it grew in the shade.

When Elisa saw her own face she was horrified to find it so brown and ugly. But as soon as she wet her slender hand, and rubbed her brow and her eyes, her fair skin showed again. Then she laid aside her clothes and plunged into the fresh water. In all the world there was no King's daughter as lovely as Elisa. When she had dressed herself and plaited her long hair, she went to the sparkling spring and drank from the hollow of her hand. She wandered deeper into the woods without knowing whither she went. She thought of her brothers, and she thought of the good Lord, who she knew would not forsake her. He lets the wild crab apples grow to feed the hungry, and he led her footsteps to a tree with its branches bent down by the weight of their fruit. Here she had her lunch. After she put props under the heavy limbs, she went on into the depths of the forest. It was so quiet that she heard her own footsteps and every dry leaf that rustled underfoot. Not a bird was in sight, not a ray of the sun could get through the big heavy branches, and the tall trees grew so close together that when she looked straight ahead it seemed as if a solid fence of lofty palings imprisoned her. She had never known such solitude.

A few steps farther on she met an old woman who had a basket of berries.
(Fritz Kredel)

The night came on, pitch black. Not one firefly glittered among the leaves as she despondently lay down to sleep. Then it seemed to her that the branches parted overhead and the Lord looked kindly down upon her, and little angels peeped out from above His head and behind Him.

When she awoke the next morning she did not know whether she had dreamed this, or whether it had really happened.

A few steps farther on she met an old woman who had a basket of berries and gave some of them to her. Elisa asked if she had seen eleven Princes riding through the forest.

"No," the old woman said. "But yesterday I saw eleven swans who wore golden crowns. They were swimming in the river not far from here."

She led Elisa a little way to the top of a hill which sloped down to a winding river. The trees on either bank stretched their long leafy branches toward each other, and where the stream was too wide for them to grow across it they had torn their roots from the earth and leaned out over the water until their branches met. Elisa told the old woman good-by, and followed the river down to where it flowed into the great open sea.

Before the young girl lay the whole beautiful sea, but not a sail nor a single boat was in sight. How could she go on? She looked at the countless pebbles on the beach, and saw how round the water had worn them. Glass, iron ore, stones, all that had been washed up, had been shaped by the water that was so much softer than even her tender hand.

"It rolls on tirelessly, and that is the way it makes such hard things smooth," she said. "I shall be just as untiring. Thank you for your lesson, you clear rolling waves. My heart tells me that some day you will carry me to my beloved brothers."

Among the wet seaweed she found eleven white swan feathers, which she collected in a sheaf. There were still drops of water on them, but whether these were spray or tears no one could say. It was very lonely along the shore but she did not mind, for the sea was constantly changing. Indeed it showed more changes in a few hours than an inland lake does in a whole year. When the sky was black with threatening clouds, it was as if the sea seemed to say, "I can look threatening too." Then the wind would blow and the waves would raise their white crests. But when the wind died down and the clouds were red, the sea would look like a rose petal.

Sometimes it showed white, and sometimes green, but however calm it might seem there was always a gentle lapping along the shore, where the waters rose and fell like the chest of a child asleep.

Just at sunset, Elisa saw eleven white swans, with golden crowns on their heads, fly toward the shore. As they flew, one behind another, they looked like a white ribbon floating in the air. Elisa climbed up and hid behind a bush on the steep bank. The swans came down near her and flapped their magnificent white wings.

As soon as the sun went down beyond the sea, the swans threw off their feathers and there stood eleven handsome Princes. They were her brothers, and, although they were greatly altered, she knew in her heart that she could not be mistaken. She cried aloud, and rushed into their arms, calling them each by name. The Princes were so happy to see their little sister. And they knew her at once, for all that she had grown tall and lovely. They laughed, and they cried, and they soon realized how cruelly their stepmother had treated them all.

"We brothers," said the eldest, "are forced to fly about disguised as wild swans as long as the sun is in the heavens, but when it goes down we take back our human form. So at sunset we must always look about us for some firm foothold, because if ever we were flying among the clouds at sunset we would be dashed down to the earth.

"We do not live on this coast. Beyond the sea there is another land as fair as this, but it lies far away and we must cross the vast ocean to reach it. Along our course there is not one island where we can pass the night, except one little rock that rises from the middle of the sea. It is barely big enough to hold us, however close together we stand, and if there is a rough sea the waves wash over us. But still we thank God for it.

"In our human forms we rest there during the night, and without it we could never come back to our own dear homeland. It takes two of the longest days of the year for our journey. We are allowed to come back to our native land only once a year, and we do not dare to stay longer than eleven days. As we fly over this forest we can see the palace where our father lives and where we were born. We can see the high tower of the church where our mother lies buried. And here we feel that even the trees and bushes are akin to us. Here the wild horses gallop across the moors as we saw them in our childhood, and the charcoal-burner sings the same old songs to which we used to dance when we were children. This is our homeland. It draws us to it, and here, dear sister, we have found you again. We may stay two days longer, and then we must fly across the sea to a land which is fair enough, but not our own. How shall we take you with us? For we have neither ship nor boat."

"How shall I set you free?" their sister asked, and they talked on for most of the night, sparing only a few hours for sleep.

In the morning Elisa was awakened by the rustling of swans' wings overhead. Her brothers, once more enchanted, wheeled above her in great circles until they were out of sight. One of them, her youngest brother, stayed with her and rested his head on her breast while she stroked his wings. They spent the whole day together, and toward evening the others returned. As soon as the sun went down they resumed their own shape.

"Tomorrow," said one of her brothers, "we must fly away, and we dare not return until a whole year has passed. But we cannot leave you like this. Have you courage enough to come with us? My arm is strong enough to carry you through the forest, so surely the wings of us all should be strong enough to bear you across the sea."

"Yes, take me with you," said Elisa.

They spent the entire night making a net of pliant willow bark and tough rushes. They made it large and strong. Elisa lay down upon it and, when the sun rose and her brothers again became wild swans, they lifted the net in their bills and flew high up toward the clouds with their beloved sister, who still was fast asleep. As the sun shone straight into her face, one of the swans flew over her head so as to shade her with his wide wings.

They were far from the shore when she awoke. Elisa thought she must still be dreaming, so strange did it seem to be carried through the air, high over the sea. Beside her lay a branch

"Yes, take me with you," said Elisa.
(Harry Clarke)

full of beautiful ripe berries, and a bundle of sweet-tasting roots. Her youngest brother had gathered them and put them there for her. She gave him a grateful smile. She knew he must be the one who flew over her head to protect her eyes from the sun.

They were so high that the first ship they sighted looked like a gull floating on the water. A cloud rolled up behind them, as big as a mountain. Upon it Elisa saw gigantic shadows of herself and of the eleven swans. It was the most splendid picture she had ever seen, but as the sun rose higher the clouds grew small, and the shadow picture of their flight disappeared.

All day they flew like arrows whipping through the air, yet, because they had their sister to carry, they flew more slowly than on their former journeys. Night was drawing near, and a storm was rising. In terror, Elisa watched the sinking sun, for the lonely rock was nowhere in sight. It seemed to her that the swans beat their wings in the air more desperately. Alas it was because of her that they could not fly fast enough. So soon as the sun went down they would turn into men, and all of them would pitch down into the sea and drown. She prayed to God from the depths of her heart, but still no rock could be seen. Black clouds gathered and great gusts told of the storm to come. The threatening clouds came on as one tremendous wave that rolled down toward them like a mass of lead, and flash upon flash of lightning followed them. Then the sun touched the rim of the sea. Elisa's heart beat madly as the swans shot down so fast that she thought they were falling, but they checked their downward swoop. Half of the sun was below the sea when she first saw the little rock below them. It looked no larger than the head of a seal jutting out of the water. The sun sank very fast. Now it was no bigger than a star, but her foot touched solid ground. Then the sun went out like the last spark on a piece of burning paper. She saw her brothers stand about her, arm in arm, and there was only just room enough for all of them. The waves beat upon the rock and washed over them in a shower of spray. The heavens were lit by constant flashes, and bolt upon bolt of thunder crashed. But the sister and brothers clasped each other's hands and sang a psalm, which comforted them and gave them courage.

At dawn the air was clear and still. As soon as the sun came up, the swans flew off with Elisa and they left the rock behind. The waves still tossed, and from the height where they soared it looked as if the white flecks of foam against the dark green waves were millions of white swans swimming upon the waters.

When the sun rose higher, Elisa saw before her a mountainous land, half floating in the air. Its peaks were capped with sparkling ice, and in the middle rose a castle that was a mile long, with one bold colonnade perched upon another. Down below, palm trees swayed and brilliant flowers bloomed as big as mill wheels. She asked if this was the land for which they were bound, but the swans shook their heads. What she saw was the gorgeous and ever changing palace of Fata Morgana. No mortal being could venture to enter it. As Elisa stared at it, before her eyes the mountains, palms, and palace faded away, and in their place rose twenty splendid churches, all alike, with lofty towers and pointed windows. She thought she heard the organ peal, but it was the roll of the ocean she heard. When she came close to the churches they turned into a fleet of ships sailing beneath her, but when she looked down it was only a sea mist drifting over the water.

Scene after scene shifted before her eyes until she saw at last the real country whither they went. Mountains rose before her beautifully blue, wooded with cedars, and studded with cities and palaces. Long before sunset she was sitting on a mountainside, in front of a large cave carpeted over with green creepers so delicate that they looked like embroidery.

"We shall see what you'll dream of here tonight," her youngest brother said, as he showed her where she was to sleep.

"I only wish I could dream how to set you free," she said.

This thought so completely absorbed her, and she prayed so earnestly for the Lord to help her that even in her sleep she kept on praying. It seemed to her that she was flying aloft to the Fata Morgana palace of clouds. The fairy who came out to meet her was fair and shining, yet she closely resembled the old woman who gave her the berries in the forest and told her of the swans who wore golden crowns on their heads.

"Your brothers can be set free," she said, "but have you the courage and tenacity to do it? The sea water that changes the shape of rough stones is indeed softer than your delicate hands, but it cannot feel the pain that your fingers will feel. It has no heart, so it cannot suffer the anguish and heartache that you will have to endure. Do you see this stinging nettle in my hand? Many such nettles grow around the cave where you sleep. Only those and the ones that grow upon graves in the churchyards may be used – remember that! Those you must gather, although they will burn your hands to blisters. Crush the nettles with your feet and you will have flax, which you must spin and weave into eleven shirts of mail with long sleeves. Once you throw these over the eleven wild swans, the spell over them is broken. But keep this well in mind! From the moment you undertake this task until it is done, even though it lasts for years, you must not speak. The first word you say will strike your brothers' hearts like a deadly knife. Their lives are at the mercy of your tongue. Now, remember what I told you!"

She touched Elisa's hand with nettles that burned like fire and awakened her. It was broad daylight, and close at hand where she had been sleeping grew a nettle like those of which she had dreamed. She thanked God upon her knees, and left the cave to begin her task.

With her soft hands she took hold of the dreadful nettles that seared like fire. Great blisters rose on her hands and arms, but she endured it gladly in the hope that she could free her beloved brothers. She crushed each nettle with her bare feet, and spun the green flax.

When her brothers returned at sunset, it alarmed them that she did not speak. They feared this was some new spell cast by their wicked stepmother, but when they saw her hands they understood that she laboured to save them. The youngest one wept, and wherever his tears touched Elisa she felt no more pain, and the burning blisters healed.

She toiled throughout the night, for she could not rest until she had delivered her beloved brothers from the enchantment. Throughout the next day, while the swans were gone she sat all alone, but never had the time sped so quickly. One shirt was made, and she set to work on the second one.

Then she heard the blast of a hunting horn on the mountainside. It frightened her, for the sound came nearer until she could hear the hounds bark. Terror-stricken, she ran into the cave, bundled together the nettles she had gathered and woven, and sat down on this bundle.

Immediately a big dog came bounding from the thicket, followed by another, and still another, all barking loudly as they ran to and fro. In a very few minutes all the huntsmen stood in front of the cave. The most handsome of these was the King of the land, and he came up to Elisa. Never before had he seen a girl so beautiful. "My lovely child," he said, "how do you come to be here?"

Elisa shook her head, for she did not dare to speak. Her brothers' deliverance and their very lives depended upon it, and she hid her hands under her apron to keep the King from seeing how much she suffered.

"Come with me," he told her. "You cannot stay here. If you are as good as you are fair I shall clothe you in silk and velvet, set a golden crown upon your head, and give you my finest palace to live in." Then he lifted her up on his horse. When she wept and wrung her hands, the King told her, "My only wish is to make you happy. Some day you will thank me for doing this." Off through the mountains he spurred, holding her before him on his horse as his huntsmen galloped behind them.

At sundown, his splendid city with all its towers and domes lay before them. The King led her into his palace, where great fountains played in the high marble halls, and where both walls and ceilings were adorned with paintings. But she took no notice of any of these things.

She was so dazzlingly beautiful.
(Ann Anderson)

She could only weep and grieve. Indifferently, she let the women dress her in royal garments, weave strings of pearls in her hair, and draw soft gloves over her blistered fingers.

She was so dazzlingly beautiful in all this splendor that the whole court bowed even deeper than before. And the King chose her for his bride, although the archbishop shook his head and whispered that this lovely maid of the woods must be a witch, who had blinded their eyes and stolen the King's heart.

But the King would not listen to him. He commanded that music be played, the costliest dishes be served, and the prettiest girls dance for her. She was shown through sweet-scented gardens, and into magnificent halls, but nothing could make her lips smile or her eyes sparkle. Sorrow had set its seal upon them. At length the King opened the door to a little chamber adjoining her bedroom. It was covered with splendid green embroideries, and looked just like the cave in which he had found her. On the floor lay the bundle of flax she had spun from the nettles, and from the ceiling hung the shirt she had already finished. One of the huntsmen had brought these with him as curiosities. "Here you may dream that you are back in your old home," the King told her. "Here is the work that you were doing there, and surrounded by all your splendor here it may amuse you to think of those times."

When Elisa saw these things that were so precious to her, a smile trembled on her lips, and the blood rushed back to her cheeks. The hope that she could free her brothers returned to her, and she kissed the King's hand. He pressed her to his heart and commanded that all the church bells peal to announce their wedding. The beautiful mute girl from the forest was to be the country's Queen.

The archbishop whispered evil words in the King's ear, but they did not reach his heart. The wedding was to take place. The archbishop himself had to place the crown on her head. Out of spite, he forced the tight circlet so low on her forehead that it hurt her. But a heavier band encircled her heart, and the sorrow she felt for her brothers kept her from feeling any hurt of the flesh. Her lips were mute, for one single word would mean death to her brothers, but her eyes shone with love for the kind and handsome King who did his best to please her. Every day she grew fonder and fonder of him in her heart. Oh, if only she could confide in him, and tell him what grieved her. But mute she must remain, and finish her task in silence. So at night she would steal away from his side into her little chamber which resembled the cave, and there she wove one shirt after another, but when she set to work on the seventh there was not enough flax left to finish it.

She knew that the nettles she must use grew in the churchyard, but she had to gather them herself. How could she go there?

"Oh, what is the pain in my fingers compared with the anguish I feel in my heart!" she thought. "I must take the risk, and the good Lord will not desert me."

As terrified as if she were doing some evil thing, she tiptoed down into the moonlit garden, through the long alleys and down the deserted streets to the churchyard. There she saw a group of vampires sitting in a circle on one of the large gravestones. These hideous ghouls took off their ragged clothes as they were about to bathe. With skinny fingers they clawed open the new graves. Greedily they snatched out the bodies and ate the flesh from them. Elisa had to pass close to them, and they fixed their vile eyes upon her, but she said a prayer, picked the stinging nettles, and carried them back to the palace.

Only one man saw her – the archbishop. He was awake while others slept. Now he had proof of what he had suspected. There was something wrong with the Queen. She was a witch, and that was how she had duped the King and all his people. In the confessional, he told the King what he had seen and what he feared. As the bitter words spewed from his mouth, the images of the saints shook their heads, as much as to say, "He lies. Elisa is innocent." The archbishop, however, had a different explanation for this. He said they were testifying against her, and shaking their heads at her wickedness.

Two big tears rolled down the King's cheeks as he went home with suspicion in his heart. That night he pretended to be asleep, but no restful sleep touched his eyes. He watched Elisa get out of bed. Every night he watched her get up and each time he followed her quietly and saw her disappear into her private little room. Day after day his frown deepened. Elisa saw it, and could not understand why this should be, but it made her anxious and added to the grief her heart already felt for her brothers. Her hot tears fell down upon her queenly robes of purple velvet. There they flashed

Only one man saw her – the archbishop.
(Fritz Kredel)

like diamonds, and all who saw this splendor wished that they were Queen.

Meanwhile she had almost completed her task. Only one shirt was lacking, but again she ran out of flax. Not a single nettle was left. Once more, for the last time, she must go to the churchyard and pluck a few more handfuls. She thought with fear of the lonely walk and the ghastly vampires, but her will was as strong as her faith in God.

She went upon her mission, but the King and his archbishop followed her. They saw her disappear through the iron gates of the churchyard, and when they came in after her they saw vampires sitting on a gravestone, just as Elisa had seen them.

The King turned away, for he thought Elisa was among them – Elisa, whose head had rested against his heart that very evening.

"Let the people judge her," he said. And the people did judge her. They condemned her to die by fire.

She was led from her splendid royal halls to a dungeon, dark and damp, where the wind whistled in between the window bars. Instead of silks and velvets they gave her for a pillow the bundle of nettles she had gathered, and for her coverlet the harsh, burning shirts of mail she had woven. But they could have given her nothing that pleased her more.

She set to work again, and prayed. Outside, the boys in the street sang jeering songs about her, and not one soul came to comfort her with a kind word. But toward evening she heard the rustle of a swan's wings close to her window. It was her youngest brother who had found her at last. She sobbed for joy. Though she knew that this night was all too apt to be her last, the task was almost done and her brothers were near her.

The archbishop came to stay with her during her last hours on earth, for this much he had promised the King. But she shook her head, and by her expression and gestures begged him to leave. This was the last night she had to finish her task, or it would all go for naught – all her pain, and her tears, and her sleepless nights. The archbishop went away, saying cruel things against her. But poor Elisa knew her own innocence, and she kept on with her task.

The little mice ran about the floor, and brought nettles to her feet, trying to help her all they could. And a thrush perched near the bars of her window to sing the whole night through, as merrily as he could, so that she would keep up her courage.

It was still in the early dawn, an hour before sunrise, when the eleven brothers reached the palace gates and demanded to see the King. This, they were told, was impossible. It was still night. The King was asleep and could not be disturbed. They begged and threatened so loudly that the guard turned out, and even the King came running to find what the trouble was. But at that instant the sun rose, and the eleven brothers vanished. Eleven swans were seen flying over the palace.

All the townsmen went flocking out through the town gates, for they wanted to see the witch burned. A decrepit old horse pulled the cart in which Elisa sat. They had dressed her in coarse sackcloth, and all her lovely long hair hung loose around her beautiful head. Her cheeks were deathly pale, and her lips moved in silent prayer as her fingers twisted the green flax. Even on her way to death she did not stop her still un-finished work. Ten shirts lay at her feet and she worked away on the eleventh. "See how the witch mumbles," the mob scoffed at her. "That's no psalm book in her hands. No, there she sits, nursing her filthy sorcery. Snatch it away from her, and tear it to bits!"

The crowd of people closed in to destroy all her work, but before they could reach her, eleven white swans flew down and made a ring around the cart with their flapping wings. The mob drew back in terror. "It is a sign from Heaven. She must be innocent," many people whispered. But no one dared say it aloud.

As the executioner seized her arm, she made haste to throw the eleven shirts over the swans, who instantly became eleven handsome Princes. But the youngest brother still had a swan's wing in place of one arm, where a sleeve was missing from his shirt. Elisa had not quite been able to finish it. "Now," she cried, "I may speak! I am innocent."

All the people who saw what had happened bowed down to her as they would before a saint. But the strain, the anguish, and the suffering had been too much for her to bear, and she fell into her brothers' arms as if all life had gone out of her.

"She is innocent indeed!" said her eldest brother, and he told them all that had happened. And while he spoke, the scent of a million roses filled the air, for every piece of wood that they had piled up to burn her had taken root and grown branches. There stood a great high hedge, covered with red and fragrant roses. At the very top a single pure white flower shone like a star. The King plucked it and put it on Elisa's breast. And she awoke, with peace and happiness in her heart.

All the church bells began to ring of their own accord, and the air was filled with birds. Back to the palace went a bridal procession such as no King had ever enjoyed before.

THE WICKED PRINCE

ONCE UPON A time there was a proud and wicked prince who thought only about how he might conquer all the nations of the earth and make his name a terror to all mankind. He plunged forth with fire and sword; his soldiers trampled down the grain in the fields, and put the torch to the peasant's cottage so that the red flames licked the very leaves from the trees, and the fruit hung roasted from black and charred limbs. Many a poor mother caught up her naked baby and tried to hide behind the smoking walls, but the soldiers followed her, and if they found her and the child, then began their devilish pleasure. Evil spirits could do no worse, but the Prince rejoiced in it all.

Day by day his power increased; his name was feared by all, and fortune followed him in all his deeds. From the conquered cities he carried away gold and precious treasures, until he had amassed in his capital riches such as were unequaled in any other place. Then he built superb palaces and temples and arches, and whoever saw his magnificence said, "What a great Prince!" Never did they think of the misery he had brought upon other lands; never did they listen to the groans and lamentations from cities laid waste by fire.

The Prince gazed upon his gold, looked at his superb buildings, and thought like the crowd, "What a great Prince!" "But I must have more, much more! There is no power that can equal – much less surpass – mine!" And so he warred with his neighbors until all were defeated. The conquered kings were chained to his chariot with chains of gold when he drove through the streets; and when he sat at table they lay at the feet of the Prince and his courtiers, eating such scraps as might be thrown to them.

Now the Prince had his own statue set up in the market places and the palaces; yes, he would even have set it in the churches, on the altars, but to this the priests said, "Prince, you are great, but God is greater! We dare not obey your orders!"

"Well," said the evil Prince, "then I shall conquer God too!" In the pride and folly of his heart he had built a splendidly constructed ship in which he could sail through the air. It was as colorful as a peacock's tail, and seemed decorated with a thousand eyes, but each eye was the barrel of a cannon. The Prince could sit in the center of the ship and, upon his touching a certain button, a thousand bullets would stream forth, and the guns would at once be reloaded. Hundreds of strong eagles were harnessed to the ship, and so it flew away, up and up toward the sun.

Far beneath lay the earth. At first its mountains and forests appeared like a plowed field, with a tuft of green peeping out here and there from the sod; then it seemed like an unrolled map, and finally it was wholly hidden in mists and clouds, as the eagles flew higher and higher.

Then God sent forth a single one of His countless angels, and immediately the Prince let fly a thousand bullets at him, but they fell back like hail from the angel's shining wings. Then one drop of blood – just one – fell from one of the angel's white wing feathers onto the ship of the Prince. There it burned itself into it, and its weight of a thousand hundredweights of lead hurled the ship back down with terrible speed to the earth. The mighty wings of the eagles were broken, the winds roared about the head of the Prince, and the clouds on every side, sprung from the smoke of burned cities, formed themselves into menacing shapes. Some were like mile-long crabs stretching out their huge claws toward him; others were like tumbling boulders or fire-breathing dragons. The Prince lay half dead in his ship, until it was finally caught in the tangled branches of a dense forest.

"I *will* conquer God!" he said. "I have sworn it; my will shall be done!" Then for seven years he built other magnificent ships in which to sail through the air, and had lightning beams forged from the hardest of steels, to batter down the battlements of heaven itself. From all the conquered countries he assembled vast armies which, when formed in battle array, covered mile after mile of ground.

They embarked in the magnificent ships, but as the Prince approached his own, God sent forth a swarm of gnats – just one little swarm – which buzzed about the Prince, and stung his face and hands. In rage he drew his sword, but he could cut only the empty air; he could not strike the gnats. Then he ordered that he be brought costly cloths, which were to be wrapped around him so that no gnat could reach him with its sting. His orders were carried out; but one little gnat had concealed itself in the innermost covering, and now it crept into the Prince's ear and stung him. It smarted like fire, and the poison rushed into his brain; he tore the clothes loose and flung them far away from him, rent his garments into rags, and danced naked before the rugged and savage soldiers. Now they could only mock at the mad Prince who had started out to conquer God and had been himself conquered by a single little gnat!

SOMETHING

"I'M GOING TO be something!" said the eldest of five brothers. "I'm going to be useful in the world, however humble a position I hold; if that which I'm doing is useful, that will be Something. I'll make bricks; people can't do without bricks, so at least I'll do Something."

"But something very unimportant," said the second brother. "What you'd be doing would be as good as nothing! That's a laborer's job and can be done by a machine. No, you'd better become a mason; that's really Something, and that's what I'm going to be. That is a position! Then you belong to a guild and become a citizen, have a banner of your own and your own quarters at the inn. Yes, and if things come out well I may get to be a master, and have workmen under me, and my wife will be known as the master's wife. That will be Something!"

"That's nothing at all," said the third. "Just think how many different classes there are in a town far above a master mason. You may be an honest man, but even as a master you'll only be what is called 'common.' No, I know Something better than that. I'll be an architect, will live among the thinkers, the artists; I'll raise myself up to the intellectual aristocracy. Of course, I may have to begin at the bottom; yes, I might as well say it – I will have to start as a carpenter's boy, wearing a cap, though I'm used to wearing a silk hat, and to fetch beer and spirits for the simple workmen, and listen to their insults. Of course, that's irritating, but I'll try to pretend it's only a masquerade. 'Tomorrow,' I'll say, 'when I'm a journeyman, I'll be on my own course, and I'll have nothing to do with the others.' Yes, I'll go to the academy, learn to draw, and get to be an architect. That is Something! That's a whole lot! I may even get a title – yes, have one placed before or after my name; and I shall build and build, as others have done before me. Yes, that's Something one can rely on; it's Something wholly worthwhile."

"But Something that I care nothing about," said the fourth. "I shouldn't care to travel on and on in the beaten track, to be only a copyist. I want to be a genius, cleverer than all of you put together. I want to create a new style, provide the idea for a building suitable to the climate and materials of our country, our national character, and the development of our age; besides, I want to build an extra floor for my own genius!"

"But suppose the climate and materials aren't good," said the fifth. "That will be very unfortunate, since they are of vital importance. As for our national character, to represent that in architecture would be sheer affectation, while the requirements of modern times may cause you to run wild, as youth frequently does. I can see that none of you will ever amount to anything, however much you yourselves think you will. But do as you like; I won't be like you. I shall consider what you do; there's something ridiculous in everything; I'll discover it, and it will be my business to expose it – that will be Something!"

He did as he promised; and people said of this fifth brother, "There's Something in him, certainly; he has plenty of brains, but he doesn't do anything!" But it was just that which made him Something.

This is only a little story, and yet as long as the world exists it will have no end.

But, then, did nothing more become of the five brothers? Listen further now, and you will hear the whole story.

The eldest brother, the brickmaker, found that every brick he made brought him in a small copper coin. It was only copper, but enough of these small copper coins added together could be changed into a bright dollar, and wherever he knocked with this – at the butcher's, the baker's, or the tailor's, yes, everywhere – the door flew open, and he was given what he wanted.

That was the virtue of his bricks. Of course, some of them crumbled or broke in two, but a use was found even for them. You see, old Mother Margaret wanted so much to build herself a little house up by the dike; so all the broken bricks were given to her, and even a few whole ones too, for though he was only a brickmaker, the eldest brother had a generous heart. The poor woman built her house with her own hands; it was very narrow; its one window was all lopsided; the door was too low, and the thatching might have been laid on the roof more skillfully, but it gave her shelter and a home and could be seen from far out at sea. The sea in all its power sometimes broke over the dike and sprinkled a salty shower over the little house, which still stood there years after he who made its bricks was dead and gone.

As for the second brother – yes, he could now build in a different fashion, as he had decided to learn. When he had served his apprenticeship, he buckled on his knapsack and started out on his travels, singing as he went. When he came back to his home town, he became a master mason there and built house after house, a whole street of houses. There they stood, looking very handsome and giving an air of dignity to the town; and these houses soon built him a little house for himself. But how can houses build a house? If you ask the houses they will give you no answer, but the people will reply, "Why, of course, the street built him his house!" It was not very large, and had only a clay floor, but when he and his young bride danced over it that floor became as smooth as if it had been polished, and from every stone in the wall sprung a flower, gay as the costliest tapestry. It was a charming house, and they were indeed a happily married couple. The banner of the Masons' Guild waved gaily outside, and workmen and apprentices shouted, "Hurray!" Yes indeed, that was Something! And at last he died – and that was Something, too!

Next comes the third brother, the architect. He had begun as a carpenter's apprentice, wearing a cap and running errands all over town; but from the academy, he had steadily risen to become a builder. If the street of houses had built a house for his brother the mason, the street took its very name from the architect; his was the handsomest house in the whole street – that was Something, and he was Something with a long title before and after his name. His children could boast of their "birth;" and when he died his widow was a lady of standing – that is Something – and his name was on the corner of the street as well as on everybody's lips – that is Something indeed!

Then comes the fourth brother, the genius who had wanted to invent something new and original and have an extra floor on top of that. But that floor gave way once beneath his feet, so that he fell and broke his neck. However, he had a splendid funeral, with music and banners, and flowery obituaries in the newspapers. Three eulogies were spoken over him, each one longer than the other, and that would have pleased him, for he had so loved being talked about. Then a monument was erected over his grave – only one story high, but still that is Something!

So now he was dead, along with his three elder brothers. The youngest one, the critic, outlived

Everyone in town was out on the ice.
(Fritz Kredel)

them all, and that was quite proper, for it gave him the last word, which to him was a matter of great importance. "He has a good head on him," people said. But at last his hour came, too; he died, and his soul went to the gates of heaven. Souls always enter in couples, so there he stood beside another soul, old Mother Margaret from the house by the dike.

"I suppose it is for the sake of contrast that I and this miserable soul should come here at the same time," said the critic. "Well, now, my good

woman," he asked, "who are you? Do you also want to go in there?"

The old woman curtsied as well as she could, thinking it was Saint Peter himself who spoke to her. "I am just a poor old soul with no family. Just old Margaret from the house near the dike."

"I see. And what have you done down below?"

"I have done really nothing in the world, nothing at all to warrant my being admitted here. It will be God's mercy, indeed, if I am allowed to pass through this gate."

It bored the critic to stand there waiting, so he felt he must talk about something. "And how did you leave the world?" he asked carelessly.

"How did I leave it? Well, I hardly know how; I was sick and miserable indeed in the last few years, and could hardly bear to creep out of bed at all in the cold and frosty weather. It has been a hard winter, but that's all past now. For a few days, as your reverence must know, the wind was quite still, but it was bitterly cold; the ice covered the water as far as you could see. Everybody in town was out on the ice, where there was what they called ski racing, and dancing, I think, with music, and entertainment. I could hear it where I lay in my poor room. And along toward evening the moon came up, but it still wasn't very bright. From my bed I looked through the window and saw a strange white cloud rising up over the sea. I lay there and watched it, watched the black spot in it grow bigger and bigger, and then I knew what it meant; you don't see that sign very often, but I was old and experienced. I knew it, and horror crept over me. Just twice before in my life had I seen that sign, and I knew it meant there would be a terrible storm and a flash flood; it would burst over the poor people who were drinking and dancing and making merry, out there on the ice. Young and old, the whole town was there; who could warn them, if no one saw the cloud or could recognize it as I could? I felt so terrified that it gave me more strength than I'd had in many years. I felt alive all over. I got out of bed and managed to get over to the window; I couldn't drag myself any farther, but I did get the window open; I could see the people dancing on the ice and the gaily colored flags, I could hear the boys shouting and the young men and women singing; all were so merry. But that white cloud with its black spot rose higher and higher. I screamed as loudly as I could, but they were all too far away to hear me. Soon the storm would break loose; the ice would be smashed into pieces, and all the people would be drowned! They could not hear me; I wasn't able to get out to them; how could I get them onto land? Then our Lord sent me the idea of setting fire to my bed; it would be better for my house to be burned to the ground than for so many people to meet a miserable death. So I made a light, and saw the red flame leap up! Somehow I got out of the door, but then I fell and lay there, for I could not rise again. But the flames burst out through the window and the roof; the people down below saw it and all ran as fast as they could to help me, the poor old woman they were afraid would be burned; there was not one who didn't come to my aid. I heard them come, but then, too, I heard a sudden roaring in the air, and then a thundering like the shots of heavy cannons; the flood was breaking up the ice, and it was all crumbling to pieces. However, the people had all come off the ice to the trenches, where the sparks were flying about me; I had saved all of them. But I

couldn't stand the cold and the fright, and so I came up here to the gates of heaven. Do you think they can be opened to such a wretched old creature as I? I have no little house now by the dike, though I guess that fact will not gain me admission here."

Then the heavenly gates opened, and the Angel bade poor old Margaret to enter. As she crossed the threshold she dropped a straw, one of the straws from the bed she had set afire to save the people on the ice, and lo! it changed into the purest gold – gold that grew and twisted itself into the most beautiful shapes!

"See, this was brought by the poor woman," said the Angel. "Now what do you bring? Yes, I know full well that you have made nothing, not even bricks. If only you could go back and return here with at least one brick, not that it would be good for anything when you had made it, but because anything, the very last thing, if done with a kindly heart, is Something. But you cannot return, and I can do nothing for you."

Then the poor soul, the old woman from the hut by the dike, spoke up for him. "His brother gave me all the bricks and broken pieces I used to build my miserable shack – that was great generosity to a poor old soul like me. Cannot all those bits and pieces, put together, be considered one brick for him? It would be an act of mercy; he needs mercy, and this is the very home of mercy."

"Your brother, he whom you called the humblest," said the Angel, "he whose honest labor seemed to you the lowliest, sends you this heavenly gift. You shall not be turned away, but shall be permitted to stand here outside and consider your manner of life below. But you shall not enter, not before you have done a good deed and thereby accomplished – Something!"

"I could have said that much better," thought the critic, but he didn't say it out loud. And for him that was already – Something!

OLE LUKOIE

THERE'S NO ONE on earth who knows so many stories as Ole Lukoie – he certainly can tell them! When night comes on and children still sit in good order around the table, or on their little stools, Ole Lukoie arrives. He comes upstairs quietly, for he walks in his socks. Softly he opens the door, and flick! he sprinkles sweet milk in the children's eyes – just a tiny bit, but always enough to keep their eyes closed so they won't see him. He tiptoes behind them and breathes softly on their necks, and this makes their heads hang heavy. Oh yes! But it doesn't hurt them, for Ole Lukoie loves children and only wants them to be quiet, and that they are only when they have been put to bed. He wants them to be quiet so that he can tell them stories.

As soon as the children fall asleep, Ole Lukoie sits down on the bed beside them. He is well dressed. His coat is made of silk, but it would be impossible to say what color it is because it gleams red, or green, or blue, as he turns about. Under each arm he carries an umbrella. One has pictures on it, and that one he opens up over good children. Then they dream the most beautiful stories all night long. The other is just a plain umbrella with nothing on it at all, and that one he opens over naughty children. Then they sleep restlessly, and when they wake up in the morning they have had no dreams at all.

Now you shall hear how for a whole week Lukoie came every evening to a little boy named Hjalmar, and what he told him. There are seven of these stories, because there are seven days to a week.

MONDAY

"Now listen," Ole Lukoie said, as soon as he got Hjalmar to bed that evening. "First, let's put things to rights."

Then all the flowers in the flower pots grew to be big trees, arching their long branches under the ceiling and along the walls until the room became a beautiful bower. The limbs were loaded with flowers, each more lovely than any rose, and their fragrance was so sweet that if you wanted to eat it – it was sweeter than jam. The fruit gleamed like gold, and besides there were dumplings bursting with currants. It was all so splendid!

Suddenly a dreadful howl came from the table drawer where Hjalmar kept his schoolbooks.

"What can the matter be?" said Ole Lukoie, as he went to the table and opened the drawer. It was the slate, which was throwing a fit and was ready to fall to pieces, because there was a mistake in the sum that had been worked on it. The slate pencil tugged and jumped at the end of its string as if it were a little dog. It wanted to correct the sum, but it could not.

Another lamentation came from Hjalmar's copybook. Oh, it was dreadful to listen to. On each page the capital letters stood one under the other, each with its little letter beside it. This was the copy. Next to these were the letters which Hjalmar had written. Though they thought they looked just like the first ones, they tumbled all over the lines on which they were supposed to stand.

"See, this is how you should hold yourselves," said the copy. "Look, slanting like this, with a bold stroke."

"Oh, how glad we would be to do that!" Hjalmar's letters replied, "but we can't. We are so weak."

"Then you must take medicine," Ole Lukoie told them.

"Oh no!" they cried, and stood up so straight that it was a pleasure to see them.

"Now we can't tell any stories," said Ole Lukoie. "I must give them their exercises. One, two! One, two!" He put the letters through their paces until they stood straight, more graceful than any copy could stand. But when Ole Lukoie left, and Hjalmar looked at them in the morning, they were just as miserable as ever.

TUESDAY

As soon as Hjalmar was in bed, Ole Lukoie touched all the furniture in the room with his little magic sprinkler. (Fritz Kredel)

As soon as Hjalmar was in bed, Ole Lukoie touched all the furniture in the room with his little magic sprinkler, and immediately everything began to talk. Everything talked about itself except the spittoon, which kept silent. It was annoyed that they should be so conceited as to talk only about themselves, and think only about themselves, without paying the least attention to it, sitting so humbly in the corner and letting everyone spit at it.

Over the chest of drawers hung a large painting in a gilt frame. It was a landscape in which one could see tall old trees, flowers in the grass, and a large lake from which a river flowed away through the woods, past many castles, far out to the open sea. Ole Lukoie touched the painting with his magic sprinkler, and the birds in it began to sing, the branches stirred on the trees, and the clouds billowed along. You could see their shadows sweep across the landscape.

Then Ole Lukoie lifted little Hjalmar up to the frame and put the boy's feet into the picture, right in the tall grass, and there he stood. The sun shone down on him through the branches of the trees, as he ran to the water and got into a little boat which was there. It was painted red and white, and its sails shone like silver. Six swans, each with a golden crown around its neck and a bright blue star upon its forehead, drew the boat through the deep woods, where the trees whispered of robbers and witches, and the flowers spoke about the dainty little elves, and about all that the butterflies had told them.

Splendid fish with scales like gold and silver swam after the boat. Sometimes they gave a leap – so that it said "splash" in the water. Birds red and blue, large and small, flew after the boat in two long lines. The gnats danced and the cockchafers went *boom, boom!* They all wanted to go with Hjalmar, and every one of them had a story to tell.

What a magnificent voyage that was! Sometimes the forest was deep and dark, and sometimes like the loveliest garden full of sun and flowers. There were palaces of marble and glass, and on the balconies stood Princesses. Hjalmar knew them well. They were all little girls with whom he had played. Each of them stretched out her hand, and each held out the prettiest sugar pig that ever a cake woman sold. Hjalmar grasped each sugar pig as he went by, and the Princess held fast, so that each got a piece of it. The Princess got the smaller piece, and Hjalmar got the larger one. Little Princes stood guard at each palace. They saluted with their swords, and caused raisins and tin soldiers to shower down. You could tell that they were Princes indeed.

Sometimes Hjalmar sailed through the forests, sometimes through great halls, or straight through a town. He also came through the town where his nurse lived, she who had carried him in her arms when he was a very small boy and had always been fond of him. She bowed and waved, and sang the pretty song which she had made up herself and sent to Hjalmar:

"I think of you as often,
Hjalmar, my little dear,
As I've kissed your lips so soft, and
Your cheeks and your eyes so clear.
I heard your first laughter and weeping,
And too soon I heard your good-bys.
May God have you in his keeping,
My angel from the skies."

All the birds sang too, and the flowers danced on their stalks, and the old trees nodded, just as if Ole Lukoie were telling stories to *them*.

WEDNESDAY

How the rain came down outdoors! Hjalmar could hear it in his sleep, and when Ole Lukoie opened the window the water had risen up to the window sill. There was a real lake outside, and a fine ship lay close to the house.

"If you will sail with me, little Hjalmar," said Ole Lukoie, "you can voyage to distant lands tonight and be back again by morning."

Immediately Hjalmar stood in his Sunday clothes aboard this splendid ship. And immediately the weather turned glorious as they sailed through the streets and rounded the church. Now everything was a great wild sea. They sailed until land was far out of sight, and they saw a flock of storks who also came from home and wanted to travel to warmer climes. These storks flew in line, one behind the other, and they had already flown a long, long way. One of them was so weary that his wings could scarcely carry him on. He was the very last in the line, and soon he was left a long way behind the others. Finally he sank with outstretched wings, lower and lower. He made a few more feeble strokes with his wings, but it was no use. Now he touched the ship's rigging with his feet, slid down the sail, and landed, *bang!* upon the deck.

The cabin boy caught him and put him in the chicken coop with the hens, ducks, and turkeys. The poor stork stood among them most dejected.

"Funny-looking fellow!" said all the hens. The turkey gobbler puffed himself as big as ever he could, and asked the stork who he was. The ducks backed off and told each other, "He's a quack! He's a quack!"

Now the stork tried to tell them about the heat of Africa; about the pyramids; and about the ostrich, how it runs across the desert like a wild horse. But the ducks did not understand him. They said to each other, "Don't we all agree that he's a fool?"

"Yes, to be sure, he's a fool," the turkey gobbler gobbled, as the stork kept silent and thought of his Africa.

"What beautiful thin legs you've got," said the turkey gobbler. "What do they cost a yard?"

"Quack, quack, quack!" The ducks all laughed, but the stork pretended not to hear them.

"You can laugh too," the gobbler told him, "for that was a mighty witty remark, or was it too deep for you? No indeed, he isn't very bright, so let's keep on being clever ourselves."

The hens cackled, the ducks went "Quick, quack! quick, quack!" and it was dreadful to see how they made fun of him among themselves. But Hjalmar opened the back door of the chicken coop and called to the stork. He hopped out on the deck. He was rested now, and he seemed to nod to Hjalmar to thank him.

Then he spread his wings and flew away to the warm countries. But the hens clucked, and the ducks quacked, and the turkey gobbler's face turned fiery red.

"Tomorrow we'll make soup out of you," said Hjalmar. With these words he woke up in his own little bed. It was a marvelous journey that Ole Lukoie had taken him on during the night.

THURSDAY

"I tell you what," Ole Lukoie said. "Don't be afraid if I show you a little mouse." He held out a hand with the quaint little creature in it. "It has come to ask you to a wedding. There are two little mice here who are to enter into the state of marriage this very night. They live under the floor of your mother's pantry, which is supposed to be the most charming quarters."

"How can I get through that little mouse hole in the floor?" Hjalmar asked.

"Leave that to me," said Ole Lukoie. "I'll make you small enough." Then he touched Hjalmar with his magic sprinkler. He immediately became shorter and shorter, until at last he was only as tall as your finger. "Now you may borrow the tin soldier's uniform. I think it will just fit you, and uniforms always look well when one is at a party."

"Oh, don't they!" said Hjalmar. Instantly he was dressed like the finest tin soldier.

"If you will be so kind as to sit in your mother's thimble," the mouse said, "I shall consider it an honor to pull you along."

"Will you really go to all that trouble, young lady?" Hjalmar cried.

And in this fashion, off they drove to the mouse's wedding. First they went down a long passage under the floor boards. It was just high enough for them to drive through in the thimble, and the whole passage was lighted with touchwood. "Doesn't it smell delightful here?" said the mouse. "This whole road has been greased with bacon rinds, and there's nothing better than that."

Now they came to the wedding hall. On the right stood all the little lady mice, whispering and giggling as if they were making fun of each other. On the left stood all the gentlemen

"Don't be afraid if I show you a little mouse."
(Fritz Kredel)

mice, twirling their mustaches with their forepaws. The bridegroom and his bride stood in a hollow cheese rind in the center of the floor, and kissed like mad, in plain view of all the guests. But of course they were engaged, and were to be married immediately.

More and more guests kept crowding in. The mice were nearly trampling each other to death, and the bridal couple had posted themselves in the doorway, so that no one could come or leave. Like the passage, this whole hall had been greased with bacon rind, and that was the complete banquet. However, for the dessert, a pea was brought in, on which a little mouse of the family had bitten the name of the bridal couple, that is to say the first letter of the name. This was a most unusual touch.

All the mice said it was a charming wedding, and that the conversation was perfect. And then Hjalmar drove home again. He had been in very high society, for all that he had been obliged to make himself very small to fit in the tin soldier's uniform.

FRIDAY

"It's astonishing how many older people are anxious to get hold of me," said Ole Lukoie. "Especially those whose consciences are bothering them. 'Good little Ole,' they say to me, 'we can't close our eyes. We lie awake all night, facing our wicked deeds which sit on the edge of our beds like ugly little fiends and soak us in hot perspiration. Won't you come and turn them out so that we can have a good night's sleep?' At that they sigh very deeply. 'We will be glad to pay you for it. Good night, Ole. The money lies on the window sill.' But I don't do things for pay," said Ole Lukoie.

"What are we going to have tonight?" little Hjalmar asked.

"I don't know whether you'd like to go to a wedding again tonight but it's quite different from the one last night. Your sister's big doll, who looks like a man and is named Herman, is to be married to the doll called Bertha. It's Bertha's birthday, too, so there'll be no end to the presents."

"Yes, I know," Hjalmar told him. "Whenever the dolls need new clothes, my sister either lets them have a birthday or hold a wedding. It must have happened a hundred times already."

"Yes, but tonight is the hundred and first wedding, and, with one hundred and one, things come to an end. That's why it's to be so splendid. Oh, look!"

Hjalmar looked over at the table. There he saw a little pasteboard house with the windows alight, and all the tin soldiers presenting arms in front of it. The bridal couple sat on the floor and leaned against the table leg. They looked thoughtful, and with good reason. Ole Lukoie, rigged out in grandmother's black petticoat, married them off. When the ceremony was over, all the furniture in the room sang the following fine song, which the pencil had written. It went to the tune of the soldier's tattoo:

"Let us lift up our voices as high as the sun,
In honor of those who today are made one.
Although neither knows quite what they've
*   done,*
And neither one quite knows who's been
*   won,*
Oh, wood and leather go well together,
So let's lift up our voices as high as the sun."

Then they were given presents, but they had refused to take any food at all, because they planned to live on love.

"Shall we go to a summer resort, or take a voyage?" the bridegroom asked. They consulted the swallow, who was such a traveler, and the old setting hen who had raised five broods of chicks. The swallow told them about the lovely warm countries where grapes hang in great ripe bunches, where the air is soft, and where the mountains have wonderful colors that they don't have here.

"But they haven't got our green cabbage," the hen said. "I was in the country with all my chickens one summer and there was a sand pit in which we could scratch all day. We also had access to a garden where cabbages grew. Oh, how green they were! I can't imagine anything lovelier."

"But one cabbage looks just like another," said the swallow, "and then we so often have bad weather. It is cold here – it freezes."

"That's good for the cabbage," said the hen. "Besides, it's quite warm at times. Didn't we have a hot summer four years ago? For five whole weeks it was so hot that one could scarcely breathe. Then too, we don't have all those poisonous creatures that infest the warm countries, and we don't have robbers. Anyone who doesn't think ours is the most beautiful country is a rascal. Why, he doesn't deserve to live here!" The hen burst into tears. "I have done my share of traveling. I once made a twelve-mile trip in a coop, and there's no pleasure at all in traveling."

"Isn't the hen a sensible woman!" said Bertha, the doll. "I don't fancy traveling in the mountains because first you go up and then you go down. No, we will move out by the sand pit and take our walks in the cabbage patch."

That settled the matter.

SATURDAY

"Shall we have some stories?" little Hjalmar asked, as soon as Ole Lukoie had put him to bed.

"There's no time for any tonight," Ole told him, as he spread his best umbrella over the boy. "Just look at these Chinamen."

The whole umbrella looked like a large Chinese bowl, with blue trees and arched bridges on which little Chinamen stood nodding their heads.

"We must have all the world spruced up by tomorrow morning," said Ole. "It's a holiday because it is Sunday. I must go to church steeples to see that the little church goblins are polishing the bells so that they will sound their best. I must go out into the fields to see whether the wind is blowing the dust off of the leaves and grass, and my biggest job of all will be to take down all the stars and shine them. I put them in my apron, but first each star must be numbered and the hole from which it comes must be numbered the same, so that they go back in their proper places, or they wouldn't stick. Then we would have too many falling stars, for one after another would come tumbling down."

"Oh I say, Mr Lukoie," said an old portrait that hung on the wall of Hjalmar's bedroom. "I am Hjalmar's great-grandfather. I thank you for telling the boy your stories, but you mustn't put wrong ideas in his head. The stars can't be taken down and polished. The stars are worlds too, just like the earth, and that's the beauty of them."

"My thanks, you old great-grandfather," said Ole Lukoie. "I thank you, indeed! You

"Oh I say, Mr Lukoie," said an old portrait that hung on the wall of Hjalmar's bedroom. (Fritz Kredel)

are the head of the family, you are the oldest of the ancestors, but I am older than you are. I am an old heathen. The Greeks and the Romans called me their god of dreams. I have been to the nobles' homes, and still go there. I know how to behave with all people, great and small. Now you may tell stories yourself." Ole Lukoie tucked his umbrella under his arm and took himself off.

"Well! It seems one can't even express an opinion these days," the old portrait grumbled. And Hjalmar woke up.

SUNDAY

"Good evening," said Ole Lukoie.

Hjalmar nodded, and ran to turn his great-grandfather's portrait to the wall so that it wouldn't interrupt them, as it had the night before.

"Now," he said, "you must tell stories; about the five peas who lived in a pod, about the rooster's foot-track that courted the hen's foot-track, and about the darning needle who gave herself such airs because she thought she was a sewing needle."

"That would be too much of a good thing," said Ole Lukoie. "You know that I would rather show you things. I shall show you my own brother. He too is named Ole Lukoie, but he comes only once to anyone. When he comes he takes people for a ride on his horse, and tells them stories. He only knows two. One is more beautiful than anyone on earth can imagine, and the other is horrible beyond description." Then Ole Lukoie lifted little Hjalmar up to the window. "There," he said, "you can see my brother, the other Ole Lukoie. He is also called Death. You can see that he doesn't look nearly as bad as they make him out to be in the picture books, where he is only bones and knuckles. No, his coat is embroidered with silver. It is the magnificent uniform of a hussar, and a cloak of black velvet floats behind him and billows over his horse. See how he gallops along."

And Hjalmar saw how the other Ole Lukoie rode off on his horse with young folk as well as old people. He took some up before him, and some behind, but first he always asked them:

"What conduct is marked on your report card?" They all said, "Good", but he said, "Indeed. Let me see for myself." Then they had to show him the card. All those who were marked "very good" or "excellent," he put on his horse in front of him, and told them a lovely story. But those who were marked "below average" or "bad" had to ride behind him, and he told them a frightful tale. They shivered and wept, and tried to jump down off the horse. But this they couldn't do. They had immediately grown fast to it.

"Why, Death is the most beautiful Ole Lukoie," Hjalmar exclaimed. "I'm not afraid of him."

"You needn't be," Ole Lukoie told him, "only be sure that you have a good report card."

"There now, that's instructive," great-grandfather's portrait muttered. "It certainly helps to speak one's mind." He was completely satisfied.

You see, that's the story of Ole Lukoie. Tonight he himself can tell you some more.

THE SWINEHERD

ONCE THERE WAS a poor Prince. He had a kingdom; it was very tiny. Still it was large enough to marry upon, and on marriage his heart was set.

Now it was certainly rather bold of him to say, "Will you have me?" to the Emperor's own daughter. But he did, for his name was famous, and far and near there were hundreds of Princesses who would have said, "Yes!" and

"Thank you!" too. But what did the Emperor's daughter say? Well, we'll soon find out.

A rose tree grew over the grave of the Prince's father. It was such a beautiful tree. It bloomed only once in five long years, and then it bore but a single flower. Oh, that was a rose indeed! The fragrance of it would make a man forget all of his sorrows and his cares. The Prince had a nightingale too. It sang as if all the sweet songs of the world were in its little throat. The nightingale and the rose were to be gifts to the Princess. So they were sent to her in two large silver cases.

The Emperor ordered the cases carried before him, to the great hall where the Princess was playing at "visitors," with her maids-in-waiting. They seldom did anything else. As soon as the Princess saw that the large cases contained presents, she clapped her hands in glee. "Oh," she said, "I do hope I get a little pussy-cat." She opened a casket and there was the splendid rose.

"Oh, how pretty it is," said all the maids-in-waiting.

"It's more than pretty," said the Emperor. "It's superb."

But the Princess poked it with her finger, and she almost started to cry. "Oh fie! Papa," she said, "it isn't artificial. It is natural."

"Oh, fie," said all her maids-in-waiting, "it's only natural."

"Well," said the Emperor, "before we fret and pout, let's see what's in the other case." He opened it, and out came the nightingale, which sang so sweetly that for a little while no one could think of a single thing to say against it.

"*Superbe!*" "*Charmant!*" said the maids-in-waiting with their smattering of French, each one speaking it worse than the next.

"How the bird does remind me of our lamented Empress's music box," said one old courtier. "It has just the same tone, and the very same way of trilling."

The Emperor wept like a child. "Ah me," he said.

"Bird?" said the Princess. "You mean to say it's real?"

"A real live bird," the men who had brought it assured her.

"Then let it fly and begone," said the Princess, who refused to hear a word about the Prince, much less to see him.

But it was not so easy to discourage him. He darkened his face both brown and black,

Now the Princess happened to be passing by with all of her maids-in-waiting.
(Ann Anderson)

pulled his hat down over his eyes, and knocked at the door.

"Hello, Emperor," he said. "How do you do? Can you give me some work about the palace?"

"Well," said the Emperor, "people are always looking for jobs, but let me see. I do need somebody to tend the pigs, because we've got so many of them."

So the Prince was appointed "Imperial Pig Tender." He was given a wretched little room down by the pigsties, and there he had to live. All day long he sat and worked, as busy as could be, and by evening he had made a neat little kettle with bells all around the brim of it. When the kettle boiled, the bells would tinkle and play the old tune:

"Oh, dear Augustin,
All is lost, lost, lost."

But that was the least of it. If anyone put his finger in the steam from this kettle he could immediately smell whatever there was for dinner in any cooking-pot in town. No rose was ever like this!

Now the Princess happened to be passing by with all of her maids-in-waiting. When she heard the tune she stopped and looked pleased, for she too knew how to play "Oh, dear Augustin." It was the only tune she did know, and she played it with one finger.

"Why, that's the very same tune I play. Isn't the swineherd highly accomplished? I say," she ordered, "go and ask him the price of the instrument."

So one of the maids had to go, in among the pigsties, but she put on her overshoes first.

"What will you take for the kettle?" she asked.

"I'll take ten kisses from the Princess," said the swineherd.

"Oo, for goodness' sakes!" said the maid.

"And I won't take less," said the swineherd.

"Well, what does he say?" the Princess wanted to know.

"I can't tell you," said the maid. "He's too horrible."

"Then whisper it close to my ear." She listened to what the maid had to whisper. "Oo, isn't he naughty!" said the Princess and walked right away from there. But she had not gone very far when she heard the pretty bells play again:

"Oh, dear Augustin,
All is lost, lost, lost."

"I say," the Princess ordered, "ask him if he will take his ten kisses from my maids-in-waiting."

"No, I thank you," said the swineherd. "Ten kisses from the Princess, or I keep my kettle."

"Now isn't that disgusting!" said the Princess. "At least stand around me so that no one can see."

So her maids stood around her, and spread their skirts wide, while the swineherd took his ten kisses. Then the kettle was hers.

And then the fun started. Never was a kettle kept so busy. They boiled it from morning till night. From the chamberlain's banquet to the cobbler's breakfast, they knew all that was cooked in town. The maids-in-waiting danced about and clapped their hands.

"We know who's having sweet soup and pancakes. We know who's having porridge and cutlets. Isn't it interesting?"

"Most interesting," said the head lady of the bedchamber.

"Now, after all, I'm the Emperor's daughter," the Princess reminded them. "Don't you tell how I got it."

"Goodness gracious, no!" said they all.

But the swineherd – that's the Prince, for nobody knew he wasn't a real swineherd – was busy as he could be. This time he made a rattle. Swing it around, and it would play all the waltzes, jigs, and dance tunes that have been heard since the beginning of time.

"Why it's *superbe*!" said the Princess as she came by. "I never did hear better music. I say, go and ask him the price of that instrument. But mind you – no more kissing!"

"He wants a hundred kisses from the Princess," said the maid-in-waiting who had been in to ask him.

"I believe he's out of his mind," said the Princess, and she walked right away from there. But she had not gone very far when she said, "After all, I'm the Emperor's daughter, and it's my duty to encourage the arts. Tell him he can have ten kisses, as he did yesterday, but he must collect the rest from my maids-in-waiting."

"Oh, but we wouldn't like that," said the maids.

"Fiddlesticks," said the Princess, "If he can kiss me he certainly can kiss you. Remember, I'm the one who gives you board and wages."

"A hundred kisses from the Princess."
(Rudolf Koivu)

So the maid had to go back to the swineherd.

"A hundred kisses from the Princess," the swineherd told her, "or let each keep his own."

"Stand around me," said the Princess, and all her maids-in-waiting stood in a circle to hide her while the swineherd began to collect.

"What can have drawn such a crowd near the pigsties?" the Emperor wondered, as he looked down from his balcony. He rubbed his eyes, and he put on his spectacles. "Bless my soul if those maids-in-waiting aren't up to mischief again. I'd better go see what they are up to now."

He pulled his easy slippers up over his heels, though ordinarily he just shoved his feet in them and let them flap. Then, my! How much faster he went. As soon as he came near the pens he took very soft steps. The maids-in-waiting were so busy counting kisses, to see that everything went fair and that he didn't get too many or too few, that they didn't notice the Emperor behind them. He stood on his tiptoes.

"Such naughtiness!" he said when he saw them kissing, and he boxed their ears with his slipper just as the swineherd was taking his eighty-sixth kiss.

"Be off with you!" the Emperor said in a rage. And both the Princess and the swineherd were turned out of his empire. And there she stood crying. The swineherd scolded, and the rain came down in torrents.

"Poor little me," said the Princess. "If only I had married the famous Prince! Oh, how unlucky I am!"

The swineherd slipped behind a tree, wiped the brown and black off his face, threw off his ragged clothes, and showed himself in such princely garments that the Princess could not keep from curtsying.

"I have only contempt for you," he told her. "You turned down a Prince's honest offer, and you didn't appreciate the rose or the nightingale, but you were all too ready to kiss a swineherd for a tinkling toy to amuse you. You are properly punished."

Then the Prince went home to his kingdom, and shut and barred the door. The Princess could stay outside and sing to her heart's content:

"Oh, dear Augustin,
All is lost, lost, lost."

THE ANGEL

EVERY TIME A good child dies, an angel of God comes down to earth. He takes the child in his arms, spreads out his great white wings, and flies with it all over the places the child loved on earth. The angel plucks a large handful of flowers, and they carry it with them up to God, where the flowers bloom more brightly than they ever did on earth. And God presses all the flowers to His bosom, but the flower that He loves the best of all He kisses. And then that flower receives a voice, and can join in the glorious everlasting hymn of praise.

You see, all this one of God's angels said as he was carrying a dead child to Heaven, and the child heard it as if in a dream. As they passed over the places where the child used to play, they came through gardens with lovely flowers. "Which flowers shall we take with us to plant in Heaven?" asked the angel.

And there stood a slender beautiful rosebush. A wicked hand had broken the stem, and the branches with their large, half-opened blossoms hung down withering.

"That poor bush!" cried the child. "Let's take it so that it may bloom again up there in God's garden."

So the angel plucked it, then kissed the child for its tender thought, and the little child half opened his eyes. They took others of the rich flowers, and even some of the despised marigolds and wild pansies.

"Now we have enough flowers," said the child, and the angel nodded. But they did not yet fly upward to God.

It was night, and it was very quiet. They remained in the great city and hovered over one of the narrowest streets, which was cluttered with straw, ashes, and refuse of all kinds. It was just after moving day, and broken plates, rags, old hats, and bits of plaster, all things that didn't look so well, lay scattered in the street.

In the rubbish the angel pointed to the pieces of a broken flowerpot and to a lump of earth which had fallen out of it. It was held together by the roots of a large withered field flower. No one could have had any more use for it, hence it had been thrown out in the street.

"We shall take that with us," said the angel. "As we fly onward, I will tell you about it." And as they flew the angel told the story.

"Down in that narrow alley, in a dark cellar, there once lived a poor sick boy who had been bedridden since childhood. The most he could ever do, when he was feeling his best, was hobble once or twice across the little room on crutches. For only a few days in midsummer the sunbeams could steal into his cellar for about half an hour or so. Then the little boy could warm himself and see the red blood in his thin, almost transparent fingers as he held them before his face. Then people would say, the boy has been out in the sunshine today.

"All he knew of the forests in the fresh breath of spring was when the neighbor's son would bring him home the first beech branch. He would hold this up over his head, and pretend he was sitting in the beech woods where the sun was shining and the birds were singing.

"One spring day the neighbor's boy brought him also some field flowers, and by chance one of them had a root to it! So it was planted in a flowerpot and placed in the window beside the little boy's bed. And tended by a loving hand, it grew, put out new shoots, and bore lovely flowers each year. It was a beautiful garden to the little sick boy – his one treasure on earth. He watered it and tended it and saw that it received every sunbeam, down to the very last that managed to struggle through the dingy cellar window.

"The flower wove itself into his dreams; for him it flowered; it spread its fragrance, and cheered his eyes, and toward it he turned his face for a last look when his Heavenly Father called him.

"He has been with God now for a year, and for a year the flower stood withered and forgotten in the window until on moving day it was thrown out on the rubbish heap in the street. That is the flower – the poor withered flower – we have added to our bouquet, for it has given more happiness than the richest flower in the Queen's garden."

The child looked up at the angel who was carrying him. "But how do you know all this?" he asked.

"I know it," said the angel, "because I myself was the sick little boy who hobbled on crutches. I know my own flower very well."

Then the child opened his eyes wide and looked up into the angel's beautiful happy face, and at that moment they found themselves in God's Heaven where there was everlasting joy and happiness. And God pressed the child to His bosom, and he received glorious white wings like the angel's, so they flew together, hand in hand. Then God pressed all the flowers to His heart, but the poor withered field flower He kissed, and it received a voice and joined the choir of the angels who floated about God's throne. Some were near, some farther out in great circles that swept to infinity, but all were supremely happy. And they all sang, the great and the small, the good blessed child and the withered field flower that had lain so long in the rubbish heap in the dark narrow alley.

THE NIGHTINGALE

THE EMPEROR OF China is a Chinaman, as you most likely know, and everyone around him is a Chinaman too. It's been a great many years since this story happened in China, but that's all the more reason for telling it before it gets forgotten.

The Emperor's palace was the wonder of the world. It was made entirely of fine porcelain, extremely expensive but so delicate that you could touch it only with the greatest of care. In the garden the rarest flowers bloomed, and to the prettiest ones were tied little silver bells which tinkled so that no one could pass by without noticing them. Yes, all things were arranged according to plan in the Emperor's garden, though how far and wide it extended not even the gardener knew. If you walked on and on, you came to a fine forest where the trees were tall and the lakes were deep. The forest ran down to the deep blue sea, so close that tall ships could sail under the branches of the trees. In these trees a nightingale lived. His song was so ravishing that even the poor fisherman, who had much else to do, stopped to listen on the nights when he went out to cast his nets, and heard the nightingale.

"How beautiful that is," he said, but he had his work to attend to, and he would forget the bird's song. But the next night, when he heard the song he would again say, "How beautiful."

From all the countries in the world travelers came to the city of the Emperor. They admired the city. They admired the palace and its garden, but when they heard the nightingale they said, "That is the best of all."

And the travelers told of it when they came home, and men of learning wrote many books about the town, about the palace, and about the garden. But they did not forget the nightingale. They praised him highest of all, and those who were poets wrote magnificent poems about the nightingale who lived in the forest by the deep sea.

These books went all the world over, and some of them came even to the Emperor of China. He sat in his golden chair and read, nodding his head in delight over such glowing descriptions of his city, and palace, and garden. *But the nightingale is the best of all.* He read it in print.

"What's this?" the Emperor exclaimed. "I don't know of any nightingale. Can there be such a bird in my empire – in my own garden – and I not know it? To think that I should have to learn of it out of a book."

Thereupon he called his Lord-in-Waiting, who was so exalted that when anyone of lower rank dared speak to him, or ask him a question, he only answered, "P", which means nothing at all.

"They say there's a most remarkable bird called the nightingale," said the Emperor. "They say it's the best thing in all my empire. Why haven't I been told about it?"

"I've never heard the name mentioned," said the Lord-in-Waiting. "He hasn't been presented at court."

"I command that he appear before me this evening, and sing," said the Emperor. "The whole world knows my possessions better than I do!"

"I never heard of him before," said the Lord-in-Waiting. "But I shall look for him. I'll find him."

But where? The Lord-in-Waiting ran upstairs and downstairs, through all the rooms and corridors, but no one he met with had ever heard tell of the nightingale. So the Lord-in-Waiting ran back to the Emperor, and said it must be a story invented by those who write books. "Your Imperial Majesty would scarcely believe how much of what is written is fiction, if not downright black art."

"But the book I read was sent me by the mighty Emperor of Japan," said the Emperor. "Therefore it can't be a pack of lies. I must hear this nightingale. I insist upon his being here this evening. He has my high imperial favor, and if he is not forthcoming I will have the whole court punched in the stomach, directly after supper."

"Tsing-pe!" said the Lord-in-Waiting, and off he scurried up the stairs, through all the rooms and corridors. And half the court ran with him, for no one wanted to be punched in the stomach after supper.

There was much questioning as to the whereabouts of this remarkable nightingale, who was so well known everywhere in the world except at home. At last they found a poor little kitchen girl, who said:

"The nightingale? I know him well. Yes, indeed he can sing. Every evening I get leave to carry scraps from table to my sick mother. She lives down by the shore. When I start back I am tired, and rest in the woods. Then I hear the nightingale sing. It brings tears to my eyes. It's as if my mother were kissing me."

"Little kitchen girl," said the Lord-in-Waiting, "I'll have you appointed scullion for life. I'll even get permission for you to watch the Emperor dine, if you'll take us to the nightingale who is commanded to appear at court this evening."

So they went into the forest where the nightingale usually sang. Half the court went along. On the way to the forest a cow began to moo.

"Oh," cried a courtier, "that must be it. What a powerful voice for a creature so small. I'm sure I've heard her sing before."

"No, that's the cow lowing," said the little kitchen girl. "We still have a long way to go."

Then the frogs in the marsh began to croak.

"Glorious!" said the Chinese court person. "Now I hear it – like church bells ringing."

"No, that's the frogs," said the little kitchen girl. "But I think we shall hear him soon."

"They say there's a most remarkable bird called the nightingale," said the Emperor. "They say it's the best thing in all my empire. Why haven't I been told about it?" (Edmund Dulac)

Then the nightingale sang.

"That's it," said the little kitchen girl. "Listen, listen! And yonder he sits." She pointed to a little gray bird high up in the branches.

"Is it possible?" cried the Lord-in-Waiting. "Well, I never would have thought he looked like that, so unassuming. But he has probably turned pale at seeing so many important people around him."

"Little nightingale," the kitchen girl called to him, "our gracious Emperor wants to hear you sing."

"With the greatest of pleasure," answered the nightingale, and burst into song.

"Very similar to the sound of glass bells," said the Lord-in-Waiting. "Just see his little throat, how busily it throbs. I'm astounded that we have never heard him before. I'm sure he'll be a great success at court."

"Shall I sing to the Emperor again?" asked the nightingale, for he thought that the Emperor was present.

"My good little nightingale," said the Lord-in-Waiting, "I have the honor to command your presence at a court function this evening, where you'll delight His Majesty the Emperor with your charming song."

"My song sounds best in the woods," said the nightingale, but he went with them willingly when he heard it was the Emperor's wish.

The palace had been especially polished for the occasion. The porcelain walls and floors shone in the rays of many gold lamps. The flowers with tinkling bells on them had been brought into the halls, and there was such a commotion of coming and going that all the bells chimed away until you could scarcely hear yourself talk.

In the middle of the great throne room, where the Emperor sat, there was a golden perch for the nightingale. The whole court was there, and they let the little kitchen girl stand behind the door, now that she had been appointed "Imperial Pot-Walloper." Everyone was dressed in his best, and all stared at the little gray bird to which the Emperor graciously nodded.

And the nightingale sang so sweetly that tears came into the Emperor's eyes and rolled down his cheeks. Then the nightingale sang still more sweetly, and it was the Emperor's heart that melted. The Emperor was so touched that he wanted his own golden slipper hung round the nightingale's neck, but the nightingale declined it with thanks. He had already been amply rewarded.

"I have seen tears in the Emperor's eyes," he said. "Nothing could surpass that. An Emperor's tears are strangely powerful. I have my reward." And he sang again, gloriously.

"It's the most charming coquetry we ever heard," said the ladies-in-waiting.
(Edmund Dulac)

"It's the most charming coquetry we ever heard," said the ladies-in-waiting. And they took water in their mouths so they could gurgle when anyone spoke to them, hoping to rival the nightingale. Even the lackeys and chambermaids said they were satisfied, which was saying a great deal, for they were the hardest to please. Unquestionably the nightingale was a success. He was to stay at court, and have his own cage. He had permission to go for a walk twice a day, and once a night. Twelve footmen attended him, each one holding tight to a ribbon tied to the bird's leg. There wasn't much fun in such outings.

The whole town talked about the marvelous bird, and if two people met, one could scarcely say "night" before the other said "gale," and then they would sigh in unison, with no need for words. Eleven pork-butchers' children were named "nightingale," but not one could sing.

One day the Emperor received a large package labeled "The Nightingale."

"This must be another book about my celebrated bird," he said. But it was not a book. In the box was a work of art, an artificial nightingale most like the real one except that it was encrusted with diamonds, rubies, and sapphires. When it was wound, the artificial bird could sing one of the nightingale's songs while it wagged its glittering gold and silver tail. Round its neck hung a ribbon inscribed: "The Emperor of Japan's nightingale is a poor thing compared with that of the Emperor of China."

"Isn't that nice?" everyone said, and the man who had brought the contraption was immediately promoted to be "Imperial-Nightingale-Fetcher-in-Chief."

"Now let's have them sing together. What a duet that will be," said the courtiers.

So they had to sing together, but it didn't turn out so well, for the real nightingale sang whatever came into his head while the imitation bird sang by rote.

"That's not the newcomer's fault," said the music master. "He keeps perfect time, just as I have taught him."

Then they had the imitation bird sing by itself. It met with the same success as the real nightingale, and besides it was much prettier to see, all sparkling like bracelets and breastpins. Three-and-thirty times it sang the selfsame song without tiring. The courtiers would gladly have heard it again, but the Emperor said the real nightingale should now have his turn. Where was he? No one had noticed him flying out the open window, back to his home in the green forest.

"But what made him do that?" said the Emperor.

All the courtiers slandered the nightingale, whom they called a most ungrateful wretch.

"Luckily we have the best bird," they said, and made the imitation one sing again. That was the thirty-fourth time they had heard the same tune, but they didn't quite know it by heart because it was a difficult piece. And the music master praised the artificial bird beyond measure. Yes, he said that the contraption was much better than the real nightingale, not only in its dress and its many beautiful diamonds, but also in its mechanical interior.

"You see, ladies and gentlemen, and above all Your Imperial Majesty, with a real nightingale one never knows what to expect, but with this artificial bird everything goes according to plan. Nothing is left to chance. I can explain it and take it to pieces, and show how the mechanical wheels are arranged, how they go around, and how one follows after another."

"Those are our sentiments exactly," said they all, and the music master was commanded to have the bird give a public concert next Sunday. The Emperor said that his people should hear it. And hear it they did, with as much pleasure as if they had all gotten tipsy on tea, Chinese fashion. Everyone said, "Oh," and held up the finger we call "lickpot," and nodded his head. But the poor fishermen who had heard the real nightingale said, "This is very pretty, very nearly the real thing, but not quite. I can't imagine what's lacking."

The real nightingale had been banished from the land. In its place, the artificial bird sat on a cushion beside the Emperor's bed. All its gold and jeweled presents lay about it, and its title was now "Grand Imperial Singer-of-the-Emperor-to-sleep." In rank it stood first from the left, for the Emperor gave pre-eminence to the left side because of the heart. Even an Emperor's heart is on the left.

The music master wrote a twenty-five-volume book about the artificial bird. It was learned, long-winded, and full of hard Chinese words, yet everybody said they read and understood it, lest they show themselves stupid and would then have been punched in their stomachs.

After a year the Emperor, his court, and all the other Chinamen knew every twitter of the artificial song by heart. They liked it all the better now that they could sing it themselves. Which they did. The street urchins sang, "Zizizi! kluk, kluk, kluk," and the Emperor sang it too. That's how popular it was.

But one night, while the artificial bird was singing his best by the Emperor's bed, something inside the bird broke with a twang. *Whir-r-r*, all the wheels ran down and the music stopped. Out of bed jumped the Emperor and sent for his own physician, but what could he do? Then he sent for a watchmaker, who conferred, and investigated, and patched up the bird after a fashion. But the watchmaker said that the bird must be spared too much exertion, for the cogs were badly worn and if he replaced them it would spoil the tune. This was terrible. Only once a year could they let the bird sing, and that was almost too much for it. But the music master made a little speech full of hard Chinese words which meant that the bird was as good as it ever was. So that made it as good as ever.

Five years passed by, and a real sorrow befell the whole country. The Chinamen loved their Emperor, and now he fell ill. Ill unto death, it was said. A new Emperor was chosen in readiness. People stood in the palace street and asked the Lord-in-Waiting how it went with their Emperor.

"P," said he, and shook his head.

Cold and pale lay the Emperor in his great magnificent bed. All the courtiers thought he was dead, and went to do homage to the new Emperor. The lackeys went off to trade gossip, and the chambermaids gave a coffee party because it was such a special occasion. Deep mats were laid in all the rooms and passageways, to muffle each footstep. It was quiet in the palace, dead quiet. But the Emperor was not yet dead. Stiff and pale he lay, in his magnificent bed with the long velvet curtains and the heavy gold tassels. High in the wall was an open window, through which moonlight fell on the Emperor and his artificial bird.

The poor Emperor could hardly breathe. It was as if something were sitting on his chest. Opening his eyes he saw it was Death who sat there, wearing the Emperor's crown, handling the Emperor's gold sword, and carrying the Emperor's silk banner. Among the folds of the great velvet curtains there were strangely familiar faces. Some were horrible, others gentle and kind. They were the Emperor's deeds, good and bad, who came back to him now that Death sat on his heart.

"Don't you remember—?" they whispered one after the other. "Don't you remember—?" And they told him of things that made the cold sweat run on his forehead.

"No, I will not remember!" said the Emperor. "Music, music, sound the great drum of China lest I hear what they say!" But they went on whispering, and Death nodded, Chinese fashion, at every word.

"Music, music!" the Emperor called. "Sing, my precious little golden bird, sing! I have given you gold and precious presents. I have hung my golden slipper around your neck. Sing, I pray you, sing!"

But the bird stood silent. There was no one to wind it, nothing to make it sing. Death kept staring through his great hollow eyes, and it was quiet, deadly quiet.

Suddenly, through the window came a burst of song. It was the little live nightingale who sat outside on a spray. He had heard of the Emperor's plight, and had come to sing of comfort and hope. As he sang, the phantoms grew pale, and still more pale, and the blood flowed quicker and quicker through the Emperor's feeble body. Even Death listened, and said, "Go on, little nightingale, go on!"

"But," said the little nightingale, "will you give back that sword, that banner, that Emperor's crown?"

And Death gave back these treasures for a song. The nightingale sang on. It sang of the quiet churchyard where white roses grow, where the elder flowers make the air sweet, and where the grass is always green, wet with the tears of those who are still alive. Death longed for his garden. Out through the windows drifted a cold gray mist, as Death departed.

"Thank you, thank you!" the Emperor said. "Little bird from Heaven, I know you of old. I banished you once from my land, and yet you have sung away the evil faces from my bed, and Death from my heart. How can I repay you?"

"You have already rewarded me," said the nightingale. "I brought tears to your eyes when first I sang for you. To the heart of a singer those are more precious than any precious stone. But sleep now, and grow fresh and strong while I sing." He sang on until the Emperor fell into a sound, refreshing sleep, a sweet and soothing slumber.

The sun was shining in his window when the Emperor awoke, restored and well. Not one of his servants had returned to him, for they thought him dead, but the nightingale still sang.

"You must stay with me always," said the Emperor. "Sing to me only when you please. I shall break the artificial bird into a thousand pieces."

"No," said the nightingale. "It did its best. Keep it near you. I cannot build my nest here, or live in a palace, so let me come as I will. Then I shall sit on the spray by your window, and sing things that will make you happy and thoughtful too. I'll sing about those who are gay, and those who are sorrowful. My songs will tell you of all the good and evil that you do not see. A little singing bird flies far and wide, to the fisherman's hut, to the farmer's home, and to many other places a long way off from you and your court. I love your heart better than I do your crown, and yet the crown has been blessed too. I will come and sing to you, if you will promise me one thing."

"All that I have is yours," cried the Emperor, who stood in his imperial robes, which he had put on himself, and held his heavy gold sword to his heart.

"One thing only," the nightingale asked. "You must not let anyone know that you have a little bird who tells you everything; then all will go even better." And away he flew.

The servants came in to look after their dead Emperor – and there they stood. And the Emperor said, "Good morning."

THE UGLY DUCKLING

IT WAS SO beautiful out in the country, it was summer – the wheat fields were golden, the oats were green, and down among the green meadows the hay was stacked. There the stork minced about on his red legs, clacking away in Egyptian, which was the language his mother had taught him. Round about the field and meadow lands rose vast forests, in which deep lakes lay hidden. Yes, it was indeed lovely out there in the country.

In the midst of the sunshine there stood an old manor house that had a deep moat around it. From the walls of the manor right down to the water's edge great burdock leaves grew, and there were some so tall that little children could stand upright beneath the biggest of them. In this wilderness of leaves, which was as dense as the forest itself, a duck sat on her nest, hatching her ducklings. She was becoming somewhat weary, because sitting is such a dull business and scarcely anyone came to see her. The other ducks would much rather swim in the moat than waddle out and squat under the burdock leaf to gossip with her.

But at last the eggshells began to crack, one after another. "Peep, peep!" said the little things, as they came to life and poked out their heads.

"Quack, quack!" said the duck, and quick as quick can be they all waddled out to have a look at the green world under the leaves. Their mother let them look as much as they pleased, because green is good for the eyes.

"How wide the world is," said all the young ducks, for they certainly had much more room now than they had when they were in their eggshells.

"Do you think this is the whole world?" their mother asked. "Why it extends on and on, clear across to the other side of the garden and right on into the parson's field, though that is further than I have ever been. I do hope you are all hatched," she said as she got up. "No, not quite all. The biggest egg still lies here. How much longer is this going to take? I am really rather tired of it all," she said, but she settled back on her nest.

"Well, how goes it?" asked an old duck who came to pay her a call.

"It takes a long time with that one egg," said the duck on the nest. "It won't crack, but look at the others. They are the cutest little ducklings I've ever seen. They look exactly like their father, the wretch! He hasn't come to see me at all."

"Let's have a look at the egg that won't crack," the old duck said. "It's a turkey egg, and you can take my word for it. I was fooled like that once myself. What trouble and care I had with those turkey children, for I may as well tell you, they are afraid of the water. I simply could not get them into it. I quacked and snapped at them, but it wasn't a bit of use. Let me see the egg. Certainly, it's a turkey egg. Let it lie, and go teach your other children to swim."

"Oh, I'll sit a little longer. I've been at it so long already that I may as well sit here half the summer."

"Suit yourself," said the old duck, and away she waddled.

At last the big egg did crack. "Peep," said the young one, and out he tumbled, but he was so big and ugly.

The duck took a look at him. "That's a frightfully big duckling," she said. "He doesn't look the least like the others. Can he really be a turkey baby? Well, well! I'll soon find out. Into the water he shall go, even if I have to shove him in myself."

Next day the weather was perfectly splendid, and the sun shone down on all the green burdock leaves. The mother duck led her whole family down to the moat. Splash! she took to the water. "Quack, quack," said she, and one duckling after another plunged in. The water went over their heads, but they came up in a flash, and floated to perfection. Their legs worked automatically, and they were all there in the water. Even the big, ugly gray one was swimming along.

"Why, that's no turkey," she said. "See how nicely he uses his legs, and how straight he holds himself. He's my very own son after all, and quite good-looking if you look at him properly. Quack, quack, come with me. I'll lead you out into the world and introduce you to the duck yard. But keep close to me so that you won't get stepped on, and watch out for the cat!"

Thus they sallied into the duck yard, where all was in an uproar because two families were fighting over the head of an eel. But the cat got it, after all.

"You see, that's the way of the world." The mother duck licked her bill because she wanted the eel's head for herself. "Stir your legs. Bustle about, and mind that you bend your necks to that old duck over there. She's the noblest of us all, and has Spanish blood in her. That's why she's so fat. See that red rag around her leg? That's a wonderful thing, and the highest distinction a duck can get. It shows that they don't want to lose her, and that she's to have

The ugly duckling.
(Mabel Lucie Attwell)

special attention from man and beast. Shake yourselves! Don't turn your toes in. A well-bred duckling turns his toes way out, just as his father and mother do – this way. So then! Now duck your necks and say quack!"

They did as she told them, but the other ducks around them looked on and said right out loud, "See here! Must we have this brood too, just as if there weren't enough of us already? And – fie! what an ugly-looking fellow that duckling is! We won't stand for him." One duck charged up and bit his neck.

"Let him alone," his mother said. "He isn't doing any harm."

"Possibly not," said the duck who bit him, "but he's too big and strange, and therefore he needs a good whacking."

"What nice-looking children you have, Mother," said the old duck with the rag around her leg. "They are all pretty except that one. He didn't come out so well. It's a pity you can't hatch him again."

"That can't be managed, your ladyship," said the mother. "He isn't so handsome, but he's as good as can be, and he swims just as well as the rest, or, I should say, even a little better than they do. I hope his looks will improve with age, and after a while he won't seem so big. He took too long in the egg, and that's why his figure isn't all that it should be." She pinched his neck and preened his feathers. "Moreover, he's a drake, so it won't matter so much. I think he will be quite strong, and I'm sure he will amount to something."

"The other ducklings are pretty enough," said the old duck. "Now make yourselves right at home, and if you find an eel's head you may bring it to me."

So they felt quite at home. But the poor duckling who had been the last one out of his egg, and who looked so ugly, was pecked and pushed about and made fun of by the ducks, and the chickens as well. "He's too big," said they all. The turkey gobbler, who thought himself an emperor because he was born wearing spurs, puffed up like a ship under full sail and bore down upon him, gobbling and gobbling until he was red in the face. The poor duckling did not know where he dared stand or where he dared walk. He was so sad because he was so desperately ugly, and because he was the laughing stock of the whole barnyard.

So it went on the first day, and after that things went from bad to worse. The poor duckling was chased and buffeted about by everyone. Even his own brothers and sisters abused him. "Oh," they would always say, "how we wish the cat would catch you, you ugly thing." And his mother said, "How I do wish you were miles away." The ducks nipped him, and the hens pecked him, and the girl who fed them kicked him with her foot.

So he ran away; and he flew over the fence. The little birds in the bushes darted up in a fright. "That's because I'm so ugly," he thought, and closed his eyes, but he ran on just the same until he reached the great marsh where the wild ducks lived. There he lay all night long, weary and disheartened.

When morning came, the wild ducks flew up to have a look at their new companion. "What sort of creature are you?" they asked, as the duckling turned in all directions, bowing his best to them all. "You are terribly ugly," they told him, "but that's nothing to us so long as you don't marry into our family."

Poor duckling! Marriage certainly had never entered his mind. All he wanted was for them to let him lie among the reeds and drink a little water from the marsh.

There he stayed for two whole days. Then he met two wild geese, or rather wild ganders – for they were males. They had not been out of the shell very long, and that's what made them so sure of themselves.

"Say there, comrade," they said, "you're so ugly that we have taken a fancy to you. Come with us and be a bird of passage. In another marsh nearby, there are some fetching wild geese, all nice young ladies who know how to quack. You are so ugly that you'll completely turn their heads."

Bing! Bang! Shots rang in the air, and these two ganders fell dead among the reeds. The water was red with their blood. *Bing! Bang!* the shots rang, and as whole flocks of wild geese flew up from the reeds another volley crashed. A great hunt was in progress. The hunters lay under cover all around the marsh, and some even perched on branches of trees that overhung the reeds. Blue smoke rose like clouds from the shade of the trees, and drifted far out over the water.

The bird dogs came *splash, splash!* through the swamp, bending down the reeds and the rushes on every side. This gave the poor duckling such a fright that he twisted his head about to hide it under his wing. But at that very moment a fearfully big dog appeared right beside him. His tongue lolled out of his mouth and his wicked eyes glared horribly. He opened his wide jaws, flashed his sharp teeth, and – *splash, splash* – on he went without touching the duckling.

"Thank heavens," he sighed, "I'm so ugly that the dog won't even bother to bite me."

He lay perfectly still, while the bullets splattered through the reeds as shot after shot was fired. It was late in the day before things became quiet again, and even then the poor duckling didn't dare move. He waited several hours before he ventured to look about him, and then he scurried away from that marsh as fast as he could go. He ran across field and meadows. The wind was so strong that he had to struggle to keep his feet.

Late in the evening he came to a miserable little hovel, so ramshackle that it did not know which way to tumble, and that was the only reason it still stood. The wind struck the duckling so hard that the poor little fellow had to sit down on his tail to withstand it. The storm blew stronger and stronger, but the duckling noticed that one hinge had come loose and the door hung so crooked that he could squeeze through the crack into the room, and that's just what he did.

Here lived an old woman with her cat and her hen. The cat, whom she called "Sonny," could arch his back, purr, and even make sparks, though for that you had to stroke his fur the wrong way. The hen had short little legs, so she was called "Chickey Shortleg." She laid good eggs, and the old woman loved her as if she had been her own child.

In the morning they were quick to notice the strange duckling. The cat began to purr, and the hen began to cluck.

"What on earth!" The old woman looked around, but she was short-sighted, and she mistook the duckling for a fat duck that had lost its way. "That was a good catch," she said. "Now I shall have duck eggs – unless it's a drake. We must try it out." So the duckling was tried out for three weeks, but not one egg did he lay.

In this house the cat was master and the hen was mistress. They always said, "We and the world," for they thought themselves half of the world, and much the better half at that. The duckling thought that there might be more than one way of thinking, but the hen would not hear of it.

"Can you lay eggs?" she asked.

"No."

"Then be so good as to hold your tongue."

The cat asked, "Can you arch your back, purr, or make sparks?"

"No."

"Then keep your opinion to yourself when sensible people are talking."

The duckling sat in a corner, feeling most despondent. Then he remembered the fresh air and the sunlight. Such a desire to go swimming on the water possessed him that he could not help telling the hen about it.

"What on earth has come over you?" the hen cried. "You haven't a thing to do, and that's why you get such silly notions. Lay us an egg, or learn to purr, and you'll get over it."

"But it's so refreshing to float on the water," said the duckling, "so refreshing to feel it rise over your head as you dive to the bottom."

"Yes, it must be a great pleasure!" said the hen. "I think you must have gone crazy. Ask the cat, who's the wisest fellow I know, whether he likes to swim or dive down in the water. Of myself I say nothing. But ask the old woman, our mistress. There's no one on earth wiser than she is. Do you imagine she wants to go swimming and feel the water rise over her head?"

"You don't understand me," said the duckling.

"Well, if we don't, who would? Surely you don't think you are cleverer than the cat and the old woman – to say nothing of myself. Don't be so conceited, child. Just thank your Maker for all the kindness we have shown you. Didn't you get into this snug room, and fall in with people who can tell you what's what? But you are such a numbskull that it's no pleasure to have you around. Believe me, I tell you this for your own good. I say unpleasant truths, but that's the only way you can know who are your friends. Be sure now that you lay some eggs. See to it that you learn to purr or to make sparks."

"I think I'd better go out into the wide world," said the duckling.

"Suit yourself," said the hen.

So off went the duckling. He swam on the water, and dived down in it, but still he was slighted by every living creature because of his ugliness.

Autumn came on. The leaves in the forest turned yellow and brown. The wind took them and whirled them about. The heavens looked cold as the low clouds hung heavy with snow and hail. Perched on the fence, the raven screamed, "Caw, caw!" and trembled with cold. It made one shiver to think of it. Pity the poor little duckling!

One evening, just as the sun was setting in splendor, a great flock of large, handsome birds appeared out of the reeds. The duckling had never seen birds so beautiful. They were dazzling white, with long graceful necks. They were swans. They uttered a very strange cry as they unfurled their magnificent wings to fly from this cold land, away to warmer countries and to open waters. They went up so high, so very high, that the ugly little duckling felt a strange uneasiness come over him as he watched them. He went around and round in the water, like a wheel. He craned his neck to follow their course, and gave a cry so shrill and strange that he frightened himself. Oh! He could not forget them – those splendid, happy birds. When he could no longer see them he dived to the very bottom, and when he came up again he was quite beside himself. He did not know what birds they were or whither they were bound, yet he loved them more than anything he had ever loved before. It was not that he envied them, for how could he ever dare dream of wanting their marvelous beauty for himself? He would have been grateful if only the ducks would have tolerated him – the poor ugly creature.

The winter grew cold – so bitterly cold that the duckling had to swim to and fro in the water to keep it from freezing over. But every night the hole in which he swam kept getting smaller and smaller. Then it froze so hard that the duckling had to paddle continuously to keep the crackling ice from closing in upon him. At last, too tired to move, he was frozen fast in the ice.

Early that morning a farmer came by, and when he saw how things were he went out on the pond, broke away the ice with his wooden shoe, and carried the duckling home to his wife. There the duckling revived, but when the children wished to play with him he thought they meant to hurt him. Terrified, he fluttered into the milk pail, splashing the whole room with milk. The woman shrieked and threw up her hands as he flew into the butter tub, and then in and out of the meal barrel. Imagine what he looked like now! The woman screamed and lashed out at him with the fire tongs. The children tumbled over each other as they tried to catch him, and they laughed and they shouted. Luckily the door was open, and the duckling escaped through it into the bushes, where he lay down, in the newly fallen snow, as if in a daze.

But it would be too sad to tell of all the hardships and wretchedness he had to endure during this cruel winter. When the warm sun shone once more, the duckling was still alive among the reeds of the marsh. The larks began to sing again. It was beautiful springtime.

Then, quite suddenly, he lifted his wings. They swept through the air much more strongly than before, and their powerful strokes carried him far. Before he quite knew what was happening, he found himself in a great garden where apple trees bloomed. The lilacs filled the air with sweet scent and hung in clusters from long, green branches that bent over a winding stream. Oh, but it was lovely here in the freshness of spring!

From the thicket before him came three lovely white swans. They ruffled their feathers and swam lightly in the stream. The duckling recognized these noble creatures, and a strange feeling of sadness came upon him.

"I shall fly near these royal birds, and they will peck me to bits because I, who am so very ugly, dare to go near them. But I don't care. Better be killed by them than to be nipped by

The smallest child cried, "Here's a new one,"
and the others rejoiced. (Harry Clarke)

THE CLASSIC FAVOURITE FAIRY TALES OF ANDERSEN & GRIMM

the ducks, pecked by the hens, kicked about by the hen-yard girl, or suffer such misery in winter."

So he flew into the water and swam toward the splendid swans. They saw him, and swept down upon him with their rustling feathers raised. "Kill me!" said the poor creature, and he bowed his head down over the water to wait for death. But what did he see there, mirrored in the clear stream? He beheld his own image, and it was no longer the reflection of a clumsy, dirty, gray bird, ugly and offensive. He himself was a swan! Being born in a duck yard does not matter, if only you are hatched from a swan's egg.

He felt quite glad that he had come through so much trouble and misfortune, for now he had a fuller understanding of his own good fortune, and of beauty when he met with it. The great swans swam all around him and stroked him with their bills.

Several little children came into the garden to throw grain and bits of bread upon the water. The smallest child cried, "Here's a new one," and the others rejoiced, "yes, a new one has come." They clapped their hands, danced around, and ran to bring their father and mother. And they threw bread and cake upon the water, while they all agreed, "The new one is the most handsome of all. He's so young and so good-looking." The old swans bowed in his honor.

Then he felt very bashful, and tucked his head under his wing. He did not know what this was all about. He felt so very happy, but he wasn't at all proud, for a good heart never grows proud. He thought about how he had been persecuted and scorned, and now he heard them all call him the most beautiful of all beautiful birds. The lilacs dipped their clusters into the stream before him, and the sun shone so warm and so heartening. He rustled his feathers and held his slender neck high, as he cried out with full heart: "I never dreamed there could be so much happiness, when I was the ugly duckling."

THE FIR TREE

OUT IN THE woods stood such a pretty little fir tree. It grew in a good place, where it had plenty of sun and plenty of fresh air. Around it stood many tall comrades, both fir trees and pines.

The little fir tree was in a headlong hurry to grow up. It didn't care a thing for the warm sunshine, or the fresh air, and it took no interest in the peasant children who ran about chattering when they came to pick strawberries or raspberries. Often when the children had picked their pails full, or had gathered long strings of berries threaded on straws, they would sit down to rest near the little fir. "Oh, isn't it a nice little tree?" they would say. "It's the baby of the woods." The little tree didn't like their remarks at all.

Next year it shot up a long joint of new growth, and the following year another joint, still longer. You can always tell how old a fir tree is by counting the number of joints it has.

"I wish I were a grown-up tree, like my comrades," the little tree sighed. "Then I could stretch out my branches and see from my top what the world is like. The birds would make me their nesting place, and when the wind blew I could bow back and forth with all the great trees."

It took no pleasure in the sunshine, nor in the birds. The glowing clouds, that sailed overhead at sunrise and sunset, meant nothing to it.

In winter, when the snow lay sparkling on the ground, a hare would often come hopping along and jump right over the little tree. Oh,

It could hardly recognize the trees it had known, when the horses pulled them out of the woods.
(Fritz Kredel)

how irritating that was! That happened for two winters, but when the third winter came the tree was so tall that the hare had to turn aside and hop around it.

"Oh, to grow, grow! To get older and taller," the little tree thought. "That is the most wonderful thing in this world."

In the autumn, woodcutters came and cut down a few of the largest trees. This happened every year. The young fir was no longer a baby tree, and it trembled to see how those stately great trees crashed to the ground, how their limbs were lopped off, and how lean they looked as the naked trunks were loaded into carts. It could hardly recognize the trees it had known, when the horses pulled them out of the woods.

Where were they going? What would become of them?

In the springtime, when swallows and storks came back, the tree asked them, "Do you know where the other trees went? Have you met them?"

The swallows knew nothing about it, but the stork looked thoughtful and nodded his head.

"Yes, I think I met them," he said. "On my way from Egypt I met many new ships, and some had tall, stately masts. They may well have been the trees you mean, for I remember the smell of fir. They wanted to be remembered to you."

"Oh, I wish I were old enough to travel on the sea. Please tell me what it really is, and how it looks."

"That would take too long to tell," said the stork, and off he strode.

"Rejoice in your youth," said the sunbeams. "Take pride in your growing strength and in the stir of life within you."

And the wind kissed the tree, and the dew wept over it, for the tree was young and without understanding.

When Christmas came near, many young trees were cut down. Some were not even as old or as tall as this fir tree of ours, who was in such a hurry and fret to go traveling. These young trees, which were always the handsomest ones, had their branches left on them when they were loaded on carts and the horses drew them out of the woods.

"Where can they be going?" the fir tree wondered. "They are no taller than I am. One was really much smaller than I am. And why are they allowed to keep all their branches? Where can they be going?"

"We know! We know!" the sparrows chirped. "We have been to town and peeped in the windows. We know where they are going. The greatest splendor and glory you can imagine awaits them. We've peeped through windows. We've seen them planted right in the middle of a warm room, and decked out with the most splendid things – gold apples, good gingerbread, gay toys, and many hundreds of candles."

"And then?" asked the fir tree, trembling in every twig. "And then? What happens then?"

"We saw nothing more. And never have we seen anything that could match it."

"I wonder if I was created for such a glorious future?" The fir tree rejoiced. "Why, that is better than to cross the sea. I'm tormented with longing. Oh, if Christmas would only come! I'm just as tall and grown-up as the trees they chose last year. How I wish I were already in the cart, on my way to the warm room where there's so much splendor and glory. Then – then something even better, something still more important is bound to happen, or why should they deck me so fine? Yes, there must be something still grander! But what? Oh, how I suffer, and how I long: I don't know what's the matter with me."

"Enjoy us while you may," the air and sunlight told him. "Rejoice in the days of your youth, out here in the open."

But the tree did not rejoice at all. It just grew. It grew and was green both winter and summer – dark evergreen. People who passed it said, "There's a beautiful tree!" And when Christmas time came again they cut it down first. The ax struck deep into its marrow. The tree sighed as it fell to the ground. It felt faint with pain. Instead of the happiness it had

expected, the tree was sorry to leave the home where it had grown up. It knew that never again would it see its dear old comrades, the little bushes and the flowers about it – and perhaps not even the birds. The departure was anything but pleasant.

The tree did not get over it until all the trees were unloaded in the yard, and it heard a man say, "That's a splendid one. That's the tree for us." Then two servants came in fine livery, and carried the fir tree into a big splendid drawing-room. Portraits were hung all around the walls. On either side of the white porcelain stove stood great Chinese vases, with lions on the lids of them. There were easy chairs, silk-covered sofas and long tables strewn with picture books, and with toys that were worth a mint of money, or so the children said.

The fir tree was planted in a large tub filled with sand, but no one could see that it was a tub, because it was wrapped in a gay green cloth and set on a many-colored carpet. How the tree quivered! What would come next? The servants and even the young ladies helped it on with its fine decorations. From its branches they hung little nets cut out of colored paper, and each net was filled with candies. Gilded apples and walnuts hung in clusters as if they grew there, and a hundred little white, blue, and even red, candles were fastened to its twigs. Among its green branches swayed dolls that it took to be real living people, for the tree had never seen their like before. And up at its very top was set a large gold tinsel star. It was splendid, I tell you, splendid beyond all words!

"Tonight," they all said, "ah, tonight how the tree will shine!"

"Oh," thought the tree, "if tonight would only come! If only the candles were lit! And after that, what happens then? Will the trees come trooping out of the woods to see me? Will the sparrows flock to the windows? Shall I take root here, and stand in fine ornaments all winter and summer long?"

That was how much it knew about it. All its longing had gone to its bark and set it to aching, which is as bad for a tree as a headache is for us.

Now the candles were lighted. What dazzling splendor! What a blaze of light! The tree quivered so in every bough that a candle set one of its twigs ablaze. It hurt terribly.

"Mercy me!" cried every young lady, and the fire was quickly put out. The tree no longer dared rustle a twig – it was awful! Wouldn't it be terrible if it were to drop one of its ornaments? Its own brilliance dazzled it.

Suddenly the folding doors were thrown back, and a whole flock of children burst in as if they would overturn the tree completely. Their elders marched in after them, more sedately. For a moment, but only for a moment, the young ones were stricken speechless. Then they shouted till the rafters rang. They danced about the tree and plucked off one present after another.

"What are they up to?" the tree wondered. "What will happen next?"

As the candles burned down to the bark they were snuffed out, one by one, and then the children had permission to plunder the tree. They went about it in such earnest that the branches crackled and, if the tree had not been tied to the ceiling by the gold star at top, it would have tumbled headlong.

The children danced about with their splendid playthings. No one looked at the tree now, except an old nurse who peered in among the branches, but this was only to make sure that not an apple or fig had been overlooked.

"Tell us a story! Tell us a story!" the children clamored, as they towed a fat little man to the tree. He sat down beneath it and said, "Here we are in the woods, and it will do the tree a lot of good to listen to our story. Mind you, I'll tell only one. Which will you have, the story of Ivedy-Avedy, or the one about Humpty-Dumpty who tumbled downstairs, yet ascended the throne and married the Princess?"

"Ivedy-Avedy," cried some. "Humpty-Dumpty," cried the others. And there was a great hullabaloo. Only the fir tree held its peace, though it thought to itself, "Am I to be left out of this? Isn't there anything I can do?" For all the fun of the evening had centered upon it, and it had played its part well.

The fat little man told them all about Humpty-Dumpty, who tumbled downstairs, yet ascended the throne and married the Princess. And the children clapped and shouted, "Tell us another one! Tell us another one!" For they wanted to hear about Ivedy-Avedy too, but after Humpty-Dumpty the story telling stopped. The fir tree stood very still as it pondered how the birds in the woods had never told it a story to equal this.

"Humpty-Dumpty tumbled downstairs, yet he married the Princess. Imagine! That must be how things happen in the world. You never can tell. Maybe I'll tumble downstairs and marry a princess too," thought the fir tree, who believed every word of the story because such a nice man had told it.

The tree looked forward to the following day, when they would deck it again with fruit and toys, candles and gold. "Tomorrow I shall not quiver," it decided. "I'll enjoy my splendor to the full. Tomorrow I shall hear about Humpty-Dumpty again, and perhaps about Ivedy-Avedy too." All night long the tree stood silent as it dreamed its dreams, and next morning the butler and the maid came in with their dusters.

"Now my splendor will be renewed," the fir tree thought. But they dragged it upstairs to the garret, and there they left it in a dark corner where no daylight ever came. "What's the meaning of this?" the tree wondered. "What am I going to do here? What stories shall I hear?" It leaned against the wall, lost in dreams. It had plenty of time for dreaming, as the days and the nights went by. Nobody came to the garret. And when at last someone did come, it was only to put many big boxes away in the corner. The tree was quite hidden. One might think it had been entirely forgotten.

"It's still winter outside," the tree thought. "The earth is too hard and covered with snow for them to plant me now. I must have been put here for shelter until springtime comes. How thoughtful of them! How good people are! Only, I wish it weren't so dark here, and so very, very lonely. There's not even a little hare. It was so friendly out in the woods when the snow was on the ground and the hare came hopping along. Yes, he was friendly even when he jumped right over me, though I did not think so then. Here it's all so terribly lonely."

"Squeak, squeak!" said a little mouse just then. He crept across the floor, and another one followed him. They sniffed the fir tree, and rustled in and out among its branches.

"It is fearfully cold," one of them said. "Except for that, it would be very nice here, wouldn't it, you old fir tree?"

"I'm not at all old," said the fir tree. "Many trees are much older than I am."

"Where did you come from?" the mice asked him. "And what do you know?" They were most inquisitive creatures.

"Tell us about the most beautiful place in the world. Have you been there? Were you ever in the larder, where there are cheeses on shelves and hams that hang from the rafters? It's the place where you can dance upon tallow candles – where you can dart in thin and squeeze out fat."

"I know nothing of that place," said the tree. "But I know the woods where the sun shines and the little birds sing." Then it told them about its youth. The little mice had never heard the like of it. They listened very intently, and said, "My! How much you have seen! And how happy it must have made you."

"I?" the fir tree thought about it. "Yes, those days were rather amusing." And he went on to tell them about Christmas Eve, when it was decked out with candies and candles.

"Oh," said the little mice, "how lucky you have been, you old fir tree!"

"I am not at all old," it insisted. "I came out of the woods just this winter, and I'm really in the prime of life, though at the moment my growth is suspended."

"How nicely you tell things," said the mice. The next night they came with four other mice to hear what the tree had to say. The more it talked, the more clearly it recalled things, and it thought, "Those were happy times. But they may still come back – they may come back again. Humpty-Dumpty fell downstairs, and yet he married the Princess. Maybe the same thing will happen to me." It thought about a charming little birch tree that grew out in the woods. To the fir tree she was a real and lovely Princess.

"Who is Humpty-Dumpty?" the mice asked it. So the fir tree told them the whole story, for it could remember it word by word. The little mice were ready to jump to the top of the tree for joy. The next night many more mice came to see the fir tree, and on Sunday two rats paid it a call, but they said that the story was not very amusing. This made the little mice to sad that they began to find it not so very interesting either.

"Is that the only story you know?" the rats asked.

"Only that one," the tree answered. "I heard it on the happiest evening of my life, but I did not know then how happy I was."

"It's a very silly story. Don't you know one that tells about bacon and candles? Can't you tell us a good larder story?"

"No," said the tree.

"Then good-by, and we won't be back," the rats said, and went away.

At last the little mice took to staying away too. The tree sighed, "Oh, wasn't it pleasant when those gay little mice sat around and listened to all that I had to say. Now that, too, is past and gone. But I will take good care to enjoy myself, once they let me out of here."

When would that be? Well, it came to pass on a morning when people came up to clean out the garret. The boxes were moved, the tree was pulled out and thrown – thrown hard – on the floor. But a servant dragged it at once to the stairway, where there was daylight again.

"Now my life will start all over," the tree thought. It felt the fresh air and the first sunbeam strike it as it came out into the courtyard. This all happened so quickly and there was so much going on around it, that the tree forgot to give even a glance at itself. The courtyard adjoined a garden, where flowers were blooming. Great masses of fragrant roses hung over the picket fence. The linden trees were in blossom, and between them the swallows skimmed past, calling, "Ti-lira-lira-lee, my love's come back to me." But it was not the fir tree of whom they spoke.

"Now I shall live again," it rejoiced, and tried to stretch out its branches. Alas, they were withered, and brown, and brittle. It was tossed into a corner, among weeds and nettles. But the gold star that was still tied to its top sparkled bravely in the sunlight.

Several of the merry children, who had danced around the tree and taken such pleasure in it at Christmas, were playing in the courtyard. One of the youngest seized upon it and tore off the tinsel star.

"Look what is still hanging on that ugly old Christmas tree," the child said, and stamped upon the branches until they cracked beneath his shoes.

The tree saw the beautiful flowers blooming freshly in the garden. It saw itself, and wished that they had left it in the darkest corner of the garret. It thought of its own young days in the deep woods, and of the merry Christmas Eve, and of the little mice who had been so pleased when it told them the story of Humpty-Dumpty.

"My days are over and past," said the poor tree. "Why didn't I enjoy them while I could? Now they are gone – all gone."

A servant came and chopped the tree into little pieces. These heaped together quite high. The wood blazed beautifully under the big copper kettle, and the fir tree moaned so deeply that each groan sounded like a muffled shot. That's why the children who were playing

A servant came and chopped the tree into little pieces. (Fritz Kredel)

nearby ran to make a circle around the flames, staring into the fire and crying, "Pif! Paf!" But as each groan burst from it, the tree thought of a bright summer day in the woods, or a starlit winter night. It thought of Christmas Eve and thought of Humpty-Dumpty, which was the only story it ever heard and knew how to tell. And so the tree was burned completely away.

The children played on in the courtyard. The youngest child wore on his breast the gold star that had topped the tree on its happiest night of all. But that was no more, and the tree was no more, and there's no more to my story. No more, nothing more. All stories come to an end.

THE SNOW QUEEN
A Tale in Seven Stories

First Story
WHICH HAS TO DO WITH A MIRROR AND ITS FRAGMENTS

NOW THEN! WE will begin. When the story is done you shall know a great deal more than you do know. He was a terribly bad hobgoblin, a goblin of the very wickedest sort and, in fact, he was the devil himself. One day the devil was in a very good humor because he had just finished a mirror which had this peculiar power: everything good and beautiful that was reflected in it seemed to dwindle to almost nothing at all, while everything that was worthless and ugly became most conspicuous and even uglier than ever. In this mirror the loveliest landscapes looked like boiled spinach, and the very best people became hideous, or stood on their heads and had no stomachs. Their faces were distorted beyond any recognition, and if a person had a freckle it was sure to spread until it covered both nose and mouth.

"That's very funny!" said the devil. If a good, pious thought passed through anyone's mind, it showed in the mirror as a carnal grin, and the devil laughed aloud at his ingenious invention.

All those who went to the hobgoblin's school – for he had a school of his own – told everyone that a miracle had come to pass. Now, they asserted, for the very first time you could see how the world and its people really looked. They scurried about with the mirror until there was not a person alive nor a land on earth that had not been distorted.

Then they wanted to fly up to heaven itself, to scoff at the angels, and our Lord. The higher they flew with the mirror, the wider it grinned. They could hardly manage to hold it. Higher they flew, and higher still, nearer to heaven and the angels. Then the grinning mirror trembled with such violence that it slipped from their hands and fell to the earth, where it shattered into hundreds of millions of billions of bits, or perhaps even more. And now it caused more trouble than it did before it was broken, because some of the fragments were smaller than a grain of sand and these went flying throughout the wide world. Once they got in people's eyes they would stay there. These bits of glass distorted everything the people saw, and made them see only the bad side of things, for every little bit of glass kept the same power that the whole mirror had possessed.

A few people even got a glass splinter in their hearts, and that was a terrible thing, for it turned their hearts into lumps of ice. Some of the fragments were so large that they were used as window panes – but not the kind of window through which you should look at your friends. Other pieces were made into spectacles, and evil things came to pass when people put them on to see clearly and to see justice done. The fiend was so tickled by it all that he laughed till his sides were sore. But fine bits of the glass are still flying through the air, and now you shall hear what happened.

Second Story
A LITTLE BOY AND A LITTLE GIRL

In the big city it was so crowded with houses and people that few found room for even a small garden and most people had to be content with a flowerpot, but two poor children who lived there managed to have a garden that was a little bigger than a flowerpot. These children were not brother and sister, but they loved each other just as much as if they had been. Their parents lived close to one another in the garrets of two adjoining houses. Where the roofs met and where the rain gutter ran between the two houses, their two small windows faced each other. One had only to step across the rain gutter to go from window to window.

In these windows, the parents had a large box where they planted vegetables for their use, and a little rose bush too. Each box had a bush, which thrived to perfection. Then it occurred to the parents to put these boxes across the gutter, where they very nearly reached from one window to the other, and looked exactly like two walls of flowers. The pea plants hung down over the boxes, and the rose bushes threw out long sprays that framed the windows and bent over toward each other. It was almost like a little triumphal arch of greenery and flowers. The boxes were very high, and the children knew that they were not to climb about on them, but they were often allowed to take their little stools out on the roof under the roses, where they had a wonderful time playing together.

Winter, of course, put an end to this pleasure. The windows often frosted over completely. But they would heat copper pennies on the stove and press these hot coins against the frost-coated glass. Then they had the finest of peepholes, as round as a ring, and behind them appeared a bright, friendly eye, one at each window – it was the little boy and the little girl who peeped out. His name was Kay and hers was Gerda. With one skip they could join each other in summer, but to visit together in the wintertime they had to go all the way downstairs in one house, and climb all the way upstairs in the other. Outside the snow was whirling.

"See the white bees swarming," the old grandmother said.

"Do they have a queen bee, too?" the little boy asked, for he knew that real bees have one.

"Yes, indeed they do," the grandmother said. "She flies in the thick of the swarm. She is the biggest bee of all, and can never stay quietly on the earth, but goes back again to the dark clouds. Many a wintry night she flies through the streets and peers in through the windows. Then they freeze over in a strange fashion, as if they were covered with flowers."

"Oh yes, we've seen that," both the children said, and so they knew it was true.

"Can the Snow Queen come in here?" the little girl asked.

"Well, let her come!" cried the boy. "I would put her on the hot stove and melt her."

But Grandmother stroked his head, and told them other stories.

That evening when little Kay was at home and half ready for bed, he climbed on the chair by the window and looked out through the little peephole. A few snowflakes were falling, and the largest flake of all alighted on the edge of one of the flower boxes. This flake grew bigger and bigger, until at last it turned into a woman, who was dressed in the finest white gauze which looked as if it had been made from millions of star-shaped flakes. She was beautiful and she was graceful, but she was ice – shining, glittering ice. She was alive, for all that, and her eyes sparkled like two bright stars, but in them there was neither rest nor peace. She nodded toward the window and beckoned with her hand. The little boy was frightened, and as he jumped down from the chair it seemed to him that a huge bird flew past the window.

She was beautiful and she was graceful, but she was ice – shining, glittering ice.
(Debra McFarlane)

The next day was clear and cold. Then the snow thawed, and springtime came. The sun shone, the green grass sprouted, swallows made their nests, windows were thrown open, and once again the children played in their little roof garden, high up in the rain gutter on top of the house.

That summer the roses bloomed their splendid best. The little girl had learned a hymn in which there was a line about roses that reminded her of their own flowers. She sang it to the little boy, and he sang it with her:

> *"Where roses bloom so sweetly in the vale,*
> *There shall you find the Christ Child,*
> *without fail."*

The children held each other by the hand, kissed the roses, looked up at the Lord's clear

sunshine, and spoke to it as if the Christ Child were there. What glorious summer days those were, and how beautiful it was out under those fragrant rose bushes which seemed as if they would never stop blooming.

Kay and Gerda were looking at a picture book of birds and beasts one day, and it was then – just as the clock in the church tower was striking five – that Kay cried:

"Oh! something hurt my heart. And now I've got something in my eye."

The little girl put her arm around his neck, and he blinked his eye. No, she couldn't see anything in it.

"I think it's gone," he said. But it was not gone. It was one of those splinters of glass from the magic mirror. You remember that goblin's mirror – the one which made everything great and good that was reflected in it appear small and ugly, but which magnified all evil things until each blemish loomed large. Poor Kay! A fragment had pierced his heart as well, and soon it would turn into a lump of ice. The pain had stopped, but the glass was still there.

"Why should you be crying?" he asked. "It makes you look so ugly. There's nothing the matter with me." And suddenly he took it into his head to say:

"Ugh! that rose is all worm-eaten. And look, this one is crooked. And these roses, they are just as ugly as they can be. They look like the boxes they grow in." He gave the boxes a kick, and broke off both of the roses.

"Kay! what are you doing?" the little girl cried. When he saw how it upset her, he broke off another rose and then leaped home through his own window, leaving dear little Gerda all alone.

Afterwards, when she brought out her picture book, he said it was fit only for babes in the cradle. And whenever Grandmother told stories, he always broke in with a "but—." If he could manage it he would steal behind her, perch a pair of spectacles on his nose, and imitate her. He did this so cleverly that it made

THE SNOW QUEEN

everybody laugh, and before long he could mimic the walk and the talk of everyone who lived on that street. Everything that was odd or ugly about them, Kay could mimic so well that people said, "That boy has surely got a good head on him!" But it was the glass in his eye and the glass in his heart that made him tease even little Gerda, who loved him with all her soul.

Now his games were very different from what they used to be. They became more sensible. When the snow was flying about one wintry day, he brought a large magnifying glass out of doors and spread the tail of his blue coat to let the snowflakes fall on it.

"Now look through the glass," he told Gerda. Each snowflake seemed much larger, and looked like a magnificent flower or a ten-pointed star. It was marvelous to look at.

"Look, how artistic!" said Kay. "They are much more interesting to look at than real flowers, for they are absolutely perfect. There isn't a flaw in them, until they start melting."

A little while later Kay came down with his big gloves on his hands and his sled on his back. Right in Gerda's ear he bawled out, "I've been given permission to play in the big square where the other boys are!" and away he ran.

In the square some of the more adventuresome boys would tie their little sleds on behind the farmer's carts, to be pulled along for quite a distance. It was wonderful sport. While the fun was at its height, a big sleigh drove up. It was painted entirely white, and the driver wore a white, shaggy fur cloak and a white, shaggy cap. As the sleigh drove twice around the square, Kay quickly hooked his little sled behind it, and down the street they went, faster and faster. The driver turned around in a friendly fashion and nodded to Kay, just as if they were old acquaintances. Every time Kay started to unfasten his little sleigh, its driver nodded again, and Kay held on, even when they drove right out through the town gate.

Then the snow began to fall so fast that the boy could not see his hands in front of him, as they sped on. He suddenly let go the slack of the rope in his hands, in order to get loose from the big sleigh, but it did no good. His little sled was tied on securely, and they went like the wind. He gave a loud shout, but nobody heard him. The snow whirled and the sleigh flew along. Every now and then it gave a jump, as if it were clearing hedges and ditches. The boy was terror-stricken. He tried to say his prayers, but all he could remember was his multiplication tables.

The snowflakes got bigger and bigger, until they looked like big white hens. All of a sudden the curtain of snow parted, and the big sleigh stopped and the driver stood up. The fur coat and the cap were made of snow, and it was a woman, tall and slender and blinding white – she was the Snow Queen herself.

"We have made good time," she said. "Is it possible that you tremble from cold? Crawl under my bear coat." She took him up in the sleigh beside her, and as she wrapped the fur about him he felt as if he were sinking into a snowdrift.

"Are you still cold?" she asked, and kissed him on the forehead. *Brer–r–r.* That kiss was colder than ice. He felt it right down to his heart, half of which was already an icy lump. He felt as if he were dying, but only for a moment. Then he felt quite comfortable, and no longer noticed the cold.

"My sled! Don't forget my sled!" It was the only thing he thought of. They tied it to one of the white hens, which flew along after them with the sled on its back. The Snow Queen kissed Kay once more, and then he forgot little Gerda, and Grandmother, and all the others at home.

"You won't get any more kisses now," she said, "or else I should kiss you to death." Kay looked at her. She was so beautiful! A cleverer and prettier face he could not imagine. She no longer seemed to be made of ice, as she

She was the Snow Queen herself.
(Edgar Maxence)

had seemed when she sat outside his window and beckoned to him. In his eyes she was perfect, and she was not at all afraid. He told her how he could do mental arithmetic even with fractions, and that he knew the size and population of all the countries. She kept on smiling, and he began to be afraid that he did not know as much as he thought he did. He looked up at the great big space overhead, as she flew with him high up on the black clouds, while the storm whistled and roared as if it were singing old ballads.

They flew over forests and lakes, over many a land and sea. Below them the wind blew cold, wolves howled, and black crows screamed as they skimmed across the glittering snow. But up above the moon shone bright and large, and on it Kay fixed his eyes throughout that long, long winter night. By day he slept at the feet of the Snow Queen.

Third Story

THE FLOWER GARDEN OF THE WOMAN SKILLED IN MAGIC

How did little Gerda get along when Kay did not come back? Where could he be? Nobody knew. Nobody could give them any news of him. All that the boys could say was that they had seen him hitch his little sled to a fine big sleigh, which had driven down the street and out through the town gate. Nobody knew what had become of Kay. Many tears were shed, and little Gerda sobbed hardest of all. People said that he was dead – that he must have been drowned in the river not far from town. Ah, how gloomy those long winter days were!

But spring and its warm sunshine came at last.

"Kay is dead and gone," little Gerda said.

"I don't believe it," said the sunshine.

"He's dead and gone," she said to the swallows.

"We don't believe it," they sang. Finally little Gerda began to disbelieve it too. One morning she said to herself:

"I'll put on my new red shoes, the ones Kay has never seen, and I'll go down by the river to ask about him."

It was very early in the morning. She kissed her old grandmother, who was still asleep, put on her red shoes, and all by herself she hurried out through the town gate and down to the river.

"Is it true that you have taken my own little playmate? I'll give you my red shoes if you will bring him back to me."

It seemed to her that the waves nodded very strangely. So she took off her red shoes that were her dearest possession, and threw them into the river. But they fell near the shore, and the little waves washed them right back to her. It seemed that the river could not take her dearest possession, because it did not have little Kay. However, she was afraid that she had not thrown them far enough, so she clambered into a boat that lay among the reeds, walked to the end of it, and threw her shoes out into the water again. But the boat was not tied, and her movements made it drift away from the bank. She realized this, and tried to get ashore, but by the time she reached the other end of the boat it was already more than a yard from the bank, and was fast gaining speed.

Little Gerda was so frightened that she began to cry, and no one was there to hear her except the sparrows. They could not carry her to land, but they flew along the shore twittering, "We are here! Here we are!" as if to comfort her. The boat drifted swiftly down the stream, and Gerda sat there quite still, in her stocking feet. Her little red shoes floated along behind, but they could not catch up with her because the boat was gathering headway. It was very pretty on both sides of the river, where the flowers were lovely, the trees were old, and the hillsides afforded pasture for cattle and sheep. But not one single person did Gerda see.

"Perhaps the river will take me to little Kay," she thought, and that made her feel more cheerful. She stood up and watched the lovely green banks for hour after hour.

Then she came to a large cherry orchard, in which there was a little house with strange red and blue windows. It had a thatched roof, and outside it stood two wooden soldiers, who presented arms to everyone who sailed past.

Gerda thought they were alive, and called out to them, but of course they did not answer her. She drifted quite close to them as the current drove the boat toward the bank. Gerda called even louder, and an old, old woman came out of the house. She leaned on a crooked stick; she had on a big sun hat, and on it were painted the most glorious flowers.

"You poor little child!" the old woman exclaimed. "However did you get lost on this big swift river, and however did you drift so far into the great wide world?" The old woman waded right into the water, caught hold of the boat with her crooked stick, pulled it in to shore, and lifted little Gerda out of it.

Gerda was very glad to be on dry land again, but she felt a little afraid of this strange old woman, who said to her:

"Come and tell me who you are, and how you got here." Gerda told her all about it. The woman shook her head and said, "Hmm, hmm!" And when Gerda had told her everything and asked if she hadn't seen little Kay, the woman said he had not yet come by, but that he might be along any day now. And she told Gerda not to take it so to heart, but to taste her cherries and to look at her flowers. These were more beautiful than any picture book, and each one had a story to tell. Then she led Gerda by the hand into her little house, and the old woman locked the door.

The windows were placed high up on the walls, and through their red, blue, and yellow panes the sunlight streamed in a strange mixture of all the colors there are. But on the

"You poor little child!" the old woman exclaimed. (Edmund Dulac)

table were the most delicious cherries, and Gerda, who was no longer afraid, ate as many as she liked. While she was eating them, the old woman combed her hair with a golden comb. Gerda's pretty hair fell in shining yellow ringlets on either side of a friendly little face that was as round and blooming as a rose.

"I've so often wished for a dear little girl like you," the old woman told her. "Now you'll see how well the two of us will get along." While her hair was being combed, Gerda gradually forgot all about Kay, for the old woman was skilled in magic. But she was not a wicked witch. She only dabbled in magic to amuse herself, but she wanted very much to keep little Gerda. So she went out into her garden and pointed her crooked stick at all the rose bushes. In the full bloom of their beauty, all of them sank down into the black earth, without leaving a single trace behind. The old woman was afraid that if Gerda saw them they would remind her so strongly of her own roses, and of little Kay, that she would run away again.

Then Gerda was led into the flower garden. How fragrant and lovely it was! Every known flower of every season was there in full bloom. No picture book was ever so pretty and gay. Gerda jumped for joy, and played in the garden until the sun went down behind the tall cherry trees. Then she was tucked into a beautiful bed, under a red silk coverlet quilted with blue violets. There she slept, and there she dreamed as gloriously as any queen on her wedding day.

The next morning she again went out into the warm sunshine to play with the flowers – and this she did for many a day. Gerda knew every flower by heart, and, plentiful though they were, she always felt that there was one missing, but which one she didn't quite know. One day she sat looking at the old woman's sun hat, and the prettiest of all the flowers painted on it was a rose. The old woman had forgotten this rose on her hat when she made the real roses disappear in the earth. But that's just the sort of thing that happens when one doesn't stop to think.

"Why aren't there any roses here?" said Gerda. She rushed out among the flower beds, and she looked and she looked, but there wasn't a rose to be seen. Then she sat down and cried. But her hot tears fell on the very spot where a rose bush had sunk into the ground, and when her warm tears moistened the earth the bush sprang up again, as full of blossoms as when it disappeared. Gerda hugged it, and kissed the roses. She remembered her own pretty roses, and thought of little Kay.

"Oh how long I have been delayed," the little girl said. "I should have been looking for Kay. Don't you know where he is?" she asked the roses. "Do you think that he is dead and gone?"

"He isn't dead," the roses told her. "We have been down in the earth where the dead people are, but Kay is not there."

"Thank you," said little Gerda, who went to all the other flowers, put her lips near them and asked, "Do you know where little Kay is?"

But every flower stood in the sun, and dreamed its own fairy tale, or its story. Though Gerda listened to many, many of them, not one of the flowers knew anything about Kay.

What did the tiger lily say?

"Do you hear the drum? *Boom, boom!* It was only two notes, always *boom, boom!* Hear the women wail. Hear the priests chant. The Hindoo woman in her long red robe stands on the funeral pyre. The flames rise around her and her dead husband, but the Hindoo woman is thinking of that living man in the crowd around them. She is thinking of him whose eyes are burning hotter than the flames – of him whose fiery glances have pierced her heart more deeply than these flames that soon will burn her body to ashes. Can the flame of the heart die in the flame of the funeral pyre?"

"I don't understand that at all," little Gerda said.

"That's my fairy tale," said the lily.

What did the trumpet flower say?

"An ancient castle rises high from a narrow path in the mountains. The thick ivy grows leaf upon leaf where it climbs to the balcony. There stands a beautiful maiden. She leans out over the balustrade to look down the path. No rose on its stem is as graceful as she, nor is any apple blossom in the breeze so light. Hear the rustle of her silk gown, sighing, 'Will he never come?'"

"Do you mean Kay?" little Gerda asked.

"I am talking about my story, my own dream," the trumpet flower replied.

What did the little snowdrop say?

"Between the trees a board hangs by two ropes. It is a swing. Two pretty little girls, with frocks as white as snow, and long green ribbons fluttering from their hats, are swinging. Their brother, who is bigger than they are, stands behind them on the swing, with his arms around the ropes to hold himself. In one hand he has

*"Between the trees a board hangs by two ropes.
It is a swing. Two pretty little girls, with
frocks as white as snow, and long green ribbons
fluttering from their hats, are swinging.*
(W. Heath Robinson)

a little cup, and in the other a clay pipe. He is
blowing soap bubbles, and as the swing flies the
bubbles float off in all their changing colors.
The last bubble is still clinging to the bowl of
his pipe, and fluttering in the air as the swing
sweeps to and fro. A little black dog, light as a
bubble, is standing on his hind legs and trying
to get up in the swing. But it does not stop.
High and low the swing flies, until the dog
loses his balance, barks, and loses his temper.
They tease him, and the bubble bursts. A
swinging board pictured in a bubble before it
broke – that is my story."

"It may be a very pretty story, but you told
it very sadly and you didn't mention Kay at
all."

What did the hyacinths say?

"There were three sisters, quite transparent
and very fair. One wore a red dress, the second
wore a blue one, and the third went all in
white. Hand in hand they danced in the clear
moonlight, beside a calm lake. They were not
elfin folk. They were human beings. The air
was sweet, and the sisters disappeared into the
forest. The fragrance of the air grew sweeter.
Three coffins, in which lie the three sisters,
glide out of the forest and across the lake. The
fireflies hover about them like little flickering
lights. Are the dancing sisters sleeping or are
they dead? The fragrance of the flowers says
they are dead, and the evening bell tolls for
their funeral."

"You are making me very unhappy," little
Gerda said. "Your fragrance is so strong that I
cannot help thinking of those dead sisters. Oh,
could little Kay really be dead? The roses have
been down under the ground, and they say no."

"Ding, dong," tolled the hyacinth bells.
"We do not toll for little Kay. We do not know
him. We are simply singing our song – the only
song we know."

And Gerda went on to the buttercup that
shone among its glossy green leaves.

"You are like a bright little sun," said Gerda.
"Tell me, do you know where I can find my
playmate?"

And the buttercup shone brightly as it
looked up at Gerda. But what sort of song
would a buttercup sing? It certainly wouldn't
be about Kay.

"In a small courtyard, God's sun was
shining brightly on the very first day of spring.
Its beams glanced along the white wall of the
house next door, and close by grew the first
yellow flowers of spring shining like gold
in the warm sunlight. An old grandmother
was sitting outside in her chair. Her grand-
daughter, a poor but very pretty maidservant,
had just come home for a little visit. She
kissed her grandmother, and there was gold,
a heart full of gold, in that kiss. Gold on her

lips, gold in her dreams, and gold above in the morning beams. There, I've told you my little story," said the buttercup.

"Oh, my poor old Grandmother," said Gerda. "She will miss me so. She must be grieving for me as much as she did for little Kay. But I'll soon go home again, and I'll bring Kay with me. There's no use asking the flowers about him. They don't know anything except their own songs, and they haven't any news for me."

Then she tucked up her little skirts so that she could run away faster, but the narcissus tapped against her leg as she was jumping over it. So she stopped and leaned over the tall flower.

"Perhaps you have something to tell me," she said.

What did the narcissus say?

"I can see myself! I can see myself! Oh, how sweet is my own fragrance! Up in the narrow garret there is a little dancer, half dressed. First she stands on one leg. Then she stands on both, and kicks her heels at the whole world. She is an illusion of the stage. She pours water from the teapot over a piece of cloth she is holding – it is her bodice. Cleanliness is such a virtue! Her white dress hangs from a hook. It too has been washed in the teapot, and dried on the roof. She puts it on, and ties a saffron scarf around her neck to make the dress seem whiter. Point your toes! See how straight she balances on that single stem. I can see myself! I can see myself!"

"I'm not interested," said Gerda. "What a thing to tell me about!"

She ran to the end of the garden, and though the gate was fastened she worked the rusty latch till it gave way and the gate flew open. Little Gerda scampered out into the wide world in her bare feet. She looked back three times, but nobody came after her. At last she could run no farther, and she sat down to rest on a big stone, and when she looked up she saw that summer had gone by, and it was late in the fall. She could never have guessed it inside the beautiful garden where the sun was always shining, and the flowers of every season were always in full bloom.

"Gracious! how long I've dallied," Gerda said. "Fall is already here. I can't rest any longer."

She got up to run on, but how footsore and tired she was! And how cold and bleak everything around her looked! The long leaves of the willow tree had turned quite yellow, and damp puffs of mist dropped from them like drops of water. One leaf after another fell to the ground. Only the blackthorn still bore fruit, and its fruit was so sour that it set your teeth on edge.

Oh, how dreary and gray the wide world looked.

Fourth Story
THE PRINCE AND THE PRINCESS

The next time that Gerda was forced to rest, a big crow came hopping across the snow in front of her. For a long time he had been watching her and cocking his head to one side, and now he said, "Caw, caw! Good caw day!" He could not say it any better, but he felt kindly inclined toward the little girl, and asked her where she was going in the great wide world, all alone. Gerda understood him when he said "alone," and she knew its meaning all too well. She told the crow the whole story of her life, and asked if he hadn't seen Kay. The crow gravely nodded his head and cawed, "Maybe I have, maybe I have!"

"What! do you really think you have?" the little girl cried, and almost hugged the crow to death as she kissed him.

"Gently, gently!" said the crow. "I think that it may have been little Kay that I saw, but if it was, then he has forgotten you for the Princess."

"Does he live with a Princess?" Gerda asked.

"Yes. Listen!" said the crow. "But it is so hard for me to speak your language. If you understand crow talk, I can tell you much more easily."

"I don't know that language," said Gerda. "My grandmother knows it, just as well as she knows baby talk, and I do wish I had learned it."

"No matter," said the crow. "I'll tell you as well as I can, though that won't be any too good." And he told her all that he knew.

"In the kingdom where we are now, there is a Princess who is uncommonly clever, and no wonder. She has read all the newspapers in the world and forgotten them again – that's how clever she is. Well, not long ago she was sitting on her throne. That's by no means as much fun as people suppose, so she fell to humming an old tune, and the refrain of it happened to run:

"Why, oh, why, shouldn't I get married?"

"'Why, that's an idea!' said she. And she made up her mind to marry as soon as she could find the sort of husband who could give a good answer when anyone spoke to him, instead of one of those fellows who merely stand around looking impressive, for that is so tiresome. She had the drums drubbed to call together all her ladies-in-waiting, and when they heard what she had in mind they were delighted.

"'Oh, we like that!' they said. 'We were just thinking the very same thing.'"

"Believe me," said the crow, "every word I tell you is true. I have a tame ladylove who has the run of the palace, and I had the whole story straight from her." Of course his ladylove was also a crow, for birds of a feather will flock together.

"The newspapers immediately came out with a border of hearts and the initials of the Princess, and you could read an announcement that any presentable young man might go to the palace and talk with her. The one who spoke best, and who seemed most at home in the palace, would be chosen by the Princess as her husband."

"Yes, yes," said the crow, "believe me, that's as true as it is that here I sit. Men flocked to the palace, and there was much crowding and crushing, but on neither the first nor the second day was anyone chosen. Out in the street they were all glib talkers, but after they entered the palace gate where the guardsmen were stationed in their silver-braided uniforms, and after they climbed up the staircase lined with footmen in gold-embroidered livery, they arrived in the brilliantly lighted reception halls without a word to say. And when they stood in front of the Princess on her throne, the best they could do was to echo the last word of her remarks, and she didn't care to hear it repeated.

"It was just as if everyone in the throne room had his stomach filled with snuff and had fallen asleep; for as soon as they were back in the streets there was no stopping their talk.

"The line of candidates extended all the way from the town gates to the palace. I saw them myself," said the crow. "They got hungry and they got thirsty, but from the palace they got nothing – not even a glass of lukewarm water. To be sure, some of the clever candidates had brought sandwiches with them, but they did not share them with their neighbors. Each man thought, 'Just let him look hungry, then the Princess won't take him!'"

"But Kay, little Kay," Gerda interrupted, "when did he come? Was he among those people?"

"Give me time, give me time! We are just coming to him. On the third day a little person, with neither horse nor carriage, strode boldly up to the palace. His eyes sparkled the way yours do, and he had handsome long hair, but his clothes were poor."

"Oh, that was Kay!" Gerda said, and clapped her hands in glee. "Now I've found him."

"He had a little knapsack on his back," the crow told her.

"No, that must have been his sled," said Gerda. "He was carrying it when he went away."

"Maybe so," the crow said. "I didn't look at it carefully. But my tame ladylove told me that when he went through the palace gates and saw the guardsmen in silver, and on the staircase the footmen in gold, he wasn't at all taken aback. He nodded and he said to them:

"'It must be very tiresome to stand on the stairs. I'd rather go inside.'

"The halls were brilliantly lighted. Ministers of state and privy councilors were walking about barefooted, carrying golden trays in front of them. It was enough to make anyone feel solemn, and his boots creaked dreadfully, but he wasn't a bit afraid."

"That certainly must have been Kay," said Gerda. "I know he was wearing new boots. I heard them creaking in Grandmother's room."

"Oh, they creaked all right," said the crow. "But it was little enough he cared as he walked straight to the Princess, who was sitting on a pearl as big as a spinning wheel. All the ladies-in-waiting with their attendants and their attendants' attendants, and all the lords-in-waiting with their gentlemen and their gentlemen's men, each of whom had his page with him, were standing there, and the nearer they stood to the door the more arrogant they looked. The gentlemen's men's pages, who always wore slippers, were almost too arrogant to look as they stood at the threshold."

"That must have been terrible!" little Gerda exclaimed. "And yet Kay won the Princess?"

"If I weren't a crow, I would have married her myself, for all that I'm engaged to another. They say he spoke as well as I do when I speak my crow language. Or so my tame ladylove tells me. He was dashing and handsome, and he was not there to court the Princess but to hear her wisdom. This he liked, and she liked him."

The Snow Queen and Kay.
(Milo Winter)

"Of course it was Kay," said Gerda. "He was so clever that he could do mental arithmetic even with fractions. Oh, please take me to the palace."

"That's easy enough to say," said the crow, "but how can we manage it? I'll talk it over with my tame ladylove, and she may be able to suggest something, but I must warn you that a little girl like you will never be admitted."

"Oh, yes I shall," said Gerda. "When Kay hears about me, he will come out to fetch me at once."

"Wait for me beside that stile," the crow said. He wagged his head and off he flew.

Darkness had set in when he got back.

"Caw, caw!" he said. "My ladylove sends you her best wishes, and here's a little loaf of bread for you. She found it in the kitchen, where they have all the bread they need, and you must be hungry. You simply can't get into the palace with those bare feet. The guardsmen in silver and the footmen in gold would never permit it. But don't you cry. We'll find a way. My ladylove knows of a little back staircase that leads up to the bedroom, and she knows where they keep the key to it."

Then they went into the garden and down the wide promenade where the leaves were falling one by one. When, one by one, the lights went out in the palace, the crow led little Gerda to the back door, which stood ajar.

Oh, how her heart did beat with fear and longing. It was just as if she were about to do something wrong, yet she only wanted to make sure that this really was little Kay. Yes, truly it must be Kay, she thought, as she recalled his sparkling eyes and his long hair. She remembered exactly how he looked when he used to smile at her as they sat under the roses at home. Wouldn't he be glad to see her! Wouldn't he be interested in hearing how far she had come to find him, and how sad they had all been when he didn't come home. She was so frightened, and yet so happy.

Now they were on the stairway. A little lamp was burning on a cupboard, and there stood the tame crow, cocking her head to look at Gerda, who made the curtsy that her grandmother had taught her.

"My fiancé has told me many charming things about you, dear young lady," she said. "Your biography, as one might say, is very touching. Kindly take the lamp and I shall lead the way. We shall keep straight ahead, where we aren't apt to run into anyone."

"It seems to me that someone is on the stairs behind us," said Gerda. Things brushed past, and from the shadows on the wall they seemed to be horses with spindly legs and waving manes. And there were shadows of huntsmen, ladies and gentlemen, on horseback.

"Those are only dreams," said the crow. "They come to take the thoughts of their royal masters off to the chase. That's just as well, for it will give you a good opportunity to see them while they sleep. But I trust that, when you rise to high position and power, you will show a grateful heart."

"Tut tut! You've no need to say that," said the forest crow.

Now they entered the first room. It was hung with rose-colored satin, embroidered with flowers. The dream shadows were flitting by so fast that Gerda could not see the lords and ladies. Hall after magnificent hall quite bewildered her, until at last they reached the royal bedroom.

The ceiling of it was like the top of a huge palm tree, with leaves of glass, costly glass. In the middle of the room two beds hung from a massive stem of gold. Each of them looked like a lily. One bed was white, and there lay the Princess. The other was red, and there Gerda hoped to find little Kay. She bent one of the scarlet petals and saw the nape of a little brown neck. Surely this must be Kay. She called his name aloud and held the lamp near him. The dreams on horseback pranced into the room again, as he awoke – and turned his head – and it was not little Kay at all.

The Prince only resembled Kay about the neck, but he was young and handsome. The Princess peeked out of her lily-white bed, and asked what had happened. Little Gerda cried and told them all about herself, and about all that the crows had done for her.

"Poor little thing," the Prince and the Princess said. They praised the crows, and said they weren't the least bit angry with them, but not to do it again. Furthermore, they should have a reward.

"Would you rather fly about without any responsibilities," said the Princess, "or would you care to be appointed court crows for life, with rights to all scraps from the kitchen?"

Both the crows bowed low and begged for permanent office, for they thought of their future and said it was better to provide for their "old age," as they called it.

The Prince got up, and let Gerda have his bed. It was the utmost that he could do. She clasped her little hands and thought, "How nice the people and the birds are." She closed her eyes, fell peacefully asleep, and all the dreams came flying back again. They looked like angels, and they drew a little sled on which Kay sat. He nodded to her, but this was only in a dream, so it all disappeared when she woke up.

The next day she was dressed from her head to her heels in silk and in velvet too. They asked her to stay at the palace and have a nice time there, but instead she begged them to let her have a little carriage, a little horse, and a pair of little boots, so that she could drive out into the wide world to find Kay.

They gave her a pair of boots, and also a muff. They dressed her as nicely as could be and, when she was ready to go, there at the gate stood a brand new carriage of pure gold. On it the coat of arms of the Prince and the Princess glistened like a star.

The coachman, the footman, and the postilions – for postilions there were – all wore golden crowns. The Prince and the Princess themselves helped her into the carriage, and wished her Godspeed. The forest crow, who was now a married man, accompanied her for the first three miles, and sat beside Gerda, for it upset him to ride backward. The other crow stood beside the gate and waved her wings. She did not accompany them because she was suffering from a headache, brought on by eating too much in her new position. Inside, the carriage was lined with sugared cookies, and the seats were filled with fruit and gingerbread.

"Fare you well, fare you well," called the Prince and Princess. Little Gerda cried and the crow cried too, for the first few miles. Then the crow said good-by, and that was the saddest leave-taking of all. He flew up into a tree and waved his big black wings as long as he could see the carriage, which flashed as brightly as the sun.

Fifth Story

THE LITTLE ROBBER GIRL

The carriage rolled on into a dark forest. Like a blazing torch, it shone in the eyes of some robbers. They could not bear it.

"That's gold! That's gold!" they cried. They sprang forward, seized the horses, killed the little postilions, the coachman, and the footman, and dragged little Gerda out of the carriage.

"How plump and how tender she looks, just as if she'd been fattened on nuts!" cried the old robber woman, who had a long bristly beard, and long eyebrows that hung down over her eyes. "She looks like a fat little lamb. What a dainty dish she will be!" As she said this she drew out her knife, a dreadful, flashing thing.

"Ouch!" the old woman howled. At just that moment her own little daughter had bitten her ear. The little girl, whom she carried on her back, was a wild and reckless creature. "You beastly brat!" her mother exclaimed, but it kept her from using that knife on Gerda.

"She shall play with me," said the little robber girl. "She must give me her muff and that pretty dress she wears, and sleep with me in my bed." And she again gave her mother such a bite that the woman hopped and whirled around in pain. All the robbers laughed, and shouted:

"See how she dances with her brat."

"I want to ride in the carriage," the little robber girl said, and ride she did, for she was too spoiled and headstrong for words. She and Gerda climbed into the carriage and away they drove over stumps and stones, into the depths of the forest. The little robber girl was no taller than Gerda, but she was stronger and much broader in the shoulders. Her skin was brown and her eyes coal-black – almost sad in their expression. She put her arms around Gerda, and said: "They shan't kill you unless I get angry with you. I think you must be a Princess."

"No, I'm not," said little Gerda. And she told about all that had happened to her, and how much she cared for little Kay. The robber girl looked at her gravely, gave a little nod of approval, and told her:

"Even if I should get angry with you, they shan't kill you, because I'll do it myself!" Then she dried Gerda's eyes, and stuck her own hands into Gerda's soft, warm muff.

The carriage stopped at last, in the courtyard of a robber's castle. The walls of it were cracked from bottom to top. Crows and ravens flew out of every loophole, and bulldogs huge enough to devour a man jumped high in the air. But they did not bark, for that was forbidden.

In the middle of the stone-paved, smoky old hall, a big fire was burning. The smoke of it drifted up to the ceiling, where it had to find its own way out. Soup was boiling in a big caldron, and hares and rabbits were roasting on the spit.

"Tonight you shall sleep with me and all my little animals," the robber girl said. After they had something to eat and drink, they went over to a corner that was strewn with rugs and straw. On sticks and perches around the bedding roosted nearly a hundred pigeons. They seemed to be asleep, but they stirred just a little when the two little girls came near them.

"They are all mine," said the little robber girl. She seized the one that was nearest to her, held it by the legs and shook it until it flapped its wings. "Kiss it," she cried, and thrust the bird in Gerda's face. "Those two are the wild rascals," she said, pointing high up the wall to a hole barred with wooden sticks. "Rascals of the woods they are, and they would fly away in a minute if they were not locked up."

"And here is my old sweetheart, Bae," she said, pulling at the horns of a reindeer that was tethered by a shiny copper ring around his neck. "We have to keep a sharp eye on him, or he would run away from us too. Every single night I tickle his neck with my knife blade, for he is afraid of that." From a hole in the wall she pulled a long knife, and rubbed it against the reindeer's neck. After the poor animal had kicked up its heels, the robber girl laughed and pulled Gerda down into the bed with her.

"Are you going to keep that knife in bed with you?" Gerda asked, and looked at it a little frightened.

"I always sleep with my knife," the little robber girl said. "You never can tell what may happen. But let's hear again what you told me before about little Kay, and about why you are wandering through the wide world."

Gerda told the story all over again, while the wild pigeons cooed in their cage overhead, and the tame pigeons slept. The little robber girl clasped one arm around Gerda's neck, gripped her knife in the other hand, fell asleep, and snored so that one could hear her. But Gerda could not close her eyes at all. She did not know whether she was to live or whether she was to die. The robbers sat around their fire, singing and drinking, and the old robber woman was turning somersaults. It was a terrible sight for a little girl to see.

Then the wood pigeons said, "Coo, coo. We have seen little Kay. A white hen was carrying his sled, and Kay sat in the Snow Queen's sleigh. They swooped low, over the trees where we lay in our nest. The Snow Queen blew upon us, and all the young pigeons died except us. Coo, coo."

"What is that you are saying up there?" cried Gerda. "Where was the Snow Queen going?

The Snow Queen.
(Edmund Dulac)

Do you know anything about it?"

"She was probably bound for Lapland, where they always have snow and ice. Why don't you ask the reindeer who is tethered beside you?"

"Yes, there is ice and snow in that glorious land," the reindeer told her. "You can prance about freely across those great, glittering fields. The Snow Queen has her summer tent there, but her stronghold is a castle up nearer the North Pole, on the island called Spitzbergen."

"Oh, Kay, little Kay," Gerda sighed.

"Lie still," said the robber girl, "or I'll stick my knife in your stomach."

In the morning Gerda told her all that the wood pigeons had said. The little robber girl looked quite thoughtful. She nodded her head, and exclaimed, "Leave it to me! Leave it to me.

"Do you know where Lapland is?" she asked the reindeer.

"Who knows it better than I?" the reindeer said, and his eyes sparkled. "There I was born, there I was bred, and there I kicked my heels in freedom, across the fields of snow."

"Listen!" the robber girl said to Gerda. "As you see, all the men are away. Mother is still here, and here she'll stay, but before the morning is over she will drink out of that big bottle, and then she usually dozes off for a nap. As soon as that happens, I will do you a good turn."

She jumped out of bed, rushed over and threw her arms around her mother's neck, pulled at her beard bristles, and said, "Good morning, my dear nanny-goat." Her mother thumped her nose until it was red and blue, but all that was done out of pure love.

As soon as the mother had tipped up the bottle and dozed off to sleep, the little robber girl ran to the reindeer and said, "I have a good notion to keep you here, and tickle you with my sharp knife. You are so funny when I do, but never mind that. I'll untie your rope, and help you find your way outside, so that you can run back to Lapland. But you must put your best leg forward and carry this little girl to the Snow Queen's palace, where her playmate is. I suppose you heard what she told me, for she spoke so loud, and you were eavesdropping."

The reindeer was so happy that he bounded into the air. The robber girl hoisted little Gerda on his back, carefully tied her in place, and even gave her a little pillow to sit on. "I don't do things half way," she said. "Here, take back your fur boots, for it's going to be bitter cold. I'll keep your muff, because it's such a pretty one. But your fingers mustn't get cold. Here are my mother's big mittens, which will come right up to your elbows. Pull them on. Now your hands look just like my ugly mother's big paws."

And Gerda shed happy tears.

"I don't care to see you blubbering," said the little robber girl. "You ought to look pleased now. Here, take these two loaves of bread and this ham along, so that you won't starve."

When these provisions were tied on the back of the reindeer, the little robber girl opened the door and called in all the big dogs. Then she cut the tether with her knife and said to the reindeer, "Now run, but see that you take good care of the little girl."

Gerda waved her big mittens to the little robber girl, and said good-by. Then the reindeer bounded away, over stumps and stones, straight through the great forest, over swamps and across the plains, as fast as he could run. The wolves howled, the ravens shrieked, and *ker-shew, ker-shew!* the red streaks of light ripped through the heavens, with a noise that sounded like sneezing.

"Those are my old Northern Lights," said the reindeer. "See how they flash." And on he ran, faster than ever, by night and day. The loaves were eaten and the whole ham was eaten – and there they were in Lapland.

Sixth Story

THE LAPP WOMAN AND THE FINN WOMAN

They stopped in front of the little hut, and a makeshift dwelling it was. The roof of it almost touched the ground, and the doorway was so low that the family had to lie on their stomachs to crawl in it or out of it. No one was at home except an old Lapp woman, who was cooking fish over a whale-oil lamp. The reindeer told her Gerda's whole story, but first he told his own, which he thought was much more important. Besides, Gerda was so cold that she couldn't say a thing.

"Oh, you poor creatures," the Lapp woman said, "you've still got such a long way to go. Why, you will have to travel hundreds of miles into the Finmark. For it's there that the Snow Queen is taking a country vacation, and burning her blue fireworks every evening. I'll jot down a message on a dried codfish, for I haven't any paper. I want you to take it to the Finn woman who lives up there. She will be able to tell you more about it than I can."

As soon as Gerda had thawed out, and had had something to eat and drink, the Lapp woman wrote a few words on a dried codfish, told Gerda to take good care of it, and tied her again on the back of the reindeer. Off he ran, and all night long the skies crackled and swished as the most beautiful Northern Lights flashed over their heads. At last they came to the Finmark, and knocked at the Finn woman's chimney, for she hadn't a sign of a door. It was so hot inside that the Finn woman went about almost naked. She was small and terribly dowdy, but she at once helped little Gerda off with her mittens and boots, and loosened her clothes. Otherwise the heat would have wilted her. Then the woman put a piece of ice on the reindeer's head, and read what was written on the codfish. She read it three times and when she knew it by heart, she put the fish into the kettle of soup, for they might as well eat it. She never wasted anything.

The reindeer told her his own story first, and then little Gerda's. The Finn woman winked a knowing eye, but she didn't say anything.

"You are such a wise woman," said the reindeer, "I know that you can tie all the winds of the world together with a bit of cotton thread. If the sailor unties one knot he gets a favorable wind. If he unties another he gets a stiff gale, while if he unties the third and fourth knots such a tempest rages that it flattens the trees in the forest. Won't you give this little girl something to drink that will make her as strong as twelve men, so that she may overpower the Snow Queen?"

"Twelve strong men," the Finn woman sniffed. " Much good that would be."

She went to the shelf, took down a big rolled-up skin, and unrolled it. On this skin strange characters were written, and the Finn woman read them until the sweat rolled down her forehead.

The reindeer again begged her to help Gerda, and little Gerda looked at her with such tearful, imploring eyes, that the woman began winking again. She took the reindeer aside in a corner, and while she was putting another piece of ice on his head she whispered to him:

"Little Kay is indeed with the Snow Queen, and everything there just suits him fine. He thinks it is the best place in all the world, but that's because he has a splinter of glass in his heart and a small piece of it in his eye. Unless these can be gotten out, he will never be human again, and the Snow Queen will hold him in her power."

"But can't you fix little Gerda something to drink which will give her more power than all those things?"

"No power that I could give could be as great as that which she already has. Don't you see how men and beasts are compelled to serve her, and how far she has come in the wide world since she started out in her naked feet? We mustn't tell her about this power. Strength lies in her heart, because she is such a sweet, innocent child. If she herself cannot reach the Snow Queen and rid little Kay of those pieces of glass, then there's no help that we can give her. The Snow Queen's garden lies about eight miles from here. You may carry the little girl there, and put her down by the big bush covered with red berries that grows on the snow. Then don't you stand there gossiping, but hurry to get back here."

The Finn woman lifted little Gerda onto the reindeer, and he galloped away as fast as he could.

"Oh!" cried Gerda, "I forgot my boots and I forgot my mittens." She soon felt the need of them in that knife-like cold, but the reindeer did not dare to stop. He galloped on until they came to the big bush that was covered with red berries. Here he set Gerda down and kissed her on the mouth, while big shining tears ran down his face. Then he ran back as fast as he could. Little Gerda stood there without boots and without mittens, right in the middle of icy Finmark.

She ran as fast as ever she could. A whole regiment of snowflakes swirled toward her, but they did not fall from the sky, for there was not a cloud up there, and the Northern Lights were ablaze.

The flakes skirmished along the ground, and the nearer they came the larger they grew. Gerda remembered how large and strange they had appeared when she looked at them under the magnifying glass. But here they were much more monstrous and terrifying. They were alive. They were the Snow Queen's advance guard, and their shapes were most strange. Some looked like ugly, overgrown porcupines. Some were like a knot of snakes that stuck out their heads in every direction, and others were like fat little bears with every hair a-bristle. All of them were glistening white, for all were living snowflakes.

It was so cold that, as little Gerda said the Lord's Prayer, she could see her breath freezing in front of her mouth, like a cloud of smoke. It grew thicker and thicker, and took the shape of little angels that grew bigger and bigger the moment they touched the ground. All of them had helmets on their heads and they carried shields and lances in their hands. Rank upon rank, they increased, and when Gerda had finished her prayer she was surrounded by a legion of angels. They struck the dread snowflakes with their lances and shivered them into a thousand pieces. Little Gerda walked on, unmolested and cheerful. The angels rubbed her hands and feet to make them warmer, and she trotted briskly along to the Snow Queen's palace.

But now let us see how little Kay was getting on. Little Gerda was furthest from his mind, and he hadn't the slightest idea that she was just outside the palace.

Seventh Story

WHAT HAPPENED IN THE SNOW QUEEN'S PALACE, AND WHAT CAME OF IT

The walls of the palace were driven snow. The windows and doors were the knife-edged wind. There were more than a hundred halls, shaped as the snow had drifted, and the largest of these extended for many a mile. All were lighted by the flare of the Northern Lights. All of the halls were so immense and so empty, so brilliant and so glacial! There was never a touch of gaiety in them; never so much as a little dance for the polar bears, at which the storm blast could have served for music, and the polar bears could have waddled about on their hind legs to show off their best manners. There was never a little party with such games as blind-bear's buff or hide the paw-kerchief for the cubs, nor even a little afternoon coffee over which the white fox vixens could gossip. Empty, vast, and frigid were the Snow Queen's halls. The Northern Lights flared with such regularity that you could time exactly when they would be at the highest and lowest. In the middle of the vast, empty hall of snow was a frozen lake. It was cracked into a thousand pieces, but each piece was shaped so exactly like the others that it seemed a work of wonderful craftsmanship. The Snow Queen sat in the exact center of it when she was at home, and she spoke of this as sitting on her "Mirror of Reason." She said this mirror was the only one of its kind, and the best thing in all the world.

Little Kay was blue, yes, almost black, with the cold. But he did not feel it, because the Snow Queen had kissed away his icy tremblings, and his heart itself had almost turned to ice.

He was shifting some sharp, flat pieces of ice to and fro, trying to fit them into every possible pattern, for he wanted to make something with them. It was like the Chinese puzzle game that we play at home, juggling little flat

The Mirror of Reason.
(Edmund Dulac)

pieces of wood about into special designs. Kay was cleverly arranging his pieces in the game of ice-cold reason. To him the patterns were highly remarkable and of the utmost importance, for the chip of glass in his eye made him see them that way. He arranged his pieces to spell out many words; but he could never find the way to make the one word he was so eager to form. The word was "Eternity." The Snow Queen had said to him, "If you can puzzle that out you shall be your own master, and I'll give you the whole world and a new pair of skates." But he could not puzzle it out.

"Now I am going to make a flying trip to the warm countries," the Snow Queen told him. "I want to go and take a look into the black caldrons." She meant the volcanos of Etna and Vesuvius. "I must whiten them up a bit. They need it, and it will be such a relief after all those yellow lemons and purple grapes."

And away she flew. Kay sat all alone in that endless, empty, frigid hall, and puzzled over the pieces of ice until he almost cracked his skull. He sat so stiff and still that one might have thought he was frozen to death.

All of a sudden, little Gerda walked up to the palace through the great gate which was a knife-edged wind. But Gerda said her evening prayer. The wind was lulled to rest, and the little girl came on into the vast, cold, empty hall. Then she saw Kay. She recognized him at once, and ran to throw her arms around him. She held him close and cried, "Kay, dearest little Kay! I've found you at last!"

But he sat still, and stiff, and cold. Gerda shed hot tears, and when they fell upon him they went straight to his heart. They melted the lump of ice and burned away the splinter of glass in it. He looked up at her, and she sang:

*"Where roses bloom so sweetly in the vale,
There shall you find the Christ Child,
without fail."*

Kay burst into tears. He cried so freely that the little piece of glass in his eye was washed right out. "Gerda!" He knew her, and cried out in his happiness, "My sweet little Gerda, where have you been so long? And where have I been?" He looked around him and said, "How cold it is here! How enormous and empty!" He held fast to Gerda, who laughed until happy tears rolled down her cheeks. Their bliss was so heavenly that even the bits of glass danced about them and shared in their happiness. When the pieces grew tired, they dropped into a pattern which made the very word that the Snow Queen had told Kay he must find before he became his own master and received the whole world and a new pair of skates.

Gerda kissed his cheeks, and they turned pink again. She kissed his eyes, and they sparkled like hers. She kissed his hands and feet, and he became strong and well. The Snow Queen might come home now whenever she pleased, for there stood the order for Kay's release, written in letters of shining ice.

Hand in hand, Kay and Gerda strolled out of that enormous palace. They talked about Grandmother, and about the roses on their roof. Wherever they went, the wind died down and the sun shone out. When they came to the bush that was covered with red berries, the reindeer was waiting to meet them. He had brought along a young reindeer mate who had warm milk for the children to drink, and who kissed them on the mouth. Then these reindeer carried Gerda and Kay first to the Finn woman. They warmed themselves in her hot room, and when she had given them directions for their journey home they rode on to the Lapp woman. She had made them new clothes, and was ready to take them along in her sleigh.

Side by side, the reindeer ran with them to the limits of the North country, where the first green buds were to be seen. Here they said good-by to the two reindeer and to the Lapp woman. "Farewell," they all said.

Now the first little birds began to chirp, and there were green buds all around them in the forest. Through the woods came riding a young girl on a magnificent horse that Gerda recognized, for it had once been harnessed to the golden carriage. The girl wore a bright red cap on her head, and a pair of pistols in her belt. She was the little robber girl, who had grown tired of staying at home, and who was setting out on a journey to the North country. If she didn't like it there, why, the world was wide, and there were many other places where she could go. She recognized Gerda at once, and Gerda knew her too. It was a happy meeting.

"You're a fine one for gadding about," she told little Kay. "I'd just like to know whether you deserve to have someone running to the end of the earth for your sake."

But Gerda patted her cheek and asked her about the Prince and the Princess.

"They are traveling in foreign lands," the girl told her.

"And the crow?"

"Oh, the crow is dead," she answered. "His tame ladylove is now a widow, and she wears a bit of black wool wrapped around her leg. She takes great pity on herself, but that's all stuff and nonsense. Now tell me what has happened to you and how you caught up with Kay."

Gerda and Kay told her their story.

"*Snip snap snurre, basse lurre*," said the robber girl. "So everything came out all right." She shook them by the hand, and promised that if ever she passed through their town she would come to see them. And then she rode away.

Kay and Gerda held each other by the hand. And as they walked along they had wonderful spring weather. The land was green and strewn with flowers, church bells rang, and they saw the high steeples of a big town. It was the one where they used to live. They walked straight to Grandmother's house, and up the stairs, and into the room, where everything was just as it was when they left it. And the clock said tick-tock, and its hands were telling the time. But the moment they came in the door they noticed one change. They were grown-up now.

The roses on the roof looked in at the open window, and their two little stools were still out there. Kay and Gerda sat down on them, and held each other by the hand. Both of them had forgotten the icy, empty splendor of the Snow Queen's palace as completely as if it were some bad dream. Grandmother sat in God's good sunshine, reading to them from her Bible:

"Except ye become as little children, ye shall not enter into the Kingdom of Heaven."

Kay and Gerda looked into each other's eyes, and at last they understood the meaning of their old hymn:

"Where roses bloom so sweetly in the vale,
There shall you find the Christ Child,
without fail."

And they sat there, grown-up, but children still – children at heart. And it was summer, warm, glorious summer.

THE RED SHOES

THERE WAS ONCE a little girl, very nice and very pretty, but so poor that she had to go barefooted all summer. And in winter she had to wear thick wooden shoes that chafed her ankles until they were red, oh, as red as could be.

In the middle of the village lived "Old Mother Shoemaker." She took some old scraps of red cloth and did her best to make them into a little pair of shoes. They were a bit clumsy, but well meant, for she intended to give them to the little girl. Karen was the little girl's name.

The first time Karen wore her new red shoes was on the very day when her mother was buried. Of course, they were not right for mourning, but they were all she had, so she put them on and walked barelegged after the plain wicker coffin.

Just then a large old carriage came by, with a large old lady inside it. She looked at the little girl and took pity upon her. And she went to the parson and said: "Give the little girl to me, and I shall take good care of her."

Karen was sure that this happened because she wore red shoes, but the old lady said the shoes were hideous, and ordered them burned. Karen was given proper new clothes. She was taught to read, and she was taught to sew. People said she was pretty, but her mirror told her, "You are more than pretty. You are beautiful."

It happened that the Queen came traveling through the country with her little daughter, who was a Princess. Karen went with all the people who flocked to see them at the castle. The little Princess, all dressed in white, came to the window to let them admire her. She didn't wear a train, and she didn't wear a gold crown, but she did wear a pair of splendid red morocco shoes. Of course, they were much nicer than the ones "Old Mother Shoemaker" had put together for little Karen, but there's nothing in the world like a pair of red shoes!

When Karen was old enough to be confirmed, new clothes were made for her, and she was to have new shoes. They went to the house of a thriving shoemaker, to have him take the measure of her little feet. In his shop were big glass cases, filled with the prettiest shoes and the shiniest boots. They looked most attractive but, as the old lady did not see very well, they did not attract her. Among the shoes there was a pair of red leather ones which were just like those the Princess had worn. How perfect they were! The shoemaker said he had made them for the daughter of a count, but that they did not quite fit her.

"They must be patent leather to shine so," said the old lady.

How perfect they were!
(W. Heath Robinson)

133

Karen couldn't resist taking a few dancing steps. (Ann Anderson)

"Yes, indeed they shine," said Karen. As the shoes fitted Karen, the old lady bought them, but she had no idea they were red. If she had known that, she would never have let Karen wear them to confirmation, which is just what Karen did.

Every eye was turned toward her feet. When she walked up the aisle to the chancel of the church, it seemed to her as if even those portraits of bygone ministers and their wives, in starched ruffs and long black gowns – even they fixed their eyes upon her red shoes. She could think of nothing else, even when the pastor laid his hands upon her head and spoke of her holy baptism, and her covenant with God, and her duty as a Christian. The solemn organ rolled, the children sang sweetly, and the old choir leader sang too, but Karen thought of nothing except her red shoes.

Before the afternoon was over, the old lady had heard from everyone in the parish that the shoes were red. She told Karen it was naughty to wear red shoes to church. Highly improper! In the future she was always to wear black shoes to church, even though they were her old ones.

Next Sunday there was holy communion. Karen looked at her black shoes. She looked at her red ones. She kept looking at her red ones until she put them on.

It was a fair, sunny day. Karen and the old lady took the path through the cornfield, where it was rather dusty. At the church door they met an old soldier, who stood with a crutch and wore a long, curious beard. It was more reddish than white. In fact it was quite red. He bowed down to the ground, and asked the old lady if he might dust her shoes. Karen put out her little foot too.

"Oh, what beautiful shoes for dancing," the soldier said. "Never come off when you dance," he told the shoes, as he tapped the sole of each of them with his hand.

The old lady gave the soldier a penny, and went on into the church with Karen. All the people there stared at Karen's red shoes, and all the portraits stared too. When Karen knelt at the altar rail, and even when the chalice came to her lips, she could think only of her red shoes. It was as if they kept floating around in the chalice, and she forgot to sing the psalm. She forgot to say the Lord's Prayer.

Then church was over, and the old lady got into her carriage. Karen was lifting her foot to step in after her when the old soldier said, "Oh, what beautiful shoes for dancing!"

Karen couldn't resist taking a few dancing steps, and once she began her feet kept on dancing. It was as if the shoes controlled her. She danced round the corner of the church – she simply could not help it. The coachman had to run after her, catch her, and lift her into the carriage. But even there her feet went on dancing so that she gave the good old lady a terrible kicking. Only when she took her shoes off did her legs quiet down. When they got home the shoes were put away in a cupboard, but Karen would still go and look at them.

Shortly afterwards the old lady was taken ill, and it was said she could not recover. She required constant care and faithful nursing, and for this she depended on Karen. But a great ball was being given in the town, and Karen was invited. She looked at the old lady, who could not live in any case. She looked at the red shoes, for she thought there was no harm in looking. She put them on, for she thought there was no harm in that either. But then she went to the ball and began dancing. When she tried to turn to the right, the shoes turned to the left. When she wanted to dance up the ballroom, her shoes danced down. They danced down the stairs, into the street, and out through the gate of the town. Dance she did, and dance she must, straight into the dark woods.

Suddenly something shone through the trees, and she thought it was the moon, but it turned out to be the red-bearded soldier. He nodded and said, "Oh, what beautiful shoes for dancing."

She was terribly frightened, and tried to take off her shoes. She tore off her stockings, but the shoes had grown fast to her feet. And dance she did, for dance she must, over fields and valleys, in the rain and in the sun, by day and night. It was most dreadful by night. She danced over an unfenced graveyard, but the dead did not join her dance. They had better things to do. She tried to sit on a pauper's grave, where the bitter fennel grew, but there was no rest or peace for her there. And when she danced toward the open doors of the church, she saw it guarded by an angel with long white robes and wings that reached from his shoulders down to the ground. His face was grave and stern, and in his hand he held a broad, shining sword.

"Dance you shall!" he told her. "Dance in your red shoes until you are pale and cold, and your flesh shrivels down to the skeleton. Dance

you shall from door to door, and wherever there are children proud and vain you must knock at the door till they hear you, and are afraid of you. Dance you shall. Dance always."

"Have mercy upon me!" screamed Karen. But she did not hear the angel answer. Her shoes swept her out through the gate, and across the fields, along highways and byways, forever and always dancing.

One morning she danced by a door she knew well. There was the sound of a hymn, and a coffin was carried out covered with flowers. Then she knew the old lady was dead. She was all alone in the world now, and cursed by the angel of God.

Dance she did and dance she must, through the dark night. Her shoes took her through thorn and briar that scratched her until she bled. She danced across the wastelands until she came to a lonely little house. She knew that this was where the executioner lived, and she tapped with her finger on his window pane.

The executioner said, "You don't seem to know who I am." (Ann Anderson)

135

"Come out!" she called. "Come out! I can't come in, for I am dancing."

The executioner said, "You don't seem to know who I am. I strike off the heads of bad people, and I feel my ax beginning to quiver."

"Don't strike off my head, for then I could not repent of my sins," said Karen. "But strike off my feet with the red shoes on them."

She confessed her sin, and the executioner struck off her feet with the red shoes on them. The shoes danced away with her little feet, over the fields into the deep forest. But he made wooden feet and a pair of crutches for her. He taught her a hymn that prisoners sing when they are sorry for what they have done. She kissed his hand that held the ax, and went back across the wasteland.

"Now I have suffered enough for those red shoes," she said. "I shall go and be seen again in the church." She hobbled to church as fast as she could, but when she got there the red shoes danced in front of her, and she was frightened and turned back.

All week long she was sorry, and cried many bitter tears. But when Sunday came again she said, "Now I have suffered and cried enough. I think I must be as good as many who sit in church and hold their heads high." She started out unafraid, but the moment she came to the church gate she saw her red shoes dancing before her. More frightened than ever, she turned away, and with all her heart she really repented.

She went to the pastor's house, and begged him to give her work as a servant. She promised to work hard, and do all that she could. Wages did not matter, if only she could have a roof over her head and be with good people. The pastor's wife took pity on her, and gave her work at the parsonage. Karen was faithful and serious. She sat quietly in the evening, and listened to every word when the pastor read the Bible aloud. The children were devoted to her, but when they spoke of frills and furbelows,

and of being as beautiful as a queen, she would shake her head.

When they went to church next Sunday they asked her to go too, but with tears in her eyes she looked at her crutches, and shook her head. The others went to hear the word of God, but she went to her lonely little room, which was just big enough to hold her bed and one chair. She sat with her hymnal in her hands, and as she read it with a contrite heart she heard the organ roll. The wind carried the sound from the church to her window. Her face was wet with tears as she lifted it up, and said, "Help me, O Lord!"

Then the sun shone bright, and the white-robed angel stood before her. He was the same angel she had seen that night, at the door of the church. But he no longer held a sharp sword. In his hand was a green branch, covered with roses. He touched the ceiling with it. There was a golden star where it touched, and the ceiling rose high. He touched the walls and they opened wide. She saw the deep-toned organ. She saw the portraits of ministers and their wives. She saw the congregation sit in flower-decked pews, and sing from their hymnals. Either the church had come to the poor girl in her narrow little room, or it was she who had been brought to the church. She sat in the pew with the pastor's family. When they had finished the hymn, they looked up and nodded to her.

"It was right for you to come, little Karen," they said.

"It was God's own mercy," she told them.

The organ sounded and the children in the choir sang, softly and beautifully. Clear sunlight streamed warm through the window, right down to the pew where Karen sat. She was so filled with the light of it, and with joy and with peace, that her heart broke. Her soul traveled along the shaft of sunlight to heaven, where no one questioned her about the red shoes.

THE SHEPHERDESS AND THE CHIMNEY-SWEEP

HAVE YOU EVER seen a very old chest, black with age, and covered with outlandish carved ornaments and curling leaves? Well, in a certain parlor there was just such a chest, handed down from some great-grandmother. Carved all up and down it, ran tulips and roses – odd-looking flourishes – and from fanciful thickets little stags stuck out their antlered heads.

Right in the middle of the chest a whole man was carved. He made you laugh to look at him grinning away, though one couldn't call his grinning laughing. He had hind legs like a goat's, little horns on his forehead, and a long beard. All his children called him "General Headquarters-Hindquarters-Gives-Orders-Front-and-Rear-Sergeant-Billygoat-Legs." It was a difficult name to pronounce and not many people get to be called by it, but he must have been very important or why should anyone have taken trouble to carve him at all?

However, there he stood, forever eyeing a delightful little china shepherdess on the table top under the mirror. The little shepherdess wore golden shoes, and looped up her gown fetchingly with a red rose. Her hat was gold, and even her crook was gold. She was simply charming!

Close by her stood a little chimney-sweep, as black as coal, but made of porcelain too. He was as clean and tidy as anyone can be, because you see he was only an ornamental chimney-sweep. If the china-makers had wanted to, they could just as easily have turned him out as a prince, for he had a jaunty way of holding his ladder, and his cheeks were as pink as a girl's. That was a mistake, don't you think? He should have been dabbed with a pinch or two of soot.

He and the shepherdess stood quite close together. They had both been put on the table where they stood and, having been placed there, they had become engaged because they suited each other exactly. Both were young, both were made of the same porcelain, and neither could stand a shock.

Near them stood another figure, three times as big as they were. It was an old Chinaman who could nod his head. He too was made of porcelain, and he said he was the little shepherdess's grandfather. But he couldn't prove it. Nevertheless he claimed that this gave him authority over her, and when General-Headquarters-Hindquarters-Gives-Orders-Front-and-Rear-Sergeant-Billygoat-Legs asked for her hand in marriage, the old Chinaman had nodded consent.

"There's a husband for you!" the old Chinaman told the shepherdess. "A husband who, I am inclined to believe, is made of mahogany. He can make you Mrs. General-Headquarters-Hindquarters-Gives-Orders-Front-and-Rear-Sergeant-Billygoat-Legs. He has the whole chest full of silver, and who knows what else he's got hidden away in his secret drawers?"

"But I don't want to go and live in the dark chest," said the little shepherdess. "I have heard people say he's got eleven china wives in there already."

"Then you will make twelve," said the Chinaman. "Tonight, as soon as the old chest commences to creak I'll marry you off to him, as sure as I'm a Chinaman." Then he nodded off to sleep. The little shepherdess cried and looked at her true love, the porcelain chimney-sweep.

"Please let's run away into the big, wide world," she begged him, "for we can't stay here."

"I'll do just what you want me to," the little chimney-sweep told her. "Let's run away right now. I feel sure I can support you by chimney-sweeping."

"I wish we were safely down off this table," she said. "I'll never be happy until we are out in the big, wide world."

He told her not to worry, and showed her how to drop her little feet over the table edge, and how to step from one gilded leaf to another down the carved leg of the table. He set up his ladder to help her, and down they came safely to the floor. But when they glanced at the old chest they saw a great commotion. All the carved stags were craning their necks, tossing their antlers, and turning their heads. General-Headquarters-Hindquarters-Gives-Orders-Front-and-Rear-Sergeant-Billygoat-Legs jumped high in the air, and shouted to the old Chinaman, "They're running away! They're running away!"

This frightened them so that they jumped quickly into a drawer of the window-seat. Here they found three or four decks of cards, not quite complete, and a little puppet theater, which was set up as well as it was possible to do. A play was in progress, and all the diamond queens, heart queens, club queens, and spade queens sat in front row and fanned themselves with the tulips they held in their hands. Behind them the knaves lined up, showing that they had heads both at the top and at the bottom, as face cards do have. The play was all about two people, who were not allowed to marry, and it made the shepherdess cry because it was so like her own story.

"I can't bear to see any more," she said. "I must get out of this drawer at once." But when they got back to the floor and looked up at the table, they saw the old Chinaman was wide awake now. Not only his head, but his whole body rocked forward. The lower part of his body was one solid piece, you see.

"The old Chinaman's coming!" cried the little shepherdess, who was so upset that she fell down on her porcelain knees.

"I have an idea," said the chimney-sweep. "We'll hide in the pot-pourri vase in the corner. There we can rest upon rose petals and lavender, and when he finds us we can throw salt in his eyes."

"It's no use," she said. "Besides, I know the pot-pourri vase was once the old Chinaman's sweetheart, and where there used to be love a little affection is sure to remain. No, there's nothing for us to do but to run away into the big wide world."

"Are you really so brave that you'd go into the wide world with me?" asked the chimney-sweep. "Have you thought about how big it is, and that we can never come back here?"

"I have," she said.

The chimney-sweep looked her straight in the face and said, "My way lies up through the chimney. Are you really so brave that you'll come with me into the stove, and crawl through the stovepipe? It will take us to the chimney. Once we get there, I'll know what to do. We shall climb so high that they'll never catch us, and at the very top there's an opening into the big wide world."

He led her to the stove door.

"It looks very black in there," she said. But she let him lead her through the stove and through the stovepipe, where it was pitch-black night.

"Now we've come to the chimney," he said. "And see! See how the bright star shines over our heads."

A real star, high up in the heavens, shone down as if it wished to show them the way. They clambered and scuffled, for it was hard climbing and terribly steep – way, way up high! But he lifted her up, held her safe, and found the best places for her little porcelain feet. At last they reached the top of the chimney, where they sat down. For they were so tired, and no wonder!

Overhead was the starry sky, and spread before them were all the housetops in the town. They looked out on the big wide world. The poor shepherdess had never thought it would

They clambered and scuffled, for it was hard climbing and terribly steep – way, way up high! (Kay Neilsen)

be like that. She flung her little head against the chimney-sweep, and sobbed so many tears that the gilt washed off her sash.

"This is too much," she said. "I can't bear it. The wide world is too big. Oh! If I only were back on my table under the mirror. I'll never be happy until I stand there again, just as before. I followed you faithfully out into the world, and if you love me the least bit you'll take me right home."

The chimney-sweep tried to persuade her that it wasn't sensible to go back. He talked to her about the old Chinaman, and of General-Headquarters-Hindquarters-Gives-Orders-Front-and-Rear-Sergeant-Billygoat-Legs, but she sobbed so hard and kissed her chimney-sweep so much that he had to do as she said, though he thought it was the wrong thing to do.

So back down the chimney they climbed with great difficulty, and they crawled through the wretched stovepipe into the dark stove. Here they listened behind the door, to find out what was happening in the room. Everything seemed quiet, so they opened the door and – oh, what a pity! There on the floor lay the Chinaman, in three pieces. When he had come running after them, he tumbled off the table and smashed. His whole back had come off in one piece, and his head had rolled into the corner. General-Headquarters-Hindquarters-Gives-Orders-Front-and-Rear-Sergeant-Billygoat-Legs was standing where he always stood, looking thoughtful.

"Oh, dear," said the little shepherdess, "poor old grandfather is all broken up, and it's entirely our fault. I shall never live through it." She wrung her delicate hands.

"He can be patched," said the chimney-sweep. "He can be riveted. Don't be so upset about him. A little glue for his back and a strong rivet in his neck, and he will be just as good as new, and just as disagreeable as he was before."

"Will he, really?" she asked, as they climbed back to their old place on the table.

"Here we are," said the chimney-sweep. "Back where we started from. We could have saved ourselves a lot of trouble."

"Now if only old grandfather were mended," said the little shepherdess. "Is mending terribly expensive?"

He was mended well enough. The family had his back glued together, and a strong rivet put through his neck. That made him as good as new, except that never again could he nod his head.

139

"It seems to me that you have grown haughty since your fall, though I don't see why you should be proud of it," General-Headquarters-Hindquarters-Gives-Orders-Front-and-Rear-Sergeant-Billygoat-Legs complained. "Am I to have her, or am I not?"

The chimney-sweep and the little shepherdess looked so pleadingly at the old Chinaman, for they were deathly afraid he would nod. But he didn't. He couldn't. And neither did he care to tell anyone that, forever and a day, he'd have to wear a rivet in his neck.

So the little porcelain people remained together. They thanked goodness for the rivet in grandfather's neck, and they kept on loving each other until the day they broke.

THE BELL

IN THE NARROW streets of the big town, toward evening when the sun was setting and the clouds shone like gold on the chimney tops, people would hear a strange sound like that of a church bell. But they heard it only for a few moments before it was lost in the rumble of city carriages and the voices of the multitudes, for such noises are very distracting. "Now the evening bell is ringing," people used to say. "The sun is setting."

People who were outside the town, where the houses were more scattered, with little gardens or fields between them, could see the evening sky in even more splendor and hear the bell more distinctly. It was as if the tones came from some church, buried in the silent and fragrant depths of the forest, and people looked solemnly in that direction.

A long time passed, and people began to say to each other, "I wonder if there really is a church out there in the woods? That bell has a mysterious, sweet tone. Let's go out there and see what it looks like."

So the rich people drove out, and the poor people walked out, but to all of them it seemed a very long way. When they reached a grove of willows on the outskirts of the woods, they sat down and looked up into the branches and imagined they were really in the heart of the forest. The town confectioner came out and set up his tent there, and then another confectioner came, and he hung a bell right above his tent; but the bell had no clapper and was all tarred over as a protection against the rain.

When the people went home again, they said it had all been very romantic, much more fun than a tea party. Three people even said that they had gone right through the forest to the far side and had still heard the strange sound of the bell, only then it seemed to be coming from the direction of town.

One of these even wrote a poem about the bell and compared its tones to those of a mother singing to a beloved child – no melody could be sweeter than the tones of that bell.

The Emperor of the country heard about the bell and issued a solemn proclamation promising that whoever discovered the source of the lovely sounds would receive the title of "Bell Ringer to the World," even it there were not really a bell there at all.

Of course, a great many people went to the woods now to try to gain that fine title, but only one of them came back with some kind of an explanation. No one had been deep enough into the forest – neither had he, for that matter – but just the same, he said the sound was made by a very large owl in an old hollow tree, a wise owl which continually knocked its head against the trunk of the tree. He wasn't quite sure whether the sound came from the bird's head or from the hollow trunk, but still he was appointed "Public Bell Ringer Number One," and every year he wrote a little treatise about the remarkable old owl. No one was much the wiser for it.

Now, on a certain Confirmation Day, the minister had preached a very beautiful and moving sermon; the children who were confirmed were deeply touched by it. It was a tremendously important day in their lives, for on this day they were leaving childhood behind and becoming grown-up persons. Their infant souls would take wing into the bodies of adults. It was a glorious, sunny day, and after the confirmation the children walked together out of the town, and from the depths of the woods the strange tolling of the bell came with a mysterious clear sweetness.

At once all the children decided to go into the woods and find the bell. All except three, that is to say. The first of these three just had to go home and try on a new ball dress; for that forthcoming ball was the very reason she had been confirmed at this time, otherwise she would have had to wait until next year's ceremony. The second was a poor boy who had borrowed his confirmation coat and boots from the landlord's son and had to give them back by a certain hour. And the third said he never went to a strange place without his parents; he had always been a dutiful child and would continue to be good, even though he was confirmed now. The others made fun of him for this, which was very wrong of them indeed.

So these three dropped out while the others started off into the woods. The sun shone, the birds sang, and the children sang too, walking along hand in hand. They had not yet received any responsibilities or high position in life – all were equal in the eye of God on that Confirmation Day.

But soon two of the smallest grew tired and returned to town; two other little girls sat down to make wreaths and so did not go any farther. The rest went on until they reached the willows where the confectioner had his tent, and then they said, "Well, here we are! You see, the bell doesn't really exist at all; it's just something people imagine!"

And then suddenly the sound of the bell came from the depths of the woods, so sweet and solemn that four or five of the young people decided to follow it still farther. The underbrush was so thick and close that their advance was most difficult. Woodruff and anemone grew almost too high; convolvuluses and blackberry brambles hung in long garlands from tree to tree, where the nightingale sang and the sunbeams played through the leaves. It was so lovely and peaceful, but it was a bad place for the girls, because they would get their dresses torn on the brambles.

There were large boulders overgrown with many-colored mosses, and a fresh spring bubbled forth among them with a strange little gurgling sound. "Cluck, cluck," it said.

"I wonder if that can be the bell," one of the children thought, lying down to listen to it. "I'd better look into this." So he remained there, and the others went on without him.

They came to a little hut, all made of branches and tree bark. Its roof was covered with roses, and over it a wild apple tree was bending as if it would shower its blessings down on the little house. The long sprays of the apple tree clustered around the gable, and on that there hung a little bell!

Could that be the one they had heard? Yes, they all – except for one boy – agreed it must be. This one boy said it was much too small and delicate to be heard so far away, and besides, its tones were very different from those that moved human hearts so strangely. The boy who spoke was a king's son, so the other children said, "Of course he thinks he knows a lot more than anybody else."

So the king's son went on alone, and as he proceeded deeper into the woods, his heart was filled more and more with the solitude of the forest. He could still hear the little bell which had satisfied the others, and when the wind was from the right direction, he could even hear the voices of the people around the confectioner's tent, singing while they were having their tea.

But above all rose the peeling of that mysterious bell. Now it sounded as if an organ were being played with it, and the tones came from the left-hand side, where the heart is.

Suddenly there was a rustling in the bushes, and a little boy stood before the king's son. He was wearing wooden shoes and such a short jacket that the sleeves did not cover his long wrists. They knew each other at once, for this was the poor boy who had had to go back to return the coat and boots to the landlord's son. This done, he had changed again into his shabby clothes and wooden shoes and come into the woods, for the bell sounded so loudly and so deeply that he had to follow its call.

"Then let's go on together," suggested the king's son.

But the poor boy in his wooden shoes was very shy, pulled at his short sleeves, and said he was afraid he could not walk as fast as the king's son; besides, he was sure the sound of the bell came from the right, because that side looked much more beautiful.

"Then I guess we can't go together," said the king's son, nodding his head to the poor boy who went in the direction he thought best, which took him into the thickest and darkest part of the forest. The thorns tore his shabby clothes and scratched his face, hands, and feet until they bled.

The king's son received some scratches too, but the sun shone on his path. And he is the one we will follow, for he was a bright young lad.

"I will and must find that bell," he said, "even if I have to go to the end of the world!"

High in the trees above him ugly monkeys sat and grinned and showed their teeth. "Let's throw things at him!" they said to each other. "Let's thrash him, 'cause he's the son of a king."

But he went on unwearied, and went farther and farther into the woods, where the most wonderful flowers were growing. There were lilies white as stars, with blood-red stamens; there were light-blue tulips that gleamed in the breeze, and apple trees with their fruit shining like big soap bubbles. Imagine how those trees sparkled in the sunlight! Around the beautiful rolling green meadows where the deer played grew massive oaks and beeches; and wherever one of the trees had a crack in the bark, mosses and long tendrils were growing out of it. In some of the meadows were quiet lakes, where beautiful white swans swam and beat the air gently with their wings. The king's son often stopped to listen, for the tones of the bell sometimes seemed to come from the depths of these lakes; then again he felt sure that the notes were coming from farther away in the forest.

Slowly the sun set, and the clouds turned a fiery red; a stillness, a deep stillness, settled over the forest. The boy fell on his knees, sang his evening hymn, and said to himself, "I'll never find what I'm seeking now. The sun is setting, and the night is coming – the dark night. But perhaps I can catch one more glimpse of the round red sun before it disappears below the horizon. I'll climb up on those rocks; they rise up as high as the tallest trees!" Seizing the roots and creepers, he slowly made his way up the slippery stones, where the water snakes writhed and the toads and frogs seemed to be barking at him. Yet he reached the summit just as the sun was going down. Oh, what a wonderful sight!

The sea, the great, the beautiful sea, rolling its long waves against the shore, lay stretched out before him, and the sun stood like a large shining altar, where ocean and heaven met; the whole world seemed to melt together in glowing colors. The forest sang, the sea sang, and the heart of the boy sang too. Nature was a vast, holy church, where the trees and drifting clouds were the pillars; flowers and

The sea, the great, the beautiful sea, rolling its long waves against the shore, lay stretched out. (Fritz Kredel)

grass made the velvet carpet, and heaven itself was the great dome. Up there, the red colors faded as the sun sank into the ocean, but then millions of stars sprang out, like millions of diamond lamps, and the king's son spread out his arms in joy toward the heavens, the sun, and the forest.

At that moment, from the right-hand path, there appeared the poor boy with the short sleeves and the wooden shoes. He had come there as quickly and by following his own path. Joyfully they ran towards each other, and held each other by the hand in the great tabernacle of Nature and Poetry, while above them sounded the invisible, holy bell. The blessed spirits floated around them and lifted up their voices in a joyful hallelujah.

THE LITTLE MATCH GIRL

IT WAS SO terribly cold. Snow was falling, and it was almost dark. Evening came on, the last evening of the year. In the cold and gloom a poor little girl, bareheaded and barefoot, was walking through the streets. Of course when she had left her house she'd had slippers on, but what good had they been? They were very big slippers, way too big for her, for they belonged to her mother. The little girl had lost them running across the road, where two carriages had rattled by terribly fast. One slipper she'd not been able to find again, and a boy had run off with the other, saying he could use it very well as a cradle some day when he had children of his own. And so the little girl walked on her naked feet, which were quite red and blue with the cold. In an old apron she carried several packages of matches, and she held a box of them in her hand. No one had bought any from her all day long, and no one had given her a cent.

Shivering with cold and hunger, she crept along, a picture of misery, poor little girl! The snowflakes fell on her long fair hair, which hung in pretty curls over her neck. In all the windows lights were shining, and there was a wonderful smell of roast goose, for it was New Year's Eve. Yes, she thought of that!

In a corner formed by two houses, one of which projected farther out into the street than the other, she sat down and drew up her little feet under her. She was getting colder and colder, but did not dare to go home, for she had sold no matches, nor earned a single cent, and her father would surely beat her. Besides, it was cold at home, for they had nothing over them but a roof through which the wind whistled even though the biggest cracks had been stuffed with straw and rags.

Her hands were almost dead with cold. Oh, how much one little match might warm her! If she could only take one from the box and rub it against the wall and warm her hands. She drew one out. *R–r–ratch!* How it sputtered and burned! It made a warm, bright flame, like a little candle, as she held her hands over it; but it gave a strange light! It really seemed to the little girl as if she were sitting before a great

She was sitting under the most beautiful Christmas tree. (Arthur Rackham)

iron stove with shining brass knobs and a brass cover. How wonderfully the fire burned! How comfortable it was! The youngster stretched out her feet to warm them too; then the little flame went out, the stove vanished, and she had only the remains of the burnt match in her hand.

She struck another match against the wall. It burned brightly, and when the light fell upon the wall it became transparent like a thin veil, and she could see through it into a room. On the table a snow-white cloth was spread, and on it stood a shining dinner service. The roast goose steamed gloriously, stuffed with apples and prunes. And what was still better, the goose jumped down from the dish and waddled along the floor with a knife and fork in its breast, right over to the little girl. Then the match went out, and she could see only the thick, cold wall. She lighted another match. Then she was sitting under the most beautiful Christmas tree. It was much larger and much more beautiful than the

one she had seen last Christmas through the glass door at the rich merchant's home. Thousands of candles burned on the green branches, and colored pictures like those in the printshops looked down at her. The little girl reached both her hands toward them. Then the match went out. But the Christmas lights mounted higher. She saw them now as bright stars in the sky. One of them fell down, forming a long line of fire.

"Now someone is dying," thought the little girl, for her old grandmother, the only person who had loved her, and who was now dead, had told her that when a star fell down a soul went up to God. She rubbed another match against the wall. It became bright again, and in the glow the old grandmother stood clear and shining, kind and lovely.

"Grandmother!" cried the child. "Oh, take me with you! I know you will disappear when the match is burned out. You will vanish like the warm stove, the wonderful roast goose and the beautiful big Christmas tree!"

And she quickly struck the whole bundle of matches, for she wished to keep her grandmother with her. And the matches burned with such a glow that it became brighter than daylight. Grandmother had never been so grand and beautiful. She took the little girl in her arms, and both of them flew in brightness and joy above the earth, very, very high, and up there was neither cold, nor hunger, nor fear – they were with God.

But in the corner, leaning against the wall, sat the little girl with red cheeks and smiling mouth, frozen to death on the last evening of the old year. The New Year's sun rose upon a little pathetic figure. The child sat there, stiff and cold, holding the matches, of which one bundle was almost burned.

"She wanted to warm herself," the people said. No one imagined what beautiful things she had seen, and how happily she had gone with her old grandmother into the bright New Year.

LITTLE TUCK

YES, THAT WAS little Tuck. As a matter of fact, his name wasn't really Tuck, but before he could speak plainly he called himself Tuck. That was supposed to mean "Carl," but "Tuck" does just as well if one only knows it.

Now he had to learn his lessons and at the same time take care of his sister Gustava, who was much smaller than he; and it was pretty hard to manage the two things at once. So the poor boy sat with his little sister on his lap, and sang to her all the songs he knew, at the same time glancing into his geography book, which was open before him. By the next morning he was supposed to know all the towns in the counties of Seeland by heart, and everything there was to know about them.

Then his mother returned, for she had been away, and took little Gustava herself. Tuck ran quickly to the window and studied until he almost read his eyes out, for it was getting darker and darker, and his poor mother could not afford candles.

Suddenly his mother looked out of the window. "There goes the old washerwoman from down the lane," she said. "She can hardly drag herself along, and she has to carry a pail of water from the well, too! Be a good boy, Tuck, and run over and help the old woman."

And Little Tuck jumped up and ran to help the old woman, but when he got home again it was quite dark. Nothing was said about candles, so all he could do was go to bed – and his bed was an old folding bench. He lay there thinking about Seeland, and his geography lesson, and everything the teacher had said. He should certainly have studied that lesson some more, but of course he couldn't do that now.

So he put his geography book under his pillow, because he had heard that this helps a great deal when you want to learn a lesson. But you can't depend on that!

There he lay, thinking and thinking, then all of a sudden it seemed as if someone kissed his eyes and lips. He slept and yet he didn't sleep, and he felt as if the old washerwoman was looking at him out of the kind eyes and saying, "It would be a great shame if you didn't know your lesson tomorrow. You helped me, and now I'll help you; and our Lord will help us both."

Then all at once the book under his pillow began to wriggle and squirm around!

"Kekelikee! Cluck, cluck!" It was a hen that came crawling out – and she was from Kjöge. "I'm a Kjöge hen," she said. And then she told him all about her town, and how many people there were in it, and about a battle that had taken place there once, though that wasn't really worth mentioning.

"Krible, kragle, bang!" Something dropped down. And a wooden bird appeared; it was the parrot from the shooting match at Praestö. The bird told the little boy very proudly that there were just as many inhabitants in its town as there were nails in its body. "Thorvaldsen used to live around the corner from me! Bang! Here I lie comfortably!"

But Little Tuck was no longer lying in bed – all of a sudden he was on horseback! Gallopy, gallopy, it went! He was sitting in front of a splendidly dressed knight, with shining helmet and nodding plume. On through the woods they galloped to the old town of Vordingborg, and that was a big and lively town. High towers rose above the royal castle, and radiant lights streamed from its windows; inside there was singing and dancing, and King Valdemar led the lovely court ladies in the dance. But soon morning came, and as the sun rose the town seemed to melt away, and the King's castle sank down, one tower after another, until at last only one tower was left standing on the hill where the castle had been, and the town had become very small and very poor. The schoolboys came along with their books under their arms, and said, "Two thousand inhabitants," but that wasn't true. There were not so many as that.

And still little Tuck lay in his bed, as if he were dreaming and not dreaming at the same time, but there seemed to be someone standing close beside him.

"Little Tuck, Little Tuck!" someone said. It was a sailor, a very little fellow, small enough to have been a midshipman, although he wasn't a midshipman. "I bring you many greetings from Korsör, that's a growing town, a lively flourishing town with steamboats and mail coaches. In olden times people used to call it ugly, but that's not true any more.

" 'I lie by the seashore,' Korsör says to you. 'I have highroads and beautiful parks, and I once gave birth to a poet who was very witty. That's more than can be said for all of them. I wanted to send a ship around the world, but I didn't. But I could have done it. Anyway, I smell deliciously, because close by my gates, the most beautiful roses bloom!'"

Little Tuck saw them, and everything was green and red before his eyes, but when the confusion of colors was over, they changed to wooden heights, sloping down to the sparkling waters of a fiord. A stately old twin-spired church towered above the waters. From out of the cliffside springs of water rushed down in bubbling streams, and nearby sat an old king with a golden crown on his long hair. It was King Hroar of the Springs, and the place is now the town of Roskilde (Hroar's Springs). Up the hill and into the old church the kings and queens of Denmark walked hand in hand, all with their golden crowns, and the organ was playing, and the springs rippled.

"Don't forget the towns of the kingdom!" said King Hroar. Then all at once everything vanished – and where had it all gone? It was like turning a leaf in a book.

Now an old peasant woman stood before Little Tuck; she was a weeding woman from Sorö, where grass grows in the market place. She had thrown her gray linen apron over her head and down her back, and it was soaking wet – it must have been raining.

"Yes, it certainly has been," she said. She knew many of the comic parts from Holberg's comedies, and all about Valdemar and Absolon.

But all at once she squatted down and wagged her head, just as if she were about to leap. "Ko-ax," she said. "It's wet! It's wet! It's quiet as a grave in Sorö!" Suddenly she was a frog, "Ko-ax!" and then she became an old woman again. "You should always dress according to the weather!" she explained. "It's wet! Very wet! My town is just like a bottle – you go in with the cork, and you have to come out the same way. In the old days I used to have beautiful fish there, and now I have red-cheeked little boys down in the bottom of the bottle. They learn a lot of wisdom there – Greek! Greek! Hebrew! Hebrew! Ko-ax!" It sounded like the croaking of frogs, or the creaking of big boots as you walk across the moor; always the same sound – so monotonous – so tiresome – yes, so tiresome that Little Tuck fell into a deep sleep, which was the best thing in the world for him.

But even in this sleep he had a dream or something like that. It seemed that his little sister, Gustava, with her blue eyes and golden curly hair, had suddenly become a grown-up beautiful lady, and she could fly without wings. Together they flew over the green forests and the deep blue waters of Seeland.

"Do you hear the cock crowing, Little Tuck? Cock-a-doodle-do! The hens are flying up out of Kjöge. You'll have a big, big chicken yard; you'll never suffer want or hunger; yes, you shall shoot the parrot, as the saying goes; you shall be a rich and happy man. Your manor shall rise up like King Valdemar's towers, and it shall be richly adorned with marble statues, like those in Praestö! Can you understand me? The fame of your name shall travel around the world, like this ship that was to sail from Korsör!" And from Roskilde town came the voice of King Hroar, "Remember the towns of the kingdom!"

"There you shall speak wisely and well, Little Tuck. And when you are in your grave you shall sleep as peacefully as—"

"As if I were in Sorö!" cried Little Tuck, and then he woke up.

It was broad daylight, and he couldn't remember the smallest part of his dream. And he wasn't supposed to either, for we shouldn't know things that are going to happen in the future.

Now he sprang quickly out of bed and read his geography book, and at once he knew the whole lesson!

And the old washerwoman put her head in the door and nodded good morning to him.

"Many thanks for your help yesterday, dear child," she said. "May the Lord make all your dreams come true!"

Little Tuck didn't know anything that he had dreamed, but you see – our Lord knew it!

THE SHADOW

IT IS IN the hot countries that the sun burns down in earnest, turning the people there a deep mahogany-brown. In the hottest countries of all they are seared into negroes, but it was not quite that hot in this country to which a man of learning had come from the colder north. He expected to go about there just as he had at home, but he soon discovered that this was a mistake. He and other sensible souls had to stay inside. The shutters were drawn and the doors were closed all day long. It looked just as if everyone were asleep or away from home. The narrow street of high houses where he lived was so situated that from morning till night the sun beat down on it – unbearably!

To this young and clever scholar from the colder north, it felt as if he were sitting in a blazing hot oven. It exhausted him so that he became very thin, and even his shadow shrank much smaller than it had been at home. Only in the evenings, after sundown, did the man and his shadow begin to recover.

This was really a joy to see. As soon as a candle was brought into the room, the shadow had to stretch itself to get its strength back. It stretched up to the wall, yes, even along the ceiling, so tall did it grow. To stretch himself,

It stretched up to the wall, yes, even along the ceiling, so tall did it grow. (Fritz Kredel)

the scholar went out on the balcony. As soon as the stars came out in the beautifully clear sky, he felt as if he had come back to life.

In warm countries each window has a balcony, and in all the balconies up and down the street people came out to breathe the fresh air that one needs, even if one is already a fine mahogany-brown. Both up above and down below, things became lively. Tailors, shoemakers – everybody – moved out in the street. Chairs and tables were brought out, and candles were lighted, yes, candles by the thousand. One man talked, another sang, people strolled about, carriages drove by, and donkeys trotted along, *ting-a-ling-a-ling*, for their harness had bells on it. There were church bells ringing, hymn singing, and funeral processions. There were boys in the street firing off Roman candles. Oh yes, it was lively as lively can be down in that street.

Only one house was quiet – the one directly across from where the scholarly stranger lived. Yet someone lived there, for flowers on the balcony grew and thrived under that hot sun, which they could not have done unless they were watered. So someone must be watering them, and there must be people in the house. Along in the evening, as a matter of fact, the door across the street was opened. But it was dark inside, at least in the front room. From somewhere in the house, farther back, came the sound of music. The scholarly stranger thought the music was marvelous, but it is quite possible that he only imagined this, for out there in the warm countries he thought everything was marvelous – except the sun. The stranger's landlord said that he didn't know who had rented the house across the street. No one was ever to be seen over there, and as for the music, he found it extremely tiresome. He said:

"It's just as if somebody sits there practicing a piece that's beyond him – always the selfsame piece. 'I'll play it right yet,' he probably says, but he doesn't, no matter how long he tries."

One night the stranger woke up. He slept with the windows to his balcony open, and as the breeze blew his curtain aside he fancied that a marvelous radiance came from the balcony across the street. The colors of all the flowers were as brilliant as flames. In their midst stood a maiden, slender and lovely. It seemed as if a radiance came from her too. It actually hurt his eyes, but that was because he had opened them too wide in his sudden awakening.

One leap, and he was out of bed. Without a sound, he looked out through his curtains, but the maiden was gone. The flowers were no longer radiant, though they bloomed as fresh and fair as usual. The door was ajar and through it came music so lovely and soft that one could really feel very romantic about it. It was like magic. But who lived there? What entrance did they use? Facing the street, the lower floor of the house was a row of shops, and people couldn't run through them all the time.

On another evening, the stranger sat out on his balcony. The candle burned in the room behind him, so naturally his shadow was cast on the wall across the street. Yes, there it sat among the flowers, and when the stranger moved, it moved with him.

"I believe my shadow is the only living thing to be seen over there," the scholar thought to himself. "See how he makes himself at home among the flowers. The door stands ajar, and if my shadow were clever he'd step in, have a look around, and come back to tell me what he had seen."

"Yes," he said as a joke, "you ought to make yourself useful. Kindly step inside. Well, aren't you going?" He nodded to the shadow, and the shadow nodded back. "Run along now, but be sure to come back."

The stranger rose, and his shadow across the street rose with him. The stranger turned around, and his shadow turned too. If anyone had been watching closely, he would have seen the shadow enter the half-open balcony door in the house across the way at the same instant that the stranger returned to his room and the curtain fell behind him.

Next morning, when the scholar went out to take his coffee and read the newspapers, he said, "What's this?" as he came out in the sunshine. "I haven't any shadow! So it really did go away last night, and it stayed away. Isn't that annoying?"

What annoyed him most was not so much the loss of his shadow, but the knowledge that there was already a story about a man without a shadow. All the people at home knew that story. If he went back and told them his story they would say he was just imitating the old one. He did not care to be called unoriginal, so he decided to say nothing about it, which was the most sensible thing to do.

That evening he again went out on the balcony. He had placed the candle directly behind him, because he knew that a shadow always likes to use its master as a screen, but he could not coax it forth. He made himself short and he made himself tall, but there was no shadow. It didn't come forth. He hemmed and he hawed, but it was no use.

This was very vexing, but in the hot countries everything grows most rapidly, and in a week or so he noticed with great satisfaction that when he went out in the sunshine a new shadow was growing at his feet. The root must have been left with him. In three weeks' time he had a very presentable shadow, and as he started north again it grew longer and longer, until it got so long and large that half of it would have been quite sufficient.

The learned man went home and wrote books about those things in the world that are true, that are good, and that are beautiful.

The days went by and the years went past, many, many years in fact. Then one evening when he was sitting in his room he heard a soft tapping at his door. "Come in," said he, but no one came in. He opened the door and was confronted by a man so extremely thin that it gave him a strange feeling. However, the man was faultlessly dressed, and looked like a person of distinction.

"With whom do I have the honor of speaking?" the scholar asked.

"Ah," said the distinguished visitor, "I thought you wouldn't recognize me, now that I've put real flesh on my body and wear clothes. I don't suppose you ever expected to see me in such fine condition. Don't you know your old shadow? You must have thought I'd never come back. Things have gone remarkably well with me since I was last with you. I've thrived in every way, and if I have to buy my freedom, I can." He rattled a bunch of valuable charms that hung from his watch, and fingered the massive gold chain he wore around his neck. Ho! how his fingers flashed with diamond rings – and all this jewelry was real.

"No, I can't get over it!" said the scholar. "What does it all mean?"

"Nothing ordinary, you may be sure," said the shadow. "But you are no ordinary person and I, as you know, have followed in your footsteps from childhood. As soon as you thought me sufficiently experienced to strike out in the world for myself, I went my way. I have been immeasurably successful. But I felt a sort of longing to see you again before you die, as I suppose you must, and I wanted to see this country again. You know how one loves his native land. I know that you have got hold of another shadow. Do I owe anything to either of you? Be kind enough to let me know."

"Well! Is it really you?" said the scholar. "Why, this is most extraordinary! I would never have imagined that one's own shadow could come back in human form."

"Just tell me what I owe," said the shadow, "because I don't like to be in debt to anyone."

"How can you talk that way?" said the student. "What debt could there be? Feel perfectly free. I am tremendously pleased to hear of your good luck! Sit down, my old friend, and tell me a bit about how it all happened, and about what you saw in that house across the street from us in the warm country."

"Yes, I'll tell you all about it," the shadow said, as he sat down. "But you must promise that if you meet me anywhere you won't tell a soul in town about my having been your shadow. I intend to become engaged, for I can easily support a family."

"Don't you worry," said the scholar. "I won't tell anyone who you really are. I give you my hand on it. I promise, and a man is as good as his word."

"And a word is as good as its – shadow," the shadow said, for he couldn't put it any other way.

It was really remarkable how much of a man he had become, dressed all in black, with the finest cloth, patent-leather shoes, and an opera hat that could be pressed perfectly flat till it was only brim and top, not to mention those things we already know about – those seals, that gold chain, and the diamond rings. The shadow was well dressed indeed, and it was just this that made him appear human.

"Now I'll tell you," said the shadow, grinding his patent-leather shoes on the arm of the scholar's new shadow, which lay at his feet like a poodle dog. This was arrogance, perhaps, or possibly he was trying to make the new shadow stick to his own feet. The shadow on the floor lay quiet and still, and listened its best, so that it might learn how to get free and work its way up to be its own master.

"Do you know who lived in the house across the street from us?" the old shadow asked. "She was the most lovely of all creatures – she was Poetry herself. I lived there for three weeks, and it was as if I had lived there three thousand years, reading all that has ever been written. That's what I said, and it's the truth! I have seen it all, and I know everything."

"Poetry!" the scholar cried. "Yes, to be sure she often lives as a hermit in the large cities. Poetry! Yes, I saw her myself, for one brief moment, but my eyes were heavy with sleep. She stood on the balcony, as radiant as the Northern Lights. Tell me! Tell me! You were on the balcony. You went through the doorway, and then—"

"Then I was in the anteroom," said the shadow. "It was the room you were always staring at from across the way. There were no candles there, and the room was in twilight. But door upon door stood open in a whole series of brilliantly lit halls and reception rooms. That blaze of lights would have struck me dead had I gone as far as the room where the maiden was, but I was careful – I took my time, as one should."

"And then what did you see, my old friend?" the scholar asked.

"I saw everything, and I shall tell everything to you, but – it's not that I'm proud – but as I am a free man and well educated, not to mention my high standing and my considerable fortune, I do wish you wouldn't call me your old friend."

"I beg your pardon!" said the scholar. "It's an old habit, and hard to change. You are perfectly right, my dear sir, and I'll remember it. But now, my dear sir, tell me of all that you saw."

"All?" said the shadow. "For I saw it all, and I know everything."

"How did the innermost rooms look?" the scholar asked. "Was it like a green forest? Was it like a holy temple? Were the rooms like the starry skies seen from some high mountain?"

"Everything was there," said the shadow. "I didn't quite go inside. I stayed in the dark anteroom, but my place there was perfect. I saw everything, and I know everything. I have been in the antechamber at the court of Poetry."

"But what did you see? Did the gods of old march through the halls? Did the old heroes fight there? Did fair children play there and tell their dreams?"

"I was there, I tell you, so you must understand that I saw all that there was to be seen. Had you come over, it would not have made a man of you, as it did of me. Also, I learned to understand my inner self, what is born in me, and the relationship between me and Poetry. Yes, when I was with you I did not think of such things, but you must remember how wonderfully I always expanded at sunrise and sunset. And in the moonlight I almost seemed more real than you. Then I did not understand myself, but in that anteroom I came to know my true nature. I was a man! I came out completely changed. But you were no longer in the warm country. Being a man, I was ashamed to be seen as I was. I lacked shoes, clothes, and all the surface veneer which makes a man.

"I went into hiding – this is confidential, and you must not write it in any of your books. I went into hiding under the skirts of the cake-woman. Little she knew what she concealed. Not until evening did I venture out. I ran through the streets in the moonlight and stretched myself tall against the walls. It's such a pleasant way of scratching one's back. Up I ran and down I ran, peeping into the highest windows, into drawing rooms, and into garrets. I peered in where no one else could peer. I saw what no one else could see, or should see. Taken all in all, it's a wicked world. I would not care to be a man if it were not considered the fashionable thing to be. I saw the most incredible behavior among men and women, fathers and mothers, and among those 'perfectly darling' children. I saw what nobody knows but everybody would like to know, and that is what wickedness goes on next door. If I had written it in a newspaper, oh, how widely it would have been read! But instead I wrote to the people directly concerned, and there was the most terrible consternation in every town to which I came. They were so afraid of me, and yet so remarkably fond of me. The professors appointed me a professor, and the tailor made me new clothes – my wardrobe is most complete. The master of the mint coined new money for me, the women called me such a handsome man; and so I became the man

I am. Now I must bid you good-by. Here's my card. I live on the sunny side of the street, and I am always at home on rainy days." The shadow took his leave.

"How extraordinary," said the scholar.

The days passed. The years went by. And the shadow called again. "How goes it?" he asked.

"Alack," said the scholar, "I still write about the true, the good, and the beautiful, but nobody cares to read about such things. I feel quite despondent, for I take it deeply to heart."

"I don't," said the shadow. "I am getting fat, as one should. You don't know the ways of the world, and that's why your health suffers. You ought to travel. I'm taking a trip this summer. Will you come with me? I'd like to have a traveling companion. Will you come along as my shadow? It would be a great pleasure to have you along, and I'll pay all the expenses."

"No, that's a bit too much," said the scholar.

"It depends on how you look at it," said the shadow. "It will do you a lot of good to travel. Will you be my shadow? The trip won't cost you a thing."

"This has gone much too far!" said the scholar.

"Well, that's the way the world goes," the shadow told him, "and that's the way it will keep on going." And away he went.

The learned man was not at all well. Sorrow and trouble pursued him, and what he had to say about the good, the true, and the beautiful, appealed to most people about as much as roses appeal to a cow. Finally he grew quite ill.

"You really look like a shadow," people told him, and he trembled at the thought.

"You must visit a watering place," said the shadow, who came to see him again. "There's no question about it. I'll take you with me, for old friendship's sake. I'll pay for the trip, and you can write about it, as well as doing your best to amuse me along the way. I need to go to a watering place too, because my beard isn't growing as it should. That's a sort of disease too, and one can't get along without a beard. Now do be reasonable and accept my proposal. We shall travel just like friends!"

So off they started. The shadow was master now, and the master was the shadow. They drove together, rode together, and walked together, side by side, before or behind each other, according to the way the sun fell. The shadow was careful to take the place of the master, and the scholar didn't much care, for he had an innocent heart, besides being most affable and friendly.

One day he said to the shadow, "As we are now fellow-travelers and have grown up together, shall we not call each other by our first names, the way good companions should? It is much more intimate."

"That's a splendid idea!" said the shadow, who was now the real master. "What you say is most open-hearted and friendly. I shall be just as friendly and open-hearted with you. As a scholar, you are perfectly well aware how strange is man's nature. Some men cannot bear the touch of gray paper. It sickens them. Others quail if they hear a nail scratched across a pane of glass. For my part, I am affected in just that way when I hear you call me by my first name. I feel myself ground down to the earth, as I was in my first position with you. You understand. It's a matter of sensitivity, not pride. I cannot let you call me by my first name, but I shall be glad to call you by yours, as a compromise." So thereafter the shadow called his one-time master by his first name.

"It has gone too far," the scholar thought, "when I must call him by his last name while he calls me by my first!" But he had to put up with it.

At last they came to the watering place. Among the many people was a lovely Princess. Her malady was that she saw things too clearly, which can be most upsetting. For instance, she immediately saw that the newcomer was a very different sort of person from all the others.

"He has come here to make his beard grow, they say. But I see the real reason. He can't cast a shadow."

Her curiosity was aroused, and on the promenade she addressed this stranger directly. Being a king's daughter, she did not have to stand upon ceremony, so she said to him straight:

"Your trouble is that you can't cast a shadow."

"Your Royal Highness must have improved considerably," the shadow replied. "I know your malady is that you see too clearly, but you are improving. As it happens, I do have a most unusual shadow. Don't you see that figure who always accompanies me? Other people have a common shadow, but I do not care for what is common to all. Just as we often allow our servants better fabrics for their liveries than we wear ourselves, so I have had my shadow decked out as a man. Why, you see I have even outfitted him with a shadow of his own. It is expensive, I grant you, but I like to have something uncommon."

"My!" the Princess thought. "Can I really be cured? This is the foremost watering place in the world, and in these days water has come to have wonderful medicinal powers. But I shan't leave just as the place is becoming amusing. I have taken a liking to this stranger. I only hope his beard won't grow, for then he would leave us."

That evening, the Princess and the shadow danced together in the great ballroom. She was light, but he was lighter still. Never had she danced with such a partner. She told him what country she came from, and he knew it well. He had been there, but it was during her absence. He had looked through every window, high or low. He had seen this and he had seen that. So he could answer the Princess and suggest things that astounded her. She was convinced that he must be the wisest man in all the world. His knowledge impressed her

And to prison he went. (Fritz Kredel)

so deeply, that while they were dancing she fell in love with him. The shadow could tell, for her eyes transfixed him, through and through. They danced again, and she came very near telling him she loved him, but it wouldn't do to be rash. She had to think of her country, and her throne, and the many people over whom she would reign.

"He is a clever man," she said to herself, "and that is a good thing. He dances charmingly, and that is good too. But is his knowledge more than superficial? That's just as important, so I must examine him."

Tactfully, she began asking him the most difficult questions, which she herself could not have answered. The shadow made a wry face.

"You can't answer me?" said the Princess.

"I knew all that in my childhood," said the shadow. "Why, I believe that my shadow over there by the door can answer you."

"Your shadow!" said the Princess. "That would be remarkable indeed!"

"I can't say for certain," said the shadow, "but I'm inclined to think so, because he has followed me about and listened to me for so many years. Yes, I am inclined to believe so. But your Royal Highness must permit me to tell you that he is quite proud of being able to pass for a man, so if he is to be in the right frame of mind to answer your questions he must be treated just as if he were human."

"I like that!" said the Princess.

So she went to the scholar in the doorway, and spoke with him about the sun and the moon, and about people, what they are inside, and what they seem to be on the surface. He answered her wisely and well.

"What a man that must be, to have such a wise shadow!" she thought. "It will be a godsend to my people, and to my country if I choose him for my consort. That's just what I'll do!"

The Princess and the shadow came to an understanding, but no one was to know about it until she returned to her own kingdom.

"No one. Not even my shadow!" said the shadow. And he had his own private reason for this.

Finally they came to the country that the Princess ruled when she was at home.

"Listen, my good friend," the shadow said to the scholar, "I am now as happy and strong as one can be, so I'll do something very special for you. You shall live with me in my palace, drive with me in my royal carriage, and have a hundred thousand dollars a year. However, you must let yourself be called a shadow by everybody. You must not ever say that you have been a man, and once a year, while I sit on the balcony in the sunshine, you must lie at my feet as shadows do. For I tell you I am going to marry the Princess, and the wedding is to take place this very evening."

"No! That's going too far," said the scholar. "I will not. I won't do it. That would be betraying the whole country and the Princess too. I'll tell them everything – that I am the man, and you are the shadow merely dressed as a man."

"No one would believe it," said the shadow. "Be reasonable, or I'll call the sentry."

"I'll go straight to the Princess," said the scholar.

"But I will go first," said the shadow, "and you shall go to prison."

And to prison he went, for the sentries obeyed the one who, they knew, was to marry the Princess.

"Why, you're trembling," the Princess said, as the shadow entered her room. "What has happened? You mustn't fall ill this evening, just as we are about to be married."

"I have been through the most dreadful experience that could happen to anyone," said the shadow. "Just imagine! Of course a poor shadow's head can't stand very much. But imagine! My shadow has gone mad. He takes himself for a man, and – imagine it! he takes me for his shadow."

"How terrible!" said the Princess. "He's locked up, I hope!"

"Oh, of course. I'm afraid he will never recover."

"Poor shadow," said the Princess. "He is very unhappy. It would really be a charitable act to relieve him of the little bit of life he has left. And, after thinking it over carefully, my opinion is that it will be necessary to put him out of the way."

"That's certainly hard, for he was a faithful servant," said the shadow. He managed to sigh.

"You have a noble soul," the Princess told him.

The whole city was brilliantly lit that evening. The cannons boomed, and the soldiers presented arms. That was the sort of wedding it was! The Princess and the shadow stepped out on the balcony to show themselves and be cheered, again and again.

The scholar heard nothing of all this, for they had already done away with him.

THE OLD HOUSE

SOMEWHERE IN THE street stood an old old house; it was almost three hundred years old, as you could tell from the date cut into the great beam. Tulips and hopbines and also whole verses of poetry were carved into the wood as people used to do in those days, and over every window a mocking face was cut into the beam. The second story hung way out over the ground floor, and right under the eaves was a leaden spout with a dragon's head. Rain water was supposed to run out of the dragon's mouth, but it came from his belly instead, for there was a hole in it.

All of the other houses in the street were so neat and modern, with large windowpanes and smooth walls, that you could easily tell they would have nothing to do with the old house.

They evidently thought, "How long do you suppose that decrepit old thing is going to stand there, making an eyesore of our street? And that bay window stands so far out we can't see from our windows what's happening in that direction. Those front steps are as broad as those of a palace, and as high as those which go up to a church tower! The iron railings – they look like the door to an old family vault! And those dreadful brass rails on them! It makes one feel ashamed!"

Across the street were other neat and modern houses, and they thought the same way. But at the window in the house directly opposite sat a little boy with bright shining eyes and fresh rosy cheeks. And he liked the old house best of all those on the street, whether by sunshine or by moonlight.

When he looked across at the wall where the mortar had fallen out, he could imagine the strangest pictures. He could see the street as it was in the old days; he could see soldiers with halberds, and the houses with their steps and projecting windows and pointed gables, and rainspouts in the shapes of dragons and serpents. Yes, to him that was indeed a house worth looking at!

An old man lived over there – an old man who wore old-fashioned plush breeches and a coat with big brass buttons, and a wig that you could plainly tell was a real one. Every morning an old male servant came, to put the rooms in order and do the marketing, but aside from that, the old man in the plush breeches lived all alone in his old house. Sometimes he came to the window and looked out, and the little boy waved to him, and the old man waved back, and so they became acquaintances and then friends. Of course, they had never spoken to each other, but that really made no difference.

One day the little boy heard his parents say, "The old man over there is very well to do, but he's terribly lonely!"

Next Sunday the little boy wrapped a small object in a piece of paper, went downstairs to his doorway, and, when the old servant who did the marketing came by, said to him, "Look, sir, will you please give this to the old gentleman across the way? I have two tin soldiers; this is one of them, and I want him to have it 'cause I know he's terribly lonely."

The old servant looked very pleased as he nodded, and took the tin soldier across to the house. And later he brought back a message inviting the little boy to come over and pay a visit. Happily the little boy asked his parents' permission, then went across to the old house.

The brass knobs on the railings shone brighter than ever – one would think they had been especially polished in honor of his visit. And the little trumpeters carved in tulips on the doorway seemed to puff out their cheeks and blow with all their might, "Tratteratra! The little boy approaches! Tratteratra!" Then the door opened.

The whole hallway was hung with old portraits of knights in armor and ladies in silken gowns, and the armor seemed to rattle and the silken gowns rustle! Then there was a flight of stairs that went a long way up and a little way down, and then the little boy came out on a balcony. It was very dilapidated, with grass and leaves growing out of holes and long crevices, for the whole balcony outside, the yard, and the walls were so overgrown that it looked like a garden. But still it was just a balcony. There were old flowerpots with faces and donkey's ears, and flowers growing out of them just as they pleased. One of the pots was almost brimming over with carnations – that is, with the green part; shoot grew by shoot, and each seemed to say quite distinctly, "The air has blessed me, and the sun has kissed me and promised me a little flower on Sunday! A little flower on Sunday!"

Now the little boy entered a room where the walls were covered with pigskin and printed with golden flowers.

"Gilding fades fast;
But pigskin will last,"

said the walls.

There were heavily carved easy chairs there, with high backs and arms on both sides. "Sit down! Sit down!" they cried. "Oh, how I creak! I know I'll get the gout, like the old cupboard! Oh!"

And at last the little boy came into the room where the bay window was, and there sat the old man.

"I thank you for the tin soldier, my young friend," he said. "And I thank you again because you came over to see me."

"Thanks! Thanks!" or perhaps "Creak! Creak!" sounded from all the furniture. And there was so much of it in the room that the pieces seemed to crowd in each other's way, trying to get a look at the little boy.

In the middle of the wall hung a painting of a beautiful lady, young and happy, but dressed as in olden times, with clothes that stood out stiffly, and with powdered hair. She neither said, "Thanks!" nor "Creak!" but just looked with mild eyes at the little boy. He promptly asked, "Where did she come from?"

"From the secondhand dealer down the street," said the old man, "where there are so many pictures. No one knows or cares anything about them, for all the people are buried. That lady has been dead and gone these fifty years, but I knew her in the old days."

In a glass frame beneath the portrait there hung a bouquet of withered flowers; they, too, must have been fifty years old – at least they looked it.

The pendulum of the great clock slowly swung to and fro, and the hands slowly turned, and everything in the room slowly became still older, but they didn't notice it.

"My mother and daddy say," said the little boy, "that you're terribly lonely."

"Oh," he answered, "the old thoughts, with what they may bring with them, come to see me, and now you come, too! I'm really very happy."

Then he took a picture book down from the shelf. There were long processions and strange coaches such as one never sees nowadays, soldiers who looked like the knave of clubs, and tradesmen with waving banners. The tailors had a banner that showed a pair of shears held by two lions; and the shoemakers had on theirs not a boot, but an eagle with two heads, for shoemakers must have everything in pairs. What a wonderful picture book that was!

And the old man went into the next room to fetch jam, apples, and nuts. Yes, the old house was a wonderful place. "I can't bear this any longer," cried the tin soldier, who was sitting on a chest of drawers. "It's so lonely and sad

here! Anyone who has been in a family circle as I have can't get used to this sort of life. I can't bear it any longer! The days are so long, and the evenings are still longer! Things here aren't the way they were over at your house, where your father and mother spoke so pleasantly, and you and the other nice children made such delightful, happy noises. How lonely this old man is! Do you think he ever gets a kiss? Do you think he ever gets a kindly look or a Christmas tree? He'll get nothing but a funeral – I simply can't stand it any longer!"

"You mustn't let it make you so sad," said the little boy. "I think it's fun here, and then all the old memories, with what they may bring with them, come to visit here."

"Yes," said the tin soldier, "but I can't see them, because I don't know them. I tell you I can't stand it!"

"But you must!" replied the little boy firmly.

Then the old man came back with his face all smiling, and with the most delicious jam and apples and nuts! So the little boy forgot about the tin soldier.

He went home, happy and pleased, and days and weeks passed, while nods and waves were exchanged to the old house and from the old house. Then he went over to call again.

Again the carved trumpeters seemed to blow, "Tratteratra! The little boy approaches! Tratteratra!" And the swords and armor on the knight's paintings rattled, and the silken gowns rustled; the pigskin spoke, and the old chairs had rheumatism in their backs – "Ouch!" It was just like the first time, for in that house one day or hour was just like another.

"I can't bear it!" wailed the tin soldier. "I've been shedding tin tears – it's too sad here! I'd rather go to the wars, and lose arms and legs; at least that would be a change! I just can't stand it! Now I know what it's like to have a visit from one's old memories and what they may bring with them. One of mine came to see me, and let me tell you that isn't a very pleasant experience! I nearly jumped down from this chest!

"Because I saw you all over there so clearly, as if you really were right here! It was again that Sunday morning which you surely remember; all you children stood before the table and sang your hymns, just as you do every Sunday. You looked so devout, with your hands folded together; and your father and mother were just as pious. Then the door was opened, and little Sister Mary was put in the room. She really shouldn't have been there because she's less than two years old, and always tries to dance when she hears any kind of music or singing. She began to dance then, but she couldn't keep time – the music was too slow. First she stood on one leg and bent her head forward, and then she stood on the other leg and bent her head again– but it wouldn't do. You all stood together, and looked very serious, although it was difficult to keep from laughing, but I did laugh to myself so hard I fell off the table and got a bump that I still have! It was very wrong of me to laugh. But it all comes back to me now in thought, and everything that I've seen all my life; these are the old memories and what they may bring with them!

"Tell me, do you still sing on Sundays? Tell me about little Mary! And how is my comrade, the other tin soldier, doing? I imagine he's happy enough! Oh, I can't stand it any more!"

"You were given away as a present," said the little boy firmly. "And you must stay here! Can't you understand that?"

Now the old man brought in a drawer in which there were many treasures – balm boxes and coin boxes and large, gilded, old playing cards, such as one never sees any more. Several drawers were opened, and then the piano was opened; landscapes were painted on the inside of its lid, and it was so squeaky when the old man played it! Then he hummed a little song.

"She used to sing that," he said softly as he nodded up at the portrait he had bought from the secondhand dealer. And the old man's eyes shone brightly.

"I'm going to the wars! I tell you I'm going to the wars!" the tin soldier shouted as loudly as he could, then he threw himself off the chest right down to the floor.

What had become of him? The old man searched, and the little boy searched, but he was gone; they couldn't find him.

"I'll find him," said the old man, but he never did; the flooring was open and full of holes, and the tin soldier had fallen into one of the many cracks in the floor and lay there as if in an open grave.

And that day passed, and the little boy went home. A week passed, and several more weeks passed.

The windows of his home were frosted over, and the little boy had to breathe hard on one to make a peephole over to the old house. Then he saw that the snow had drifted into all the carving and inscriptions and up over the steps, just as if there were no one there. And there wasn't, really. For the old man was dead!

That evening a hearse drove up before the door, and the old man's coffin was borne into it; he was going out into the country now, to lie in his grave. And so he was driven away, but there was no one to follow him, for all the old man's friends were dead. There was only the little boy who blew a kiss to the coffin as it was driven away.

A few days later the old house was sold at auction, and from his window the little boy watched them carry away the old knights and their ladies, and the long-eared flowerpots, the old chairs, and the old cupboards; some pieces landed here and others landed there; the portrait that had come from the secondhand dealer went back to the secondhand dealer again, and there it hung, for no one knew the lady any more, and no one cared about the old picture.

In the spring the house was torn down, for everybody said it was nothing but a ruin. One could see from the street right into the room with the pigskin hangings, which were slashed and torn; and the green foliage about the balcony hung wild among the falling beams. The site was cleared.

"Good riddance," said the neighboring houses.

Then a fine house was built there, with large windows and smooth white walls; but in front of it, where the old house used to stand, a little garden was laid out, with a wild grapevine running up the wall of the neighboring house. Before the garden was a large railing with an iron gate; it looked quite splendid, and many people stopped to peer in. Scores of sparrows fluttered in the vines and chattered away to each other as fast as they could, but they didn't talk about the old house, for they couldn't remember it. So many years had passed.

Yes, many years had passed, and the little boy had grown up now to be a fine man; yes, an able man, and a great joy to his old parents. He had just been married and, with his pretty little wife, came to live in the new house where the garden was.

He was standing beside her in the garden while she planted a wild flower she was so fond of. She bedded it in the ground with her little hand and pressed the earth around it with her fingers. Ouch, what was that! She had pricked herself. There was something there, pointed straight up in the soft dirt. Yes, it was – just imagine, the little tin soldier! The same one that had been lost in the old man's room. He had tumbled and tossed about among the gravel and the timber and at last had lain for years in the ground.

The young wife wiped the dirt off the soldier, first with a green leaf and then with her delicate handkerchief, which had such a delightful scent that it woke the soldier up from his trance.

"Let me see him," said the young man. Then he laughed and shook his head. "No, it couldn't be he, but he certainly reminds me of a tin soldier I had when I was a little boy." Then he told her all about the old house and the old man and the tin soldier that had been sent over to keep him company because he was so terribly lonely. He told it just as it had happened, and the tears came into the eyes of his young wife – tears of pity for the old house and the old man.

"It might just possibly be the same tin soldier," she said gently. "I'll keep it, and remember everything you've told me. But you must show me the old man's grave."

"But I don't know where it is," he replied. "Nobody knows. All his friends were dead, and there was no one to take care of it. I was then just a little boy."

"How terribly lonely he must have been!" she murmured.

"Terribly lonely!" repeated the tin soldier. "But it's wonderful not to be forgotten!"

"Wonderful!" cried something else close by, but only the tin soldier saw that it was a scrap of the pigskin hanging. It had lost all of its gilding and looked like a piece of wet clay, but it still had its opinion, and gave it:

> *"Gilding fades fast;*
> *But pigskin will last!"*

But the tin soldier didn't really believe it.

THE HAPPY FAMILY

THE BIGGEST LEAF we have in this country is certainly the burdock leaf. If you hold one in front of your little stomach, it's just like a real apron; and in rainy weather, if you lay it on your head, it does almost as well as an umbrella. It's really amazingly large. Now, a burdock never grows alone; no, when you see one you'll always see others around it. It's a splendid sight; and all this splendor is nothing more than food for snails – the big white snails which the fine people in olden days used to have made into fricassees. When they had eaten them, they would smack their lips and say, "My! How good that is!" For somehow they had the idea that the snails tasted delicious. You see, these snails lived on the burdock leaves, and that's why the burdock was first grown.

There was a certain old manor house where the people didn't eat snails any more. The snails had almost died out, but the burdock hadn't. These grew and grew on all the walks and flower beds – they couldn't be stopped – until the whole place was a forest of burdocks. Here and there stood an apple or a plum tree, but except for that, people wouldn't have thought there had ever been a garden there. Everywhere was burdock, and among the burdocks lived the last two incredibly old snails!

They themselves didn't know how old they were, but they could remember very clearly that once there had been a great many more of them, that they had descended from a prominent foreign family, and they knew perfectly well that the whole forest had been planted just for them and their family.

They had never been away from home, but they did know that somewhere there was something called a manor house, and that there you were boiled until you turned black, and were laid on a silver dish; but what happened afterwards they hadn't the least idea. Furthermore, they couldn't imagine what it would be like to be boiled and laid on a silver dish, but everyone said it must be very wonderful and a great distinction. Neither the cockchafer nor the toad nor the earthworm, whom they asked about it, could give them any information. None of their families had ever been boiled or laid on silver dishes.

So the old white snails knew they were by far the most important people in the world. The forest was there just for their sake, and the manor house existed just so that they could be boiled and laid on silver dishes!

The two old snails led a quiet and happy life, and since they were childless they had adopted a little orphan snail, which they were bringing up as their own child. He wouldn't grow very large, for he was only a common snail; but

the two old snails – and especially the mother snail – thought it was easy to see how well he was growing. And she begged the father snail to touch the little snail's shell, if he couldn't see it, and so he felt it and found that she was right.

One day it rained very hard.

"Just listen to it drum on the burdock leaves!" cried Father Snail. "Rum-dum-dum! Rum-dum-dum!"

"Drops are also coming down here!" said the mother. "It's coming straight down the stalks, and it'll be wet down here before you know it. I'm certainly glad we have our own good houses and the little one has his own. We're better off than any other creatures; it's quite plain that we're the most important people in the world. We have our own houses from our very birth, and the burdock forest has been planted just for us. I wonder how far it extends, and what lies beyond it."

"There can't be anything beyond," said Father Snail, "that's any better than we have here. I have nothing in the world to wish for."

"Well, I have," said the mother. "I'd like to be taken to the manor house and boiled and laid on a silver dish. All our ancestors had that done to them, and, believe me, it must be something quite uncommon!"

"Maybe the manor house has fallen to pieces," suggested Father Snail. "Or perhaps the burdock forest has grown over it, so that the people can't get out at all. Don't be in such a hurry – but then you're always hurrying so. And the little one is beginning to do the same thing. Why, he's been creeping up that stalk for three days. It really makes my head dizzy to watch him go!"

"Don't scold him," said Mother Snail. "He crawls very carefully. He'll bring us much joy, and we old folk don't have anything else to live for. But have you ever thought where we can find a wife for him? Don't you think there might be some more of our kind of people farther back in the burdock woods?"

"I suppose there may be black snails back there," said the old man.

"Black snails without houses! Much too vulgar! And they're conceited, anyway. But let's ask the ants to find out for us; they're always running around as if they had important business. They're sure to know of a wife for our little snail."

"Certainly, I know a very beautiful bride," said one of the ants. "But I don't think she'd do, because she's a queen!"

"That doesn't matter," said Mother Snail emphatically. "Does she have a house?"

"She has a castle!" replied the ant. "The most beautiful ant's castle, with seven hundred corridors!"

"Thank you very much," said Mother Snail, "but our boy shall not go into an anthill! If you don't know of anything better, we'll ask the white gnats to find out for us. They flit around in the rain and sunshine, and they know this forest inside and out."

"We have just the wife for him," said the gnats. "A hundred man-steps from here a little snail with a house is sitting on a gooseberry bush. She is all alone in the world, and quite old enough to marry. It's only a hundred man-steps from here!"

"Fine, but she must come to him," said the old couple. "Our child has a whole burdock forest, and she has only a bush."

And so the gnats had the little maiden snail come over. It took her eight days to get there, but that was the wonderful part of it – for it showed she had the right sort of dignity.

And then they had a fine wedding! Six glow-worms lighted up the place as well as they could, but aside from that it was a very quiet ceremony, for the old people did not care for feasting or merriment. A charming speech was made by Mother Snail, but Father Snail couldn't say a word; he was too deeply moved. And so she gave the young couple the whole burdock forest for a dowry, and repeated what she had always said –

that it was the finest place in the world, and that the young people, if they lived honorably and had many children, would someday be taken with their young ones to the manor house, to be boiled black and laid on a silver dish. And when Mother Snail's speech was finished, the old people crept into their houses and never came out again, for they went to sleep.

Now the young couple ruled the forest and did have many children. But since none of them were ever boiled and laid in silver dishes, they decided that the manor house must have fallen into ruins and that all the people in the world had died out. And since nobody contradicted them, I think they must have been right. So the rain beat on the burdock leaves, to play the drum for them, and the sun shone, to color the forest for them; and they were very happy. The whole family was happy – extremely happy, indeed they were.

THE STORY OF A MOTHER

A MOTHER SAT BY her little child. She was so sad, so afraid he would die. The child's face was pallid. His little eyes were shut. His breath came faintly now, and then heavily as if he were sighing, and the mother looked more sadly at the dear little soul.

There came a knocking at the door, and a poor old man hobbled into the house. He was wrapped in a thick horseblanket. It kept him warm and he needed it to keep out the wintry cold, for outside the world was covered with snow and ice, and the wind cut like a knife.

As the child was resting quietly for a moment, and the old man was shivering from the cold, the mother put a little mug of beer to warm on the stove for him. The old man rocked the cradle and the mother sat down near it to watch her sick child, who labored to draw each breath. She lifted his little hand, and asked:

"You don't think I shall lose him, do you? Would the good Lord take him from me?"

The old man was Death himself. He jerked his head strangely, in a way that might mean yes or might mean no. The mother bowed her head and tears ran down her cheeks. Her head was heavy.

For three days and three nights she had not closed her eyes. Now she dozed off to sleep, but only a moment. Something startled her and she awoke, shuddering in the cold.

Out there in the snow sat a woman, dressed in long black garments. (Fritz Kredel)

"What was that?" she said, looking everywhere about the room. But the old man had gone and her little child had gone. Death had taken the child away. The old clock in the corner whirred and whirred. Its heavy lead weight dropped down to the floor with a thud. *Bong!* the clock stopped. The poor mother rushed wildly out of the house, calling for her child.

Out there in the snow sat a woman, dressed in long black garments. "Death," she said, "has been in your house. I just saw him hurrying away with your child in his arms. He goes faster than the wind. And he never brings back what he has taken away."

"Tell me which way he went," said the mother. "Only tell me the way, and I will find him."

"I know the way," said the woman in black, "but before I tell you, you must sing to me all those songs you used to sing to your child. I am night. I love lullabies and I hear them often. When you sang them I saw your tears."

"I shall sing them again – you shall hear them all," said the mother, "but do not stop me now. I must catch him. I must hurry to find my child."

Night kept silent and still, while the mother wrung her hands, and sang, and wept. She sang many songs, but the tears that she shed were many, many more. At last Night said to her, "Go to the right. Go into the dark pine woods. I saw Death go there with your child."

Deep into the woods the mother came to a crossroad, where she was at a loss which way to go. At the crossroad grew a blackthorn bush, without leaf or flower, for it was wintertime and its branches were glazed with ice.

"Did you see Death go by with my little child?"

"Yes," said the blackthorn bush. "But I shall not tell you which way he went unless you warm me against your heart. I am freezing to death. I am stiff with ice."

She pressed the blackthorn bush against her heart to warm it, and the thorns stabbed so deep into her flesh that great drops of red blood flowed. So warm was the mother's heart that the blackthorn bush blossomed and put forth green leaves on that dark winter's night. And it told her the way to go.

Then she came to a large lake, where there was neither sailboat nor rowboat. The ice on the lake was too thin to hold her weight, and yet not open or shallow enough for her to wade. But across the lake she must go if ever she was to find her child. She stooped down to drink the lake dry, and that of course was impossible for any human being, but the poor

woman thought that maybe a miracle would happen.

"No, that would never do," the lake objected. "Let us make a bargain between us. I collect pearls, and your two eyes are the clearest I've ever seen. If you will cry them out for me, I shall carry you over to the great greenhouse where Death lives and tends his trees and flowers. Each one of them is a human life."

"Oh, what would I not give for my child," said the crying mother, and she wept till her eyes dropped down to the bottom of the lake and became two precious pearls. The lake took her up as if in a swing, and swept her to the farther shore.

Here stood the strangest house that ever was. It rambled for many a mile. One wouldn't know whether it was a cavernous, forested mountain, or whether it was made of wood. But the poor mother could not see this, for she had cried out her eyes.

"Where shall I find Death, who took my child from me?" she cried.

"He has not come back yet," said the old woman who took care of the great greenhouse while Death was away. "How did you find your way here? Who helped you?"

"The Lord helped me," she said. "He is merciful, and so must you be. Where can I find my child?"

"I don't know him," said the old woman, "and you can't see to find him. But many flowers and trees have withered away in the night, and Death will be along soon to transplant them. Every human being, you know, has his tree or his flower of life, depending on what sort of person he is. These look like other plants, but they have a heart that beats. A child's heart beats too. You know the beat of your own child's heart. Listen and you may hear it. But what will you give me if I tell you what else you must do?"

"I have nothing left," the poor mother said, "but I will go to the ends of the earth for you."

"I have nothing to do there," said the old woman, "but you can give me your long black hair. You know how beautiful it is, and I like it. I'll give you my white hair for it. White hair is better than none."

"Is that all you ask?" said the mother. "I will gladly give it to you." And she gave her beautiful long black tresses in exchange for the old woman's white hair.

Then they went into Death's great greenhouse, where flowers and trees were strangely intertwined. In one place delicate hyacinths were kept under glass bells, and around them great hardy peonies flourished. There were water plants too, some thriving where the stalks of others were choked by twisting water snakes, or gnawed away by black crayfish. Tall palm trees grew there, and plane trees, and oaks. There grew parsley and sweet-smelling thyme. Every tree or flower went by the name of one particular person, for each was the life of someone still living in China, in Greenland, or in some other part of the world. There were big trees stunted by the small pots which their roots filled to bursting, and elsewhere grew languid little flowers that came to nothing, for all the care that was lavished upon them, and for all the rich earth and the mossy carpet where they grew. The sad, blind mother bent over the tiniest plants and listened to the beat of their human hearts, and among so many millions she knew her own child's heartbeat.

"This is it," she cried, groping for a little blue crocus, which had wilted and dropped to one side.

"Don't touch that flower," the old woman said. "Stay here. Death will be along any minute now, and you may keep him from pulling it up. Threaten him that, if he does, you will pull up other plants. That will frighten him, for he has to account for them to the Lord. Not one may be uprooted until God says so."

Suddenly an icy wind blew through the place, and the blind mother felt Death come near.

"How did you find your way here?" he asked her. "How did you ever get here before me?"

"I am a mother," she said.

Then Death stretched out his long hand toward the wilted little flower, but she held her hands tightly around it, in terror lest he touch a single leaf. Death breathed upon her hands, and his breath was colder than the coldest wind. Her hands fell, powerless.

"You have no power to resist me," Death told her.

"But our Lord has," she said.

"I only do his will," said Death, "I am His gardener. I take His flowers and trees and plant them again in the great Paradise gardens, in the unknown land. But how they thrive, and of their life there, I dare not speak."

"Give me back my child," the mother wept and implored him. Suddenly she grasped a beautiful flower in each hand and as she clutched them she called to Death: "I shall tear out your flowers by the roots, for I am desperate."

"Do not touch them!" Death told her. "You say you are desperate, yet you would drive another mother to the same despair."

"Another mother!" The blind woman's hands let go the flowers.

"Behold," said Death, "you have your eyes again. I saw them shining as I crossed the lake, and fished them up, but I did not know they were yours. They are clearer than before. Take them and look deep into this well. I shall tell you the names of the flowers you were about to uproot and you shall see the whole future of those human lives that you would have destroyed and disturbed."

She looked into the well, and it made her glad to see how one life became a blessing to the world, for it was so kind and happy. Then she saw the other life, which held only sorrow, poverty, fear, and woe.

"Both are the will of God," said Death.

"Which one is condemned to misery, and which is the happy one?" she asked.

"That I shall not tell you," Death said. "But I tell you this. One of the flowers belongs to your own child. One life that you saw was your child's fate, your own child's future."

Then the mother shrieked in terror, "Which was my child? Tell me! Save my innocent child. Spare him such wretchedness. Better that he be taken from me. Take him to God's kingdom.

Forget my tears. Forget the prayers I have said, and the things I have done."

"I do not understand," Death said. "Will you take your own child back or shall I take him off to a land unknown to you?"

Then the mother wrung her hands, fell on her knees, and prayed to God:

"Do not hear me when I pray against your will. It is best. Do not listen, do not listen!" And she bowed her head, as Death took her child to the unknown land.

IT'S QUITE TRUE!

"IT'S A DREADFUL story!" said a hen, and she said it in a part of town, too, where it had not taken place. "It's a dreadful story to happen in a henhouse. I'm afraid to sleep alone tonight; it's a good thing there are many of us on the perch!" And then she told a story that made the feathers of the other hens stand on end and the rooster's comb fall. It's quite true!

But we will begin at the beginning and tell what had happened in a henhouse at the other end of town.

The sun went down, and the hens flew up. One of them was a white-feathered and short-limbed hen who laid her eggs according to the regulations and who was a respectable hen in every way. As she settled herself on the perch, she plucked herself with her beak, and a tiny feather came out.

"There it goes," she said. "No doubt the more I pluck, the more beautiful I will get." But she said it only in fun, for she was considered the jolliest among the hens, although, as we've said before, most respectable. Then she fell asleep.

There was darkness all around, and the hens sat closely together. But the hen that sat closest to the white hen was not asleep; she had heard and had not heard, as one should do in this world, if one wishes to live in peace. But

still she couldn't resist telling it to her nearest neighbour.

"Did you hear what was said? Well, I don't want to mention any names, but there is a hen here who intends to pluck out all her feathers just to make herself look well. If I were a rooster, I would despise her."

Right above the hens lived a mother owl with a father owl and all her little owls. They had sharp ears in that family, and they all heard every word that their neighbor hen had said. They all rolled their eyes, and the mother owl flapped her wings and said; "Don't listen to it. But I suppose you all heard what was said. I heard it with my own ears, and one must hear a great deal before they fall off. One of the hens has so completely forgotten what is becoming conduct to a hen that she plucks out all her feathers, while the rooster watches her."

"Little pitchers have long ears," said the father owl. "Children shouldn't hear such talk."

"I must tell it to the owl across the road," said the mother owl. "She is such a respectable owl!" And away flew Mamma.

"Hoo-whoo! Hoo-whoo!" they both hooted to the pigeons in the pigeon house across the road. "Have you heard it? Have you heard it? Hoo-whoo! There is a hen who has plucked out all her feathers just to please the rooster.

She must be freezing to death; that is, if she isn't dead already. Hoo-whoo! Hoo-whoo!"

"Where? Where?" cooed the pigeons.

"In the yard across the way. I have as good as seen it myself. It is almost not a proper story to tell, but it's quite true!"

"True, true, every word of it," said the pigeons, and cooed down into their poultry yard. "There is a hen, and some say there are two hens, who have plucked out all their feathers in order to look different from the rest and to attract the attention of the rooster."

"Wake up! Wake up!" crowed the rooster, and flew up on the fence. He was still half asleep, but he crowed just the same. "Three hens have died of a broken heart, all for the sake of a rooster, and they have plucked all their feathers out! It's a dreadful story, but I will not keep it to myself. Tell it everywhere!"

"Tell it everywhere!" shrieked the bats; and the hens clucked and the roosters crowed. "Tell it everywhere!"

And so the story traveled from henhouse to henhouse until at last it was carried back to the very same place from where it had really started.

"There are five hens," now ran the tale, "who all have plucked out all their feathers to show which of them had lost the most weight through unhappy love for their rooster. And then they pecked at each other till they bled and all five dropped dead, to the shame and disgrace of their families, and to the great loss of their owner."

And the hen who had lost the little loose feather naturally didn't recognize her own story; and as she was a respectable hen, she said, "I despise such hens, but there are many of that kind! Such stories should not be hushed up, and I'll do my best to get the story into the newspapers. Then it will be known all over the country; that will serve those hens right, and their families, too." And it got to the newspapers, and it was printed. And it is quite true. One little feather may grow till it becomes five hens.

THE GOBLIN AND THE GROCER

THERE WAS A student, who lived in the garret and didn't own anything. There was also a grocer, who kept shop on the ground floor and owned the whole house. The household goblin stuck to the grocer, because every Christmas Eve it was the grocer who could afford him a bowl of porridge with a big pat of butter in it. So the goblin stayed in the grocery shop, and that was very educational.

One evening the student came in by the back door to buy some candles and cheese. He had no one to send, and that's why he came himself. He got what he came for, paid for it, and the grocer and his wife nodded, "Good evening." There was a woman who could do more than just nod, for she had an unusual gift of speech. The student nodded too, but while he was reading something on the piece of paper which was wrapped around his cheese, he suddenly stopped. It was a page torn out of an old book that ought never to have been put to this purpose, an old book full of poetry.

"There's more of it," the grocer told him. "I gave an old woman a few coffee beans for it. If you will give me eight pennies, you shall have the rest."

"If you please," said the student, "let me have the book instead of the cheese. There's no harm in my having plain bread and butter for supper, but it would be sinful to tear the book to pieces. You're a fine man, a practical man, but you know no more about poetry than that tub does."

Now this was a rude way to talk, especially to the tub. The grocer laughed and the student laughed. After all, it was said only as a joke, but the goblin was angry that anyone should dare say such a thing to a grocer, a man who owned the whole house, a man who sold the best butter.

That night, when the shop was shut and everyone in bed except the student, the goblin borrowed the long tongue of the grocer's wife, who had no use for it while she slept. And any object on which he laid this tongue became as glib a chatterbox as the grocer's wife herself. Only one object could use the tongue at a time, and that was a blessing, for otherwise they would all have spoken at once. First the goblin laid the tongue on the tub in which old newspapers were kept.

"Is it really true," asked the goblin, "that you don't know anything about poetry?"

"Of course, I know all about poetry," said the tub. "It's the stuff they stick at the end of a newspaper column when they've nothing better to print, and which is sometimes cut out. I dare say I've got more poetry in me than the student has, and I'm only a small tub compared to the grocer."

Then the goblin put the tongue on the coffee mill – how it did chatter away. He put it on the butter-cask and on the cash-box, he put it on everything around the shop, until it was back upon the tub again. To the same question everyone gave the same answer as the tub, and the opinion of the majority must be respected.

"Oh, won't I light into that student," said the goblin, as he tiptoed up the back stairs to the garret where the student lived. A candle still burned there, and by peeping through the keyhole the goblin could see that the student was reading the tattered old book he had brought upstairs with him.

But how bright the room was! From the book a clear shaft of light rose, expanding into a stem and a tremendous tree which spread its branching rays above the student. Each leaf on the tree was evergreen, and every flower

So he tiptoed away, back to the shop.
(Fritz Kredel)

was the face of a fair lady, some with dark and sparkling eyes, some with eyes of the clearest blue. Every fruit on the tree shone like a star, and the room was filled with song.

Never before had the little goblin imagined such splendor. Never before had he seen or heard anything like it. He stood there on tiptoe, peeping and peering till the light went out. But even after the student blew out his lamp and went to bed, the little fellow stayed to listen outside the door. For the song went on, soft but still more splendid, a beautiful cradle song lulling the student to sleep.

"No place can compare with this," the goblin exclaimed. "I never expected it. I've a good notion to come and live with the student." But he stopped to think, and he reasoned, and he weighed it, and he sighed, "The student has no porridge to give me."

So he tiptoed away, back to the shop, and high time too. The tub had almost worn out the tongue of the grocer's wife. All that was right-side-up in the tub had been said, and it was just turning over to say all the rest that was in it, when the goblin got back and returned the tongue to its rightful owner. But forever afterward the whole shop, from the cash-box right down to the kindling wood, took all their ideas from the tub. Their respect for it was so great and their confidence so complete that, whenever the grocer read the art and theatrical reviews in the evening paper, they all thought the opinions came out of the tub.

But the little goblin was no longer content to sit listening to all the knowledge and wisdom down there. No! as soon as the light shone again in the garret, he felt as if a great anchor rope drew him up there to peep through the keyhole. And he felt the great feeling that we feel when watching the ever-rolling ocean as a storm passes over it. And he started to cry, for no reason that he knew, but these were tears that left him strong and glad. How glorious it would be to sit with the student under the tree of light! He couldn't do that. He was content with the keyhole. There he stood on the cold landing, with wintry blasts blowing full upon him from the trapdoor to the roof. It was cold, so cold, but the little fellow didn't feel it until the light went out and the song gave way to the whistle of the wind. Ugh! he shivered and shook as he crept down to his own corner, where it was warm and snug. And when Christmas came round – when he saw that bowl of porridge and the big pat of butter in it – why then it was the grocer whose goblin he was.

But one midnight, the goblin was awakened by a hullabaloo of banging on the shutters. People outside knocked their hardest on the windows, and the watchman blasted away on his horn, for there was a house on fire. The whole street was red in the light of it. Was it the grocer's house? Was it the next house? Where? Everybody was terrified! The grocer's wife was so panicky that she took off her gold earrings and put them in her pocket to save them. The grocer ran to get his stocks and bonds, and the servant for the silk mantilla she had scrimped so hard to buy. Everyone wanted to rescue what he treasured most, and so did the little goblin. With a leap and a bound he was upstairs and into the garret. The student stood calmly at his window, watching the fire which was in the neighbor's house. The goblin snatched the wonderful book from the table, tucked it in his red cap, and held it high in both hands. The treasure of the house was saved! Off to the roof he ran. Up to the top of the chimney he jumped. There he sat, in the light of the burning house across the street, clutching with both hands the cap which held his treasure.

Now he knew for certain to which master his heart belonged. But when they put the fire out, and he had time to think about it, he wasn't so sure.

"I'll simply have to divide myself between them," he decided. "I can't give up the grocer, because of my porridge."

And this was all quite human. Off to the grocer all of us go for our porridge.

THE ICE MAIDEN

LET US VISIT Switzerland. Let us take a look at that magnificent land of mountains, where the forests creep up the sides of the steep rocky walls; let us climb to the dazzling snow-fields above, and descend again to the green valleys below, where the rivers and streams rush along as if afraid they will be too late to reach the ocean and disappear. The burning rays of the sun shine in the deep dales and also on the heavy masses of snow above, so that the ice blocks which have been piling for years melt and turn to thundering avalanches or heaped-up glaciers.

Two such glaciers lie in the broad ravines under the Schreckhorn and the Wetterhorn, near the little mountain town of Grindelwald.

They are strange to look at, and for that reason, in summer-time many travelers come here from all parts of the world. They cross the lofty, snow-capped hills, and they come through the deep valleys; then they have to climb for several hours, and as they ascend, the valleys seem to become deeper and deeper, until they look as if they are being viewed from a balloon. Often the clouds hang around the towering peaks like thick curtains of smoke, while down in the valley dotted with brown wooden houses, a ray of the sun may be shining brightly, throwing into sharp relief a brilliant patch of green, until it seems transparent. The water foams and roars, and rushes along below, but up above the water murmurs and tinkles; it looks as if silver ribbons were streaming down over the rocks. .

On both sides of the ascending road are wooden houses. Each house has its little

Let us visit Switzerland.
(Fritz Kredel)

potato garden, and this is a real necessity; for within those doors are many hungry mouths – there are many children, and children are often wasteful with food. From all the cottages they swarm out and besiege travelers, whether these be on foot or in carriages. All the children are little merchants; they offer for sale charming toy wooden houses, replicas of those that are built here in the mountains.

Some twenty years ago there often stood here, but always somewhat apart from the other children, a little boy who was also eager to do some business. He would stand there with an earnest, grave expression, holding his chip-box tightly with both hands, as if afraid of losing it; but it was this seriousness, and the fact that he was so small, that caused him to be noticed and called forward, so that he often sold more than all the others – he didn't exactly know why himself.

His grandfather lived high up on the mountain, where he carved out the neat, pretty little houses. In a room up there he had an old chest full of all sorts of carved things – nutcrackers, knives, forks, boxes with cleverly carved scrollwork, and leaping chamois – everything that would please a child's eye. But little Rudy, as he was called, gazed with greater interest and longing at the old gun that hung under the beams of the roof. "He shall have it some day," his grandfather had said, "but not until he's big and strong enough to use it."

Small as the boy was, he took care of the goats. If knowing how to climb along with the goats meant that he was a good goatherd, then Rudy certainly was an excellent goatherd; he could even go higher than the goats, for he loved to search for birds' nests high up in the tops of the trees. He was bold and daring. No one ever saw him smile, except when he stood near the roaring waterfall or heard the rolling of an avalanche.

He never played with the other children; in fact, he never went near them except when his grandfather sent him down to sell the things he had carved. And Rudy didn't care much for that; he would much rather climb about in the mountains or sit home with his grandfather and hear him tell stories of ancient times and of the people at nearby Meiringen, where he was born. This race, he said, had not always lived there; they were wanderers from other lands; they had come from the far North, where their people still lived, and were called "Swedes." This was a good deal for Rudy to learn, but he learned still more from other teachers – the animals that lived in the house. There was a big dog, Ajola, which had belonged to Rudy's father, and there was a tomcat. Rudy had much to thank the tomcat for – the Cat had taught him to climb.

"Come on out on the roof with me!" the Cat had said one day, very distinctly and intelligibly, too. For to a little child who can hardly speak, the language of hens and ducks, cats and dogs, is almost as easily understood as that of fathers and mothers. But you must be very young indeed then; those are the days when Grandpa's stick neighs and turns into a horse, with head, legs, and tail.

Some children keep these thoughts longer than others, and people say that these are exceedingly backward, and remain children too long. But people say so much!

"Come on out on the roof with me, little Rudy!" was one of the first things the Cat said, and Rudy could understand him.

"It's all imagination to think you'll fall; you won't fall unless you're afraid! Come on! Put one of your paws here, and another there, and then feel your way with your forepaws. Use your eyes and be very active in your limbs. If there's a hole, jump over it the way I do."

And that's what little Rudy did. Very often he sat on the sloping roof of the house with the Cat, and often in the tops of the trees, and even high up among the towering rocks, where the Cat never went.

"Higher! Higher!" the trees and bushes said. "Can't you see how we climb – how high we go, and how tightly we hold on, even on the narrowest ledge of rock?"

And often Rudy reached the top of the hill even before the sun; there he took his morning draft of fresh, strengthening mountain air, that drink which only Our Lord can prepare, and which human beings call the early fragrance from the mountain herbs and the wild thyme and mint in the valley. Everything that is heavy in the air is absorbed by the overhanging clouds and carried by the winds over the pine woods, while the essence of fragrance becomes light and fresh air – and this was Rudy's morning draft.

Sunbeams, daughters of the sun who bring his blessings with them, kissed his cheeks. Dizziness stood nearby watching, but dared not approach him. The swallows from his grandfather's house below (there were at least seven nests) flew up toward him and the goats, singing, "We and you, and you and we!" They brought greetings from his home, even from the two hens, who were the only birds in the house; however, Rudy had never been very intimate with them.

Young as he was he had traveled, and quite a good deal for such a little fellow. He was born in Canton Valais, and brought from there over the hills. He had recently traveled on foot to the nearby Staubbach, that seems to flutter like a silver veil before the snow-clad, glittering white Jungfrau. And he had been to the great glaciers near Grindelwald, but there was a sad story connected with that trip; his mother had met her death there, and it was there, as his grandfather used to say, that "little Rudy had lost all his childish happiness." When he was less than a year old he laughed more than he cried, as his mother had written; but from the time he fell into the crevasse his whole nature had changed. His grandfather didn't talk about this very much, but it was known all over the mountain.

Rudy's father had been a coach driver, and the big dog that now shared the boy's home had always gone with him on his journeys over the Simplon down to Lake Geneva. Rudy's relatives on his father's side lived in the Rhone valley, in Canton Valais, where his uncle was a celebrated chamois hunter and a famous Alpine guide. Rudy was only a year old when he lost his father, and his mother decided to return with the child to her own family in the Berner Oberland. Her father lived a few hours' journey from Grindelwald; he was a wood carver, and his trade enabled him to live comfortably.

With her infant in her arms she set out toward home in June, accompanied by two chamois hunters, over the Gemmi toward Grindelwald. They had made the greater part of the journey, had climbed the highest ridges to the snow fields and could already see her native valley with the familiar scattered cottages; they now had only to cross the upper part of one great glacier. The newly fallen snow concealed a crevasse, not deep enough to reach the abyss below where the water rushed along, but deeper than a man's height.

As she was carrying her child the young woman suddenly slipped, sank down, and instantly disappeared. Not a shriek or groan was heard, only the wailing of a little child. It was over an hour before her two companions could obtain ropes and poles from the nearest house to pull her out; and after tremendous labor they brought from the crevasse what they thought were two dead bodies. Every means of restoring life was tried, and at last they managed to save the child, but not the mother. Thus the old grandfather received in his house, not a daughter, but a daughter's son, the little one who laughed more than he cried. But a change seemed to have come over him since his terrible experience in the glacier crevasse – that cold, strange ice world, where the Swiss peasant believes the souls of the damned are imprisoned till doomsday.

The glacier lies like a rushing stream, frozen and pressed into blocks of green crystal, one huge mass of ice balanced on another; the swelling stream of ice and snow tears along in the depths beneath, while within it yawn deep hollows, immense crevasses. It is a wondrous palace of crystal, and in it dwells the Ice Maiden, queen of the glaciers. She, the slayer, the crusher, is half the mighty ruler of the rivers, half a child of the air. Thus it is that she can soar to the loftiest haunts of the chamois, to the towering summits of the snow-covered hills, where the boldest mountaineer has to cut footrests for himself in the ice; she sails on a light pine twig over the foaming river below, and leaps lightly from one rock to another, with her long, snow-white hair fluttering about her, and her blue-green robe glistening like the water in the deep Swiss lakes.

"To crush! To hold fast! That is my power!" she says. "And yet a beautiful boy was snatched from me – one whom I had kissed, but not yet kissed to death! He is again among human beings – he tends his goats on the mountain peaks; he is always climbing higher and still higher, far, far from other humans, but never from me! He is mine! I will fetch him!"

So she commanded Dizziness to undertake the mission; it was in the summertime and too hot for the Ice Maiden in the valley where the green mint grew; so Dizziness mounted and dived. Now Dizziness has a flock of sisters – first one came, then three of them – and the Ice Maiden selected the strongest of those who wield their power indoors and out. They perch on the banisters of steep staircases and the guard rails of lofty towers; they run like squirrels along the mountain ridges and, leaping away from them, tread the air as a swimmer treads water, luring a victim onward to the abyss beneath.

Dizziness and the Ice Maiden both reach out for mankind, as the polypus reaches after whatever comes near it. The mission of Dizziness was to seize Rudy.

"Seize him, you say!" said Dizziness. "I can't do it. That wretched Cat has taught him its skill.

The Ice Maiden.
(Chester Loomis)

the air like the echo of church bells pealing; it was the harmonious tones of a chorus of other spirits of Nature, the mild, soft, and loving daughters of the rays of the sun. Every evening they encircle the mountain peaks and spread their rosy wings, which, as the sun sinks, become redder and redder until the lofty Alps seem blazing. Mountaineers call this the Alpine glow. When the sun has set, they retire into the white snow on the peaks and sleep there until they appear again at sunrise. Greatly do they love flowers and butterflies and mankind, and they had taken a great fancy to little Rudy.

"You shall not catch him! You shall not have him!" they sang.

"I have caught greater and stronger ones than he!" said the Ice Maiden.

Then the daughters of the sun sang of the traveler whose cap was torn from his head by the whirlwind, and carried away in stormy flight. The wind had power to take his cap, but not the man himself. "You can seize him, but you cannot hold him, you children of strength. The human race is stronger and more divine even than we are; they alone can mount higher than our mother the sun. They know the magic words that can compel the wind and waves to obey and serve them. Once the heavy, dragging weight of the body is loosened, it soars upward."

Thus sounded the glorious bell-like chorus.

And every morning the sun's rays shone on the sleeping child through the one tiny window of the old man's house. The daughters of the sun kissed the boy; they tried to thaw, to wipe out the ice kiss given him by the queen of the glaciers when, in his dead mother's arms, he lay in the deep ice crevasse from which he had only been rescued as if by a miracle.

That human child has a power within himself that keeps me away. I can't touch the little fellow when he hangs from branches out over the abyss, or I'd be glad to tickle his feet and send him flying down through the air. I can't do it!"

"We can seize him!" said the Ice Maiden. "Either you or I! I will! I will!"

"No! No!" A whisper, a song, broke upon

THE JOURNEY TO THE NEW HOME

Now Rudy was eight years old. His uncle, who lived in the Rhone valley on the other side of the mountain, wanted to take the boy, so that he could have a better education and be

taught to take care of himself. The grandfather thought this would be better for the boy, so agreed to part with him.

As the time for Rudy's departure drew near,

there were many others besides Grandfather to take leave of. First there was Ajola, the old dog.

"Your father was the coachman, and I was the coachman's dog," said Ajola. "We often traveled back and forth, and I know both dogs and men on the other side of the mountains. I never had the habit of speaking very much, but now that we have so little time to talk to each other, I'll say a little more than I usually do, and tell you a story that I've been thinking about for a long time. I can't understand it, and you can't either, but that doesn't matter. I have learned this: the good things of this world aren't dealt out equally either to dogs or to men; not everyone is born to lie in someone's lap or to drink milk. I've never been accustomed to such luxury. But I've often seen a puppy dog traveling inside a post carriage, taking up a human being's seat, while the lady to whom he belonged, or rather who belonged to him, carried a bottle of milk from which she fed him. She also offered him sweet candy, but he wouldn't bother to eat it; he just sniffed at it, so she ate it herself. I was running in the mud beside the carriage, about as hungry as a dog could be, but I had only my own bitter thoughts to chew on. Things weren't quite as they ought to be, but then there is much that is not! I hope you get to ride inside carriages, and ride softly, but you can't make all that happen by yourself. I never could either by barking or yawning."

That was Ajola's lecture, and Rudy threw his arms around the dog's neck and kissed his wet nose. Then he took the Cat in his arms, but he struggled to be free, and cried, "You're getting much too strong for me, but I won't use my claws against you. Climb away over the mountains – I've taught you how to climb. Never think about falling, but hold tightly; don't be afraid, and you'll be safe enough."

Then the Cat ran off, for he didn't want Rudy to see how sorry he was.

The hens were hopping about the floor. One of them had lost its tail, for a traveler, who thought himself a sportsman, had shot it off, mistaking the poor hen for a game bird.

"Rudy is going over the mountains," said one of the hens.

"He's in a hurry," said the other, "and I don't like farewells." So they both hopped away.

And the goats also said their farewells. "Maeh! Maeh!" they bleated; it sounded so sad.

Just at that time there happened to be two experienced guides about to cross the mountains; they planned to descend the other side of the Gemmi, and Rudy would go with them on foot. It was a hard trip for such a little fellow, but he had considerable strength, and was untiring and courageous.

The swallows accompanied him a little way, and sang to him, "We and you, and you and we."

The travelers' route led across the foaming Lütschine, which falls in many small rivulets from the dark clefts of the Grindelwald glaciers. Fallen tree trunks made bridges, and pieces of rock served here as steppingstones. Soon they had passed the alder thicket, and began to climb the mountain near where the glaciers had loosened themselves from the cliff. They went around the glacier and over the blocks of ice.

Rudy crept and walked. His eyes sparkled with joy as he firmly placed his iron-tipped mountain shoes; it seemed as if he wished to leave behind him an impression of each footstep. The patches of black earth, tossed onto the glacier by the mountain torrents, gave it a burned look, but still the blue-green, glassy ice shone through. They had to circle the little pools that seemed damned up by detached masses of ice. On this route they approached a huge stone which was balanced on the edge of an ice crevasse. Suddenly the rock lost its balance and toppled into the crevasse; the echo of its thunderous fall resounded faintly from the deep abyss of the glacier, far, far below.

Upward, always upward, they climbed; the glacier stretched up like a solid stream of masses of ice piled in wild confusion, wedged between bare and rugged rocks. For a moment Rudy remembered what had been told him, how he had lain in his mother's arms, buried in one of these terrible crevasses. But he soon threw off such gloomy thoughts, and considered the tale as only one of the many stories he had heard. Occasionally, when the guides thought the way was too difficult for a such a little boy, they held out their hands to help him; but he didn't tire, and he crossed the glacier as sure-footedly as a chamois itself.

From time to time they reached rocky ground; they walked between mossless stones, and sometimes between low pine trees or out on the green pastures – always changing, always new. About them towered the lofty, snow-capped peaks, which every child in the country knows by name – the Jungfrau, the Eiger, and the Mönch.

Rudy had never before been up so high, had never before walked on the wide ocean of snow with its frozen billows of ice, from which the wind occasionally swept little clouds of powdery snow as it sweeps the whitecaps from the waves of the sea. Glacier stretched beside glacier, almost as if they were holding hands; and each is a crystal palace of the Ice Maiden, whose joy and in whose power it is to seize and imprison her victims.

The sun shone warmly, and the snow dazzled the eye as if it were covered with the flashing sparks of pale blue diamonds. Countless insects, especially butterflies and bees, lay dead in heaps on the snow; they had winged their way too high, or perhaps the wind had carried them up to the cold regions that to them meant death. Around the Wetterhorn there hung a threatening cloud, like a large mass of very fine dark wool; it sank, bulging with what was concealed within – a foehn, the Alpine south wind that foretells a storm, fearfully violent in its power when it should break loose.

This whole journey – the stops for the nights high up in the mountains, the wild route, the deep crevasses where the water, during countless ages of time, had cut through the solid stone – made an unforgettable impression on little Rudy's mind.

A deserted stone hut, beyond the snowfields, gave them shelter and comfort for the night. Here they found charcoal and pine branches, and a fire was soon kindled. Sleeping quarters were arranged as well as possible, and the men settled near the blazing fire; they smoked their tobacco and drank some of the warm, spiced beverage they had prepared – and they didn't forget to give Rudy some.

The talk turned to the mysterious creatures who haunt the high Alps: the huge, strange snakes in the deep lakes – the night riders – the spectral host that carry sleepers through the air to the wonderful, floating city of Venice – the wild herdsman, who drives his black sheep over the green pastures: these had never been seen, although men had heard the sound of their bells and the frightful noise of the phantom herd.

Rudy listened to these superstitious tales with intense interest, but with no fear, for that he had never known; yet while he listened he imagined he could hear the roar of that wild, spectral herd. Yes! It became more and more distinct, until the men heard it too. They stopped their talking and listened to it, and then they told Rudy that he must not fall asleep.

It was a foehn that had risen – that violent tempest which whirls down from the mountains into the valley below, and in its fury snaps large trees like reeds, and tosses the wooden houses from one bank of a river to the other, as easily as we would move chessmen.

After an hour they told Rudy the wind had died down and he might go to sleep safely; and, weary from his long walk, he followed their instructions and slept.

Early next morning, they set off again. That day the sun shone for Rudy on new mountains, new glaciers, and new snowfields. They had entered Canton Valais, on the other side of the ridge of mountains visible from Grindelwald; but they still had a long way to go to his new home.

More mountain clefts, pastures, woods, and new paths unfolded themselves; then Rudy saw other houses and other people. But what kind of human beings were these? They were misshapen, with frightful, disgusting, fat, yellowish faces, the hideous flesh of their necks hanging down like bags. They were the cretins – miserable, diseased wretches, who dragged themselves along and stared with stupid, dead eyes at the strangers who crossed their path; the women were even more disgusting than the men. Were these the sort of people who lived in his new home?

THE UNCLE

When Rudy arrived in his uncle's house he thanked God to see people such as he was accustomed to. There was only one cretin, a poor imbecile boy, one of those unfortunate beings who, in their poverty, which amounts to utter destitution, always travel about in Canton Valais, visiting different families in turn and staying a month or two in each house. Poor Saperli happened to be living in the house of Rudy's uncle when the boy arrived.

This uncle was a bold hunter, and a cooper by trade, while his wife was a lively little person, with a face somewhat like a bird's, eyes like an eagle's, and a long, skinny, fuzz-covered neck.

Everything was strange and new to Rudy – dress, customs, employment, even the language, though his young ear would soon learn to understand that. A comparison between his grandfather's little home and his uncle's domicile greatly favored the latter. The room they lived in was larger; the walls were decorated with chamois heads and brightly polished guns; a painting of the Virgin Mary hung over the door, with fresh Alpine roses and a constantly burning lamp before it.

As you have learned, his uncle was one of the most famous chamois hunters of the canton, and also the most experienced and best guide.

Rudy became the pet of the house, but there was another pet too – a blind, lazy old dog, of not much use any more. But he had been useful once, and his value in former years was remembered, so he now lived as one of the family, with every comfort. Rudy patted him, but the dog didn't like strangers and still considered Rudy one. But the boy did not long remain so, for soon he won his way into everyone's heart.

"Things are not so bad here in Canton Valais," said his uncle. "We have plenty of chamois; they don't die off as fast as the wild goats. Things are much better now than in the old days, however much we praise the olden times. A hole has been burst in the bag, so now we have a little fresh air in our cramped valley. When you do away with out-of-date things you always get something better," he said.

When the uncle became really talkative, he would tell the boy about his own and his father's childhood. "In those days Valais was," he called it, "just a closed bag full of too many sick people – miserable cretins. But the French soldiers came, and they made excellent doctors – they soon killed the disease, and the patients too. They knew how to strike – yes, to strike in many different ways; even their girls knew how to strike!" Then he winked at his wife, who was French by birth, and laughed. "The French knew how to split solid stones if they wanted to. It was they who cut out of solid rock the road over the Simplon Pass – yes, and made such a road that I could tell a three-year-old child to go to Italy! You just have to keep on the highway, and there you are!" Then the uncle sang a French song, and ended by shouting "hurrah!" for Napoleon Bonaparte.

It was the first time Rudy had ever heard of France or of Lyons, that great city on the Rhone which his uncle had visited.

In a few years Rudy would become an expert chamois hunter, for he showed quite a flair for it, said the uncle. He taught the boy to hold, load, and fire a gun; in the hunting season he took him up into the hills and made him drink warm chamois blood to ward off hunter's giddiness; he taught him to know the times when, on different slopes of the mountains, avalanches were likely to fall, in the morning or evening, whenever the sun's rays had the greatest effect. He taught him to observe the movements of the chamois and copy their leaps, so that he might alight firmly on his feet. He told him that if there was no footing in the rock crevices, he must support himself by the pressure of his elbows, and the muscles of his thighs and calves; if necessary even the neck could be used.

The chamois is cunning and places sentinels on guard, so the hunter must be still more cunning, and scent them out. Sometimes he could cheat them by arranging his hat and coat on his alpine staff, so that the chamois would mistake the dummy for the man. The uncle played this trick one day when he was out hunting with Rudy.

It was a narrow mountain path – indeed, scarcely a path at all; it was nothing more than a slight ledge close to the yawning abyss. The snow there was half thawed, and the rock crumbled away under the pressure of a boot; so that the uncle lay down at full length and inched his way forward. Every fragment of rock that crumbled off fell, knocking and bouncing from one side of the wall to the other, until it came to rest in the depths far below. Rudy stood on the edge of the last point of solid rock, about a hundred paces behind his uncle, and

from there he suddenly saw, wheeling through the air and hovering just above his uncle, an enormous vulture, which, with one stroke of its tremendous wings, could easily have hurled the creeping form into the abyss beneath, and there fed on his carcass.

The uncle had eyes for nothing but the chamois, which had appeared with its young kid on the other side of the crevasse. But Rudy kept watching the bird, with his hand on his gun to fire the instant it became necessary, for he understood its intention. Suddenly the chamois leaped upward; the uncle fired, and the animal was hit by the deadly bullet; but the kid escaped as skillfully as if it had had a lifelong experience of danger and flight. The huge bird, frightened by the report, wheeled off in another direction; and the uncle was saved from a danger of which he knew nothing until Rudy told him about it later.

As they were making their way homeward in high good humor, the uncle humming an air he remembered from his childhood, they heard a strange noise very close to them. They looked all around, and then upward; and there, on the slope of the mountain high above, the heavy snow covering was lifted up and heaving as a stretched linen sheet heaves when the wind creeps under it. Then the great mass cracked like a marble slab, broke, and changed into a foaming cataract, rushing down on them with a rumbling noise like distant thunder. An avalanche was coming, not directly toward Rudy and his uncle, but close to them – much too close!

"Hang on, Rudy!" he cried. "Hang on with all your might!"

Rudy threw his arms around the trunk of a nearby tree, while his uncle climbed higher and clung to the branches of the tree. The avalanche roared past a little distance away, but the gale of wind that swept behind it, the tail of a hurricane, snapped trees and bushes all around them as if they had been dry rushes, and hurled them about in wild confusion. Rudy was flung to the ground, for the trunk of his tree looked as if it had been sawed in two, and the upper part was tossed a great distance. And there, among the shattered branches, Rudy found his poor uncle, with a fractured skull! His hands were still warm, but his face was unrecognizable. Rudy turned pale and trembled, for this was the first real shock of his life, the first terror he had ever experienced.

Late that evening he brought the fatal news to his home – his home, which was now to be the home of grief. The wife stood like a statue, uttering no word, shedding no tear; it was not until the corpse was brought home that her sorrow found utterance. The poor cretin crept into his bed, and was not seen throughout the whole next day. But the following evening he came to Rudy.

"Write a letter for me please!" he said. "Saperli can't write. Saperli can only take letter to post office."

"A letter for you?" Rudy asked. "To whom?"

"To our Lord Christ!"

"What do you mean?"

And the half-wit, as he was called, looked at Rudy with a touching expression, clasped his hands, and said solemnly and reverently, "Jesus Christ! Saperli would send Him a letter to pray Him that Saperli lie dead, and not the master of the house here."

And Rudy pressed his hand. "That letter wouldn't reach up there. That letter wouldn't restore him to us."

He found it very difficult to convince Saperli how impossible his request was.

"Now you must be the support of the house," said his aunt. And Rudy became just that.

BABETTE

"Who is the best hunter in Canton Valais?" The chamois knew well. "Beware of Rudy!" they might have said to each other. And, "Who is the handsomest hunter?" "Oh, it's Rudy!" the girls said. But they didn't add, "Beware of Rudy!" And their serious mothers didn't say so either, for he bowed as politely to them as to the young girls.

He was so brave and happy; his cheeks were so brown, his teeth so white, his dark eyes so sparkling! He was a handsome fellow, just twenty years old. The most icy water never seemed too cold for him to go swimming; in fact, he was like a fish in water. He could outclimb anyone else; he could cling as tightly as a snail to the cliffs. There were steel muscles and sinews in him; that was clear whenever he jumped. He had learned how to leap, first from the Cat, and later from the chamois. Rudy was considered the best mountain guide, and he could have made a great deal of money in that vocation. His uncle had also taught him the trade of a cooper, but he had no inclination for that. He was interested in nothing but chamois hunting; that was his greatest pleasure, and it also brought in good money. Everybody said Rudy would be an excellent match, if only he didn't set his sights too high. He was the kind of graceful dancer that the girls dreamed about; and more than one carried him in her thoughts while she was awake.

"He kissed me while we were dancing!" the schoolmaster's daughter, Annette, told her dearest friend; but she shouldn't have told it, even to her dearest friend. Such secrets are seldom kept; they ooze out, like sand from a bag that has holes in it. Consequently, however well behaved and good Rudy was, the rumor soon spread about that he kissed his dancing partners. And yet he had never kissed the one he really wanted to kiss.

"Watch him!" said an old hunter. "He has kissed Annette. He has begun with A, and he's going to kiss his way through the whole alphabet!"

A kiss in the dance was all the gossips so far could find to bring against Rudy; but he certainly had kissed Annette, and yet she wasn't the real flower of his heart.

Down at Bex, among the great walnut trees near a small rushing mountain stream, there lived a rich miller. His home was a large house, three stories high, with small turrets; it was made of wood, and covered with tin plates, which shone both in sunshine and moonlight. On the highest turret was a weather vane, a shining arrow piercing an apple – an allusion to Wilhelm Tell's famous arrow shot. The mill was prominent and prosperous looking and allowed itself to be sketched and written about, but the miller's daughter did not permit herself to be described in painting or writing, at least so Rudy would have said. Yet her image was engraved on his heart; her eyes sparkled in it so that it was quite on fire. This fire had, like most fires, begun suddenly. The strangest part of it was that the miller's daughter, the lovely Babette, had no suspicion of it, for she and Rudy had never spoken so much as two words to each other.

The miller was rich, and because of his wealth Babette was rather high to hope for. "But nothing is so high," Rudy told himself, "that one may not reach it. You must climb on, and if you have confidence you won't fall." This was how he had been taught as a child.

Now it so happened that Rudy had some business in Bex. It was quite a journey, for in those days there was no railroad. From the Rhone glaciers, at the very foot of the Simplon, the broad valley of Canton Valais stretches among many and often-shifting mountain peaks, with its mighty Rhone River, whose rising waters often overflow its banks, covering fields and roads, destroying everything. Between the towns of Sion and St. Maurice the valley bends sharply like an elbow, and below St. Maurice it

narrows until there is room only for the bed of the river and the narrow carriage road. Canton Valais ends here, and an old tower stands on the side of the mountain like the guardian of the canton, commanding a view across the stone bridge to the customhouse on the other side, where Canton Vaud commences. And the closest of the nearby towns is Bex. Fruitfulness and abundance increase here with every step forward; one enters, so to speak, a grove of chestnut and walnut trees. Here and there cypresses and pomegranates peep out; it is as warm here as if one were in Italy.

Rudy reached Bex, and after finishing his business he took a walk about town; but he saw no one belonging to the mill, not even Babette. And that wasn't what he wanted.

Evening came on; the air was heavy with the fragrance of the wild thyme and the blossoming lime trees; a shining veil of sky-blue seemed to lie over the wooded green hills; and a stillness was everywhere. It was not the stillness of sleep or of death – no, it was as if nature were holding her breath, as if posing, for her image to be photographed on the blue surface of the heavens above. Here and there among the trees in the green field stood poles that carried the telegraph wires through the silent valley. Against one of them there leaned an object, so motionless that it might have been the dead trunk of a tree; it was Rudy, standing there as still as the world around him at that moment. He wasn't sleeping, nor was he dead; but just as great events of the world, or matters of the highest importance to individuals often are transmitted through the telegraph wires without those wires betraying them by the slightest movement or the faintest sound, so there passed through Rudy's mind the one, mighty, overwhelming thought that now constantly occupied him – the thought of his life's happiness. His eyes were fixed on a single point before him – a light that glimmered through the foliage from the parlor of the miller's house, where Babette lived. Rudy stood as still as if he were taking aim at a chamois; but at that moment he was like the chamois itself, which could stand as if chiseled from rock, and in the next instant, if only a stone rolled past, would spring into life and leave the hunter far behind. And so it was with Rudy, for a thought passed through his mind.

"Never give up!" he said. "Visit the mill; say good evening to the miller, and good day to Babette. You won't fall unless you're afraid of falling. If I'm going to be Babette's husband, she'll have to see me sooner or later!"

Then Rudy laughed, and in good spirits, he went to the mill. He knew what he wanted; he wanted Babette!

The river with its yellowish-white water was rolling along, overhung with willows and lime trees. Rudy went along the path, and, as the old nursery rhyme says,

> "Found to the miller's house his way;
> But no one was at home
> Except a pussycat at play!"

The cat, which was standing on the steps, arched its back and mewed, but Rudy was not inclined to pay any attention to it. He knocked at the door, but no one heard him; no one opened the door. "Meow!" said the cat. If Rudy had still been a little boy, he would have understood the cat's language, and known that it said, "No one is home!" But now he had to go over to the mill to find out; and there he was told that the miller had gone on a long journey to Interlaken – "Inter Lacus, among the lakes," as the highly learned schoolmaster, Annette's father, had explained the name. There was going to be a great shooting match held there, to begin the next morning and last for eight days. The Swiss from all the German cantons were assembling there, and the miller and Babette had gone too.

"Poor Rudy" we may well say. It wasn't a lucky time for him to have come to Bex. He could only go home again, which he did, taking the road over St. Maurice and Sion to his own valley, his own mountains. But he wasn't disheartened. The next morning when the sun rose he was in good spirits, for they had never been really depressed.

"Babette is in Interlaken, a good many days' journey from here," he said to himself. "It's a long way if you follow the highway, but not so far if you cut across the mountain, and that's the best way for a chamois hunter. I've traveled that route before; over there is my first home, where I lived with my grandfather when I was a little boy. And there are shooting matches at Interlaken; I'll show I'm the best one there, and I'll be with Babette there too, after I've made her acquaintance."

With his musket and gamebag, and his light knapsack packed with his Sunday best, Rudy went up the mountain; it was the shortest way, though still fairly long. But the shooting matches would only begin that day, and were to last more than a week. During all that time, he had been told, the miller and Babette would be staying with their relatives at Interlaken. So Rudy crossed the Gemmi; he planned to descend near Grindelwald.

Happily and in good health he walked along, enjoying the fresh, pure, invigorating mountain air. The valley sank below him; the horizon widened, showing here one snow-capped summit, there another, until the whole of the bright shining Alpine range was visible. Rudy well knew every snow-covered mountain peak. He was now approaching the Schreckhorn, which pointed its white, powdered stone finger high toward the blue vault above.

At last he had crossed the highest mountain ridge. Now the pasture lands sloped down to the valley that was his old home. The air was light, and his thoughts were light; mountain and valley were blooming with flowers and foliage, and his heart was blooming with the bright dreams of youth. He felt as if old age and death would never approach him; life, power, and enjoyment would be before him always. Free as a bird, light as a bird, was Rudy; and as the swallows flew past him they sang as in the days of his childhood, "We and you, and you and we!" Everything was light and happy.

Down below lay the green-velvet meadows, dotted with brown wooden houses; and the river Lütschine murmured and rolled along. He could see the glacier, with its edges like green glass bordering the dirty snow, and looking down into the deep crevasses, he saw both the upper and lower glacier. The pealing of the church bells came to his ears, as if they were welcoming him to his old home. His heart beat faster, and so many old memories filled his mind that for a moment he almost forgot Babette.

He was again passing along the same road where, as a little boy, he had stood with the other children to sell the carved wooden toy houses. His grandfather's house still stood over above the pine trees, but strangers lived there now. As in the olden days, the children came running to sell their wares. One of them offered him an Alpine rose, and Rudy took it as a good omen, thinking of Babette. Soon he came to the bridge where the two Lütschines unite; here the foliage was heavier and the walnut trees gave grateful shade. Then he could make out waving flags, the white cross on the red ground – the standard of Switzerland as of Denmark – and before him lay Interlaken.

To Rudy it certainly seemed like a wonderful town – a Swiss town in its Sunday dress. Unlike other market towns, it was not a heap of heavy stone buildings, stiff, cold, foreign looking. No, it looked as if the wooden chalets from the hills above had moved down into the green valley below, with its clear stream rushing swiftly as an arrow, and had ranged themselves in rows, somewhat unevenly, to be sure, to form a street. And most beautiful of all, the streets, which had

been built since Rudy had last been there as a child, seemed to be made up of all the prettiest wooden houses his Grandfather had carved and that had filled the cupboard at home. They seemed to have transplanted themselves down here and to have grown very much in size, as the old chestnut trees had done.

Every house was a so-called hotel, with carved wooden grillwork around the windows and balconies, and with projecting roofs; they were very neat and dainty. Between each house and the wide, hard-surfaced highway was a flower garden. Near these houses, though on only one side of the road, there stood other houses; if they had formed a double row they would have cut off from view the fresh green meadows where cattle grazed, their bells jingling as in the high Alpine pastures. The valley was surrounded by high mountains, with a little break on one side that revealed the glittering, snow-white Jungfrau, in form the most beautiful of all the Swiss mountains.

What a multitude of gayly dressed ladies and gentlemen from foreign countries! What crowds of country people from the nearby cantons! The marksmen carried the number of their posts in a garland round their hats. There were shouting and racket and music of all kinds, from singing to hand organs and wind instruments. The houses and bridges were decorated with flags and verses. Banners waved, and shot after shot was being fired; to Rudy's ears that was the best music. In all this excitement he almost forgot Babette, though it was for her sake alone that he had gone there.

The marksmen were crowding around the targets. Rudy quickly joined them, and he was the best shot of them all, for he always made a bull's-eye.

"Who's that strange fellow, that very young marksman?" people asked. "He speaks the French of Canton Valais; but he can also express himself fluently in our German," said some.

"He is supposed to have lived in the valley, near Grindelwald, when he was a child," someone explained.

The lad was full of life; his eyes sparkled; his aim and his arm were steady, so his shots were always perfect. Good luck brings courage, and Rudy always had courage. Soon a whole circle of admirers was around him; they showed him their esteem and honored him. Babette had almost disappeared from his thoughts. But suddenly a heavy hand was laid on his shoulder, and a deep voice spoke to him in French.

"You're from Canton Valais?"

Rudy turned and saw a fat man with a jolly face. It was the rich miller from Bex, his broad body hiding the slender, lovely Babette; however, she soon came forward, her dark eyes sparkling brightly. The rich miller was very proud that it was a marksman from his own canton who proved to be the best shot, and was so much admired and praised. Rudy was truly the child of good fortune; that which he had traveled so far to find, but had nearly forgotten since his arrival, now sought him out.

When in a far land one meets people from his own part of the country, it is easy to make friends, and people speak as if they were well acquainted. Rudy was the foremost at the shooting matches, as the miller was foremost at Bex, because of his money and his fine mill. So, though they had never met before, the two men shook hands warmly. Babette, too, gave the young man her hand frankly, and he pressed it and gazed at her in such a way that it made her blush.

The miller spoke of the long trip they had made and of the many large towns they had seen; it had been quite a journey, for they had traveled partly by railroad and partly by post.

"I came the shorter way," said Rudy. "I came over the mountains. There's no road so high that you can't try it."

"But you can also break your neck," said the miller. "And you look as if you probably will break your neck some day; you're so daring."

"One never falls so long as one doesn't think of it," said Rudy.

The miller's relatives at Interlaken, with whom he and Babette were staying, invited Rudy to visit them, since he came from the same canton as their kinfolk. It was a wonderful invitation for Rudy. Luck was running with him, as it always does with those who are self-reliant and remember that "Our Lord gives nuts to us, but He does not crack them for us!"

And Rudy sat with the miller's relatives, almost like one of the family. They drank a toast in honor of the best marksman; Babette clinked glasses with Rudy too, and he in return thanked them for the toast.

In the evening the whole party walked on the lovely avenue, past the gay-looking hotels under the walnut trees, and there was such a large crowd that Rudy had to give Babette his arm. He explained to her how happy he was to have met people from Canton Vaud, for Vaud and Valais were good neighbors. He expressed himself so cordially about this that Babette could not keep from squeezing his hand. As they walked there, they seemed almost like old friends, and she was such a lively, pretty little person. Rudy was greatly amused at her remarks about the absurd affectations in the dress of some of the foreign ladies, and the airs they put on; but she really didn't mean to make fun of them, because there must be some nice people among them – yes, some sweet and lovely people, she was sure, for her godmother was a very superior English lady. Eighteen years before, when Babette was christened, that lady had lived in Bex, and had given Babette the valuable brooch she was wearing. Her godmother had written her twice, and this year they were to have met her here at Interlaken, where she was bringing her daughters; they were old maids, almost thirty, said Babette – she herself was just eighteen.

Her pretty little mouth was not still for an instant, and everything she said appeared to Rudy to be of the greatest importance, and he in turn told her all he had to tell, how he had been to Bex, and how well he knew the mill, and how often he had seen her, though, of course, she had never noticed him. He told her he had been too disappointed for words when he found she and her father were far away; but still it wasn't far enough to keep him from climbing the wall that made the road so long.

Yes, he said all this, and a great deal more, too. He told her how fond he was of her, and how it was for her sake, and not because of the shooting matches, that he had come to Interlaken.

Babette became very silent now; all this that he confided to her was almost too much to listen to.

As they walked on, the sun set behind the mighty peaks, and the Jungfrau stood in all her glory, encircled by the dark green woods of the surrounding mountains. The big crowd stopped to gaze at it; even Rudy and Babette enjoyed the magnificent scene.

"Nowhere is it more beautiful than it is here!" said Babette.

"Nowhere!" agreed Rudy, with his eyes fixed on Babette.

"Tomorrow I must leave," he said a little later.

"Come and visit us at Bex," Babette whispered. "My father will be very pleased!"

ON THE WAY HOME

Oh, what a load Rudy had to carry the next day, when he started his return home over the mountains! He had two handsome guns, three silver cups, and a silver coffeepot – this last would be useful when he set up his own home. But these valuable prizes were not the heaviest burden he had to bear; a still weightier load he had to carry – or did it carry him? – across the high mountains.

The weather was dismal, gloomy, and rainy; the clouds hung like a mourning veil over the mountain summits, and shrouded the shining peaks. The last stroke of the ax had resounded from the woods, and down the side of the mountain rolled the great tree trunks. From the vast heights above they looked like matchsticks, but were nevertheless as big as masts of ships. The Lütschine River murmured its monotonous song; the wind whistled, and the clouds sailed swiftly by.

Suddenly there appeared next to Rudy a young girl; he had not noticed her until she was quite near him. She also was planning to cross the mountain. Her eyes had a peculiar power that compelled one to look into them; they were so clear and deep – bottomless.

"Do you have a sweetheart?" asked Rudy, whose thoughts were filled with love.

"I have none," she laughed, but it seemed as if she were not speaking the truth. "Let us not take the long way around; let us keep to the left – it is shorter."

"Yes, and easier to fall into some crevasse," said Rudy. "You ought to know the route better if you're going to be the guide."

"I know the way very well," she said, "and I have my thoughts collected. Your thoughts are down there in the valley; but up here you should think of the Ice Maiden. People say she is not friendly to the human race."

"I'm not a bit afraid of her," said Rudy. "She couldn't keep me when I was a child, and she won't catch me now that I'm a grown-up man."

Now it became very dark. First rain fell, then snow, and its whiteness was quite blinding.

"Give me your hand, and I shall help you climb," said the girl, touching him with her icy fingers.

"You help me?" said Rudy. "I don't yet need a woman's help in climbing!"

Then he walked on away from her quickly. The falling snow thickened about him like a curtain, the wind moaned, and behind him he could hear the girl laughing and singing. It sounded very strange. Surely it must be a specter in the service of the Ice Maiden; Rudy had heard of these things when, as a little boy, he had spent that night on the mountain, during his trip across the mountains.

The snow no longer fell so thickly, and the clouds lay far below him. He looked back, but there was no one to be seen; he could only hear laughing and jeering that did not seem to come from a human being.

When at last he reached the highest part of the mountain, where the path led down into the Rhone valley, he saw in the clear blue heaven, toward Chamonix, two glittering stars. They shone brightly; and he thought of Babette, of himself, and of his good fortune. And these thoughts made him warm.

THE VISIT TO THE MILL

"What grand prizes you have brought home," said his old foster mother. And her strange, birdlike eyes sparkled, as she twisted her thin, wrinkled neck even more strangely and faster than usual. "You carry good luck with you, Rudy. I must kiss you, my dear boy!"

Rudy allowed himself to be kissed, but one could read in his face that he did not enjoy this affectionate greeting.

"How handsome you are, Rudy!" said the old woman.

"Oh, stop your flattery," Rudy laughed; but still the compliment pleased him.

"I repeat it," said the old woman. "And fortune smiles on you."

"Yes, I think you're right there," he said, thinking of Babette. Never before had he longed so for the deep valley.

"They must have come home by now," he told himself. "It's more than two days past the day they intended to return. I must go to Bex!"

So to Bex he went, and the miller and his daughter were home. He was received in friendly fashion, and many messages of remembrance were given him from the family at Interlaken. Babette spoke very little; she had become quite silent, but her eyes spoke, and that was enough for Rudy. The miller, who usually had plenty to say, and was accustomed to making jokes and having them laughed at,

for he was "the rich miller," seemed to prefer listening to Rudy's adventures – hearing him tell of the hardships and risks that the chamois hunters had to undergo on the mountain heights, how they had to crawl along the treacherous snowy cornices on the edges of cliffs, attached to the rocks only by the force of wind and weather, and cross the frail bridges cast by the snowstorms over deep ravines.

Rudy looked very handsome, and his eyes flashed as he described the life of a hunter, the cunning of the chamois and the wonderful leaps they made, the powerful foehn, and the rolling avalanche. He noticed that every new description held the miller's interest more and more, and that he was particularly fascinated by the youth's account of the vulture and the great royal eagle.

Not far from there, in Canton Valais, there was an eagle's nest, built cleverly under a projecting platform of rock, in the face of a cliff; and in it there was an eaglet, but it was impossible to get at it.

A few days before an Englishman had offered Rudy a whole handful of gold if he would bring him the eaglet alive.

"But there is a limit to everything," said Rudy. "You can't get at that eaglet up there; it would be madness to try."

As the wine flowed freely, and the conversation flowed just as freely, Rudy thought the

The visit to the mill.
(Fritz Kredel)

evening was much too short, although it was past midnight when he left the miller's house after this, his first visit.

For a little while the lights shone through the windows, and through the green branches of the trees, while out from the open skylight on the roof crept the Parlor Cat, and along the drainpipe the Kitchen Cat came to meet her.

"Is there any news at the mill?" said the Parlor Cat. "There's some secret love-making in this house! The father doesn't know anything about it yet. Rudy and Babette have been stepping on each other's paws under the table all evening. They trod on me twice, but I didn't mew; that would have aroused suspicion."

"Well, *I* would have mewed," said the Kitchen Cat.

"What would go in the kitchen wouldn't do in the parlor," said the Parlor Cat. "I certainly would like to know what the miller will say when he hears about this engagement."

Yes, what would the miller say? That Rudy also was most anxious to know; and he couldn't make himself wait very long. Before many days had passed, when the omnibus crossed the bridge between Cantons Valais and Vaud, Rudy sat in it, with his usual self-confidence and happy thoughts of the favorable answer he would hear that evening.

And later that evening, when the omnibus was driving back along the same road, Rudy was sitting in it again, going home, while the Parlor Cat was running over to the mill with the news.

"Look here, you kitchen fellow, the miller knows everything now. The affair has come to a fine end. Rudy came here toward evening, and he and Babette found a great deal to whisper about, as they stood in the hallway outside the miller's room. I lay at their feet, but they had neither eyes nor thoughts for me.

" 'I'll go straight to your father,' said Rudy. 'My proposal is perfectly honorable.'

" 'Do you want me to go with you?' said Babette, 'to give you courage?'

" 'I have enough courage,' said Rudy, 'but if you're with me he'll have to be friendly, whether he likes it or not.'

"So they went in. Rudy stepped hard on my tail – he's awfully clumsy. I mewed, but neither he nor Babette had any ears for me. They opened the door, and went in together, and I too. I jumped up on the back of a chair, for I didn't know if Rudy would kick me. But it was the miller who kicked – and what a kick! Out of the door and back up to the mountains and the chamois! Rudy could take care of them, but not of our little Babette!"

"But what was said?" asked the Kitchen Cat.

"Said? Oh, they said everything that people say when they're wooing! 'I love her, and she loves me; and if there's milk in the can for one, there's milk in the can for two.'

" 'But she's much above you,' said the miller.

'She sits on heaps of grain, golden grain – as you know. You can't reach up to her!'

" 'There's nothing so high that one can't reach it, if one has the will to do it!' said Rudy, for he is a determined fellow.

" 'But you said a little while ago that you couldn't reach the eaglet in its nest! Babette is still higher than that.'

" 'I'll take them both,' said Rudy.

" 'Yes,' said the miller. 'I'll give her to you when you bring me the eaglet alive!' Then he laughed until the tears stood in his eyes. 'But now, thank you for your visit, Rudy. Come again tomorrow; then you'll find nobody home! Good-by, Rudy!'

"Then Babette said farewell too, as meekly as a little kitten that can't see its mother.

" 'A promise is a promise, and a man's a man!' said Rudy. 'Don't cry, Babette. I'll bring the eaglet.'

" 'I hope you break your neck!' said the miller. 'And then we'll be spared your visits here!' That's what I call kicking him out! Now Rudy's gone, and Babette just sits and cries; but the miller sings German songs he learned in his travels. I'm not going to worry myself about the matter; it wouldn't do any good."

"But it would look better if you pretended," said the Kitchen Cat.

THE EAGLE'S NEST

From the mountain path there sounded lively yodeling that meant good humor and gay courage. The yodeler was Rudy; he was going to see his friend Vesinand.

"You must help me," he said. "We'll take Ragli with us. I have to capture the eaglet up there on the top of the cliff!"

"Better try to capture the moon first. That would be about as easy a job," said Vesinand. "I see you're in good spirits."

"Yes; I'm thinking about marrying. But now, seriously, you must know how things stand with me."

And soon Vesinand and Ragli knew what Rudy wanted.

"You're a daring fellow," they said. "But you won't make it. You'll break your neck."

"One doesn't fall, so long as one doesn't think of it!" said Rudy.

They set out about midnight, with poles, ladders and ropes. The road led through brushwood and over loose stones, up, always up, up through the dark night. The water roared below, and the water trickled down from above; damp clouds swept heavily along. At last the hunters reached the edge of the precipice, where it was even darker, for the rock walls almost met, and the sky could only be seen through the narrow opening above. Close by was a deep abyss, with the hoarsely roaring water far beneath them.

All three sat quite still. They had to await daybreak, for when the parent eagle flew out, they would have to shoot it if they were to have any hopes of capturing the young one. Rudy was as still as if he were a part of the rock on which he was sitting. He held his gun ready; his eyes were fixed steadily on the highest part of the cleft, where the eagle's nest was hidden under the projecting rock. The three hunters had a long time to wait.

But at last they suddenly heard high above them a crashing, whirring sound, and the air was darkened by a huge object. Two guns took aim at the enormous eagle the moment it left the nest. A shot blazed out; for an instant the outspread wings fluttered, and then the bird slowly began to sink. It seemed that with its tremendous size and wingspread it would fill the whole chasm, and in its fall drag the hunters down with it. The eagle disappeared in the abyss below; the hunters could hear the crashing of trees and bushes, crushed by the fall of the bird.

And now the men began to get busy. Three of the longest ladders were tied tightly together. They were supposed to reach the last stepping place on the margin of the abyss, but they did not reach far enough; and the perpendicular rock side was smooth as a brick wall on up to where the nest was hidden under the highest projecting rock overhang. After some discussion they agreed that the only thing to do was to tie two more ladders together, let them down into the chasm from above, and attach these to the three already raised. With immense difficulty they dragged the two ladders up, binding them with ropes to the top; they were then let out over the rock and hung there swaying in the air over the bottomless abyss. Rudy was already seated on the lowest rung. It was an icy-cold morning, and the mist was rising heavily from the dark chasm below. Rudy was like a fly sitting on some bit of a straw that a bird, while building its nest, might have dropped on the edge of a tall factory chimney; but the insect could fly if the straw gave way, while Rudy could only break his neck. The wind howled about him, while far below in the abyss the gushing water roared out from the melting glacier – the palace of the Ice Maiden.

He then made the ladder swing to and fro, like the spider swings its body when it wants to catch anything in its slender thread; and when he, for the fourth time, touched the top of the ladders set up from below, he got a good hold on them, and bound them together with sure and skillful hands, though they swayed as if they hung on worn-out hinges.

The five long ladders, which now reached the nest, seemed like a swaying reed knocking against the perpendicular cliff. And now the most dangerous part of the job was to be done, for he had to climb as a cat climbs. But Rudy could do that, for a cat had taught him. He never noticed the presence of Dizziness, who floated in the air behind him, and stretched forth her embracing arms toward him. At last

The eagle's nest.
(Fritz Kredel)

he reached the last step of the highest ladder, and then he found that he was still not high enough even to see into the nest. He would have to use his hands to raise himself up to it; he tried the lowest part of the thick, interwoven branches, forming the base of the nest, to learn if it was sufficiently strong; then having secured a firm hold on a heavy, strong branch, he swung himself up from the ladder, until his head and chest were level with the nest. Then there swept over him a horrible stench of carrion, for putrefied lambs, chamois, and birds littered the nest.

Dizziness, who had little power over him, blew the poisonous odor into his face to make him faint; while down below, on the dank, foaming waters of the yawning ravine, sat the Ice Maiden herself, with her long pale-green hair, staring at him with eyes as deadly as two gun barrels. "Now I will catch you!"

In a corner of the nest Rudy could see the eaglet sitting – a big powerful bird, even though it could not yet fly. Staring straight at it, Rudy somehow held on with one hand, while with the other he cast a noose around the bird. Thus it was captured alive; its legs were held by the tightened cord, and Rudy flung the noose over his shoulder, so that the bird hung a good distance below him. Then he held on to a rope, flung out to help him, until his toes at last touched the highest rung of the ladder.

"Hold tightly; don't be afraid of falling and you won't fall!" That was his early training, and Rudy acted on it. He held tightly, climbed down, and believing he couldn't fall, he didn't fall.

Then there arose loud and joyous yodeling. He stood safely on the firm rocky ledge, with his eaglet.

WHAT NEWS THE PARLOR CAT HAD TO TELL

"Here's what you asked for!" said Rudy, as he entered the miller's house at Bex, and placed a large basket on the floor. When he took the lid off two yellow eyes surrounded by dark rings glared out, eyes so flashing, so fierce, that they looked as though they would burn or blast anything they saw. The neck was red and downy; the short strong beak opened to bite.

"The eaglet!" cried the miller. Babette screamed and sprang back, but could not tear her eyes from Rudy and the eaglet.

"Nothing frightens you!" said the miller to Rudy.

"And you always keep your word," said Rudy. "Everyone has his principles."

"But how did it happen that you didn't break your neck?" asked the miller.

"Because I held tightly," said Rudy. "And so I'm doing now – holding tightly to Babette."

"Better wait till you get her!" laughed the miller; and Babette knew that was a good sign.

"Let's take the eaglet out of the basket; it's horrible to see its eyes glaring. How did you manage to capture it?"

And Rudy had to describe his adventure. As he talked the miller's eyes opened wider and wider.

"With your courage and good luck you could take care of three wives!" said the miller.

"Thank you! Thank you!" cried Rudy.

"But you won't get Babette just yet!" said the miller, slapping the young hunter good-humoredly on the shoulder.

"Do you know the latest news at the mill?" said the Parlor Cat to the Kitchen Cat. "Rudy has brought us the eaglet, and takes Babette in exchange. They have actually kissed each other, and her father saw it! That's as good as an engagement! The old man didn't make any fuss at all; he kept his claws pulled in, took his afternoon nap, and left the two of them to sit and spoon. They have so much to tell each other that they won't have finished until Christmas!"

And they hadn't finished by Christmas, either. The wind shook down the yellow leaves; the snow drifted up in the valleys as well as on the high mountains; the Ice Maiden sat in her stately palace, which grew larger during the winter. The cliffs were covered with sleet, and icicles, big and heavy as elephants, hung down. Where in summer the mountain streams poured down, there were now enormous masses of icy tapestry; fantastic garlands of crystal ice hung over the snow-covered pine trees. Over the deepest valleys the Ice Maiden rode the howling wind. The carpet of snow spread down as far as Bex, so she could go there and see Rudy in the house where he spent so much time with Babette. The wedding was to take place the following summer; and their ears often tingled, for their friends often talked about it.

Then everything was sunny, and the most beautiful Alpine rose bloomed. The lovely, laughing Babette was as charming as the early spring itself – the spring which makes all the birds sing of the summertime and weddings.

"How those two do sit and drool over each other!" said the Parlor Cat. "I'm tired of their mewing now!"

THE ICE MAIDEN

Spring has unfolded her fresh green garlands of walnut and chestnut trees which burst into bloom, especially in the country extending from the bridge at St. Maurice to Lake Geneva and along the banks of the Rhone. With wild speed the river rushes from its sources beneath the green glaciers – the Ice Palace, home of the Ice Maiden, from where she allows herself to be carried on the biting wind up to the highest fields of snow, there to recline on their drifting masses in the warm sunshine. Here she sat and gazed down into the deep valleys below where she could see human beings busily bustling about, like ants on a sunlit stone.

" 'Mental giants,' the children of the sun call you," said the Ice Maiden. "You are only vermin! One rolling snowball, and your houses and villages are crushed, wiped out!" Then she raised her proud head still higher, and stared with death-threatening eyes about and below her. Then from the valley there arose a strange sound; it was the blasting of rocks – the labors of men – the building of roadbeds and tunnels for the coming of the railroad.

"They work like moles," she said, "digging passages in the rocks, and therefore are heard these sounds like the reports of guns. If I move my palaces, the noise is stronger than the roar of thunder itself."

Then up from the valley there arose thick smoke – moving forward like a fluttering veil, a waving plume – from the locomotive which on the new railway was drawing a train, carriage linked to carriage, looking like a winding serpent. It shot past with the speed of an arrow.

"They think they're the masters down there, these 'mental giants!'" said the Ice Maiden.

"But the powers of nature are still the real rulers!"

And she laughed and sang, and it made the valley tremble.

"It's an avalanche!" the people down there said.

But the children of the sun sang still more loudly of the power of mankind's thought. It commands all, it yokes the wide ocean, levels mountains, fills valleys; the power of thought makes mankind lord over the powers of nature.

At that moment a party of climbers crossed the snowfield where the Ice Maiden sat; they had roped themselves together, to form one large body on the slippery ice, near the deep abyss.

"Vermin!" she said. "*You* the lords of the powers of nature!" And she turned from them and gazed scornfully into the deep valley, where the railway train was rushing along.

"There they sit, those thoughts! But they are in the power of nature's force. I see every one of them! One sits alone like a king, others sit in a group, and half of them are asleep! And when the steam dragon stops, they climb out and go their way. Then the thoughts go out into the world!" And she laughed.

"There's another avalanche!" said the people in the valley.

"It won't reach us!" said two who sat together in the train – "two minds with but a single thought," as we say. They were Rudy and Babette, and the miller was going with them.

"Like baggage," he said. "I'm along with them as sort of extra baggage!"

The Ice Maiden.
(Edmund Dulac)

"There sit those two!" said the Ice Maiden. "Many a chamois have I crushed, millions of Alpine flowers have I snapped and broken, leaving no root behind – I destroy them all!

Thoughts! 'Mental giants,' indeed!" Again she laughed.

"That's another avalanche!" said those down in the valley.

THE GODMOTHER

At Montreux, one of the nearby towns which, with Clarens, Bernex, and Crin, encircle the northeast shore of Lake Geneva, lived Babette's godmother, the highborn English lady, with her daughters and a young relative. They had been there only a short while, but the miller had already visited them, announced Babette's engagement, and told them about Rudy and the visit to Interlaken and the young eagle – in short, the whole story. It had pleased them greatly, and they felt very kindly toward Rudy and Babette, and even the miller himself. They insisted upon all three of them coming to Montreux, and that's why they went. Babette wanted to see her godmother, and her godmother wanted to see her.

At the little village of Villeneuve, at the end of Lake Geneva, lay the steamboat which, in a voyage of half an hour, went from there to Bernex, a little below Montreux. That coast has often been celebrated by poets in song and story. There, under the walnut trees, beside the deep, blue-green lake Byron sat, and wrote his melodious verses about the prisoner in the dark, mountain Castle of Chillon. There, where Clarens is reflected amid weeping willows in the clear water, Rousseau wandered, dreaming of his Héloïse. The Rhone River glides beneath the lofty, snow-capped hills of Savoy, and near its mouth here there is a small island, so tiny that from the shore it looks as if it were a ship floating in the water. It is just a patch of rocky ground, which a century before a lady had walled around and covered with earth, where three acacia trees were planted, which now overshadowed the whole island. Babette was enchanted with this little spot; to her it was the

loveliest place to be seen on the whole trip. She said they ought to land there – they must land there – it would be so charming under those beautiful trees. But the steamer passed by and did not stop until it reached Bernex.

The little party passed up among the white sunlit walls that surrounded the vineyards before the little mountain town of Montreux, where the peasants' cottages are shaded by fig trees, and laurels and cypresses grow in the gardens. Halfway up the mountain was the hotel where the godmother lived.

The meeting was very cordial. The godmother was a stout, pleasant-looking woman, with a smiling, round face. As a child she must certainly have resembled one of Raphael's cherubs; it was still an angel's head, but older, with silver-white hair. The daughters were tall and slender, well-dressed and elegant looking. The young cousin with them, who had enough golden hair and golden whiskers for three gentlemen, was dressed in white from head to foot, and promptly began to pay devoted attention to little Babette.

Beautifully bound books and music and drawings were on the large table. The balcony door was open, and from the balcony there was a lovely view of the calm lake, so bright and clear that the villages, woods, and snow-peaks of Savoy were reflected in it.

Rudy, who was generally so lively and gay, found himself very ill at ease. He moved about as if he were walking on peas over a slippery floor. How slowly the time passed – it was like being in a treadmill! And now they had to go out for a walk! And that was just as tiresome. Rudy had to take two steps forward and one back to keep abreast of the others. They went down to Chillon, the gloomy old castle on the island, to look at dungeons and instruments of torture, rusty chains hanging from rocky walls, stone benches for those condemned to death, trap doors through which the doomed were hurled down onto iron spikes amid the surge. They called it a pleasure to look at these things! It was a dreadful place of execution, elevated by Byron's verse into the world of poetry – but to Rudy still only a place of execution. He leaned out of one of the great windows and gazed down into the blue-green water, and over to the lonely little island with the three acacias. How he longed to be there, free from the whole chattering party!

But Babette was very happy. She had had a wonderful time, she said later; and the cousin she thought was perfect!

"Yes, perfectly flippant!" said Rudy; and that was the first time he had ever said anything to her that did not please her.

The Englishman had given her a little book as s souvenir of Chillon; it was Byron's poem, *The Prisoner of Chillon*, translated into French so that she could read it.

"The book may be all right," said Rudy, "but the finely combed fellow who gave it to you didn't make a hit with me."

"He looks like a flour sack without any flour!" said the miller, laughing at his own wit.

Rudy laughed too, and said that he was exactly right.

THE COUSIN

When Rudy went to visit the mill a couple of days later, he found the young Englishman there. Babette had just set a plate of boiled trout before him, which she herself had decorated with parsley, to make it look appetizing, no doubt. Rudy thought that was entirely unnecessary. What did he want there? What was his business? To be served and pampered by Babette? Rudy was jealous, and that pleased Babette. It amused her to see revealed all the feelings of his heart – the weak as well as the strong.

Love was still an amusement to her, and she played with Rudy's heart; but it must be said that he was still the center of all her thoughts, the dearest and most cherished in the world. Still, the gloomier he looked the more merrily she laughed at him with her eyes. She would even have kissed the blond Englishman with the golden whiskers if it would have made Rudy rush out in a fury; for it would have shown her how much he loved her.

This was not the fair nor the wise thing for little Babette to do, but she was only nineteen. She had no intention of being unkind to Rudy; still less did she think how her conduct would appear to the young Englishman, or how light and improper it was for the miller's modest, newly betrothed daughter.

Where the road from Bex passes beneath the snow-clad peaks, which in the language of the country are called *diablerets*, the mill stood, near a rushing, grayish-white mountain stream that looked as if it were covered with soapsuds. It wasn't that stream that turned the mill wheel, but a smaller one which came tumbling down the rocks on the other side of river. It ran through a reservoir dammed up by stones in the road beneath, and forced itself up with violence and speed into an enclosed wooden basin, formed by a wide dam across the rushing river, where it turned the large mill wheel. When the water had piled up behind the dam it overflowed, and made the path so wet and slippery that it was difficult for anyone who wanted to take this short cut to the mill to do so without falling into the water. However, the young Englishman thought he would try it.

Dressed in white like a mill worker, he was climbing the path one evening, following the light that shone from Babette's window. He had never learned to climb, and so almost went head first into the stream, but escaped with wet arms and spattered trousers. Soaking wet and covered with mud, he arrived beneath Babette's window, climbed the old linden tree, and there began to make a noise like an owl, which was the only bird he could even try to imitate. Babette heard it and peeped out through the thin curtains, but when she saw the man in white, and realized who he was, her little heart pounded with fright, but also with anger. Quickly she put out her light, made sure the window was securely fastened, and then left him to his hooting and howling.

How terrible it would be, she thought, if Rudy were now at the mill! But Rudy wasn't at the mill – no, it was much worse – he was standing right under the tree. Loud words were spoken – angry words – they might come to blows, or even murder!

Babette hurried to open her window, and called down to Rudy to go away, adding that she couldn't let him stay there.

"You won't let me stay here!" he cried. "Then this is an appointment! You're expecting some good friend – someone you'd rather see than me! Shame on you, Babette!"

"You are very nasty!" said Babette, and started to cry. "I hate you! Go away! Go away!"

"I haven't deserved anything like this," said Rudy as he went away, his cheeks burning, his heart on fire.

Babette threw herself on her bed and cried. "And you can think that of me, Rudy, of me who loves you so!"

She was angry, very angry, and that was good for her; for otherwise she would have been deeply hurt. As it was, she could fall asleep and enjoy youth's refreshing slumber.

EVIL POWERS

Rudy left Bex, and started homeward, following the mountain path, with its cold fresh air, and where the snow is deep and the Ice Maiden reigns. The trees with their thick foliage were so far below him that they looked like potato tops; the pines and bushes became smaller; the Alpine roses were blanketed with snow, which lay in isolated patches like linen put out to be bleached. A single blue gentian stood in his path, and he crushed it with the butt of his gun. Higher up two chamois became visible, and Rudy's eyes sparkled as his thoughts turned into another course, but he wasn't near enough for a good shot. Still higher he climbed, to where only a few blades of grass grew between the rocks. The chamois passed calmly over the snowfields as Rudy pressed on.

The thick mists enshrouded him, and suddenly he found himself on the brink of a steep rock precipice. Then the rain began to fall in torrents. He felt a burning thirst; his head was hot, and his limbs were cold. He reached for his hunting flask, but found it was empty; he had not given it a thought when he rushed away, up the mountain. He had never been sick in his life, but now he suddenly felt that he was ill. He felt exhausted, and wanted only to lie down and sleep; but the rain was streaming down around him. He tried to pull himself out of it, but every object seemed to dance strangely before his eyes.

Suddenly he became aware of something he had never before seen in that place – a small, newly built hut leaning against the rock; and in the doorway stood a young girl. First he thought she was the schoolmaster's daughter, Annette, whom he had once kissed while dancing with her; but she wasn't Annette. But he was sure he had seen her before, perhaps near Grindelwald the evening he went home from the Interlaken shooting matches.

"How did you get here?" he asked.

"I'm home," she said. "Watching my flocks."

"Your flocks! Where do they find grass? There's nothing here but snow and rocks!"

"You know a lot about it!" she said and laughed. "A little way down behind here is a very nice pasture, where my goats go. I take good care of them, and never lose one. What's mine is mine!"

"You're very brave," said Rudy.

"And so are you," she answered.

"If you have any milk, please give me some; I have a terrible thirst."

"I have something much better than milk," she replied, "and you may have some. Yesterday some travelers came here with guides, and left half a flask of wine behind them, such wine as you have never tasted. They won't come back for it, and I don't drink it, so you may have it."

She brought the wine, poured some into a wooden goblet, and gave it to Rudy.

"That's fine!" he said. "I have never tasted a wine so warming and reviving!" His eyes sparkled with life; a glowing thrill of happiness swept over him, as if every sorrow and vexation had vanished from his mind; a carefree feeling awoke in him.

"But surely you are Annette, the schoolmaster's daughter!" he exclaimed. "Give me a kiss!"

"Yes, but first give me that pretty ring you're wearing on your finger!"

"My engagement ring?"

"Yes, just that ring," said the girl, then refilling the goblet, she held it to his lips, and he drank again. A feeling of joy seemed to flow through his blood. The whole world was his, he seemed to think, so why torture himself! Everything is created for our pleasure and enjoyment. The stream of life is the stream of happiness; let yourself be carried away on it – that is joy. He looked at the young girl. She was Annette, and yet not Annette; but still less was she the magical phantom, as he had called the one he had met near Grindelwald. This girl on the mountain was fresh as newly fallen snow, as blooming as an Alpine rose, as lively as a young lamb; yet still she was formed from Adam's rib, a human being like Rudy himself.

Then the Ice Maiden kissed him.
(Fritz Kredel)

He flung his arms about her and gazed into her marvelously clear eyes. It was only for a second, but how can that second be expressed or described in words? Was it the life of the soul or the life of death that took possession of his being? Was he carried up high, or did he sink down into the deep and deathly icy crevasse, deeper, always deeper? He beheld the ice walls shining like blue-green glass; bottomless crevasses yawned about him; the waters dripped, sounding like the chimes of bells, and were as clear as a pearl glowing with pale blue flames. Then the Ice Maiden kissed him – a kiss that sent an icy shiver through his whole body. He gave a cry of pain, tore himself away from her, stumbled, and fell; all went dark before his eyes, but he opened them again. The powers of evil had played their game.

The Alpine girl was gone, and the sheltering hut was gone; water streamed down on the bare rocks, and snow lay everywhere. Rudy was shivering with cold, soaked through to the skin, and his ring was gone – the engagement ring

Babette had given him. His gun lay on the snow beside him, but when he took it up and tried to fire it as a signal, it missed fire. Damp clouds filled the chasm like thick masses of snow. Dizziness sat there, glaring at her helpless prey, while there rang through the deep crevasse beneath her a sound as if a mass of rock had fallen, and was crushing and carrying away everything that obstructed its course.

Back at the miller's Babette sat and wept. It was six days since Rudy had been there – Rudy, who had been in the wrong, and should ask her pardon, for she loved him with all her heart.

AT THE MILLER'S HOUSE

"It's lot of nonsense with those people!" said the Parlor Cat to the Kitchen Cat. "It's all off now between Babette and Rudy. She just sits and cries, and he doesn't think about her any more."

"I don't like that," said the Kitchen Cat.

"I don't either," said the Parlor Cat. "But I'm not going to mourn about it. Babette can take golden whiskers for her sweetheart. He hasn't been here since the night he tried to climb onto the roof!"

The powers of evil carry out their purposes around us and within us. Rudy understood this, and thought about it. What was it that had gone on about him and inside him up there on the mountain? Was it sin or just a feverish dream? He had never known illness or fever before. While he blamed Babette, he also searched his own heart. He remembered the wild tornado, the hot whirlwind that had broken loose in there. Could he confess everything to Babette – every thought which in that hour of temptation almost brought about his action? He had lost her ring, and by that very loss she had won him back. Would she be able to confess to him? When his thoughts turned to her, so many memories crowded his mind that he felt that his heart was breaking. He saw her as a laughing, happy child, full of life; the many loving words she had addressed to him from the fullness of her heart gladdened his soul like a ray of light, and soon there was only sunshine there for Babette.

However, she would have to confess to him, and he would see that she did so.

So he went to the mill, and there was a confession; it began with a kiss, and ended with Rudy's being the sinner. His great fault was that he could have doubted for one moment Babette's faithfulness – that was very wicked of him! Such distrust, such violence, might bring misery to both of them. Yes, that was very true! Babette preached him a little sermon, which pleased her greatly and which was very becoming to her. But Rudy was right about one thing – the godmother's nephew was a babbler. She'd burn the book he had given her, and wouldn't keep the slightest thing that would remind her of him.

"Now that's all over with," said the Parlor Cat. "Rudy's back again, and they've made up; and they say that's the greatest of happiness."

"Last night," said the Kitchen Cat, "I heard the rats saying that their greatest happiness was to eat candle grease and have plenty of tainted bacon. Which of them should we believe, the lovers or the rats?"

"Neither of them," said the Parlor Cat. "That's always the safest."

Rudy's and Babette's greatest happiness was drawing near, the most beautiful day, as they call it, was coming – their wedding day!

But the wedding was not to take place in the church at Bex, nor in the miller's house; the godmother had asked that the party be held at her house, and that the ceremony be performed in the pretty little church at Montreux. And the miller was very insistent that they should agree to this arrangement, for he alone knew what the godmother intended giving the young couple –

her wedding gift would be well worth such a small concession to her wishes. The day was agreed upon. They would go to Villeneuve the evening before, then proceed to Montreux by boat the next morning, so that the godmother's daughters would have time to dress the bride.

"I suppose there'll be a second ceremony in this house," said the Parlor Cat. "Or else I know I wouldn't give a mew for the whole business."

"There's going to be a feast here, too," said the Kitchen Cat. "The ducks have been killed, the pigeons plucked, and a whole deer is hanging on the wall. My mouth waters when I look at all the food. Tomorrow they start their journey."

Yes, tomorrow! That evening Rudy and Babette sat in the miller's house for the last time as an engaged couple. Outside, the evening glow was on the Alps; the vesper bells were chiming; and the daughters of the sun sang, "That which is best shall come to pass!"

VISIONS IN THE NIGHT

The sun had gone down, and the clouds lay low in the valley of the Rhone between the tall mountains; the wind blew from the south, an African wind; it suddenly sprang up over the high summits like a foehn, which swept the clouds away; and when the wind had fallen everything for a moment was perfectly still. The scattered clouds hung in fantastic shapes between the wooded hills skirting the rushing Rhone; they hung in the shapes of sea monsters of the prehistoric world, of eagles hovering in the air, of frogs leaping in a marsh; they settled down on the swift river and seemed to sail on it, yet they were floating in the air. The current swept along an uprooted pine tree, with the water making circles around it. It was Dizziness and some of her sisters dancing in circles on the foaming stream. The moon lighted up the snow-covered mountain peaks, the dark woods, and the strange white clouds – those visions of the night that seemed to be the powers of nature. The mountain peasant saw them through his window; they sailed past in great numbers before the Ice Maiden, who had come from her glacier palace. She was sitting on a frail boat, the uprooted pine, as the waters from the glacier carried her down the river to the open lake.

"The wedding guests are coming!" was sung and murmured in the air and in the water.

There were visions outside and visions inside. And Babette had a very strange dream.

It seemed to her that she had been married to Rudy for many years. He had gone chamois hunting, leaving her at home; and the young Englishman with the golden whiskers was sitting beside her. His eyes were passionate, his words seemed to have a magic power in them. He held out his hand to her, and she was obliged to follow him; they walked away from her home, always downward. And Babette felt a weight in her heart that became heavier every moment. She was committing a sin against Rudy – a sin against God Himself. And suddenly she found herself alone; her dress had been torn to pieces by thorns, and her hair had turned gray. In deep grief she looked upward, and saw Rudy on the edge of a mountainous ridge. She stretched up her arms to him, but dared neither pray nor call out to him; and neither would have been of any avail, for she soon discovered it was not Rudy, but only his cap and shooting jacket hanging on an alpenstock, as hunters often place them to deceive the chamois. In miserable grief Babette cried, "Oh, if I had only died on my wedding day – the happiest day of my life! Oh, Lord, my God, that would have been a blessing! That would have been the best thing that could have happened for me and Rudy. No one knows his future!" Then in godless despair she hurled herself down into the deep chasm. A thread seemed to break, and the echo of sorrowful tones was heard.

Babette awoke; the dream was ended, and although partly forgotten she knew it had been a frightful one, and that she had dreamed about the young Englishman whom she had not seen or thought of for several months. She wondered if he still was at Montreux, and if she would see him at the wedding. A faint shadow passed over Babette's pretty mouth, her brows knitted; but soon there came a smile, and the sparkle returned to her eye. The sun was shining brightly outside, and tomorrow was her and Rudy's wedding day!

When she came down he was already in the parlor, and soon they set off for Villeneuve. They were both so happy, and so was the miller. He laughed and joked, and was in excellent humor, for he was a kind father and an honest soul.

"Now we are the masters of the house," said the Parlor Cat.

THE CONCLUSION

It was not yet evening when the three happy people reached Villeneuve, and sat down to dinner. The miller settled himself in a comfortable armchair with his pipe, and had a little nap. The young bridal couple went out of the town arm in arm, along the highway, under the wooded hills by the side of the deep blue-green lake. The clear water reflected the gray walls and heavy towers of gloomy-looking Chillon. The little island with its three acacias seemed quite close, looking like a bouquet lying on the lake.

"How lovely it must be over there!" said Babette, who again felt a great desire to go to the island; and her desire could be satisfied at once, for a boat was lying near the bank, and it was easy to undo the rope securing it. There was no one around of whom they could ask permission, so they got into the boat anyway.

Rudy knew how to use the oars. Like the fins of a fish, the oars divided the water, so pliant and yet so powerful, with a back for carrying and a mouth for swallowing – gentle, smiling, calmness itself, yet terrible and mighty in destruction. Foamy wake stretched out behind the boat, and in a few minutes they arrived at the little island, where they landed. There was just room for the two of them to dance.

Rudy whirled Babette around two or three times. Then they sat on the little bench under the drooping acacia, and held each other's hands and looked deep into each other's eyes, while the last rays of the setting sun streamed about them. The pine forests on the mountains took on a purplish-red tint like that of blooming heather, and where the trees stopped and the bare rocks began, they glowed as if the mountain itself were transparent. The clouds in the sky glowed a brilliant crimson; the whole lake was like a fresh, blushing rose petal. As the shades of evening gathered, the snow-capped mountains of Savoy turned a dark blue, but the highest summits still shone like red lava and for a moment reflected their light on the mountains before the vast masses were lost in darkness. It was the Alpine glow, and Rudy and Babette thought they had never before seen so magnificent a sight. The snow-covered Dents du Midi glistened like the disk of the full moon when it rises above the horizon.

"Oh, what beauty! What happiness!" both of them said.

"Earth can give me no more," said Rudy. "An evening like this is like a whole life. How often have I realized my good fortune, as I realize it now, and thought that if everything ended for me at once now I have still had a happy life! What a blessed world this is! One day passes, and a new one, even more beautiful than the other, begins. Our Lord is infinitely good, Babette!"

"I'm so happy!" she said.

"Earth can give me no more," exclaimed Rudy. Then the vesper bells sounded from the Savoy mountains and the mountains of Switzerland. The dark-blue Jura stood up in golden splendor in the west.

"God give you all that is brightest and best!" exclaimed Babette.

"He will," said Rudy. "Tomorrow I shall have that wish. Tomorrow you'll be wholly mine – my own lovely, little wife!"

"The boat!" Babette suddenly cried.

For the boat that was to take them back had broken loose and was drifting away from the island.

"I'll get it!" said Rudy, and he stripped off his coat and boots, plunged into the lake, and swam with vigorous strokes after the boat.

The clear blue-green water from the mountain glacier was icy and deep. Rudy looked down into the depths; he took only a single glance, and yet, he thought he saw a gold ring trembling, glittering, wavering there! He thought of his lost engagement ring, and the ring became larger and spread out into a glittering circle, within which appeared the clear glacier. Endless deep chasms yawned about it, and the dropping water tinkled like the sound of bells and glowed with pale blue flames. In a second he beheld what will take us many long words to describe!

Young hunters and young girls, men and women who had once fallen into the glacier's crevasses, stood there as in life, with open eyes and smiling lips, while far below them arose from buried villages the chimes of church bells. The congregation knelt beneath the church roofs; icicles made the organ pipes, and the mountain torrents furnished the music. And the Ice Maiden sat on the clear, transparent ground. She stretched herself up toward Rudy and kissed his feet, and there shot through his limbs a deadly chill like an electric shock – ice and fire, one could not be distinguished from the other in that brief touch.

"Mine! Mine!" sounded around him and within him. "I kissed you when you were little – kissed you on the mouth! Now I kiss you on your toes and your heels – now you belong to me!"

And he disappeared in the clear blue water.

All was still. The church bells had ceased their ringing; their last tones had died away with the glow on the red clouds above.

"You are mine!" sounded from the depths below. "You are mine!" resounded from beyond the heights – from infinity itself!

How wonderful to pass from love to love, from earth to heaven!

A thread seemed to break, and sorrowful tones echoed around. The icy kiss of death had conquered what was mortal; the prelude to the drama of life had ended before the play itself had begun. And discord had resolved itself into harmony.

Do you call this a sad story?

Poor Babette! For her it was the hour of anguish. The boat drifted farther and farther away. No one on the mainland knew that the bridal couple had crossed over to the little island. Evening came on, the clouds gathered, and darkness settled down. Alone, despairing and crying, she stood there. A storm broke out; lightning flashed over the Jura mountains and over the peaks of Savoy and Switzerland; from all sides came flash after flash, while one peal of thunder followed the other for minutes at a time. One instant the lightning was so vivid that the surroundings were bright as day – every single vine stem was as distinct as at high noon – and in the next instant everything was plunged back into the blackest darkness. The lightning formed circles and zigzagged, then darted into the lake; and the increasing noise of the rolling thunder echoed from the surrounding mountains. On the mainland the boats had been drawn far up the beach, while all living things sought shelter. And now the rain poured down in torrents.

"Where can Rudy and Babette be in this terrible storm?" said the miller.

Babette sat with folded hands, her head in her lap, utterly worn out by grief, tears, and screams for help.

"In the deep water," she said to herself, "far down there as if under a glacier, he lies!"

Then she thought of what Rudy had told her about his mother's death, and of his escape, how he was lifted up out of the cleft of the glacier almost dead. "The Ice Maiden has him again!"

Then there came a flash of lightning as dazzling as the rays of the sun on white snow. Babette jumped up; at that moment the lake rose like a shining glacier; there stood the Ice Maiden, majestic, bluish, pale, glittering, with Rudy's corpse at her feet.

"Mine!" she said, and again everything was darkness and torrential rain.

"Horrible!" groaned Babette. "Ah, why should he die when our day of happiness was so near? Dear God, make me understand; shed light into my heart! I cannot understand the ways of your almighty power and wisdom!"

And God enlightened her heart. A memory – a ray of mercy – her dream of the night before – all rushed vividly through her mind. She remembered the words she had spoken, the wish for the best for herself and Rudy.

"Pity me! Was it the seed of sin in my heart? Was my dream, a glimpse into the future, whose course had to be violently changed to save me from guilt? How miserable I am!"

In the pitch-black night she sat weeping. And now in the deep stillness around her she seemed to hear the last words he had spoken here, "Earth can give me no more." They had been spoken in the fullest of joy; they echoed in the depths of great sorrow.

A few years have passed since that night. The lake smiles; its shores are smiling; the vines yield luscious grapes; steamboats with waving pennants glide swiftly by; pleasure boats with their two sails unfurled skim like white butterflies over the mirrored water; the railway beyond Chillon is open now, leading far into the valley of the Rhone. At every station strangers get out, studying in their little red guidebooks what sights they should see. They visit Chillon, see the little island with the three acacias, and read in their books about a bridal couple who in 1856 rowed over to it one evening – how not until the next morning could the bride's despairing cries be heard on the mainland.

But the guidebooks tell nothing about Babette's quiet life in her father's house – not at the mill, for strangers live there now – in the pretty house near the railway station, where many an evening she gazes from her window beyond the chestnut trees to the snowy mountains over which Rudy had loved to range. In the evening hours she can see the Alpine glow – up there where the daughters of the sun settle down, and sing again their song about the traveler whose coat the whirlwind snatched off, taking it, but not the man himself.

There is a rosy glow upon the mountain's snowfields; there is a rosy tint in every heart in which lives the thought, "God wills what is best for us!" But it is not always revealed to us as it was revealed to Babette in her dream.

THE BUTTERFLY

THE BUTTERFLY WANTED a sweetheart, and naturally he wanted one of the prettiest of the dear little flowers. He looked at each of them; there they all sat on their stalks as quiet and modest as little maidens ought to sit before they are engaged; but there were so many to choose from that it would be quite difficult to decide. So the Butterfly flew down to the Daisy, whom the French call "Marguerite."

They know she can tell fortunes. This is the way it's done: the lovers pluck off the little petals one by one, asking questions about each other, "Does he love me from the heart? A little? A lot? Or loves he not at all?" – or something like that; everyone asks in his own language. So the Butterfly also came to ask, but he wouldn't bite off the leaves; instead he kissed each one in turn, thinking that kindness is the best policy.

"Sweet Miss Marguerite Daisy," he said, "you're the wisest woman of all the flowers – you can tell fortunes! Tell me, should I choose this one or that one? Which one am I to have? When you have told me, I can fly straight to her and propose."

But Marguerite answered not a word. She resented his calling her "a woman," for she was unmarried and quite young. He put his question a second time, and then a third time, and when he still couldn't get a word out of her he gave up and flew away to begin his wooing.

It was early spring; the snowdrops and crocuses were growing in abundance. "They're really very charming," said the Butterfly. "Neat little schoolgirls, but a bit too sweet." For, like all very young men, he preferred older girls. So he flew to the anemones, but they were a bit too bitter for his taste. The violets were a little too sentimental, the tulips much too gay. The lilies too middle class, the linden blossoms too small, and, besides, there were too many in their family. He admitted the apple blossoms looked like roses, but if they opened one day and the wind blew they fell to pieces the very next; surely such a marriage would be far too brief. He liked the sweet pea best of all; she was red and white, dainty and delicate, and belonged to that class of domestic girl who is pretty yet useful in the kitchen. He was about to propose to her when he noticed a pea pod hanging near by, with a withered flower clinging to it. "Who's that?" he asked.

But Marguerite answered not a word.
(Fritz Kredel)

"It's my sister," said the pea flower.

"Oh, so that's how you'll look later on!" This frightened the Butterfly, and away he flew.

Honeysuckles hung over the hedges; there were plenty of those girls, long-faced and with yellow complexions. No, he didn't like that kind at all. Yes, but what *did* he like? You ask him!

Spring passed and summer passed; then autumn came, and he was still no nearer making up his mind. Now the flowers wore beautiful, colorful dresses, but what good did that do? The fresh, fragrant youth had passed, and it is fragrance the heart needs as one grows older; and of course dahlias and hollyhocks have no particular fragrance. So the Butterfly went to see the mint.

"It's not exactly a flower – or rather it's all flower, fragrant from root to top, with sweet scent in every leaf. Yes, she's the one I want!" So at last he proposed to her.

But the mint stood stiff and silent, and at last said, "Friendship, if you like, but nothing else. I'm old, and you're old, too. It would be all right to live for each other, but marriage – no! Don't let's make fools of ourselves in our old age!"

And so the Butterfly did not find a sweetheart at all. He had hesitated too long, and one shouldn't do that! The Butterfly became an old bachelor, as we call it.

Now it was a windy and wet late autumn; the wind blew cold down the backs of the poor trembling old willows. And that made them creak all over. When the weather is like that it isn't pleasant to fly about in summer clothing, outside. But the Butterfly was not flying out-of-doors; he had happened to fly into a room where there was a fire in the stove and the air was as warm as summer. Here he could at least keep alive. "But just to keep alive isn't enough," he said. "To live you must have sunshine and freedom and a little flower to love!"

And he flew against the windowpane, was noticed by people, admired, and set on a needle to be stored in a butterfly collection. This was the most they could do for him.

"Now I'm sitting on a stalk, just like the flowers," said the Butterfly. "It isn't very much fun; it's just like being married, you're bound up so tightly!" He comforted himself with this reflection.

"A poor consolation, after all," said the pot plants in the room.

"But you can't take the opinion of pot plants," thought the Butterfly. "They converse too much with human beings!"

THE DRYAD

WE'RE GOING TO Paris to see the exposition! Now we're there! It was a speedy journey, done completely without witchcraft – we went by steam, in a ship and on a railroad. Our time is indeed a time of fairy tales.

Now we are in a large hotel in the middle of Paris. The staircase is decorated with flowers, and soft carpets are spread over the steps. Our room is pleasant; the balcony door is open, and we can look out onto a large square. Down there is spring, which has come to Paris, having arrived at the same time we did, in the form of a big, young chestnut tree with delicate leaves beginning to open. How much more richly that tree is dressed in the beauty of spring than the other trees on the square! One of them has stepped out of the row of living trees and lies on the ground with its roots torn up. Where that tree stood the young chestnut will be planted, and there it will grow.

It is still standing high up on the heavy wagon that brought it to Paris this morning from many miles out in the country. For years it had stood out there, close to a mighty oak, under which

We went by steam, in a ship and on a railroad.
(Fritz Kredel)

the pious old pastor often used to sit and tell his stories to the listening children. Of course, the young chestnut tree had also listened.

The Dryad that lived in this tree was then but a child; she could remember way back when the chestnut tree was so small it could hardly peep over the tall grass blades and ferns. These were then as large as they ever would be; but the tree grew bigger every year, drinking in air and sunshine, dew and rain; the powerful winds shook it and bent it back and forth, which was an important part of its education.

The Dryad was pleased with her life and enjoyed living, was pleased with the sunshine and the songs of birds; but she liked best of all the human voice for she knew the language of people as well as that of the animals. Butterflies, cockchafers, and dragonflies – indeed, everything that could fly came to visit her, and everyone that came would gossip. They talked about the villages, the vineyards, the woods, and the old castle with its park, in which there were dikes and canals; down there in water also dwelt beings who in their own way could fly from place to place – beneath the water – beings with knowledge and imagination, but who said nothing, for they were too wise. The swallow, which often dived down deep into the water, told about the bright goldfish, the fat turbot, the sturdy perch, and the old moss-covered carp. The swallow gave very good descriptions, but it's always better to go and look for oneself, it said. But how could the Dryad ever see all these things? She had to be satisfied with the beautiful landscape and the buzz of human activity.

Everything was delightful, but most delightful when the old pastor stood there under the oak tree and talked about France and about the great deeds of men and women whose names are remembered through the ages with admiration. The Dryad heard of the shepherd maid, Joan of Arc, of Charlotte Corday; she learned of ancient times, and the times of Henry IV and Napoleon I, and she even heard of the genius and glory of our own times. She heard of names that were deep in the hearts of the people, and that France is the world's country, the world's gathering place of genius, with the Cradle of Liberty at its center.

The village children listened attentively, and the Dryad just as attentively; she became a school child like the rest. In the shapes of the drifting clouds she could see many pictures of those things she had learned. The cloudy sky was her picture book.

The Dryad.
(John William Waterhouse)

She had thought she was very happy in this beautiful France, but she began to believe that the birds – in fact, all creatures that could fly – were much better off than she. Even the fly could look far beyond her horizon. France was so large and so beautiful, but she could see only a very small part of it. France was as broad as the world, with vineyards and forests and great cities, and of all these Paris was the greatest and most glorious! The birds could fly there, but she, never!

Among the village children there was a little girl so ragged and so poor, but very pretty to look upon. She was always singing and laughing, and often tied red flowers in her black hair.

"Don't go to Paris!" said the old pastor. "Poor child, if you go there it will be the ruin of you!"

And yet she went. The Dryad often thought of her, for they had both had the same desire and yearning to see the great city.

Spring came, and then summer; autumn came, and then winter. A couple of years went by.

The Dryad's tree was bearing its first chestnut blossoms, and the birds chirped around them in the bright sunlight. A noble lady came driving along the road in a grand carriage. She herself was driving the beautiful and spirited horses, with a smartly dressed little groom sitting behind her. The Dryad recognized her; the old pastor knew her. He shook his head and said sadly, "You did go there, and it proved your ruin, poor Marie!"

"She, poor?" thought the Dryad. "No! What a change! She's dressed like a duchess; that's what she got in the city of enchantment. Oh, if only I were there in all that light and splendor! When I look over there where I know the city is, I can see how it lights up the clouds in the night."

Indeed, she would look in that direction every evening, every night; there she could see the brightness along the horizon. On clear, moonlit nights she missed the bright cloudiness; she missed the drifting clouds that showed her pictures of the great city and its history.

The child clings to its picture book. The Dryad clings to her cloud book, her book of thoughts.

A balmy, cloudless sky was like a blank page to her, and it had now been several days since she had seen one like that. It was summertime, and the days were hot and sultry, without a cooling breeze; every flower and leaf was drowsy, and people were, too.

The clouds rose at that corner of the horizon where in the night the brightness announced, "Here is Paris!" All the clouds gathered and rose together, forming what appeared to be whole mountains; they pushed through the air and spread out over the entire countryside as far as the Dryad could see. They were heaped in mighty, rocklike, thundery-blue masses, layer on layer, high into the air. Then flashes of light shot out from them. "These are also the servants of God our Master," the old pastor had said. And then out flashed a bluish, blinding light, a blaze of lightning, which tried to rival the sun itself; it shattered the piled-up clouds.

The lightning struck down, down at the mighty old oak tree, splitting it to its very roots; the crown was shattered, the trunk torn apart. The tree crashed down and fell as if spreading itself out to receive the messenger of light. Not even the mightiest cannon could roar through the air and over the land at the birth of a King's son as did the thunder in saluting the passing of the old oak tree.

The rain streamed down. A refreshing breeze sprang up; the storm was over, and a holiday calm settled on the countryside. The villagers gathered around the fallen old oak tree; the old pastor spoke a few words in praise of it, and a painter made a sketch of the old tree as a lasting souvenir.

"Everything passes on," said the Dryad, "passes on as the clouds do, never to return."

Never again did the pastor come there. The roof of the schoolhouse had crashed in, and the pulpit was broken. No more did the children come. But autumn came, and winter came, and then spring. And during this time the Dryad's eyes were turned toward that corner on the distant horizon where every evening and night the lights of Paris shone like a belt of radiance. Out of Paris sped locomotive after locomotive, train after train, whistling and roaring, constantly. At every hour, in the evenings, at midnight, in the morning, and throughout the day, the trains arrived, and from these, and into these, people from all countries of the world pushed. A new wonder of the world drew them to Paris. How did this wonder show itself?

"A gorgeous flower of art and industry," people said, "has sprung up on the barren sands of the Champ de Mars. It's a gigantic sunflower, and from its leaves you can study geography or statistics, or become as wise as a councilman, or be inspired by art and poetry, or learn about the products and greatness of every country."

"It's a fairy-tale flower," others said, "a colored lotus, spreading its green leaves like a velvet carpet, the leaves that shot up in the early spring. Summer will see it in its greatest glory, and the storms of autumn will blow it away, leaving neither leaves nor roots."

Before the military school, the Champ de Mars lay stretched out in time of peace, a field without grass and straw, a piece of sandy desert cut from the African wilderness, where Fata Morgana shows her mysterious air castles and hanging gardens; they were more magnificent, more wondrous, now on the Champ de Mars, for they had been converted into reality by human skill.

"They have built the palace of the modern Aladdin," it was said. "Day after day, hour after hour, it unfolds more and more of its new splendors."

There was an endless array of halls in marble and many colors. The giant with bloodless veins moved his steel and iron limbs there in the great circular hall. Works of art in metal, in stone, in tapestry, loudly proclaimed the powerful genius that labored in all the lands of the world. There were picture gallery and flower show. Everything that hand and brain could create was on exhibition in the workshop of the mechanic. Even relics from ancient castles and peat moors were to be found there. The overwhelmingly great, colorful show should have been reproduced in miniature and squeezed into the dimensions of a toy, to be seen and appreciated in its entirety.

There on the Champ de Mars stood, as on a huge Christmas table, Aladdin's castle of art and industry, and around it were knick-knacks of greatness from every country; every nation found a memory of its home.

There was the royal palace of Egypt, and there a caravanserai from the desert. The Bedouin from the land of the hot sun galloped past; and there were the Russian stables, with beautiful fiery horses from the steppes. Over there was the small thatched cottage of a Danish peasant, with Dannebrog, the flag of Denmark, next to Gustavus Vasa's beautifully carved wooden cottage from Dalarne. American log cabins, English cottages, French pavilions, mosques, churches, and theaters were all spread about in a wonderful manner. And in the middle of all this was the fresh green turf, with clear running water, flowering shrubs, rare trees, and glass houses where one might imagine oneself in a tropical forest. Complete rose gardens, brought from Damascus, bloomed in glory under glass roofs. What colors and fragrance! Artificial grottoes contained specimens of various fishes in fresh- and salt-water ponds – it was like standing at the bottom of the ocean there among the fishes and polyps.

Word spread that all these things were now being exhibited on the Champ de Mars, and an immense crowd of human beings crawled all over this richly decked feast table like a swarm of ants on a journey. Some went on foot or were drawn in wagons, for not everyone's legs can endure such tiresome traveling.

From early dawn until late at night they came there. Steamer after steamer, crowded with visitors, glided down the Seine. The mass of carriages was continually increasing, and the multitude of travelers on foot and horseback increased; streetcars and buses were jammed, packed, and spilling over with human beings. All these currents flowed toward one goal – the Paris Exposition!

Every entrance was bright with the flag of France, and around the bazaar of all nations waved the flags of the various countries. A burring and buzzing sounded from the hall of the machines, and chimes rang out from the towers, while the tones of the organs sounded from the churches, mingled with hoarse, nasal strains from Oriental coffeehouses. It was a Babel empire, a Babel language, a wonder of the world.

All this really happened – at least, according to reports. Who hasn't heard about it? The Dryad knew all about it; she knew everything that has been told here of the world's new wonder in the city of cities. "Hurry, all you birds, fly there and see it; then come back and tell me about it!" was the prayer of the Dryad.

Her longing grew until it became a great desire; it became the one thought of her life. And then …

In the silent, solemn night the full moon was shining, and from its face the Dryad saw a spark come forth, as bright as a falling star, and fall to the foot of the tree, whose branches shivered as if shaken by a tempest – and then a mighty, shining figure stood there. It spoke with a tender voice, and yet as powerfully as the judgment-day trumpet that kisses to life and calls to judgment.

"You shall go to the city of enchantments! There you shall take root and enjoy the air and the sunshine, but your life shall be shortened. The long procession of years that awaited you here in the open country will shrink to a small number. Poor Dryad, it will be your ruin! Your longing will grow and your great desire and craving will increase until the tree itself will be a prison to you. You will leave your shelter and change your nature; you will fly forth to mingle with human beings, and then your years will shrink to half of a May fly's lifetime – to one night only! The flame of your life will be blown out. The leaves of the tree will wither and blow away, never to return."

So said the voice; thus it rang out. And then the shining being disappeared – but not the Dryad's longing and desire; she trembled in a violent fever of anticipated joy. Rejoicingly she said, "I shall go to the city of cities. Life will begin for me – floating like the clouds, whither no one knows!"

The time of fulfillment came at early dawn, when the moon had grown pale and the skies had reddened; then the words of promise were to come true. Men came with spades and poles. They dug carefully around and deep under the roots of the tree. Then they lifted the tree out of the ground with its roots and the earth about them, and wound straw mats around the roots to make a warm foot bag. And then the tree was set on a wagon and tied securely. Now it was to go on a journey to Paris, and it was to remain and grow in the great metropolis of France, the city of cities.

The branches and leaves of the chestnut tree trembled as they began to move it. The Dryad trembled, too, but with the joy of expectation.

"Away! Away!" sounded every heartbeat. "Away! Away!" rang the trembling words of longing. The Dryad forgot to say "Farewell" to her old home, to the swaying blades of grass and the innocent daisies that had looked up to her as to a great lady in the garden of our

Father, a young princess playing shepherdess in the country.

The chestnut tree on the wagon nodded "Farewell" or "Away!" – the Dryad didn't know which. Her thoughts and dreams were of the wonderful new and yet familiar life which would soon unfold itself. Neither the happy heart of an innocent child nor the heart filled with passion was ever more filled with thought than hers was on her journey to Paris.

Not "Farewell!" – but "Away! Away!" The wagon wheels turned round and round; the distance came near and then soon lay behind. The country changed, as the clouds above changed. New vineyards, woods, villages, villas, and gardens came into view, came closer, and then rolled past. The chestnut tree moved on, and the Dryad moved on with it. Locomotive after locomotive roared past. They blew clouds that took on the shapes of figures, which spoke of Paris, where they came from and where the Dryad was going.

Of course, everything around her knew where she was going. It seemed to her that every tree she passed stretched its branches toward her and begged, "Take me with you! Take me with you!" In every tree there lived a yearning dryad.

What a change! What a trip! The houses seemed to come springing right up out of the ground, more and more of them, closer and closer together. Chimneys appeared like flowerpots, placed side by side, one after another, on the roofs. Huge inscriptions, in letters a yard long, and colorfully painted figures covered the walls from ground to roofs, and shone brightly.

"Where does Paris begin, and when will I be there?" the Dryad asked herself.

There were increasing crowds of people; the tumult and noise grew louder. Carriage followed carriage; people were on foot and on horseback. There were shops on all sides, and music, song, talking, and screaming.

Carriage followed carriage; people were on foot and on horseback. (Fritz Kredel)

Now the Dryad, in her tree, was in the center of Paris.

The big, heavy wagon stopped in a little square where trees were planted and around which were high houses. Every window had its own balcony, and from these people looked down at that fresh, young chestnut tree which had been driven there to be planted in the place of the dead, uprooted tree that lay on the ground. People passing by stopped for a while to smile at that fresh green bit of early spring. The older trees, their leaves yet scarcely budding, greeted it with rustling branches, "Welcome! Welcome!" And the fountain, which spouted its water into the air so that it splashed into the basin, let the wind carry a few drops to the new arrival, to give it a welcome drink.

The Dryad felt the tree being taken down from the wagon and then being put into its destined home. The roots were covered with earth, and fresh green turf was laid on top of that. Blooming shrubs were planted, and earthen pots with flowers in them were placed about. Thus a whole little garden appeared in the midst of the square.

The dead, uprooted tree, killed by gas fumes, hearth smoke, and all the stifling city air, was thrown upon the wagon and hauled away. The crowd watched; old people and children sat upon the bench in the little park, looking at the leaves of the newly planted tree. And we, who tell you about all this, stood on our balcony, gazing down on the young tree that had just come from the fresh air of the country and said what the old pastor would have said if he had been there: "Poor Dryad!"

"How happy I am, how happy!" said the Dryad. "And yet I can't quite understand it. I can't explain how I feel; it all seems to be the way I thought it would be, and yet it isn't quite what I expected!"

The houses were so high and so close. The sun shone upon only one wall; that was covered with posters and placards, and people crowded and thronged around it. Carriages rushed by, light ones and heavy ones. Buses, filled to overflowing, rattled by like moving houses. Carts and carriages squabbled over the right of way.

"Won't these overgrown houses standing so stiflingly close," thought the Dryad, "move away and make room for other shapes and forms, the way the clouds do in the sky? Why don't they move aside, so I can really see Paris and beyond Paris?" She felt she had to see Notre-Dame, the Vendôme Column, and the many wonderful works that had drawn and were still drawing so many people there.

But the houses didn't move from their places.

The lamps were lighted while it was still daylight, and the gaslight gleamed from all the shopwindows, lighting up the branches of the trees; it was almost like summer sunlight. But the stars above looked exactly the same as the Dryad had seen them back home. She thought she felt a clean and mild breeze come from there. She felt uplifted, strengthened, and could feel a new vigor flow through the tree from the very tips of the leaves to its roots. She then realized that she was in the world of living people and felt she was looked upon with kindly eyes; all around her were tumult and tones, colors and lights. The tones of wind

instruments came to her from the side streets, hurdy-gurdies playing dance-provoking melodies. Yes, for dancing, for dancing! for pleasure and amusement, these were played. It was a music to make men and horses, even carriages, trees, and houses, dance, if they could. All this fanned an intoxicating yearning for pleasure in the heart of the Dryad.

"How glorious! How beautiful all this is!" she cried rejoicingly. "I'm in Paris!"

The day that came, and the night that followed it, and then the following day brought the same display, the same uproar, the same life, changing and yet always the same.

"By now I know every tree and flower in this square; I know every house, balcony, and shop in this little corner where they've stuck me and where I can see nothing of the great and mighty city. Where is the Arc de Triomphe, and the boulevards, and that wonder of the world? I can't see anything of all this. I stand as if imprisoned in a cage here among these high houses, which I know by heart now, with all their inscriptions, posters, and placards – all the painted delicacies for which I have no more appetite. Where is that which I've heard so much about, which I have known and longed for, the reason I wanted to come here? What have I got – gained, found? I yearn as much as I did before. I know the life I want. I want to go out among the living people and mingle with them; I want to fly like the birds and see and feel and become like a human being! I would rather really live for half a day than spend a lifetime of years in daily idleness and languor, becoming sick, sinking, falling like dew in the meadow, and then disappearing! I want to sail like the clouds, bathe in the sun of life, look down on everything below as the clouds do, and then disappear as they do – where, no one knows!"

This was the sigh of the Dryad, going aloft as a prayer.

"Take from me all my years of life and grant me but half of a May fly's life! Free me from my prison; give me human life and human happiness, though it be but for a fleeting moment, for only this one night, and then punish me, if you wish, for my longing for life! Free me, even if this dwelling of mine, this fresh young tree, wither, be cut down, turned to ashes, and blown away by the winds!"

There was a rustling among the boughs of the tree, and a strange sensation came over it. Every leaf shivered, and fiery sparks seemed to shoot forth from them. A gust of wind shook the crown of the tree. And then there came forth a feminine form – the Dryad herself! In the same instant she found herself beneath the green boughs, rich with leaves and lit by gaslight from all sides. She was as young and beautiful as poor Marie, to whom one had said, "The great city will be your ruin!"

The Dryad sat at the foot of the tree, which she had locked and whose key she had thrown away. So young, so lovely! The stars saw her, and they twinkled; the gas lamps saw her as they glittered, beckoning to her. How slender she was, and yet so strong, a child and yet a full-grown maiden! Her dress was as smooth as silk, as green as the freshly unfolded leaves of the crown of the tree. In her nut-brown hair was a half-opened chestnut blossom. She looked like the Goddess of Spring.

For a brief moment she sat there motionless, and then she bounded off around the corner like a gazelle. She ran and darted the way reflected sunbeams dart here and there from a mirror being moved in the sunshine. If one had looked closely and could have seen what was there to see, how wondrous this would have been to him! Whenever she rested a moment, the color of her dress and of her figure was changed, according to the nature of the place where she stood and the lights that fell on her.

She reached the boulevards, where there was an ocean of light from the gas flames in the street lamps, stores, and cafés. There were rows of young and slender trees, each of which shielded its dryad from the artificial sunlight. The whole vast sidewalk was like one large dining room, with tables of all sorts of refreshments, from champagne and chartreuse to coffee and beer. There were exhibits of flowers, of pictures, statues, books, and colored materials.

From the crowd by the high houses she watched the roaring streams between the rows of trees; there was a surging river of rolling wagons, cabriolets, chariots, buses, coaches, men on horseback, and marching troops. Life and limb were endangered by any attempt to cross to the other side. Now a blue light shone the brightest, and then the gaslight was again the most brilliant; a rocket had suddenly shot up – from where, to where?

Surely this must be the greatest highway of the world's greatest city! There were charming Italian melodies, and Spanish songs with castanet accompaniment. But the strains from Minutet's music box drowned all the other sounds – that exciting cancan music which Orpheus never knew and Helen never heard. Even the wheelbarrow would have danced on its one wheel if it could have. The Dryad did dance; she whirled and soared, and changed colors like a hummingbird in the sunshine, every house and its interior being reflected on her.

As the glorious lotus flower, torn from its roots, is carried away by the whirling river, so was the Dryad carried along, and whenever she stopped she changed into a new form; consequently, no one could follow her, recognize her, or even view her. Everything passed by her like cloud pictures – face after face – but she recognized none of them; she saw no familiar forms from home. Before her mind came two bright eyes, and she thought at once of Marie. Poor Marie, that ragged, gay child with the red flowers in her black hair. She was here in this worldly city – rich and charming, as when she had driven by the pastor's house, the Dryad's tree and the old oak. More than likely, she was somewhere in this deafening uproar; perhaps she had just alighted from that magnificent carriage waiting over there. Brilliant carriages, with richly liveried coachmen and footmen wearing silk stockings, were drawn up in a line, and the nobility alighting from them were all ladies beautifully dressed. They passed through the open gates and ascended the broad, high steps that led into that stately building with the marble columns. Could this, perhaps, be the great wonder of the world? Surely Marie must be there!

"Sancta Maria!" was being sung within. The fragrance of incense rolled out under the high, painted and gilded arch, where it was always twilight. This was the Church of the Madeleine.

Dressed in the most costly black, fashioned after the finest and newest modes, the ladies of the aristocracy glided over the polished floor. Crests sparkled from the clasps of magnificent prayerbooks bound in velvet and were embroidered on perfumed handkerchiefs bordered with costly Brussels lace. A few of the women knelt in silent prayer before the high altar; others went to the confessionals. The Dryad felt an uneasiness, a fear, as if she were in a place where she should not be. It was a house of silence, a great hall of mystery and secrecy. Everything was said in whispers or in silent trust.

Now the Dryad realized that she was wrapped in silk and a lace veil, like the ladies of wealth and noble birth. Was every one of them a child of desire and longing like herself?

A deep, painful sigh was heard; did it come from the confessional or from the bosom of the Dryad? She drew the veil more closely about her. She was breathing in incense fumes and not the fresh air. This was not the place she had longed for.

"Away, away! Take flight, without rest! The May fly that lives but a day has no rest; her flight is her life!"

The Dryad was out again among the bright gas lamps and the magnificent fountains.

"Not all the water from the fountain can wash away the blood of the innocents slain here!"

Those words were spoken. Here stood many strangers who spoke in loud and lively tones, which no one had dared to do in the great hall of secrecy from which she had just come.

A big stone slab was turned and then raised – why, she did not understand. She saw an opening into the depths of the earth. The strangers stepped down, leaving the starlit sky, the brilliant gaslights, and all the life of the living.

"I'm afraid!" said one of the women who stood here. "I don't dare go down! I care little about seeing the wonders there. Stay here with me!"

"And go home?" said a man. "Leave Paris without having seen the most remarkable thing of all, the wonderwork of modern times, the result of one man's mind and skill?"

"I'll not go down there," was the reply.

"The wonderwork of modern times," it had been said. And the Dryad had heard this and understood. At last she was to reach the goal of her greatest longing, and here was the entrance – down to the vast depths beneath Paris. She had not expected this, but now she had heard about it, and had seen the strangers descend, and she followed them.

The steps were of cast iron, spiral-shaped, broad and comfortable; a lamp was burning below, and deeper down there was another. She found herself in a labyrinth of endless passages and halls crossing each other. Every street and lane in Paris could be seen there, as if reflected in a mirror. Their names could be read, and every house above had its number here, and its root, which led down under the hard, lonely walk that squeezed its way along the wide canal with its onward-rolling drainage. Above this was the aqueduct of fresh running water, and still higher gas pipes and telegraph wire hung like a network. Lamps shone in the distance, as if they were reflected images from the worldly city above. Now and then a rumbling could be heard overhead; it came from the heavy wagons crossing the bridges. Where was the Dryad?

You have heard of the catacombs; they are nothing compared with this underground world, this wonder of our times, the sewers of Paris! That was where the Dryad was, and not at the World's Fair on the Champ de Mars.

On all sides were heard exclamations of astonishment, wonder, and approval.

"Out of the deep here," they said, "come health and long life for the thousands above. Our age is the age of progress, with all its blessings!"

That was the opinion of people, the talk of people, but not that of the scavengers who were born here and built their homes and lived here – the rats. From the cracks of an old stone wall the rats squeaked so loudly and distinctly that the Dryad could understand them. A big, old rat, whose tail had been bitten off, piped in a shrill voice of his feelings, his anguish, and the only idea in his mind; and his whole family approved of every word he said.

"I am disgusted by the miaow, the human miaow, the ignorant talk! Indeed, everything is very fine now, with gas and oil, but I don't eat such things. It has become so clean and light here that one is ashamed and doesn't know what one is ashamed of. I wish we lived in the good old days of the tallow candles; those times are not so far back – those romantic times, as people call them."

"What are you talking about?" asked the Dryad. "I've never seen you before. What are you talking about?"

"The wonderful old days," said the rat, "the days when Greatgrandfather and Great-grandmother rat were young. At that time it was a great adventure to come down here.

Those were the days for the rats of Paris! Mother Pest used to live down here then; she would kill human beings, but never rats. Robbers and smugglers could breathe freely down here. Then this was the asylum for the most fascinating characters I ever saw, such characters as one sees nowadays only in the melodramatic plays. Those romantic days have gone, even for us rats; we have fresh air now – and petroleum!"

Thus the rat squeaked, squeaked over the new times, and in honor of the good old days with Mother Pest.

Now they came to a carriage, a sort of open bus, drawn by two small, lively ponies. The group entered and drove along the Boulevard Sébastopol – that is, along the underground boulevard. Right above them, in Paris, was the real boulevard of that name, crowded with people.

The carriage disappeared in the twilight, and the Dryad disappeared, too, but she came to light again in the fresh, open air under the glare of the gas lamps. Here the wonder was to be found, and not in the damp atmosphere of the crossing and recrossing passages. Here she found the wonder of the world, which she had been seeking in her short lifetime. It burst forth in far richer glory than all the gaslights above, stronger than the moon, which was now gliding by.

Yes, indeed, she saw it greet her; it winked and twinkled like Venus in the heavens.

She saw a brilliant gate open into a little garden gay with light and dance music. Colored gas lamps shone on small artificial lakes and ponds, where water plants, artistically made of bent and painted tinsel, were displayed, and these hurled jets of water high into the air from their chalices, the water sparkling under the brilliant lights. Graceful weeping willows – real, spring weeping willows – trailed their fresh green branches in curving waves, like a transparent and yet screening veil. A bowl of light among the shrubbery threw its red glow over half-lit bowers made of green foliage, while magic tones of music thrilled the ears, teasing and alluring and chasing the blood through the human limbs.

She saw beautiful young women in evening dress, with innocent smiles on their lips, and laughing with the carelessness of youth. There was a Marie with roses in her hair, but with no carriage or footmen. How they whirled about; how they swung in that wild dance, now up, now down! They laughed and smiled, and leaped as if smitten by the tarantella dance; they looked so joyous, so gay, as if ready to embrace the whole world through pure happiness!

The Dryad felt herself irresistibly drawn into the dance. Her small, delicate feet were

The dance was Bacchanalian, wild.
(Fritz Kredel)

shod in silken shoes as brown as the ribbon that fluttered from her hair onto her bare shoulders. The large folds of the green silk dress enveloped her, but could not hide the perfectly shaped legs and the dainty feet, which seemed to be trying to draw a magic circle in the air before her dancing cavalier's head. Was she in the enchanted garden of Armida? What was the name of this place? In bright gas flames outside shone the name "Mabille."

There were shouts and applause, rockets and running water, and the popping of champagne bottles. The dance was Bacchanalian, wild. And above all this the moon was sailing across the sky, its face sloping a bit. The sky was cloudless, clear and pure, and one thought of looking right into heaven from Mabille.

A consuming intoxication seized the Dryad, like the after-effect of opium. Her eyes spoke, and her lips spoke, but her words were drowned by the tones of flute and violin. Her cavalier whispered words in her ear with the rhythm of the cancan; she did not understand them, nor do we understand them. He stretched his arms out to her, around her – but embraced only the transparent, gas-filled air! The Dryad was carried away by the wind like a rose petal; and high in the air she saw a flame ahead, a brilliant light at the top of a tower. This light came from the goal of her desires, from the red lighthouse of the Fata Morgana of the Champ de Mars. The spring breeze carried her to it. She circled around the tower, and the workmen thought it was a butterfly that had come too early in the spring and was fluttering down to die.

The moon was shining, and so were the gaslights and lanterns in the great halls, and throughout the widespread buildings of all nations they shone on the green hills and on the rocks that human skill had created and over which waterfalls were precipitated by the power of the "bloodless giant."

The depths of the oceans and of bodies of fresh water – the realm of fishes – were displayed there. One could imagine oneself at the bottom of the sea – deep down in a diving bell, with the water pressing hard on all sides against the thick glass walls. Fathom-long polyps, flexible, bending like eels, trembling with living thorns, swayed to and fro and held fast to the bottom of the sea.

A large flounder lay close by in deep thought, spreading himself out comfortably. A crab, resembling an enormous spider, crawled over him, while the shrimps moved about swiftly and restlessly, as if they were the moths and butterflies of the ocean.

Many beautiful plants were growing in the fresh water. Goldfish had arranged themselves in rows like red cows in a pasture, with all their heads in one direction, so that the stream would flow into their mouths. Thick, fat tenches stared with dull eyes at the glass walls; they knew they were in the Paris Exposition; they knew they had completed a tiring journey in tubs filled with water, and had been on a railroad train, where they had become landsick as men become seasick on the ocean. They had also come to see the Exposition, and they saw it from their own salt- or fresh-water "loges," gazing at the swarms of humans that passed by from morning to night. All the countries of the world had sent their specimens of humanity there, so that the old tenches and breams, the perch and moss-covered carps, might look at the creatures and give their opinions about the various tribes.

"Man is a scalefish," said a slimy little carp, "changing his scales two or three times a day. They make mouth noises – speaking, they call it. We don't change our scales, and we make ourselves understood much more easily, by the motions of the corners of our mouths and the look in our eyes. We have many advantages over men."

"But they've learned how to swim," said a small fresh-water fish. "I come from the great inland lake, and in the hot days of summer people go into the water there, but first they strip off their scales and then they swim. The frogs have taught them how to do it; the hind legs push and the front legs row, but they can't do it very long. They think they can rival us, but they can't. Poor people!"

The fishes stared; they thought that the crowd of people there now was the same one they had seen in the bright daylight; yes, and they even believed those figures were the same ones that had beaten against their nerves of observation on the very first day.

A little perch with pretty, mottled skin and an enviably rounded back said he was sure that the same "human scum" was still there.

"I can see it, too, very plainly," said a golden tench. "I distinctly see a beautiful, well-shaped human, a 'long-legged lady,' or whatever it is they call her. She has mouth corners and staring eyes like us, two balloons in the back, a folded umbrella hanging down in front, and a lot of seaweed on her dingling and dangling. She ought to throw all that off and go about the way we do, in nature's gift, and then she would look like an honorable tench – that is, as much as a human can look like us."

"What's become of that laced one, that he-human?"

"He was riding around here in a wheel chair, sitting there with paper, ink, and a pen, and writing everything down. What was he doing? They called him a journalist."

"He is still riding around!" said a moss-covered, old-maid carp who had a bit of worldly temptation stuck in her throat, making her quite hoarse. She had once swallowed a fishhook and since then had been swimming about tolerantly with the hook in her throat. "Journalist," she said; "that's spoken like a fish. It really means a sort of octopus among men!"

Thus the fishes talked on in their own way. But amid this artificial grotto and its water-filled tanks there sounded hammer blows and the songs of workmen, who had to work at night in order to get everything completed. These songs resounded in the midsummer night's dream of the Dryad, who stood there herself, but was soon to fly again and disappear.

"These are goldfish," she said, and nodded to them. "I'm glad to have been able to see you. Yes, I know you and have known you for a long time! The swallow told me all about you in my own home. How pretty and shining and charming you are! I could kiss each and every one of you! I know the others, too. That must be a crucian, and this is a delicate bream, and there's an old moss-covered carp. I know you, but you don't know me."

The fishes just stared, unable to understand a word she said; they gazed through the dim twilight.

The Dryad was gone; she was in the open air again, where the world's "wonder flower" spread its fragrance from many lands – from the rye-bread land, the codfish seashore, the Russian-leather country, the eau-de-cologne valley, and the rose-oil Orient.

When we drive home half asleep in our carriage after a ball, the melodies we have heard continue to ring plainly in our ears, and we may sing each of them again. And as in the dead man's eye the last impression received in life remains photographed for some time, so the impression of the day's tumult and brilliance remained yet upon the eye of the night; it was neither absorbed nor quite blown away. The Dryad could see it and knew that it would persist even into the morrow.

Now the Dryad was among fragrant roses; she thought she recognized them as being from her own country, from the castle park and the garden of the pastor. She also saw a red pomegranate blossom; it was one like this that Marie had worn in her coal-black hair. The memory of her childhood home in the country rushed back into her thoughts; eagerly she drank in the sights around her, while a feverish desire seized her and carried her through the wondrous halls.

She was tired, and her fatigue increased. She felt a yearning to rest on the soft Oriental cushions and carpets, or to duck into the clear water as did the branches of the weeping willow. But the May fly has no rest. In a few minutes the day would end. Her thoughts and her limbs trembled, and she sank in the grass beside the babbling stream.

"You spring from the earth with eternal life," she said. "Cool my tongue; give me a refreshing drink!"

"I am no living spring," answered the water. "I run by machinery!"

"Give me some of your freshness, you green grass!" begged the Dryad. "Give me one of the fragrant flowers!"

"We shall die if we are torn from our plants," answered grass blade and flower.

"Kiss me, you cooling breeze! Give me but a single kiss!"

"Soon the sun will kiss the clouds red," said the wind, "and then you will be among the dead, gone as all this glory will be gone before the year is out. And then I can once more play with the light, loose sand in this place and blow the dust over the earth and into the air. Dust! Nothing but dust!"

The Dryad felt a terror creep over her, like a woman who, bleeding to death in the bath from a severed artery, still wishes to live, while her strength gradually leaves her from loss of blood. She rose, staggered a few steps forward, and then sank again before a little church. The door was open; a light burned on the altar, and the organ sounded. What music! The Dryad never had heard such tones before, though she seemed to hear familiar voices; they came from the depths of the great heart of creation. She thought she heard the whistling of the old oak tree; she thought she heard the old pastor speaking of the great deeds of famous men and of what a creation of God could and might give to the coming ages and thus win himself eternal life. The tones of the organ swelled and rang out; they spoke in song:

"Your desire and longing tore your roots from the place God had given them. That became your ruin, poor Dryad!"

Then the tones from the organ grew soft and gentle; they sounded like weeping and then died away like a weeping whisper. The clouds in the sky began to redden with the dawn. The wind whispered, and sang, "Go away, you dead, for the sun is rising!" The first ray fell upon the Dryad; her figure was radiant with changing colors, like a soap bubble before it bursts, vanishes, and becomes a drop, a tear, which falls and disappears. Poor Dryad, a dewdrop, only a tear, wept, and swept away!

The sun shone down on the Champ de Mars' Fata Morgana, shone over mighty Paris, over the little square with its trees and its rippling fountain, and between the high houses, where the chestnut tree stood, its branches now drooping, its leaves withered, the tree that only yesterday had stood as erect and fresh as spring itself. It was dead now, said the people, for the Dryad had left it, had passed away like the clouds – where, no one knew. On the ground there lay a withered, crumpled chestnut blossom. All the holy water of the church could not recall it to life. Human feet soon stepped on it and crushed it into the dust.

All this has happened and been experienced. We ourselves have seen it, at the Paris Exposition in 1867, in our time, the great and wonderful time of fairy tales.

Dryads and Naiads.
(Walter Crane)

212

THE BROTHERS GRIMM'S FAIRY TALES
INTRODUCTION BY PETER HARNESS

"How happy am I!" cried he; "nobody was ever so lucky as I." Then up he got with a light heart, free from all his troubles, and walked on till he reached his mother's house, and told her how very easy the road to good luck was.

Hans in Luck

Grimm's Fairy Tales or *Household Tales*, first published in Germany in 1812, is far and away the most popular volume of folktales ever gathered together. Most households across Europe can boast a copy, and in Germany, it is the second bestselling book of all time (the first, of course, being the Bible). It is not difficult to see why it has weaved such an enduring and enchanting spell over the past two centuries. The tales catch and fire the imagination. They conjure up magical, terrifying worlds, populated by strange and unusual creatures. They are beautifully written in plain and simple language, and are easy to remember and pass on to others. They form part of our own childhood landscape, that of our parents and that of many generations preceding them: hundreds of thousands of people have grown up listening to the stories of Snow White, Cinderella, Hansel and Gretel and Rumpelstiltskin. Yet, although many of these tales are so familiar to us as to seem almost part of ourselves; the circumstances behind their production are perhaps not so well known. Who were the mysterious Brothers Grimm? And how did they come to produce such a magical and all-pervasive collection?

Jacob Ludwig Grimm was born in 1785, the eldest of six children, of whom his brother Wilhelm Carl was the second, born scarcely a year after Jacob, in 1786. Theirs

was a happy childhood. Their father, Phillip, was a prosperous and ambitious lawyer, who would go on to be a district judge in the area (Hanau, in the Hesse region of Germany); their mother, Dorothea, was the daughter of a local politician, and was a kind and caring parent to them. The boys were educated at a well-to-do school, and seemed to have a rosy future ahead of them. Unfortunately, however, tragedy struck: in 1796, at the early age of forty-four, Phillip Grimm died unexpectedly. As well as casting a terrible and understandable emotional shadow, his death had a ruinous effect on the family finances: the Grimms were forced to move out of their comfortable and expensive house, and to dismiss their domestic staff. With no breadwinner available, the burden was to fall on the elder brothers.

Fortunately, Jacob and Wilhelm were well prepared to go out and seek employment. From a very early age, they had been excellent students; they studied every hour that God sent, and graduated from their respective schools at the top of their classes. Their poverty of background, however, meant that they had to apply for special permission to study law at the University of Marburg: they did not come from a good enough family to warrant an automatic offer of a place. This indignity, along with the snobbery they encountered among their teachers and fellow students, gave rise to keen nolitical sensibility in the brothers. Throughout their lives, they would stand firm and fast for their principles: they despised social injustice and battled corrupt aristocratic privilege wherever they encountered it.

The brothers were temperamentally quite different: chalk and cheese, even, to some observers. The elder, Jacob, was quiet, withdrawn, somewhat awkward in company, but strong-willed and tough. Wilhelm was an extrovert, optimistic and talkative, but dogged by ill-health (a chest complaint haunted him from infancy). These differences did not seem to affect their relationship, however. From an early age, the Brothers Grimm were powerfully bonded: almost never seen apart, and always eager to protect and take care of each other.

Soon after leaving university, Jacob gained employment as a research assistant to a certain Professor Savigny, who was the acknowledged German authority on the history of law. Savigny's approach to his subject – that to understand the law as it now stands, it is necessary to trace its roots and gain knowledge of the cultural conditions under which legislation was originally made – had a strong impact on Jacob and Wilhelm. They became obsessed with philology – the study of language and its derivation – as well as cultural and social history. All of the many works which they published, jointly and separately, over the course of their long careers, were concerned with researchink and uncovering the linguistic and contextual history of their subject.

The brothers' catalogue of academic publications is impressive. There are treatises upon medieval history and literature; a massive scholarly volume about German grammar; another similarly ambitious history of German law; a tome dealing with the emergence of the German heroic legend, as well as many collections of folksongs, religious stories and legends. They were the originators of the law of Consonantal Drift – a theory which explains how pronunciation changes over the decades and centuries; and they were the first scholars to attempt to create a full, etymological dictionary of the German language (similar to John Murray's enormous *Oxford English Dictionary* in England), and, although it was not actually finished until nearly a century after their deaths, this is a testament to their academic zeal and ambitious intelligence.

Yet they came to their most famous project almost by accident. In the sixteenth and seventeenth centuries, there was a rising interest, all across Europe, in the collecting and publishing of folktales. from the oral tradition. This trend had begun in the sixteenth century with Giovan Francesco Straparola's collection *Le Tredici Piacevole Notti* ('Thirteen Pleasant Nights'), and continued in Italy with Giambattista Basile's work *Il Pentamerone*. Arguably the best-known collection prior to that of the Grimms had been the Parisian author Charles Perrault's *Les Contes de ma Mère l'Oye* ('Tales of Mother Goose'), but similar work was also being done in Germany by a young Romantic author called Clemens von Brentano. It is Brentano whom we have to thank for getting the Brothers Grimm interested in fairy tales in the first place. He was a friend of the Grimms who had published a collection of folksongs, *Des Knaben Wunderhorn* (which translates as 'The Boy's Magic Horn'), and who asked the brothers for help in compiling a new volume of folktales.

The brothers – generous to a fault when it came to helping others with research – duly set to work gathering stories for Brentano to include in his book. They would seek out storytellers from far and wide, and invite them to their home. The teller would then unfold his or her tale, and, after a few renditions, the brothers would have perfectly recorded the story, word for word. The sources the brothers found were an unusual assortment. Some of them were young middle-class ladies (one of whom, Dorothea 'Dortchen' Wild, Wilhelm would later marry), some of them were servants (the Grimms' housekeeper, Marie Muller, for example), and some were aristocrats (the family of Werner von Haxthausen, with a large country estate in Paderborn, provided several stories for the second volume). Another was a retired soldier, Johann Krause, who was extremely poor, and would tell them his wonderful tales in return for their discarded clothing. Perhaps the most valuable and voluble contributor was an old woman called Frau Viehmann, who lived in the small village of Zwehrn. Dubbed *die Märchenfrau* by the brothers, she had dozens of tales committed to memory, and her style of telling them was so fluent and correct that most of them made it into the collection virtually untouched. However, when the brothers came to send their first bundle of folktales to Brentano, they found he had lost interest in the project. So, reluctantly, the Grimms tidied and trimmed the tales a little, and published them under their own name.

The collection was not a success straight away, but this is understandable as its first edition was a scholarly-looking tome, with footnotes and a commentary. Yet, as it went through subsequent editions, and became more of a work for children, with illustrations and less of an academic spin to it, sales began to pick up,

and the *Household Tales* became well known all across Europe. Their fame, however, had little effect on the studiously minded Grimms. They continued working in universities, in libraries, and as members of parliament. They took up political causes, and frequently resigned over matters of principle. Wilhelm died in 1859, leaving the introverted Jacob (who never married) heartbroken and alone with his work. Within ten years of the remaining brother's death in 1863, their folktales would be included on school and university curricula all across Europe, and would be anthologised all over the world.

The *Household Tales,* as well as the many hundreds of other folktales, fairy stories and allegories that the brothers published during their lifetime, have understandably been subject to a great deal of critical interpretation and evaluation over the years. As might have been expected, they were first taken up by German nationalists to support their political ideas. At the time when the Grimms were working, Germany was in a state of almost continual upheaval and change: the Napoleonic wars were raging; Germany was invaded by France for a time, before she eventually withdrew in ignominy; there were revolutions and counter-revolutions and the aristocracy rose and fell; and the 'Iron Chancellor', Bismarck, was busily building his Prussian empire. Clearly, in such a state of flux, Germany was keen to seize on anything that suggested a continuity of national history or national identity, and the work of the Grimms provided this. Their folktales gave a clear indication of a shared German heritage, and highlighted the nobility and imagination of the national peasant culture. In the twentieth century, the Nazi party and their supporters went even further in their nationalistic appropriation of the Grimms' work. They took an Aryan approach, shoe-horning themes of racial purity and German superiority into the tales which, although apparent in some of

Brentano's collections of folklore and those of Johan Herder (another contemporary), are clearly not to be found in the Brothers Grimm.

Over the past few decades, analysis of the work of the Brothers Grimm has spread to many different academic fields and disciplines. Psychologists and psychiatrists have pounced on the underlying meanings of 'Cinderella', 'Snow White', *et al.*, and discovered Oedipal complexes, repressed sexual terror and dream-symbols of childhood anxiety. This work was originated by Freud, and taken up by other notable psychologists of all the major twentieth-century schools: Carl Jung, Bruno Bettelheim and André Favat to name but a few. Elsewhere, critics have examined the stories in terms of feminism, Marxism, racism, new historicism and any number of other 'isms' you might care to name. Clearly, interest in Grimms' fairy tales, and folk tales in general, continues unabated, and shows no sign of diminishing.

Understandably, it has been professional folklorists who have spent the greatest amount of time writing and lecturing about the *Household Tales*, from shortly after their original publication right up to the present day. The stories thave been categorised and organised according to their place in world folklore, and their roots have been traced across the world. Although a great deal of this research is highly technical, reliant on complicated classification techniques, and not particularly appealing to the general reader, some of it makes very interesting reading indeed. It is a little surprising to learn that some of the most familiar stories have, in one form or another, been in existence for thousands of years, and in locations as various as China, Greece, Egypt and Russia, as well as in all of mainland Europe. Cinderella, for instance, goes under almost as

many different names as there are languages: Ashputtel (as in this volume), Pisk-i-aske, Zamarashka, Pepeleshka, etc.

Clearly, there is something universal about the fairy tale, something that speaks to all races and all extremities of the human condition. Where it comes from and what precisely it is, who can say? All we can do is surrender ourselves to the uplifting, disturbing and compelling influence of the strange web it weaves. The tales may have been around for hundreds of years before the brothers wrote them down, but the dazzling collection you have before you now will ensure that they will endure for as long as human beings need them.

Sleeping Beauty.
(Maxfield Parrish)

The Brothers Grimm's Fairy Tales

The Golden Bird

A CERTAIN KING HAD a beautiful garden, and in the garden stood a tree which bore golden apples. These apples were always counted, and about the time when they began to grow ripe it was found that every night one of them was gone. The king became very angry at this, and ordered the gardener to keep watch all night under the tree. The gardener set his eldest son to watch; but about twelve o'clock he fell asleep, and in the morning another of the apples was missing. Then the second son was ordered to watch; and at midnight he too fell asleep, and in the morning another apple was gone. Then the third son offered to keep watch; but the gardener at first would not let him, for fear some harm should come to him: however, at last he consented, and the young man laid himself under the tree to watch. As the clock struck twelve he heard a rustling noise in the air, and a bird came flying that was of pure gold; and as it was snapping at one of the apples with its beak, the gardener's son jumped up and shot an arrow at it. But the arrow did the bird no harm; only it dropped a golden feather from its tail, and then flew away. The golden feather was brought to the king in the morning, and all the council was called together. Everyone agreed that it was worth more than all the wealth of the kingdom: but the king said, "One feather is of no use to me, I must have the whole bird."

Then the gardener's eldest son set out and thought to find the golden bird very easily; and when he had gone but a little way, he came to a wood, and by the side of the wood he saw a fox sitting; so he took his bow and made ready to shoot at it.

The gardener's son jumped up and shot an arrow at it.

Then the fox said, "Do not shoot me, for I will give you good counsel; I know what your business is, and that you want to find the golden bird. You will reach a village in the evening; and when you get there, you will see two inns opposite to each other, one of which is very pleasant and beautiful to look at: go not in there, but rest for the night in the other, though it may appear to you to be very poor and mean."

217

But the son thought to himself, "What can such a beast as this know about the matter?" So he shot his arrow at the fox; but he missed it, and it set up its tail above its back and ran into the wood.

Then he went his way, and in the evening came to the village where the two inns were; and in one of these were people singing, and dancing, and feasting; but the other looked very dirty, and poor. "I should be very silly," said he, "if I went to that shabby house, and left this charming place;" so he went into the smart house, and ate and drank at his ease, and forgot the bird, and his country too.

Time passed on and as the eldest son did not come back, and no tidings were heard of him, the second son set out, and the same thing happened to him. He met the fox, who gave

him the good advice: but when he came to the two inns, his elder brother was standing at the window where the merrymaking was, and called to him to come in; and he could not withstand the temptation, but went in, and forgot the golden bird and his country in the same manner.

Time passed on again, and the youngest son too wished to set out into the wide world to seek for the golden bird; but his father would not listen to his entreaties for a long while, for he was very fond of his son, and was afraid that some ill luck might happen to him also, and prevent his coming back. However, at last it was agreed he should go, for he would not rest at home; and as he came to the wood, he met the fox, and heard the same good counsel. But he was thankful to the fox, and did not attempt his life as his brothers had done; so the fox said, "Sit upon my tail, and you will travel faster." So he sat down, and the fox began to run, and away they went over hill and dale so quick that their hair whistled in the wind.

When they came to the village, the son followed the fox's counsel, and without looking about him went to the shabby inn and rested there all night at his ease. In the morning came the fox again and met him as he was beginning his journey, and said, "Go straight forward till you come to a castle, before which lie a whole troop of soldiers fast asleep and snoring: take no notice of them, but go into the castle and pass on and on till you come to a room, where the golden bird sits in a wooden cage; close by it stands a beautiful golden cage; but do not try to take the bird out of the shabby cage and put it into the handsome one, otherwise you will repent it." Then the fox stretched out his tail again, and the young man sat himself down, and away they went over hill and dale till their hair whistled in the wind.

Before the castle gate all was as the fox had said: so the son went in and found the chamber where the golden bird hung in a wooden cage, and below stood the golden cage, and the three golden apples that had been lost were lying close by it. Then thought he to himself, "It will be a very droll thing to bring away such a fine bird in this shabby cage;" so he opened the door and took hold of it and put it into the golden cage. But the bird set up such a loud scream that all the soldiers awoke, and they took him prisoner and carried him before the king. The next morning the court sat to judge him; and when all was heard, it sentenced him to die, unless he should bring the king the golden horse which could run as swiftly as the wind; and if he did this, he was to have the golden bird given him for his own.

So he set out once more on his journey, sighing, and in great despair, when on a sudden his friend the fox met him, and said,

"You see now what has happened on account of your not listening to my counsel. I will still, however, tell you how to find the golden horse, if you will do as I bid you. You must go straight on till you come to the castle where the horse stands in his stall: by his side will lie the groom fast asleep and snoring: take away the horse quietly, but be sure to put the old leathern saddle upon him, and not the golden one that is close by it." Then the son sat down on the fox's tail, and away they went over hill and dale till their hair whistled in the wind.

All went right, and the groom lay snoring with his hand upon the golden saddle. But when the son looked at the horse, he thought it a great pity to put the leathern saddle upon it. "I will give him the good one," said he; "I am sure he deserves it." As he took up the golden saddle the groom awoke and cried out so loud that all the guards ran in and took him prisoner, and in the morning he was again brought before the court to be judged, and was sentenced to die. But it was agreed, that, if he could bring thither the beautiful princess, he should live, and have the bird and the horse given him for his own.

Then he went his way very sorrowful; but the old fox came and said, "Why did you not listen to me? If you had, you would have carried away both the bird and the horse; yet will I once more give you counsel. Go straight on, and in the evening you will arrive at a castle. At twelve o'clock at night the princess goes to the bathing-house: go up to her and give her a kiss, and she will let you lead her away; but take care you do not suffer her to go and take leave of her father and mother." Then the fox stretched out his tail, and so away they went over hill and dale till their hair whistled again.

As they came to the castle, all was as the fox had said, and at twelve o'clock the young man met the princess going to the bath and gave her the kiss, and she agreed to run away with him, but begged with many tears that he would let her take leave of her father. At first he refused, but she wept still more and more, and fell at his feet, till at last he consented; but the moment she came to her father's house the guards awoke and he was taken prisoner again.

Then he was brought before the king, and the king said, "You shall never have my daughter unless in eight days you dig away the hill that stops the view from my window."

Now this hill was so big that the whole world could not take it away: and when he had worked for seven days, and had done very little, the fox came and said, "Lie down and go to sleep; I will work for you." And in the morning he awoke and the hill was gone; so he went merrily to the king, and told him that now that it was removed he must give him the princess.

Then the king was obliged to keep his word, and away went the young man and the princess; and the fox came and said to him, "We will have all three, the princess, the horse, and the bird."

"Ah!" said the young man, "that would be a great thing, but how can you contrive it?"

"If you will only listen," said the fox, "it can be done. When you come to the king, and he asks for the beautiful princess, you must say, "Here she is!" Then he will be very joyful; and you will mount the golden horse that they are to give you, and put out your hand to take leave of them; but shake hands with the princess last. Then lift her quickly on to the horse behind you; clap your spurs to his side, and gallop away as fast as you can."

All went just so. Then the fox said, "When you come to the castle where the bird is, I will stay with the princess at the door, and you will ride in and speak to the king; and when he sees that it is the right horse, he will bring out the bird; but you must sit still, and say that you want to look at it, to see whether it is the true golden bird; and when you get it into your hand, ride away."

The son followed the fox's counsel, and without looking about him went to the shabby inn and rested there all night at his ease. (Noel Pocock)

This, too, happened as the fox said; the young man carried off the bird, the princess mounted again, and they rode on to a great wood. Then the fox came, and said, "Pray kill me, and cut off my head and my feet." But the young man refused to do it: so the fox said, "I will at any rate give you good counsel: beware of two things; ransom no one from the gallows, and sit down by the side of no river." Then away he went.

"Well," thought the young man, "it is no hard matter to keep that advice."

He rode on with the princess, till at last he came to the village where he had left his two brothers. And there he heard a great noise and uproar; and when he asked what was the matter, the people said, "Two men are going to be hanged."

As he came nearer, he saw that the two men were his brothers, who had turned robbers; so he said, "Cannot they in any way be saved?"

But the people said no, not unless he would bestow all his money upon the rascals and buy their liberty. Then he did not stay to think about the matter, but paid what was asked, and his brothers were given up, and went on with him towards their home.

And as they came to the wood where the fox first met them, it was so cool and pleasant that the two brothers said, "Let us sit down by the side of the river, and rest a while, to eat and drink."

So he said, "Yes," and forgot the fox's counsel, and sat down on the side of the river; and while he suspected nothing, they came behind, and threw him down the bank, and took the princess, the horse and the bird, and went home to the king their master, and said. "All this have we won by our labour." Then there was great rejoicing made; but the horse would not eat, the bird would not sing, and the princess wept.

The youngest son fell to the bottom of the river's bed: luckily it was nearly dry, but his bones were almost broken, and the bank was so steep that he could find no way to get out. Then the old fox came once more, and scolded him for not following his advice; otherwise no evil would have befallen him. "Yet," said he, "I cannot leave you here, so lay hold of my tail and hold fast." Then he pulled him out of the river, and said to him, as he got upon the bank, "Your brothers have set watch to kill you, if they find you in the kingdom."

So he dressed himself as a poor man, and came secretly to the king's court, and was scarcely within the doors when the horse began to eat, and the bird to sing, and the princess left off weeping. Then he went to the king, and told him all his brothers' roguery; and they were seized and punished, and he had the princess given to him again; and after the king's death he was heir to his kingdom.

A long while after, he went to walk one day in the wood, and the old fox met him, and besought him with tears in his eyes to kill him, and cut off his head and feet. And at last he did so, and in a moment the fox was changed into a man, and turned out to be the brother of the princess, who had been lost a very great many years.

HANS IN LUCK

SOME MEN ARE born to good luck: all they do or try to do comes right, all that falls to them is so much gain, all their geese are swans, all their cards are trumps – toss them which way you will, they will always, like poor puss, alight upon their legs, and only move on so much the faster. The world may very likely not always think of them as they think of themselves, but what care they for the world? What can it know about the matter?

One of these lucky beings was neighbour Hans. Seven long years he had worked hard for his master. At last he said, "Master, my time is up; I must go home and see my poor mother once more; so pray pay me my wages and let me go."

And the master said, "You have been a faithful and good servant, Hans, so your pay shall be handsome." Then he gave him a lump of silver as big as his head.

Hans took out his pocket-handkerchief, put the piece of silver into it, threw it over his shoulder, and set off on his road homewards. As he went lazily on, dragging one foot after another, a man came in sight, trotting gaily along on a capital horse. "Ah!" said Hans aloud, "what a fine thing it is to ride on horseback! There he sits as easy and happy as if he was at home, in the chair by his fireside; he trips against no stones, saves shoe-leather and gets where he's going he hardly knows how."

Hans did not speak softly so the horseman heard it all. "Well, friend, why do you go on foot then?" he asked.

"Ah!" said Hans, "I have this load to carry: to be sure it is silver, but it is so heavy that I can't hold up my head, and I can tell you it hurts my shoulder sadly."

"What do you say of making an exchange?" said the horseman. "I will give you my horse, and you shall give me the silver; which will save you a great deal of trouble in carrying such a heavy load about with you."

"With all my heart," said Hans: "but as you are so kind to me, I must tell you one thing – you will have a weary task to draw that silver about with you."

Undeterred, the horseman got off, took the silver, helped Hans up, gave him the bridle into one hand and the whip into the other, and said, "When you want to go very fast, smack your lips loudly together, and cry 'Jip!'"

Hans was delighted as he sat on the horse, drew himself up, squared his elbows, turned out his toes, cracked his whip, and rode merrily off, one minute whistling a merry tune, and another singing,

> *"No care and no sorrow,*
> *A fig for the morrow!*
> *We'll laugh and be merry,*
> *Sing neigh down derry!"*

After a time he thought he should like to go a little faster, so he smacked his lips and cried "Jip!" Away went the horse at full gallop; and before Hans knew what he was about, he was thrown off, and lay on his back by the roadside. His horse would have run off, if a shepherd who was coming by, driving a cow, had not stopped it. Hans soon came to himself, and got upon his legs again, sadly vexed, and said

Hans in luck. (James Linton)

to the shepherd, "This riding is no joke for a man who has the luck to get upon a beast like this that stumbles and flings him off as if it would break his neck. However, I'm off now once and for all! I like your cow now a great deal better than this smart beast that played me this trick, and has spoiled my best coat, as you see, in this puddle; which, by the by, smells not very like a nosegay. One can walk along at one's leisure behind that cow – keep good company, and have milk, butter and cheese every day into the bargain. What would I give to have such a prize!"

"Well," said the shepherd, "if you are so fond of her, I will change my cow for your horse; I like to do good to my neighbours, even though I lose by it myself."

"Done!" said Hans, merrily. "What a noble heart that good man has!" thought he. Then the shepherd jumped upon the horse, wished Hans and the cow good-morning, and away he rode.

Hans brushed his coat, wiped his face and hands, rested a while, and then drove off his cow quietly, and thought his bargain a very lucky one. "If I have only a piece of bread (and I certainly shall always be able to get that), I can, whenever I like, eat my butter and cheese with it; and when I am thirsty I can milk my cow and drink the milk: who could wish for more?" When he came to an inn, he halted, ate up all his bread, and gave away his last penny for a glass of beer. When he had rested himself he set off again, driving his cow towards his mother's village. But the heat grew greater as soon as noon came on, till at last, as he found himself on a wide heath that would take him more than an hour to cross, he began to be so hot and parched that his tongue cleaved to the roof of his mouth. "I can find a cure for this," thought he; "now I will milk my cow and quench my thirst": so he tied her to the stump of a tree, and held his leathern cap to milk into; but not a drop was to be had. Who would have thought that this cow, which was to bring him milk and butter and cheese, was all the time utterly dry? Hans had not even considered the possibility.

While he was trying his luck in milking, and managing the matter very clumsily, the uneasy beast began to think him very troublesome; and at last she gave him such a kick on the head that she knocked him down; and there he lay a long while senseless. Luckily a butcher soon came by, pushing a pig in a wheelbarrow.

"What is the matter with you, my man?" said the butcher, as he helped him up.

Hans told him what had happened, how he was dry, and wanted to milk his cow, but found the cow was dry too. Then the butcher gave him a flask of ale, saying, "There, drink and refresh yourself; your cow will give you no milk: don't you see she is an old beast, good for nothing but the slaughterhouse?"

"Alas, alas!" said Hans, "who would have thought it? What a shame to take my horse, and give me only a dry cow! If I kill her, what will she be good for? I hate cow-beef; it is not tender enough for me. If she were a pig now – like that fat gentleman you are wheeling along at his ease – one could do something with her; she would at any rate make sausages."

"Well," said the butcher, "I don't like to say no, when one is asked to do a kind, neighbourly thing. To please you I will change, and give you my fine fat pig for the cow."

"Heaven reward you for your kindness and self-denial!" said Hans, as he gave the butcher the cow; and taking the pig off the wheelbarrow, drove it away, holding it by the string that was tied to its leg.

So on he jogged, and all seemed now to go right with him: he had met with some misfortunes, to be sure; but he was now well repaid for all. How could it be otherwise with such a travelling companion as he had at last got?

The next man he met was a countryman carrying a fine white goose. The countryman stopped to ask him the time; this led to further chat; and Hans told him all his luck, how he had had so many good bargains, and how all the world had seemed to be smiling with him. The countryman then began to tell his tale, and said he was going to take the goose to a christening. "Feel," said he, "how heavy it is, and yet it is only eight weeks old. Whoever roasts and eats it will find plenty of fat upon it, it has lived so well!"

"You're right," said Hans, as he weighed it in his hands; "but if you talk of fat, my pig is no trifle."

Meantime the countryman began to look grave, and shook his head. "Hark ye," said he, "my worthy friend, you seem a good sort of fellow, so I can't help doing you a kind turn. Your pig may get you into a scrape. In the village I just came from, the squire has had a pig stolen out of his sty. I was dreadfully afraid when I saw you that you had got the squire's pig. If you have, and they catch you, it will be a bad job for you. The least they will do will be to throw you into the horse-pond. Can you swim?"

Poor Hans was sadly frightened. "Good man," cried he, "pray get me out of this scrape. I know nothing of where the pig was either bred or born; but he may have been the squire's for aught I can tell: you know this country better than I do, take my pig and give me the goose."

"I ought to have something into the bargain," said the countryman; "give a fat goose for a pig, indeed! 'Tis not everyone would do so much for you as that. However, I will not be hard upon you, as you are in trouble."

Then he took the string in his hand, and drove off the pig by a side path, while Hans went on the way homewards free from care. "After all," thought he, "that chap is pretty well taken in. I don't care whose pig it is, but wherever it came from, in this it has been a very good friend to me. I have much the best of the bargain. First there will be a capital roast; then the fat will find me in goose-grease for six months; and then there are all the beautiful white feathers. I will put them into my pillow, and then I am sure I shall sleep soundly without rocking. How happy my mother will be! Talk of a pig, indeed! Give me a fine fat goose."

As he came to the next village, he saw a scissor-grinder with his wheel, working and singing,

"O'er hill and o'er dale
So happy I roam,
Work light and live well,
All the world is my home;
Then who so blithe, so merry as I?"

Hans stood looking on for a while, and at last said, "You must be well off, master grinder! You seem so happy at your work."

"Yes," said the other, "mine is a golden trade; a good grinder never puts his hand into his pocket without finding money in it – but where did you get that beautiful goose?"

"I did not buy it, I gave a pig for it."

"And where did you get the pig?"

"I gave a cow for it."

"And the cow?"

"I gave a horse for it."

"And the horse?"

"I gave a lump of silver as big as my head for it."

"And the silver?"

"Oh! I worked hard for that seven long years."

"You have thrived well in the world hitherto," said the grinder, "now if you could find money in your pocket whenever you put your hand in it, your fortune would be made."

"Very true, but how is that to be managed?"

"How? Why, you must turn grinder like myself," said the other; "you only want a grindstone; the rest will come of itself. Here is one that is but little the worse for wear. I would not ask more than the value of your goose for it – will you buy?"

"How can you ask?" said Hans. "I should be the happiest man in the world, if I could have money whenever I put my hand in my pocket: what could I want more? There's the goose."

"Now," said the grinder, as he gave him a common rough stone that lay by his side, "this is a most capital stone; do but work it well enough, and you can make an old nail cut with it."

Hans took the stone, and went his way with a light heart; his eyes sparkled for joy, and he said to himself, "Surely I must have been born in a lucky hour; everything I could want or wish for comes of itself. People are so kind; they seem really to think I do them a favour in letting them make me rich, and giving me good bargains."

Meantime he began to be tired, and hungry too, for he had given away his last penny in his joy at getting the cow.

At last he could go no farther, for the stone tired him sadly, and he dragged himself to the side of a river, that he might take a drink of water, and rest a while. He laid the stone carefully by his side on the bank: but, as he stooped down to drink, he forgot it, pushed it a little, and down it rolled, plump into the stream.

For a while he watched it sinking in the deep clear water – then sprang up and danced for joy, and again fell upon his knees and thanked heaven, with tears in his eyes, for its kindness in taking away his only plague, the ugly heavy stone.

"How happy am I!" cried he; "nobody was ever so lucky as I." Then up he got with a light heart, free from all his troubles, and walked on till he reached his mother's house, and told her how very easy the road to good luck was.

JORINDA AND JORINDEL

THERE WAS ONCE an old castle, that stood in the middle of a deep gloomy wood, and in the castle lived an old fairy. Now this fairy could take any shape she pleased. All the day long she flew about in the form of an owl, or crept about the country like a cat; but at night she always became an old woman again. When any young man came within a hundred paces of her castle, he became quite fixed, and could not move a step till she came and set him free; which she would not do till he had given her his word never to come there again. But when any pretty maiden came within that space she was changed into a bird, and the fairy put her into a cage, and hung her up in a chamber in the castle. There were seven hundred of these cages hanging in the castle, and all with beautiful birds in them.

Now there was once a maiden whose name was Jorinda. She was prettier than all the pretty girls that ever were seen before, and a shepherd lad, whose name was Jorindel, was very fond of her, and they were soon to be married.

One day they went to walk in the wood, that they might be alone; and Jorindel said, "We must take care that we don't go too near to the fairy's castle." It was a beautiful evening; the last rays of the setting sun shone bright through the long stems of the trees upon the green underwood beneath, and the turtle-doves sang from the tall birches.

Jorinda sat down to gaze upon the sun; Jorindel sat by her side and both felt sad, they knew not why; but it seemed as if they were to be parted from one another for ever. They had wandered a long way; and when they looked to see which way they should go home, they found themselves at a loss to know what path to take.

The sun was setting fast, and already half of its circle had sunk behind the hill. Jorindel on a sudden looked behind him, and saw through the bushes that they had, without knowing it, sat down close under the old walls of the castle. Then he shrank for fear, turned pale, and trembled. Jorinda was just singing,

"The ring-dove sang from the willow spray,
Well-a-day! Well-a-day!
He mourn'd for the fate of his darling
  mate,
Well-a-day!"

when her song stopped suddenly. Jorindel turned to see the reason, and beheld his Jorinda changed into a nightingale, so that her song ended with a mournful "jug, jug". An owl with fiery eyes flew three times round them, and three times screamed: "Tu whu! Tu whu! Tu whu!"

Jorindel could not move; he stood fixed as a stone, and could neither weep, nor speak, nor stir hand or foot. And now the sun went quite down; the gloomy night came; the owl flew into a bush; and a moment after the old fairy came forth pale and meagre, with staring eyes, and a nose and chin that almost met one another.

She crept about the country like a cat
(Arthur Rackham)

She mumbled something to herself, seized the nightingale, and went away with it in her hand. Poor Jorindel saw the nightingale was gone – but what could he do? He could not speak, he could not move from the spot where he stood. At last the fairy came back and sang with a hoarse voice:

> *"Till the prisoner is fast,*
> *And her doom is cast,*
> *There stay! Oh, stay!*
> *When the charm is around her,*
> *And the spell has bound her,*
> *Hie away! away!"*

On a sudden Jorindel found himself free. Then he fell on his knees before the fairy, and prayed her to give him back his dear Jorinda;

but she laughed at him, and said he should never see her again; then she went her way.

He prayed, he wept, he sorrowed, but all in vain. "Alas!" he said, "what will become of me?" He could not go back to his own home, so he went to a strange village, and employed himself in keeping sheep. Many a time did he walk round and round as near to the hated castle as he dared go, but all in vain; he neither heard nor saw anything of Jorinda.

At last he dreamt one night that he found a beautiful purple flower, and that in the middle of it lay a costly pearl; and he dreamt that he plucked the flower, and went with it in his hand into the castle, and that everything he touched with it was disenchanted, and that there he found his Jorinda again.

In the morning when he awoke, he began to search over hill and dale for this pretty flower. For eight long days he sought for it in vain, but on the ninth day, early in the morning, he found the beautiful purple flower; and in the middle of it was a large dewdrop, as big as a costly pearl. Then he plucked the flower, and set out and travelled day and night till he came again to the castle.

He walked nearer than a hundred paces to it, and yet he did not become fixed as before, but found that he could go quite close up to the door. Jorindel was very glad indeed to see this. Then he touched the door with the flower, and it sprang open; so that he went in through the court, and listened when he heard so many birds singing. At last he came to the chamber where the fairy sat, with the seven hundred birds singing in the seven hundred cages. When she saw Jorindel she was very angry, and screamed with rage; but she could not come within two yards of him, for the flower he held in his hand was his safeguard. He looked around at the birds, but alas! there were many, many nightingales, and he was at a loss to find out which was his Jorinda. While he was thinking what to do, he saw the fairy had taken down one of the cages, and was making off with it through the door. He ran – or flew – after her, touched the cage with the flower, and Jorinda stood before him, and threw her arms round his neck looking as beautiful as ever, as beautiful as when they walked together in the wood.

Then he touched all the other birds with the flower, so that they all took their old forms again; and he took Jorinda home, where they were married, and lived happily together many years: and so did a good many other lads, whose maidens had been forced to sing in the old fairy's cages by themselves much longer than they liked.

THE TRAVELLING MUSICIANS

AN HONEST FARMER had once an ass that had been a faithful servant to him a great many years, but was now growing old and every day more and more unfit for work. His master therefore was tired of keeping him and began to think of putting an end to him; but the ass, who saw that some mischief was in the wind, took himself slyly off, and began his journey towards the great city, "For there," thought he, "I may turn musician."

After he had travelled a little way, he spied a dog lying by the roadside and panting as if he were tired. "What makes you pant so, my friend?" said the ass.

"Alas!" said the dog, "my master was going to knock me on the head, because I am old and weak, and can no longer make myself useful to him in hunting; so I ran away; but what can I do to earn my livelihood?"

"Hark ye!" said the ass, "I am going to the great city to turn musician: suppose you come with me, and see what you can do in the same way?" The dog said he was willing, and they jogged on together.

They had not gone far before they saw a cat sitting in the middle of the road and making a most rueful face.

"Pray, my good lady," said the ass, "what's the matter with you? You look quite out of spirits!"

"Ah, me!" said the cat, "how can one be in good spirits when one's life is in danger? Because I am beginning to grow old, and had rather lie at my ease by the fire than run about the house after the mice, my mistress laid hold of me, and was going to drown me; and though I have been lucky enough to get away from her, I do not know what I am to live upon."

"Oh," said the ass, "by all means come with us to the great city; you are a good night singer, and may make your fortune as a musician." The cat was pleased with the thought, and joined the party.

Soon afterwards, as they were passing by a farmyard, they saw a cock perched upon a gate, and screaming out with all his might and main. "Bravo!" said the ass; "upon my word, you make a famous noise; pray what is all this about?"

"Why," said the cock, "I was just now saying that we should have fine weather for our washing-day, and yet my mistress and the cook don't thank me for my pains, but threaten to cut off my head tomorrow, and make broth of me for the guests that are coming on Sunday!"

"Heaven forbid!" said the ass, "come with us Master Chanticleer; it will be better, at any rate, than staying here to have your head cut off! Besides, who knows? If we care to sing in tune, we may get up some kind of a concert; so come along with us."

"With all my heart," said the cock; so they all four went on jollily together.

They could not, however, reach the great city the first day; so when night came on, they went into a wood to sleep. The ass and the dog laid themselves down under a great tree, and the cat climbed up into the branches; while the cock, thinking that the higher he sat the safer he should be, flew up to the very top of the tree, and then, according to his custom, before he went to sleep, looked out on all sides of him to see that everything was well. In doing this, he saw afar off something bright and shining and calling to his companions said, "There must be a house no great way off, for I see a light."

"If that be the case," said the ass, "we had better change our quarters, for our lodging is not the best in the world!"

"Besides," added the dog, "I should not be the worse for a bone or two, or a bit of meat."

So they walked off together towards the spot where Chanticleer had seen the light, and as they drew near it became larger and brighter, till they at last came close to a house in which a gang of robbers lived.

The ass, being the tallest of the company, marched up to the window and peeped in. "Well, donkey," said Chanticleer, "what do you see?"

"What do I see?" replied the ass. "Why, I see a table spread with all kinds of good things, and robbers sitting round it making merry."

"That would be a noble lodging for us," said the cock. "Yes," said the ass, "if we could only get in;" so they consulted together how they should contrive to get the robbers out; and at

The travelling musicians.
(Jan Baptist Lodewyck Maes)

last they hit upon a plan. The ass placed himself upright on his hind legs, with his forefeet resting against the window; the dog got upon his back; the cat scrambled up to the dog's shoulders; and the cock flew up and sat upon the cat's head. When all was ready a signal was given, and they began their music. The ass brayed, the dog barked, the cat mewed and the cock screamed; and then they all broke through the window at once, and came tumbling into the room, among the broken glass, with a most hideous clatter! The robbers, who had been not a little frightened by the opening concert, had now no doubt that some frightful hobgoblin had broken in upon them, and scampered away as fast as they could.

The coast once clear, our travellers soon sat down and dispatched what the robbers had left, with as much eagerness as if they had not expected to eat again for a month. As soon as they had satisfied themselves, they put out the lights, and each once more sought out a resting-place to his own liking. The donkey laid himself down upon a heap of straw in the yard, the dog stretched himself upon a mat behind the door, the cat rolled herself up on the hearth before the warm ashes, and the cock perched upon a beam on the top of the house; and, as they were all rather tired with their journey, they soon fell asleep.

But about midnight, when the robbers saw from afar that the lights were out and that all seemed quiet, they began to think that they had been in too great a hurry to run away; and one of them, who was bolder than the rest, went to see what was going on. Finding everything still, he marched into the kitchen, and groped about till he found a match in order to light a candle; and then, espying the glittering fiery eyes of the cat, he mistook them for live coals, and held the match to them to light it. But the cat, not understanding this joke, sprang at his face, and spat, and scratched at him. This frightened him dreadfully, and away he ran to the back door; but there the dog jumped up and bit him in the leg; and as he was crossing over the yard the ass kicked him; and the cock, who had been awakened by the noise, crowed with all his might. At this the robber ran back as fast as he could to his comrades, and told the captain how a horrid witch had got into the house, and had spat at him and scratched his face with her long bony fingers; how a man with a knife in his hand had hidden himself behind the door, and stabbed him in the leg; how a black monster stood in the yard and struck him with a club, and how the devil had sat upon the top of the house and cried out, "Throw the rascal up here!" After this the robbers never dared to go back to the house; but the musicians were so pleased with their quarters that they took up their abode there; and there they are, I dare say, at this very day.

OLD SULTAN

A SHEPHERD HAD A faithful dog, called Sultan, who was grown very old, and had lost all his teeth. And one day when the shepherd and his wife were standing together before the house the shepherd said, "I will shoot old Sultan tomorrow morning, for he is of no use now."

But his wife said, "Pray let the poor faithful creature live; he has served us well a great many years, and we ought to give him a livelihood for the rest of his days."

"But what can we do with him?" said the shepherd, "he has not a tooth in his head, and the thieves don't fear him at all; to be sure he has served us, but then he did it to earn his livelihood; tomorrow shall be his last day, depend upon it."

Poor Sultan, who was lying close by them,

Old Sultan (Arthur Rackham)

heard all that the shepherd and his wife said to one another, and was very much frightened to think tomorrow would be his last day; so in the evening he went to his good friend the wolf, who lived in the wood, and told him all his sorrows, and how his master meant to kill him in the morning. "Make yourself easy," said the wolf, "I will give you some good advice. Your master, you know, goes out every morning very early with his wife into the field; and they take their little child with them, and lay it down behind the hedge in the shade while they are at work. Now do you lie down close by the child, and pretend to be watching it, and I will come out of the wood and run away with it; you must run after me as fast as you can, and I will let it drop; then you may carry it back, and they will think you have saved their child, and will be so thankful to you that they will take care of you as long as you live."

The dog liked this plan very well; and accordingly so it was managed. The wolf ran with the child a little way; the shepherd and his wife screamed out; but Sultan soon overtook him, and carried the poor little thing back to his master and mistress.

Then the shepherd patted him on the head, and said, "Old Sultan has saved our child from the wolf, and therefore he shall live and be well taken care of, and have plenty to eat. Wife, go home, and give him a good dinner, and let him have my old cushion to sleep on as long as he lives." So from this time forward Sultan had all that he could wish for.

Soon afterwards the wolf came and wished him joy, and said, "Now, my good fellow, you must tell no tales, but turn your head the other way when I want to taste one of the old shepherd's fine fat sheep."

"No," said the Sultan; "I will be true to my master." However, the wolf thought he was jesting, and came one night to get a dainty morsel. But Sultan had told his master what the wolf meant to do; so he lay in wait for him behind the barn door, and when the wolf was busy looking out for a good fat sheep, he had a stout cudgel laid about his back that combed his locks for him finely.

Then the wolf was very angry, and called Sultan "an old rogue", and swore he would have his revenge. So the next morning the wolf sent the boar to challenge Sultan to come into the wood to fight the matter. Now Sultan had nobody he could ask to be his second but the shepherd's old three-legged cat; so he took her with him, and as the poor thing limped along with some trouble, she stuck her tail straight up in the air.

The wolf and the wild boar were first on the ground; and when they espied their enemies coming, and saw the cat's long tail standing straight in the air, they thought she was carrying a sword for Sultan to fight with; and every time she limped, they thought she was picking up a stone to throw at them; so they said they should not like this way of fighting, and the boar lay down behind a bush, and the wolf jumped up into a tree. Sultan and the cat soon came up, and looked about and wondered that no one was there. The boar, however, had not quite hidden himself, for his ears stuck out of the bush; and when he shook one of them a little, the cat, seeing something move, and thinking it was a mouse, sprang upon it, and bit and scratched it, so that the boar jumped up and grunted, and ran away, roaring out, "Look up in the tree, there sits the one who is to blame." So they looked up, and espied the wolf sitting among the branches; and they called him a cowardly rascal, and would not suffer him to come down till he was heartily ashamed of himself, and had promised to be good friends again with old Sultan.

THE SLEEPING BEAUTY

A KING AND QUEEN once upon a time reigned in a country a great way off, where there were in those days fairies. Now this king and queen had plenty of money, and plenty of fine clothes to wear, and plenty of good things to eat and drink, and a coach to ride out in every day; but though they had been married many years they had no children, and this grieved them very much indeed. But one day, as the queen was walking by the side of the river at the bottom of the garden, she saw a poor little fish that had thrown itself out of the water and lay gasping and nearly dead on the bank. Then the queen took pity on the little fish, and threw it back again into the river; and before it swam away it lifted its head out of the water and said, "I know what your wish is, and it shall be fulfilled, in return for your kindness to me – you will soon have a daughter."

What the little fish had foretold soon came to pass: the queen had a little girl, so very beautiful that the king could not cease looking on her for joy, and said he would hold a great feast and make merry, and show the child to all the land. So he asked his kinsmen, and nobles, and friends, and neighbours.

But the queen said, "I will have the fairies also, that they might be kind and good to our little daughter."

Now there were thirteen fairies in the kingdom; but as the king and queen had only twelve golden dishes for them to eat out of, they were forced to leave one of the fairies without asking her. So twelve fairies came, each with a high red cap on her head, and red shoes with high heels on her feet, and a long white wand in her hand; and after the feast was over they gathered round in a ring and gave all their best gifts to the little princess. One gave her goodness, another beauty, another riches, and so on till she had all that was good in the world.

Just as eleven of them had done blessing her, a great noise was heard in the courtyard,

Sleeping Beauty. (John Collier)

and word was brought that the thirteenth fairy was come, with a black cap on her head, and black shoes on her feet, and a broom-stick in her hand: and presently up she came into the dining-hall. Now, as she had not been asked to the feast she was very angry, and scolded the king and queen very much, and set to work to take her revenge. So she cried out, "The king's daughter shall, in her fifteenth year, be wounded by a spindle, and fall down dead."

Then the twelfth of the friendly fairies, who had not yet given her gift, came forward, and said that the evil wish must be fulfilled, but that she could soften its mischief; so her gift was that the king's daughter, when the spindle wounded her, should not really die, but should only fall asleep for a hundred years.

However, the king hoped still to save his dear child altogether from the threatened evil; so he ordered that all the spindles in the kingdom should be bought up and burnt. All the gifts of the first eleven fairies were in the meantime fulfilled; for the princess was so beautiful, and well behaved, and good, and wise, that everyone who knew her loved her.

It happened that, on the very day she was fifteen years old, the king and queen were not at home, and she was left alone in the palace. So she roved about by herself, and looked at all the rooms and chambers, till at last she came to an old tower, up which there was a narrow staircase ending with a little door. In the door there was a golden key, and when she turned it the door sprang open and there sat an old lady spinning away very busily. "Why, how now, good mother," said the princess; "what are you doing there?"

"Spinning," said the old lady, and nodded her head, humming a tune, while buzz! went the wheel. "How prettily that little thing turns round!" said the princess, and took the spindle and began to try and spin. But scarcely had she touched it, before the fairy's prophecy was fulfilled; the spindle wounded her, and she fell down lifeless on the ground.

However, she was not dead, but had only fallen into a deep sleep; and the king and the queen, who had just come home, and all their court, fell asleep too; and the horses slept in the stables, and the dogs in the court, the pigeons on the house-top, and the very flies slept upon the walls. Even the fire on the hearth left off blazing, and went to sleep; the jack stopped, and the spit that was turning about with a goose upon it for the king's dinner stood still; and the cook, who was at that moment pulling the kitchen-boy by the hair to give him a box on the ear for something he had done amiss, let him go, and both fell asleep; the butler, who was slyly tasting the ale, fell asleep with the jug at his lips: and thus everything stood still, and slept soundly.

A large hedge of thorns soon grew round the palace, and every year it became higher and thicker; till at last the old palace was surrounded and hidden, so that not even the roof or the chimneys could be seen. But there went a report through all the land of the beautiful sleeping Briar Rose (for so the king's daughter was called), so that, from time to time, several kings' sons came, and tried to break through the thicket into the palace. This, however, none of them could ever do; for the thorns and bushes laid hold of them, as it were with hands; and there they stuck fast, and died wretchedly.

After many, many years there came a king's son into that land, and an old man told him the story of the thicket of thorns: how a beautiful palace stood behind it, and how a wonderful princess, called Briar Rose, lay in it asleep, with all her court. He told, too, how he had heard from his grandfather that many, many princes had come, and had tried to break through the thicket, but that they had all stuck fast in it, and died. Then the young prince said, "All this does not frighten me; I will go and see this Briar Rose." The old man tried to hinder him, but he was bent upon going.

Now that very day the hundred years were ended; and as the prince came to the thicket he saw nothing but beautiful flowering shrubs, through which he went with ease, and they shut in after him as thick as ever. Then he came at last to the palace, and there in the court lay the dogs asleep; and the horses were standing in the stables; and on the roof sat the pigeons fast asleep, with their heads under their wings. And when he came into the palace, the flies were sleeping on the walls; the spit was standing still; the butler had the jug of ale at his lips, going to drink a draught; the maid sat with a fowl in her lap ready to be plucked; and the cook in the kitchen was still holding up her hand, as if she was going to strike the boy.

Then he went in farther, and all was so still that he could hear every breath he drew, till at last he came to the old tower, and opened the door of the little room in which Briar Rose was; and there she lay, fast asleep on a couch by the window. She looked so beautiful that he could not take his eyes off her, so he stooped down and gave her a kiss. And the moment he kissed her she opened her eyes and awoke, and smiled upon him; and they went out together; and soon the king and queen also awoke, and all the court, and gazed on each other with great wonder. And the horses shook themselves, and the dogs jumped up and barked; the pigeons took their heads from under their wings, and looked about and flew into the fields; the flies on the walls buzzed again; the fire in the kitchen blazed up; round went the jack, and round went the spit, with the goose for the king's dinner upon it; the butler finished his draught of ale; the maid went on plucking the fowl; and the cook gave the boy the box on his ear.

And then the prince and Briar Rose were married, and the wedding feast was given; and they lived happily together all their lives long.

THE DOG AND THE SPARROW

A SHEPHERD'S DOG HAD a master who took no care of him, but often let him suffer the greatest hunger. At last he could bear it no longer; so he took to his heels, and off he ran in a very sad and sorrowful mood.

On the road he met a sparrow that said to him, "Why are you so sad, my friend?"

"Because," said the dog, "I am very very hungry, and have nothing to eat."

"If that be all," answered the sparrow, "come with me into the next town, and I will soon find you plenty of food." So on they went together into the town, and as they passed by a butcher's shop, the sparrow said to the dog, "Stand there a little while till I peck you down a piece of meat." So the sparrow perched upon the shelf, and having first looked carefully about her to see if anyone was watching her, she pecked and scratched at a steak that lay upon the edge of the shelf, till at last down it fell. Then the dog snapped it up, and scrambled away with it into a corner, where he soon ate it all up. "Well," said the sparrow, "you shall have some more if you will; so come with me to the next shop, and I will peck you down another steak." When the dog had eaten this too, the sparrow said to him, "Well, my good friend, have you had enough now?"

"I have had plenty of meat," answered he, "but I should like to have a piece of bread to eat after it."

"Come with me then," said the sparrow, "and you shall soon have that too." So she took him to a baker's shop, and pecked at two rolls that lay in the window, till they fell down; and as the dog still wished for more, she took him to another shop and pecked down some more for him.

When they were eaten, the sparrow asked him whether he had had enough now. "Yes," said he; "and now let us take a walk a little way out of the town." So they both went out upon the high road; but as the weather was warm, they had not gone far before the dog said, "I am very much tired – I should like to take a nap."

"Very well," answered the sparrow, "do so, and in the meantime I will perch upon that bush." So the dog stretched himself out on the road, and fell fast asleep. While he slept, there came by a carter with a cart drawn by three horses, and loaded with two casks of wine. The sparrow, seeing that the carter did not turn out of the way but would go on in the track in which the dog lay so as to drive over him, called out, "Stop! stop, Mr Carter! or it shall be the worse for you."

But the carter, grumbling to himself, "You make it the worse for me, indeed! What can you do?" cracked his whip, and drove his cart over the poor dog, so that the wheels crushed him to death.

"There," cried the sparrow, "thou cruel villain, thou hast killed my friend the dog. Now mind what I say. This deed of thine shall cost thee all thou art worth."

"Do your worst, and welcome," said the brute, "what harm can you do me?" and passed on. But the sparrow crept under the tilt of the cart, and pecked at the bung of one of the casks till she loosened it; and then all the wine ran out, without the carter seeing it. At last he looked round, and saw that the cart was dripping, and the cask quite empty. "What an unlucky wretch I am!" cried he.

"Not wretch enough yet!" said the sparrow, as she alighted upon the head of one of the horses, and pecked at him till he reared up and kicked. When the carter saw this, he drew out his hatchet and aimed a blow at the sparrow, meaning to kill her; but she flew away, and the blow fell upon the poor horse's head with such force that he fell down dead. "Unlucky wretch that I am!" cried he.

"Not wretch enough yet!" said the sparrow. And as the carter went on with the other two horses, she again crept under the tilt of the cart, and pecked out the bung of the second cask, so that all the wine ran out. When the carter saw this, he again cried out, "Miserable wretch that I am!"

But the sparrow answered, "Not wretch enough yet!" and perched on the head of the second horse, and pecked at him too. The carter ran up and struck at her again with his hatchet; but away she flew, and the blow fell upon the second horse and killed him on the spot. "Unlucky wretch that I am!" said he.

"Not wretch enough yet!" said the sparrow; and perching upon the third horse, she began to peck him too. The carter was mad with fury, and without looking about him, or caring what he was about, struck again at the sparrow and killed his third horse as he had done the other two. "Alas! miserable wretch that I am!" cried he.

"Not wretch enough yet!" answered the sparrow as she flew away; "now will I plague and punish thee at thy own house."

The carter was forced at last to leave his cart behind him, and to go home overflowing with rage and vexation. "Alas!" said he to his wife, "what ill luck has befallen me! – my wine is all spilt, and my horses all three dead."

"Alas! husband," replied she, "and a wicked bird has come into the house, and has brought with her all the birds in the world, I am sure, and they have fallen upon our corn in the loft, and are eating it up at such a rate!" Away ran the husband upstairs, and saw thousands of birds sitting upon the floor eating up his corn, with the sparrow in the midst of them. "Unlucky wretch that I am!" cried the carter; for he saw that the corn was almost all gone.

"Not wretch enough yet!" said the sparrow; "thy cruelty shall cost thee thy life yet!" and away she flew.

The carter seeing that he had thus lost all that he had, went down into his kitchen; and was still not sorry for what he had done, but sat himself angrily and sulkily in the chimney corner.

But the sparrow sat on the outside of the window, and cried "Carter! Thy cruelty shall cost thee thy life!"

With that he jumped up in a rage, seized his hatchet, and threw it at the sparrow; but it missed her, and only broke the window.

The sparrow now hopped in, perched upon the window-seat, and cried, "Carter! It shall cost thee thy life!"

Then he became mad and blind with rage, and struck the window-seat with such force that he cleft it in two: and as the sparrow flew from place to place, the carter and his wife were so furious that they broke all their furniture, glasses, chairs, benches, the table and at last the walls, without touching the bird at all. In the end, however, they caught her and the wife said, "Shall I kill her at once?"

"No," cried he, "that is letting her off too easily; she shall die a much more cruel death: I will eat her."

But the sparrow began to flutter about, and stretch out her neck and cried, "Carter! It shall cost thee thy life yet!"

With that he could wait no longer, so he gave his wife the hatchet, and cried, "Wife, strike at the bird and kill her in my hand." And the wife struck; but she missed her aim, and hit her husband on the head so that he fell down dead, and the sparrow flew quietly home to her nest.

The twelve dancing princesses. (Kay Neilsen)

THE TWELVE DANCING PRINCESSES

THERE WAS A king who had twelve beautiful daughters. They slept in twelve beds all in one room; and when they went to bed, the doors were shut and locked up; but every morning their shoes were found to be quite worn through as if they had been danced in all night; and yet nobody could find out how it happened, or where they had been.

Then the king made it known to all the land that if any man could discover the secret, and find out where it was that the princesses danced in the night, he should have the one he liked best for his wife, and should be king after his death; but whoever tried and did not succeed, after three days and nights should be put to death.

A king's son soon came. He was well entertained, and in the evening was taken to the chamber next to the one where the princesses lay in their twelve beds. There he was to sit and watch where they went to dance; and, in order that nothing might pass without his hearing it, the door of his chamber was left open. But the king's son soon fell asleep; and when he awoke in the morning he found that the princesses had all been dancing, for the soles of their shoes were full of holes. The same thing happened the second and third night, so the king ordered his head to be cut off. After him came several others; but they had all the same luck, and all lost their lives in the same manner.

Now it chanced that an old soldier, who had been wounded in battle and could fight no longer, passed through the country where this king reigned, and as he was travelling through a wood, he met an old woman, who asked him where he was going. "I hardly know where I am going, or what I had better do," said the soldier; "but I think I should like very well to find out where it is that the princesses dance, and then in time I might be a king."

"Well," said the old dame, "that is no very hard task, only take care not to drink any of the wine which one of the princesses will bring to you in the evening; and as soon as she leaves you pretend to be fast asleep." Then she gave him a cloak, and said, "As soon as you put that on you will become invisible, and you will then be able to follow the princesses wherever they go."

When the soldier heard all this good counsel, he determined to try his luck: so he went to the king, and said he was willing to undertake the task. He was as well received as the others had been, and the king ordered fine royal robes to be given him; and when the evening came he was led to the outer chamber. Just as he was going to lie down, the eldest of the princesses brought him a cup of wine; but the soldier threw it all away secretly, taking care not to drink a drop. Then he laid himself down on his bed, and in a little while began to snore very loud as if he was fast asleep.

When the twelve princesses heard this they laughed heartily; and the eldest said, "This fellow too might have done a wiser thing than lose his life in this way!"

Then they rose up and opened their drawers and boxes, and took out all their fine clothes, and dressed themselves at the glass, and skipped about as if they were eager to begin dancing. But the youngest said, "I don't know why it is, but while you are all so happy I feel very uneasy; I am sure some mischance will befall us."

"You simpleton," said the eldest, "you are always afraid; have you forgotten how many kings' sons have already watched in vain? And as for this soldier, even if I had not given him his sleeping draught, he would have slept soundly enough."

When they were all ready, they went and looked at the soldier; but he snored on, and did not stir hand or foot, so they thought they were quite safe; and the eldest went up to her own bed and clapped her hands, and the bed sank into the floor and a trap-door flew open. The soldier saw them going down through the trap-door one after another, the eldest leading the way; and thinking he had no time to lose, he jumped up, put on the cloak which the old woman had given him, and followed them; but in the middle of the stairs he trod on the gown of the youngest princess, and she cried out to her sisters, "All is not right; someone took hold of my gown."

"You silly creature!" said the eldest, "it is nothing but a nail in the wall."

Then down they all went, and at the bottom they found themselves in a most delightful grove of trees; and the leaves were all of silver, and glittered and sparkled beautifully. The soldier wished to take away some token of the place; so he broke off a little branch, and there came a loud noise from the tree. Then the youngest daughter said again, "I am sure all is not right – did not you hear that noise? That never happened before."

But the eldest said, "It is only our princes, who are shouting for joy at our approach."

Then they came to another grove of trees, where all the leaves were of gold; and afterwards to a third, where the leaves were all glittering diamonds. And the soldier broke a branch from each; and every time there was a loud noise, which made the youngest sister tremble with fear; but the eldest still said, it was only the princes, who were crying for joy. So they went on till they came to a great lake; and at the side of the lake there lay twelve little boats with twelve handsome princes in them, who seemed to be waiting there for the princesses.

One of the princesses went into each boat, and the soldier stepped into the same boat as the youngest. As they were rowing over the lake, the prince who was in the boat with the

youngest princess and the soldier said, "I do not know why it is, but though I am rowing with all my might we do not get on so fast as usual, and I am quite tired: the boat seems very heavy today."

"It is only the heat of the weather," said the princess. "I feel very warm too."

On the other side of the lake stood a fine illuminated castle, from which came the merry music of horns and trumpets. There they all landed, and went into the castle, and each prince danced with his princess; and the soldier, who was all the time invisible, danced with them too; and when any of the princesses had a cup of wine set by her, he drank it all up, so that when she put the cup to her mouth it was empty. At this, too, the youngest sister was terribly frightened, but the eldest always silenced her. They danced on till three o'clock in the morning, and then all their shoes were worn out, so that they were obliged to leave off. The princes rowed them back again over the lake (but this time the soldier placed himself in the boat with the eldest princess); and on the opposite shore they took leave of each other, the princesses promising to come again the next night.

When they came to the stairs, the soldier ran on before the princesses, and laid himself down; and as the twelve sisters slowly came up, very much tired, they heard him snoring in his bed; so they said, "Now all is quite safe;" then they undressed themselves, put away their fine clothes, pulled off their shoes, and went to bed. In the morning the soldier said nothing about what had happened, but determined to see more of this strange adventure, and went again the second and third night; and everything happened just as before; the princesses danced each time till their shoes were worn to pieces, and then returned home. However, on the third night the soldier carried away one of the golden cups as a token of where he had been.

As soon as the time came when he was to declare the secret, he was taken before the king with the three branches and the golden cup; and the twelve princesses stood listening behind the door to hear what he would say. And when the king asked him. "Where do my twelve daughters dance at night?" he answered, "With twelve princes in a castle under ground." And then he told the king all that had happened, and showed him the three branches and the golden cup which he had brought with him. Then the king called for the princesses, and asked them whether what the soldier said was true; and when they saw that they were discovered, and that it was of no use to deny what had happened, they confessed it all. And the king asked the soldier which of them he would choose for his wife; and he answered, "I am not very young, so I will have the eldest." And they were married that very day, and the soldier was chosen to be the king's heir.

THE FISHERMAN AND HIS WIFE

THERE WAS ONCE a fisherman who lived with his wife in a pigsty, close by the seaside. The fisherman used to go out fishing all day long, and one day, as he sat on the shore with his rod, looking at the sparkling waves and watching his line, all of a sudden his float was dragged away deep into the water, and in drawing it up he pulled out a great fish. But the fish said, "Pray let me live! I am not a real fish; I am an enchanted prince. Put me in the water again, and let me go!"

"Oh, ho!" said the man, "you need not make so many words about the matter; I will have nothing to do with a fish that can talk; so swim away, sir, as soon as you please!" Then he put him back into the water, and the fish darted straight down to the bottom, and left a long streak of blood behind him on the wave.

When the fisherman went home to his wife in the pigsty, he told her how he had caught a great fish, and how it had told him it was an enchanted prince, and how, on hearing it speak, he had let it go again. "Did you not ask it for anything?" said the wife. "We live very wretchedly here, in this nasty dirty pigsty; do go back and tell the fish we want a snug little cottage."

The fisherman did not much like the business: however, he went back to the seashore; and

The fish said, "Pray let me live! I am not a real fish; I am an enchanted prince. Put me in the water again, and let me go!" (Daryll Lorette)

when he got there the water looked all yellow and green. And he stood at the water's edge, and said:

"O man of the sea!
Hearken to me!
My wife Ilsabill
Will have her own will,
And hath sent me to beg a boon of thee!"

Then the fish came swimming to him, and said, "Well, what is her will? What does your wife want?"

"Ah!" said the fisherman, "she says that when I had caught you, I ought to have asked you for something before I let you go; she does not like living any longer in the pigsty, and wants a snug little cottage."

"Go home, then," said the fish; "she is in the cottage already!" So the man went home, and saw his wife standing at the door of a nice trim little cottage. "Come in, come in!" said she. "Is not this much better than the filthy pigsty we had?" And there was a parlour, and a bedchamber, and a kitchen; and behind the cottage there was a little garden, planted with all sorts of flowers and fruits; and there was a courtyard behind, full of ducks and chickens.

"Ah!" said the fisherman, "how happily we shall live now!"

"We will try to do so, at least," said his wife.

Everything went right for a week or two, and then Dame Ilsabill said, "Husband, there is not nearly room enough for us in this cottage; the courtyard and the garden are a great deal too small; I should like to have a large stone castle to live in. Go to the fish again and tell him to give us a castle."

"Wife," said the fisherman, "I don't like to go to him again, for perhaps he will be angry; we ought to be content with this pretty cottage to live in."

"Nonsense!" said the wife; "he will do it very willingly, I know; go along and try!"

The fisherman went, but his heart was very heavy: and when he came to the sea, it looked blue and gloomy, though it was very calm; and he went close to the edge of the waves, and said:

"O man of the sea!
Hearken to me!
My wife Ilsabill
Will have her own will,
And hath sent me to beg a boon of thee!"

"Well, what does she want now?" said the fish.

"Ah!" said the man, dolefully, "my wife wants to live in a stone castle."

"Go home, then," said the fish; "she is standing at the gate of it already."

So away went the fisherman, and found his wife standing before the gate of a great castle. "See," said she, "is not this grand?"

With that they went into the castle together, and found a great many servants there, and the rooms all richly furnished, and full of golden chairs and tables; and behind the castle was a garden, and around it was a park half a mile long, full of sheep, and goats, and hares, and deer; and in the courtyard were stables and cow-houses.

"Well," said the man, "now we will live cheerful and happy in this beautiful castle for the rest of our lives."

"Perhaps we may," said the wife; "but let us sleep upon it, before we make up our minds to that." So they went to bed.

The next morning when Dame Ilsabill awoke it was broad daylight, and she jogged the fisherman with her elbow, and said, "Get up, husband, and bestir yourself, for we must be king of all the land."

"Wife, wife," said the man, "why should we wish to be the king? I will not be king."

"Then I will," said she.

"But, wife," said the fisherman, "how can you be king – the fish cannot make you a king!"

"Husband," said she, "say no more about it, but go and try! I will be king."

So the man went away quite sorrowful to think that his wife should want to be king. This time the sea looked a dark grey colour, and was overspread with curling waves with ridges of foam as he cried out:

"O man of the sea!
Hearken to me!
My wife Ilsabill
Will have her own will,
And hath sent me to beg a boon of thee!"

"Well, what would she have now?" said the fish. "Alas!" said the poor man, "my wife wants to be king."

"Go home," said the fish; "she is king already."

Then the fisherman went home; and as he came close to the palace he saw a troop of soldiers, and heard the sound of drums and trumpets. And when he went in he saw his wife sitting on a throne of gold and diamonds, with a golden crown upon her head; and on each side of her stood six fair maidens, each a head taller than the other. "Well, wife," said the fisherman, "are you king?"

"Yes," said she, "I am king."

And when he had looked at her for a long time, he said, "Ah, wife! What a fine thing it is to be king! Now we shall never have anything more to wish for as long as we live."

"I don't know how that may be," said she; "never is a long time. I am king, it is true; but I begin to be tired of that, and I think I should like to be emperor."

"Alas, wife! Why should you wish to be emperor?" said the fisherman.

"Husband," said she, "go to the fish! I say I will be emperor."

"Ah, wife!" replied the fisherman, "the fish cannot make an emperor, I am sure, and I should not like to ask him for such a thing."

"I am king," said Ilsabill, "and you are my slave; so go at once!"

So the fisherman was forced to go; and he muttered as he went along, "This will come to no good, it is too much to ask; the fish will be tired at last, and then we shall be sorry for what we have done."

He soon came to the seashore; and the water was quite black and muddy, and a mighty whirlwind blew over the waves and rolled them about, but he went as near as he could to the water's brink, and said:

"O man of the sea!
Hearken to me!
My wife Ilsabill
Will have her own will,
And hath sent me to beg a boon of thee!"

"What would she have now?" said the fish.

"Ah!" said the fisherman, "she wants to be emperor."

"Go home," said the fish; "she is emperor already."

So he went home again; and as he came near he saw his wife Ilsabill sitting on a very lofty throne made of solid gold, with a great crown on her head full two yards high; and on each side of her stood her guards and attendants in a row, each one smaller than the other, from the tallest giant down to a little dwarf no bigger than my finger. And before her stood princes, and dukes, and earls; and the fisherman went up to her and said, "Wife, are you emperor?"

"Yes," said she, "I am emperor."

"Ah!" said the man, as he gazed upon her, "what a fine thing it is to be emperor!"

"Husband," said she, "why should we stop at being emperor? I will be pope next."

"O wife, wife!" said he, "how can you be pope? There is but one pope at a time in Christendom."

"Husband," said she, "I will be pope this very day."

"But," replied the husband, "the fish cannot make you pope."

"What nonsense!" said she; "if he can make an emperor, he can make a pope. Go and try him."

So the fisherman went. But when he came to the shore the wind was raging and the sea was tossed up and down in boiling waves, and the ships were in trouble, and rolled fearfully upon the tops of the billows. In the middle of the heavens there was a little piece of blue sky, but towards the south all was red, as if a dreadful storm was rising. At this sight the fisherman was dreadfully frightened, and he trembled so that his knees knocked together, but still he went down near to the shore, and said:

"O man of the sea!
Hearken to me!
My wife Ilsabill
Will have her own will,
And hath sent me to beg a boon of thee!"

"What does she want now?" said the fish.

"Ah!" said the fisherman, "my wife wants to be pope."

"Go home," said the fish; "she is pope already."

Then the fisherman went home, and found Ilsabill sitting on a throne that was two miles high. And she had three great crowns on her head, and around her stood all the pomp and power of the Church. And on each side of her were two rows of burning lights, of all sizes, the greatest as large as the highest and biggest tower in the world, and the least no larger than a small rushlight.

"Wife," said the fisherman, as he looked at all this greatness, "are you pope?"

"Yes," said she, "I am pope."

"Well, wife," replied he, "it is a grand thing to be pope; and now you must be content, for you can be nothing greater."

"I will think about that," said the wife. Then they went to bed, but Dame Ilsabill could not sleep all night for thinking what she should be next. At last, just as she was falling asleep, morning broke and the sun rose. "Ha!"

thought she, as she woke up and looked at it through the window, "after all I cannot prevent the sun rising."

At this thought she was very angry, and wakened her husband, and said, "Husband, go to the fish and tell him I must be lord of the sun and moon."

The fisherman was half asleep, but the thought frightened him so much that he started and fell out of bed. "Alas, wife!" said he, "can you not be content with being pope?"

"No," said she, "I am very uneasy as long as the sun and moon rise without my leave. Go to the fish at once!"

Then the man went shivering with fear; and as he was going down to the shore a dreadful storm arose, so that the trees and the very rocks shook. And all the heavens became black with stormy clouds, and the lightning played and the thunder rolled; and you might have seen in the sea great black waves, swelling up like mountains with crowns of white foam upon their heads. And the fisherman crept towards the sea, and cried out, as well as he could:

"O man of the sea!
Hearken to me!
My wife Ilsabill
Will have her own will,
And hath sent me to beg a boon of thee!"

"What does she want now?" said the fish.

"Ah!" said he, "she wants to be lord of the sun and moon."

"Go home," said the fish, "to your pigsty again."

And there they live to this very day.

THE WILLOW-WREN AND THE BEAR

ONCE IN SUMMERTIME the bear and the wolf were walking in the forest, and the bear heard a bird singing so beautifully that he said: "Brother wolf, what bird is it that sings so well?"

"That is the king of birds," said the wolf, "before whom we must bow down." In reality the bird was the willow-wren.

"If that's the case," said the bear, "I should very much like to see his royal palace; come,

THE WILLOW-WREN AND THE BEAR

take me thither."

"That is not done quite as you seem to think," said the wolf; "you must wait until the queen comes."

Soon afterwards, the queen arrived with some food in her beak, and the lord king came too, and they began to feed their young ones.

The bear would have liked to go at once, but the wolf held him back by the sleeve, and said: "No, you must wait until the lord and lady queen have gone away again." So they took stock of the hole where the nest lay, and trotted away.

The bear, however, could not rest until he had seen the royal palace, and when a short time had passed he went to it again. The king and queen had just flown out, so he peeped in and saw five or six young ones lying there. "Is that the royal palace?" cried the bear; "it is a wretched palace, and you are not king's children, you are disreputable children!"

When the young wrens heard that, they were frightfully angry, and screamed: "No, that we are not! Our parents are honest people! Bear, you will have to pay for that!"

The bear grew uneasy and went back to his hole. The young willow-wrens, however, continued to cry and scream, and when their parents again brought food they said: "We will not so much as touch one fly's leg, no, not if we were dying of hunger, until you have settled whether we are respectable children or not; the bear has been here and has insulted us!"

Then the old king said: "Be easy, he shall be punished," and he at once flew with the queen to the bear's cave, and called in: "Old Growler, why have you insulted my children? You shall suffer for it – we will punish you with a bloody war."

Thus war was announced to the bear, and all four-footed animals were summoned to take part in it: oxen, asses, cows, deer, and every other animal the earth contained. And the willow-wren summoned everything which flew in the air; not only birds, large and small, but midges and hornets, bees and flies had to come.

When the time came for the war to begin, the willow-wren sent out spies to discover who was the enemy's commander-in-chief. The gnat, who was the most crafty, flew into the forest where the enemy was assembled, and hid herself beneath a leaf of a tree.

There stood the bear, and he called the fox before him and said: "Fox, you are the most cunning of all animals, you shall be general and lead us."

"Good," said the fox, "but what signal shall we agree upon?" No one spoke, so the fox said: "I have a fine long bushy tail, which almost looks like a plume of red feathers. When I lift my tail up quite high, all is going well, and you must charge; but if I let it hang down, run away as fast as you can."

When the gnat had heard that, she flew away again, and revealed everything, down to the minutest detail, to the willow-wren. When day broke, and the battle was to begin, all the four-footed animals came running up with such a noise that the earth trembled. The willow-wren with his army also came flying through the air with such a humming, and whirring, and swarming that everyone was uneasy and afraid, and on both sides they advanced against each other. But the willow-wren sent down the hornet, with orders to settle beneath the fox's tail, and sting with all his might. When the fox felt the first string, he winced with pain, but he bore it, and still kept his tail high in the air; at the second sting, he was forced to put it down for a moment; at the third, he could hold out no longer, screamed, and put his tail between his legs. When the animals saw that, they thought all was lost, and began to flee, each into his hole, and the birds had won the battle.

Then the king and queen flew home to their children and cried: "Children, rejoice, eat and drink to your heart's content, we have won the battle!"

But the young wrens said: "We will not eat yet, the bear must come to the nest, and beg for pardon and say that we are honourable children, before we will do that."

Then the willow-wren flew to the bear's hole and cried: "Growler, you are to come to the nest to my children, and beg their pardon, or else every rib of your body shall be broken."

So the bear crept thither in the greatest fear, and begged their pardon. And then at last the young wrens were satisfied, and sat down together and ate and drank, and made merry till quite late into the night.

THE FROG PRINCE

ONE FINE EVENING, a young princess put on her bonnet and clogs, and went out to take a walk by herself in a wood; and when she came to a cool spring of water, that rose in the midst of it, she sat herself down to rest a while. Now she had a golden ball in her hand, which was her favourite plaything; and she was always tossing it up into the air, and catching it again as it fell. After a time she threw it up so high that she missed catching it as it fell, and the ball bounded away, and rolled along upon the ground, till at last it fell down into the spring. The princess looked into the spring after her ball, but it was very deep, so deep that she could not see the bottom of it. Then she began to bewail her loss, and said, "Alas! if I could only get my ball again, I would give all my fine clothes and jewels, and everything that I have in the world."

While she was speaking, a frog put his head out of the water, and said, "Princess, why do you weep so bitterly?"

"Alas!" said she, "what can you do for me, you nasty frog? My golden ball has fallen into the spring."

The frog said, "I want not your pearls, and jewels, and fine clothes; but if you will love me, and let me live with you and eat from off your golden plate and sleep upon your bed, I will bring you your ball again."

"What nonsense," thought the princess, "this silly frog is talking! He can never even get out of the spring to visit me, though he may

"Alas!" said she, "what can you do for me, you nasty frog? My golden ball has fallen into the spring." (Ann Anderson)

be able to get my ball for me, and therefore I will tell him he shall have what he asks." So she said to the frog, "Well, if you will bring me my ball, I will do all you ask."

Then the frog put his head down, and dived deep under the water; and after a little while he came up again, with the ball in his mouth, and threw it on to the edge of the spring. As soon as the young princess saw her ball, she ran to pick it up; and she was so overjoyed to have it in her hand again, that she never thought of the frog, but ran home with it as fast as she could. The frog called after her, "Stay, princess, and take me with you as you said," but she did not stop to hear a word.

The next day, just as the princess had sat down to dinner, she heard a strange noise – tap, tap – plash, plash – as if something was coming up the marble staircase, and soon afterwards there was a gentle knock at the door, and a little voice cried out and said:

"Open the door, my princess dear,
Open the door to thy true love here!
Remember the words that thou and I said
By the fountain cool, in the greenwood
shade."

Then the princess ran to the door and opened it, and there she saw the frog, whom she had quite forgotten. At this sight she was sadly frightened, and shutting the door as fast as she could came back to her seat. The king, her father, seeing that something had frightened her, asked her what was the matter. "There is a nasty frog," said she, "at the door, that lifted my ball for me out of the spring last evening. I told him that he should live with me here, thinking that he could never get out of the spring; but there he is at the door, and he wants to come in."

While she was speaking the frog knocked again at the door, and said:

"Open the door, my princess dear,
Open the door to thy true love here!
Remember the words that thou and I said
By the fountain cool, in the greenwood
shade."

Then the king said to the young princess, "As you have given your word you must keep it; so go and let him in." She did so, and the frog hopped into the room, and then straight on – tap, tap – plash, plash – from the bottom

Then the princess ran to the door and opened it, and there she saw the frog, whom she had quite forgotten. (Arthur Rackham)

of the room to the top, till he came up close to the table where the princess sat. "Pray lift me upon chair," said he to the princess, "and let me sit next to you." As soon as she had done this, the frog said, "Put your plate nearer to me, that I may eat from it." This she did, and when he had eaten as much as he could, he said, "Now I am tired; carry me upstairs, and put me into your bed." And the princess, though very unwilling, took him up in her hand, and put him upon the pillow of her own bed, where he slept all night long.

As soon as it was light he jumped up, hopped downstairs, and went out of the house. "Now, then," thought the princess, "at last he is gone, and I shall be troubled with him no more."

But she was mistaken; for when night came again she heard the same tapping at the door; and the frog came once more, and said:

"Open the door, my princess dear,
Open the door to thy true love here!
Remember the words that thou and I said
By the fountain cool, in the greenwood
shade."

And when the princess opened the door the frog came in, ate with her and slept upon her pillow as before, till the morning broke. And the third night he did the same.

But when the princess awoke on the following morning she was astonished to see, instead of the frog, a handsome prince, gazing on her with the most beautiful eyes she had ever seen, and standing at the head of her bed.

He told her that he had been enchanted by a spiteful fairy, who had changed him into a frog; and that he had been fated so to abide till some princess should take him out of the spring, and let him eat from her plate, and sleep upon her bed for three nights. "You," said the prince, "have broken his cruel charm, and now I have nothing to wish for but that you should go with me into my father's kingdom, where I will marry you, and love you as long as you live."

The young princess, you may be sure, was not long in giving her consent; and as they spoke a magnificent coach drove up, drawn by eight beautiful horses, decked with plumes of feathers and golden harness; and behind the coach rode the prince's servant, faithful Heinrich, who had bewailed the misfortunes of his dear master during his enchantment so long and so bitterly that his heart had well-nigh burst.

They then took leave of the king, and got into the coach, and all set out, full of joy and merriment, for the prince's kingdom, which they reached safely; and there they lived happily a great many years.

CAT AND MOUSE IN PARTNERSHIP

A CERTAIN CAT HAD made the acquaintance of a mouse, and had said so much to her about the great love and friendship she felt for her, that at length the mouse agreed that they should live and keep house together.

"But we must make a provision for winter, or else we shall suffer from hunger," said the cat; "and you, little mouse, cannot venture everywhere, or you will be caught in a trap someday."

The good advice was followed, and a pot of fat was bought, but they did not know where to put it. At length, after much consideration, the cat said: "I know no place where it will be better stored up than in the church, for no one dares take anything away from there. We will set it beneath the altar, and not touch it until we are really in need of it."

So the pot was placed in safety, but it was not long before the cat had a great yearning for it, and said to the mouse: "I want to tell you something, little mouse; my cousin has brought a little son into the world, and has asked me to be godmother; he is white with brown spots, and I am to hold him over the font at the christening. Let me go out today, and you look after the house by yourself."

"Yes, yes," answered the mouse, "by all means go, and if you get anything very good to eat, think of me. I should like a drop of sweet red christening wine myself."

All this, however, was untrue; the cat had no cousin, and had not been asked to be godmother. She went straight to the church, stole to the pot of fat and began to lick at it until she had licked the top layer off. Then she took a walk upon the roofs of the town, looked

The cat crept behind the town walls to the church. (Arthur Rackham)

out for opportunities, and then stretched herself in the sun, and licked her lips whenever she thought of the pot of fat. Not until it was evening did she return home.

"Well, here you are again," said the mouse, "no doubt you have had a merry day."

"All went off well," answered the cat.

"What name did they give the child?"

"Top-off!" said the cat quite coolly.

"Top-off!" cried the mouse. "That is a very odd and uncommon name – is it a usual one in your family?"

"So what if it is," said the cat, "it is no worse than Crumb-stealer, as your godchildren are called."

Before long the cat was seized by another fit of yearning. She said to the mouse: "You must do me a favour, and once more manage the house for a day alone. I am again asked to be

godmother, and as the child has a white ring round its neck, I cannot refuse."

The good mouse consented, but the cat crept behind the town walls to the church, and devoured half the pot of fat. "Nothing ever seems so good as what one keeps to oneself," said she, and was quite satisfied with her day's work.

When she went home the mouse enquired: "And what was the child christened?"

"Half-done," answered the cat.

"Half-done! What are you saying? I never heard the name in my life. I'll wager anything it is not in any dictionary of names!"

The cat's mouth soon began to water for some more licking. "All good things go in threes," said she. "I am asked to stand godmother again. The child is quite black; it does have white paws, but with that exception, it has not a single white hair on its whole body; this only happens once every few years; you will let me go, won't you?"

"Top-off! Half-done!" answered the mouse. "They are such odd names, they make me very thoughtful."

"You sit at home," said the cat, "in your dark-grey fur coat and long tail, and are filled with fancies; that's because you do not go out in the daytime." During the cat's absence the mouse cleaned the house, and put it in order, but the greedy cat entirely emptied the pot of fat. "When everything is eaten up one has some peace," said she to herself, and well filled and sleek she did not return home till night.

The mouse at once asked what name had been given to the third child. "It will not please you more than the others," said the cat. "He is called All-gone."

"All-gone," cried the mouse. "That is the most suspicious name of all! I have never seen it in print. All-gone; what can that mean?" and she shook her head, curled herself up and lay down to sleep.

From this time forth no one invited the cat to be godmother, but when the winter had come and there was no longer anything to be found outside, the mouse thought of their provision, and said: "Come, cat, we will go to our pot of fat which we have stored up for ourselves – we shall enjoy that."

"Yes," answered the cat, "you will enjoy it as much as you would enjoy sticking that dainty tongue of yours out of the window."

They set out on their way, and when they arrived the pot certainly was still in its place, but it was empty. "Alas!" said the mouse, "now I see what has happened, now it comes to light! You are some true friend! You have devoured all when you were standing godmother. First Top-off, then Half-done, then — "

"Will you hold your tongue?" cried the cat. "One word more, and I will eat you too."

"All-gone" was already on the poor mouse's lips; scarcely had she spoken it before the cat sprang on her, seized her and swallowed her down. Verily, that is the way of the world.

THE GOOSE GIRL

THE KING OF a great land died, and left his queen to take care of their only child. This child was a daughter, who was very beautiful; and her mother loved her dearly, and was very kind to her. And there was a good fairy too, who was fond of the princess, and helped her mother to watch over her. When she grew up, she was betrothed to a prince who lived a great way off; and as the time drew near for her to be married, she got ready to set off on her journey to his country. Then the queen her mother packed up a great many costly things: jewels, and gold, and silver; trinkets, and fine dresses, and in short everything that became a royal bride. And she gave her a waiting-maid to ride with her and give her into the bridegroom's hands; and each had a horse for the journey. Now the princess's horse was the fairy's gift, and it was called Falada, and could speak.

When the time came for them to set out, the fairy went into her bedchamber, and took a little knife, and cut off a lock of her hair, and gave it to the princess, and said, "Take care of it, dear child; for it is a charm that may be of use to you on the road." Then they all took a sorrowful leave of the princess; and she put the lock of hair into her bosom, got upon her horse, and set off on her journey to her bridegroom's kingdom.

One day, as they were riding along by a brook, the princess began to feel very thirsty: and she said to her maid, "Pray get down and fetch me some water in my golden cup out of yonder brook, for I want to drink."

"Nay," said the maid, "if you are thirsty, get off yourself, and stoop down by the water and drink; I shall not be your waiting-maid any longer."

Then she was so thirsty that she got down, and knelt over the little brook, and drank; for she was frightened, and dared not bring out her golden cup; and she wept and said, "Alas! what will become of me?"

And the lock answered her, and said:

"Alas! alas! if thy mother knew it,
Sadly, sadly, would she rue it."

But the princess was very gentle and meek, so she said nothing about her maid's ill behaviour, but got upon her horse again.

Then all rode farther on their journey, till the day grew so warm, and the sun so scorching, that the bride began to feel very thirsty again; and at last, when they came to a river, she forgot her maid's previous rude speech, and said, "Pray get down, and fetch me some water to drink in my golden cup."

But the maid answered her, and even spoke even more haughtily than before: "Drink if you will, but I shall not be your waiting-maid."

Then the princess was so thirsty that she got off her horse, and lay down, and held her head over the running stream, and cried and said, "What will become of me?"

And the lock of hair answered her again:

"Alas! alas! if thy mother knew it,
Sadly, sadly, would she rue it."

And as she leaned down to drink, the lock of hair fell from her bosom, and floated away with the water.

Now she was so frightened that she did not see it; but her maid saw it, and was very glad, for she knew it was a charm; and she saw that the poor bride would be in her power, now that she had lost the hair.

So when the bride had done drinking, and would have got upon Falada again, the maid said, "I shall ride upon Falada, and you may have my horse instead;" so she was forced to give up her horse, and soon afterwards to take off her royal clothes and put on her maid's shabby ones.

At last, as they drew near the end of their journey, this treacherous servant threatened to kill her mistress if she ever told anyone what had happened. But Falada saw it all, and marked it well.

Then the waiting-maid rode on upon Falada, and the real bride rode upon the other horse, and they went on in this way till at last they came to the royal court. There was great joy at their coming, and the prince flew to meet them, and lifted the maid from her horse, thinking she was the one who was to be his wife; and she was led upstairs to the royal chamber; but the true princess was told to stay in the court below.

Now the old king happened just then to have nothing else to do; so he amused himself by sitting at his kitchen window, looking at what was going on; and he saw her in the courtyard.

The goose girl. (Gustaf Theodor Wallen)

As she looked very pretty, and too delicate for a waiting-maid, he went up into the royal chamber to ask the bride who it was she had brought with her but had thus left standing in the court below.

"I brought her with me for the sake of her company on the road," said she; "pray give the girl some work to do, that she may not be idle."

The old king could not for some time think of any work for her to do; but at last he said, "I have a lad who takes care of my geese; she may go and help him." Now the name of this lad that the real bride was to help in watching the king's geese was Curdken.

But the false bride said to the prince, "Dear husband, pray do me one piece of kindness."

"That I will," said the prince.

"Then tell one of your slaughterers to cut off the head of the horse I rode upon, for it was very unruly, and plagued me sadly on the road." But the truth was, she was very much

Early the next morning, as she and Curdken went out through the gate. (Rie Cramer)

afraid lest Falada should someday or other speak, and tell all she had done to the princess. She had her way, and the faithful Falada was killed; but when the true princess heard of it, she wept, and begged the man to nail up Falada's head in a large dark gateway of the city, through which she had to pass every morning and evening, that there she might still see him sometimes. Then the slaughterer said he would do as she wished; and cut off the head, and nailed it up in the dark gateway.

Early the next morning, as she and Curdken went out through the gate, she said sorrowfully: "Falada, Falada, there thou hangest!" and the head answered:

> *"Bride, bride, there thou gangest!*
> *Alas! alas! if thy mother knew it,*
> *Sadly, sadly, would she rue it."*

Then they went out of the city, and drove the geese on. And when she came to the meadow, she sat down upon a bank there, and let down her waving locks of hair, which were all of pure silver; and when Curdken saw it glitter in the sun, he ran up, and would have pulled some of the locks out, but she cried:

> *"Blow, breezes, blow!*
> *Let Curdken's hat go!*
> *Blow, breezes, blow!*
> *Let him after it go!*
> *O'er hills, dales, and rocks,*
> *Away be it whirl'd*
> *Till the silvery locks*
> *Are all comb'd and curl'd!"*

Then there came a wind so strong that it blew off Curdken's hat; and away it flew over the hills: and he was forced to turn and run after it. By the time he came back, she had done combing and curling her hair, and had put it up again safe. Then he was very angry and sulky, and would not speak to her at all; but they watched the geese until it grew dark in the evening, and then drove them homewards.

The next morning, as they were going through the dark gateway, the poor girl looked up at Falada's head, and cried: "Falada, Falada, there thou hangest!" and the head answered:

> *"Bride, bride, there thou gangest!*
> *Alas! alas! if they mother knew it,*
> *Sadly, sadly, would she rue it."*

Then she drove on the geese, and sat down again in the meadow, and began to comb out her hair as before; and Curdken ran up to her, and wanted to take hold of it; but she cried out quickly:

> *"Blow, breezes, blow!*
> *Let Curdken's hat go!*
> *Blow, breezes, blow!*
> *Let him after it go!*
> *O'er hills, dales, and rocks,*
> *Away be it whirl'd*
> *Till the silvery locks*
> *Are all comb'd and curl'd!"*

Then the wind came and blew away his hat; and off it flew a great way, over the hills and far away, so that he had to run after it; and when he came back she had bound up her hair again, and all was safe. So they watched the geese till it grew dark.

In the evening, after they came home, Curdken went to the old king, and said, "I cannot have that strange girl to help me to keep the geese any longer."

"Why?" said the king.

"Because, instead of doing any good, she does nothing but tease me all day long."

Then the king made him tell him what had happened. And Curdken said, "When we go in the morning through the dark gateway with

Then the wind came and blew away his hat.
(Helen Stratton)

our flock of geese, she cries and talks with the head of a horse that hangs upon the wall, and says: "Falada, Falada, there thou hangest!" and the head answers:

> *"Bride, bride, there thou gangest!*
> *Alas! alas! if they mother knew it,*
> *Sadly, sadly, would she rue it."*

And Curdken went on to tell the king what had happened upon the meadow where the geese fed: how his hat was blown away, and how he was forced to run after it, and to leave his flock of geese to themselves.

The old king told the boy to go out again the next day, and when morning came, he placed himself beside the dark gateway, and heard how she spoke to Falada, and how Falada answered. Then he went into the field, and hid himself in a bush by the meadow's side; and he soon saw with his own eyes how they drove the flock of geese; and how, after a little time, she let down her hair that glittered in the sun. And then he heard her say:

> *"Blow, breezes, blow!*
> *Let Curdken's hat go!*
> *Blow, breezes, blow!*
> *Let him after it go!*
> *O'er hills, dales, and rocks,*
> *Away be it whirl'd*
> *Till the silvery locks*
> *Are all comb'd and curl'd!"*

And soon came a gale of wind, and carried away Curdken's hat, and away went Curdken after it, while the girl went on combing and curling her hair. All this the old king saw, and then he went home without being seen. When the little goose girl came back in the evening he called her aside, and asked her why she behaved as she did; she burst into tears, and said, "That I must not tell you or any man, or I shall lose my life."

But the old king begged so hard that she had no peace till she had told him all the tale, from beginning to end, word for word. And it was

251

very lucky for her that she did so, for when she had done the king ordered royal clothes to be put upon her, and gazed on her with wonder, she was so beautiful. Then he called his son and told him that he had only a false bride, one who was merely a waiting-maid, while the true bride stood by. And the young king rejoiced when he saw her beauty, and heard how meek and patient she had been; and without saying anything to the false bride, the king ordered a great feast to be got ready for all his court. The bridegroom sat at the top, with the false princess on one side, and the true one on the other; but nobody recognised her, for her beauty was quite dazzling to their eyes; and she did not seem at all like the little goose girl, now that she had her brilliant dress on.

When they had eaten and drunk, and were very merry, the old king said he would tell them a tale. So he began, and told all the story of the princess, as if it was one that he had once heard; and he asked the true waiting-maid what she thought ought to be done to anyone who would behave thus.

"Nothing better," said this false bride, "than that she should be thrown into a cask stuck round with sharp nails, and that two white horses should be put to it, and should drag it from street to street till she was dead."

"Thou art she!" said the old king; "and as thou hast judged thyself, so shall it be done to thee."

And the young king was then married to his true wife, and they reigned over the kingdom in peace and happiness all their lives; and the good fairy came to see them, and restored the faithful Falada to life again.

THE ADVENTURES OF CHANTICLEER AND PARTLET

HOW THEY WENT TO THE MOUNTAINS TO EAT NUTS

"The nuts are quite ripe now," said Chanticleer to his wife Partlet; "suppose we go together to the mountains, and eat as many as we can, before the squirrel takes them all away."

"With all my heart," said Partlet; "let us go and make a holiday of it together."

So they went to the mountains; and as it was a lovely day, they stayed there till the evening. Now, whether it was that they had eaten so many nuts that they could not walk, or whether they were lazy and would not, I do not know: however, they took it into their heads that it did not become them to go home on foot. So Chanticleer began to build a little carriage of nutshells, and when it was finished, Partlet jumped into it and sat down, and bid Chanticleer harness himself to it and draw her home. "That's a good joke!" said Chanticleer; "no, that will never do; I had rather walk home than do that; I'll sit on the box and

be coachman, if you like, but I'll not draw." While this was passing, a duck came quacking up and cried out, "You thieving vagabonds, what business have you in my grounds? I'll pay you for your insolence!" and upon that she fell upon Chanticleer most lustily. But Chanticleer was no coward, and returned the duck's blows with his sharp spurs so fiercely that she soon began to cry out for mercy; which was only granted her upon condition that she would draw the carriage home for them. This she agreed to do; and Chanticleer got up on the box, and drove, crying, "Now, duck, get on as fast as you can." And away they went at a pretty good pace.

After they had travelled along a little way, they met a needle and a pin walking together along the road; and the needle cried out, "Stop, stop!" and said it was so dark that they could hardly find their way, and so muddy underfoot that they could not get on at all; he told them that he and his friend, the pin, had been at a public-house a few miles off, and had sat drinking till they had forgotten how late it was; he begged therefore that the travellers would be so kind as to give them a lift in their carriage. Chanticleer observing that they were but thin fellows, and not likely to take up much room, told them they might ride, but made them promise not to dirty the wheels of the carriage in getting in, nor to tread on Partlet's toes.

Late at night they arrived at an inn; and as it was bad travelling in the dark, and the duck seemed rather tired, and waddled about a good deal from one side to the other, they made up their minds to fix their quarters there; but the landlord at first was unwilling, and said his house was full, thinking they might not be very respectable company; however, they spoke civilly to him, and gave

him the egg which Partlet had laid by the way, and said they would give him the duck, who was in the habit of laying one every day: so at last he let them come in, and they ordered a handsome supper, and spent the evening very jollily.

Early in the morning, before it was quite light, and when nobody was stirring in the inn, Chanticleer awakened his wife, and, fetching the egg, they pecked a hole in it, ate

it up, and threw the shell into the fireplace; they then went to the pin and needle, who were fast asleep, and seizing them by the heads, stuck one into the landlord's easy chair and the other into his handkerchief; and, having done this, they crept away as softly as possible. However, the duck, who slept in the open air in the yard, heard them coming, and jumping into the brook which ran close by the inn, soon swam out of their reach.

An hour or two afterwards the landlord got up, and took his handkerchief to wipe his 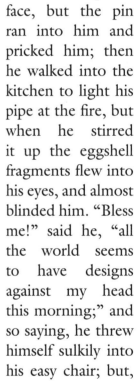 face, but the pin ran into him and pricked him; then he walked into the kitchen to light his pipe at the fire, but when he stirred it up the eggshell fragments flew into his eyes, and almost blinded him. "Bless me!" said he, "all the world seems to have designs against my head this morning;" and so saying, he threw himself sulkily into his easy chair; but, oh dear! the needle ran into him; and this time the pain was not in his head. He now flew into a very great passion, and, suspecting the company who had come in the night before, he went to look for them, but they were nowhere to be found; so he swore that he never again would take in such a troop of vagabonds, who ate a great deal, paid no reckoning, and gave him nothing for his trouble but their apish tricks.

HOW CHANTICLEER AND PARTLET WENT TO VISIT MR KORBES

Another day, Chanticleer and Partlet wished to ride out together; so Chanticleer built a handsome carriage with four red wheels, and harnessed six mice to it; and then he and Partlet got into the carriage, and away they drove.

Soon afterwards a cat met them, and said, "Where are you going?"

And Chanticleer replied,

"All on our way
A visit to pay
To Mr Korbes, the fox, today."

Then the cat said, "Take me with you."
Chanticleer said,

"With all my heart; get up behind, and be
sure you do not fall off.
Take care of this handsome coach of mine,
Nor dirty my pretty red wheels so fine!
Now, mice, be ready,
And, wheels, run steady!
For we are going a visit to pay
To Mr Korbes, the fox, today."

Soon after up came a millstone, an egg, a duck and a pin; and Chanticleer gave them all leave to get into the carriage and go with them.

When they arrived at Mr Korbes's house, he was not at home; so the mice drew the carriage into the coach-house, Chanticleer and Partlet flew up on to a beam, the cat sat down in the fireplace, the duck got into the washing cistern, the pin stuck himself into the bed pillow, the millstone laid himself over the house-door and the egg rolled himself up in the towel.

When Mr Korbes came home, he went to the fireplace to make a fire, but the cat threw all the ashes in his eyes; so he ran to the kitchen to wash himself, but there the duck splashed all the water in his face; and when he tried to wipe himself, the egg broke to pieces in the towel all over his face and eyes. Then he was very angry, and went without his supper to bed; but when he laid his head on the pillow, the pin ran into his cheek; at this he became quite furious, and, jumping up, would have run out of the house, but when he came to the door, the millstone fell down on his head and killed him on the spot.

HOW PARTLET DIED, AND WAS BURIED, AND HOW CHANTICLEER DIED OF GRIEF

Another day, Chanticleer and Partlet agreed to go again to the mountains to eat nuts; and it was settled that all the nuts which they found should be shared equally between them. Now Partlet found a very large nut, but she said nothing about it to Chanticleer, and kept it all to herself; however, it was so big that she could not swallow it, and it stuck in her throat. Then she was in a great fright, and cried out to Chanticleer, "Pray run as fast as you can, and fetch me some water, or I shall be choked."

Chanticleer ran as fast as he could to the river, and said, "River, give me some water, for Partlet lies in the mountain, and will be choked by a great nut."

The river said, "Run first to the bride, and ask her for a silken cord to draw up the water."

Chanticleer ran to the bride, and said, "Bride, you must give me a silken cord, for then the river will give me water, and the water I will carry to Partlet, who lies on the mountain, and will be choked by a great nut."

But the bride said, "Run first and bring me my garland that is hanging on a willow in the garden."

Then Chanticleer ran to the garden, and took the garland from the bough where it hung, and brought it to the bride; and then the bride gave him the silken cord, and he took the silken cord to the river; and the river gave him water, and he carried the water to Partlet; but in the meantime she had been choked by the great nut, and lay quite dead, and never moved again.

Then Chanticleer was very sorry, and cried bitterly; and all the beasts came and wept with him over poor Partlet. And six mice built a little hearse to carry her to her grave; and when it was ready they harnessed themselves before it, and Chanticleer drove them.

On the way they met the fox. "Where are you going, Chanticleer?" said he.

"To bury my Partlet," said the other.

"May I go with you?" said the fox.

"Yes; but you must get up behind, or my horses will not be able to draw you."

Then the fox got up behind; and presently the wolf, the bear, the goat and all the beasts of the wood came and climbed upon the hearse.

So on they went till they came to a rapid stream.

"How shall we get over?" said Chanticleer.

Then said a straw, "I will lay myself across, and you may pass over upon me."

But as the mice were going over, the straw slipped away and fell into the water, and the six mice all fell in and were drowned.

What was to be done?

Then a large log of wood came and said, "I am big enough; I will lay myself across the stream, and you shall pass over upon me."

So he laid himself down; but they managed so clumsily that the log of wood fell in and was carried away by the stream.

Then a stone, who saw what had happened, came up and kindly offered to help poor Chanticleer by laying himself across the stream; and this time he got safely to the other side with the hearse, and managed to get Partlet out of it; but the fox and the other mourners, who were sitting behind, were too heavy, and fell back into the water and were all carried away by the stream and drowned.

Thus Chanticleer was left alone with his dead Partlet; and having dug a grave for her, he laid her in it, and made a little hillock over her. Then he sat down by the grave, and wept and mourned, till at last he died too; and so all were dead.

RAPUNZEL

THERE WERE ONCE a man and a woman who had long in vain wished for a child. At length it seemed that God was about to grant their desire.

These people had a little window at the back of their house from which a splendid garden could be seen, which was full of the most beautiful flowers and herbs. It was, however, surrounded by a high wall, and no one dared to go into it because it belonged to an enchantress who had great power and was dreaded by all the world. One day the woman was standing by this window and looking down into the garden, when she saw a bed which was planted with the most beautiful rampion (sometimes called rapunzium), and it looked so fresh and green that she longed for it; she quite pined away, and began to look pale and miserable.

Then her husband was alarmed, and asked: "What ails you, dear wife?"

"Ah," she replied, "if I can't eat some of the rampion which is in the garden behind our house, I shall die."

The man, who loved her, thought: "Sooner than let your wife die, bring her some of the rampion yourself, let it cost what it will."

At twilight, he clambered down over the wall into the garden of the enchantress, hastily clutched a handful of rampion and took it to his wife. She at once made herself a salad of it, and ate it greedily. It tasted so good to her – so very good – that the next day she longed for it three times as much as before. If he was to have any rest, her husband must once more descend into the garden. In the gloom of evening therefore, he let himself down again; but when he had clambered down the wall he was terribly afraid, for he saw the enchantress standing before him.

"How can you dare," said she, fixing him with an angry look, "descend into my garden and steal my rampion like a thief? You shall suffer for it!"

"Ah," answered he, "let mercy take the place of justice. I only made up my mind to do it out of necessity. My wife saw your rampion from the window, and felt such a longing for it that she would have died if she had not got some to eat."

Then the enchantress allowed her anger to be softened, and said to him: "If the case be as you say, I will allow you to take away with you as much rampion as you will, only I make one condition: you must give me the child which your wife will bring into the world; it shall be well treated, and I will care for it like a mother."

The man in his terror consented to everything, and when the woman was brought to bed, the enchantress appeared at once, gave the child the name of Rapunzel, and took it away with her.

Rapunzel grew into the most beautiful child under the sun. When she was twelve years old, the enchantress shut her into a tower, which lay in a forest. It had neither stairs nor door, but quite at the top was a little window. When the enchantress wanted to go in, she placed herself beneath it and cried: "Rapunzel, Rapunzel, let down your hair to me."

Rapunzel had magnificent long hair, fine as spun gold, and when she heard the voice of the enchantress she unfastened her braided tresses, wound them round one of the hooks of the window above, and let the hair fall twenty metres down, whereupon the enchantress climbed up by it.

When she was twelve years old, the enchantress shut her into a tower, which lay in a forest.
(Ernst Liebermann)

After a year or two, it came to pass that the king's son rode through the forest and passed by the tower. Coming from it he heard a song, which was so charming that he stood still and listened. This was Rapunzel, who in her solitude passed her time in letting her sweet voice resound. The king's son wanted to climb up to her, and looked for the door of the tower, but none was to be found. He rode home, but the singing had so deeply touched his heart that every day he went out into the forest and listened to it. Once, when he was thus standing behind a tree, he saw that an enchantress came there, and he heard how she cried: "Rapunzel, Rapunzel, let down your hair to me." Then Rapunzel let down the braids of her hair, and the enchantress climbed up to her.

"If that is the ladder by which one mounts, I too will try my fortune," said he, and the next day when it began to grow dark, he went to the tower and cried: "Rapunzel, Rapunzel, let down your hair to me." Immediately the hair fell down and the king's son climbed up.

At first Rapunzel was terribly frightened when a man, such as her eyes had never yet beheld, came to her; but the king's son began to talk to her quite like a friend, and told her that his heart had been so stirred that it had let

Immediately the hair fell down and the king's son climbed up. (Ernst Liebermann)

him have no rest, and he had been determined to see her.

Then Rapunzel lost her fear, and when he asked her if she would take him for her husband, and she saw that he was young and handsome, she did not hesitate; she thought: "He will love me more than old Dame Gothel does;" and she said yes, and laid her hand in his. She said: "I will willingly go away with you, but I do not know how to get down. Bring with you a skein of silk every time that you come, and I will weave a ladder with it, and when that is ready I will descend, and you will take me away on your horse." They agreed that until that time he should come to her every evening, for the old woman came by day.

The enchantress remarked nothing of this, until one day Rapunzel thoughtlessly said to her: "Tell me, Dame Gothel, how it happens that you are so much heavier for me to draw up than the king's young son – he is with me in a moment."

"Ah! you wicked child," cried the enchantress. "What do I hear you say! I thought I had separated you from all the world, and yet you have deceived me!"

In her anger she clutched Rapunzel's beautiful tresses, wrapped them twice round her left hand, seized a pair of scissors with the

right, and snip, snap, they were cut off, and the lovely braids lay on the ground. And she was so pitiless that she banished poor Rapunzel to a desert where she had to live in great grief and misery.

On the same day that she cast out Rapunzel, however, the enchantress fastened the braids of hair which she had cut off to the hook of the window, and when the king's son came and cried: "Rapunzel, Rapunzel, let down your hair to me," she let the hair down.

The king's son ascended, but instead of finding his dearest Rapunzel, he found the enchantress, who gazed at him with wicked and venomous looks.

"Aha!" she cried mockingly, "you would fetch your dearest, but the beautiful bird sits no longer singing in the nest; the cat has got it, and will scratch out your eyes as well. Rapunzel is lost to you; you will never see her again."

The king's son was beside himself with pain, and in his despair he leapt down from the tower. He escaped with his life, but the thorns into which he fell pierced his eyes. Then he wandered quite blind about the forest, ate nothing but roots and berries, and did naught but lament and weep over the loss

At first Rapunzel was terribly frightened when a man, such as her eyes had never yet beheld, came to her. (Ernst Liebermann)

257

of his dearest wife. Thus he roamed about in misery for some years, and at length came to the desert where Rapunzel, with the twins to which she had given birth, a boy and a girl, lived in wretchedness.

He heard a voice, and it seemed so familiar to him that he went towards it, and when he approached, Rapunzel knew him and fell on his neck and wept. Two of her tears wetted his eyes and they grew clear again, and he could see with them as before. He led her to his kingdom where he was joyfully received, and they lived for a long time afterwards, happy and contented.

THE VALIANT LITTLE TAILOR

ONE SUMMER'S MORNING a little tailor was sitting on his table by the window; he was in good spirits, and sewed with all his might.

Then came a peasant woman down the street crying: "Good jams, cheap! Good jams, cheap!"

This rang pleasantly in the tailor's ears; he stretched his delicate head out of the window, and called: "Come up here, dear woman; here you will get rid of your goods."

The woman came up the three steps to the tailor with her heavy basket, and he made her unpack all the pots for him.

He inspected each one, lifted it up, put his nose to it, and at length said: "The jam seems to me to be good, so weigh me out four ounces, dear woman, and if it is a quarter of a pound that is of no consequence."

The woman who had hoped to find a good sale, gave him what he desired, but went away quite angry and grumbling.

"Now, this jam shall be blessed by God," cried the little tailor, "and give me health and strength;" so he brought the bread out of the cupboard, cut himself a piece right across the loaf and spread the jam over it. "This won't taste bitter," said he, "but I will just finish the jacket before I take a bite."

He laid the bread near him and sewed on, in his joy making bigger and bigger stitches. In the meantime the smell of the sweet jam rose to where the flies were sitting in great numbers, and they were attracted and descended on it in hosts.

"Hi! Who invited you?" said the little tailor, and drove the unbidden guests away.

The flies, however, who understood not a word, would not be turned away, but came back again in ever-increasing companies. The little tailor at last lost all patience, and drew a piece of cloth from the hole under his work-table, and, saying: "Wait, and I will give it to you," struck it mercilessly on them.

When he drew it away and counted, there lay before him no fewer than seven, dead and with legs stretched out.

"Are you a fellow of that sort?" said he, and could not help admiring his own bravery. "The whole town shall know of this!" And the little tailor hastened to cut himself a girdle, stitched it, and embroidered on it in large letters: "Seven at one stroke".

"Why stop at the town?" he continued. "The whole world shall hear of it!" and his heart wagged with joy like a lamb's tail.

The tailor put on the girdle, and resolved to go forth into the world, because he thought his workshop was too small for his valour. Before he went away, he sought about in the house to see if there was anything which he could take with him; however, he found nothing but an old cheese, and that he put in his pocket. In front of the door he observed a bird which had caught itself in the thicket. It had to go into his pocket with the cheese. Now he took to the road boldly, and as he was light and nimble, he felt no fatigue. The road led him up a mountain, and when he had reached the highest point of it, there sat a powerful giant looking peacefully about him.

The little tailor went bravely up, spoke to him, and said: "Good-day, comrade, so you are sitting there overlooking the widespread world! I am just on my way thither, and want to try my luck. Have you any inclination to go with me?"

The giant looked contemptuously at the tailor, and said: "You ragamuffin! You miserable creature!"

"Oh, indeed?" answered the little tailor and, unbuttoning his coat, showed the giant the girdle. "There may you read what kind of a man I am!"

The giant read: "Seven at one stroke", and thought that they had been men whom the tailor had killed, and began to feel a little respect for the tiny fellow. Nevertheless, he wished to try him first, and took a stone in his hand and squeezed it together so that water dropped out of it. "Do that likewise," said the giant, "if you have strength."

"Is that all?" said the tailor; "that is child's play with us!" and put his hand into his pocket, brought out the soft cheese, and pressed it until the liquid ran out of it. "Faith," said he, "that was a little better, wasn't it?"

The giant did not know what to say, and could not believe it of the little man. Then the giant picked up a stone and threw it so high that the eye could scarcely follow it. "Now, little mite of a man, do that likewise."

"Well thrown," said the tailor; "but after all the stone came down to earth again; I will throw you one which shall never come back at all," and he put his hand into his pocket, took out the bird, and threw it into the air. The bird, delighted with its liberty, rose, flew away and did not come back. "How does that shot please you, comrade?" asked the tailor.

"You can certainly throw," said the giant; "but now we will see if you are able to carry anything properly."

The valiant little tailor. (Alexander Zick)

He took the little tailor to a mighty oak tree which lay there felled on the ground, and said: "If you are strong enough, help me to carry the tree out of the forest."

"Readily," answered the little man; "take you the trunk on your shoulders, and I will raise up the branches and twigs; after all, they are the heaviest." The giant took the trunk on his shoulder, but the tailor seated himself on a branch, and the giant, who could not look round, had to carry away the whole tree, and the little tailor into the bargain; he, behind, was quite merry and happy, and whistled the song "Three tailors rode forth from the gate", as if carrying the tree were child's play.

The giant, after he had dragged the heavy burden part of the way, could go no farther, and cried: "Hark you, I shall have to let the tree fall!"

The tailor sprang nimbly down, seized the tree with both arms as if he had been carrying it, and said to the giant: "You are such a great fellow, and yet cannot even carry the tree!"

They went on together, and as they passed a cherry tree, the giant laid hold of the top of the tree where the ripest fruit was hanging, bent it down, gave it into the tailor's hand, and bade him eat. But the little tailor was much too weak to hold the tree, and when the giant let it go, it sprang back again, and the tailor was tossed into the air with it.

When he had fallen down again without injury, the giant said: "What is this? Have you not strength enough to hold a weak twig?"

"There is no lack of strength," answered the little tailor. "Do you think that could be anything to a man who has struck down seven at one blow? I leapt over the tree because the huntsmen are shooting down there in the thicket. Jump, as I did, if you can do it."

The giant made the attempt but he could not get over the tree, and remained hanging in the branches, so that in this also the tailor kept the upper hand.

The giant said: "If you are such a valiant fellow, come with me into our cavern and spend the night with us."

The little tailor was willing, and followed him. When they went into the cave, other giants were sitting there by the fire, and each of them had a roasted sheep in his hand and was eating it. The little tailor looked round and thought: "It is much more spacious here than in my workshop." The giant showed him a bed, and said he was to lie down in it and sleep. The bed, however, was too big for the little tailor; he did not lie down in it, but crept into a corner.

When it was midnight, and the giant thought that the little tailor was lying in a sound sleep, he got up, took a great iron bar, cut through the bed with one blow, and thought he had finished off the grasshopper for good.

With the earliest dawn the giants went into the forest, and had quite forgotten the little tailor, when all at once he walked up to them quite merrily and boldly. The giants were terrified, they were afraid that he would strike them all dead, and ran away in a great hurry.

The little tailor went onwards, always following his own pointed nose. After he had walked for a long time, he came to the courtyard of a royal palace, and as he felt weary, he lay down on the grass and fell asleep.

While he lay there, the people came and inspected him on all sides, and read on his girdle: "Seven at one stroke".

"Ah!" said they, "what does the great warrior want here in the midst of peace? He must be a mighty lord." They went and announced him to the king, and gave it as their opinion that if war should break out, this would be a weighty and useful man who ought on no account to be allowed to depart. The counsel pleased the king, and he sent one of his courtiers to the little tailor to offer him military service when he awoke. The ambassador remained standing by the sleeper, waited until he stretched his limbs and opened his eyes, and then conveyed to him this proposal.

"For this very reason have I come here," the tailor replied. "I am ready to enter the king's service."

He was therefore honourably received, and a special dwelling was assigned him.

The soldiers, however, were set against the little tailor, and wished him a thousand miles away. "What is to be the end of this?" they said among themselves. "If we quarrel with him, and he strikes about him, seven of us will fall at every blow; not one of us can stand against him."

They came therefore to a decision, betook themselves in a body to the king, and begged for their dismissal. "We are not prepared," said they, "to stay with a man who kills seven at one stroke."

The king was sorry that for the sake of one he should lose all his faithful servants, wished that he had never set eyes on the tailor, and would willingly have been rid of him again. But he did not venture to give him his dismissal, for he dreaded lest he should strike him and all his people dead and place himself on the royal throne. He thought about it for a long time, and at last found good counsel. He sent to the little tailor and caused him to be informed that, as he was a great warrior, he had one request to make to him.

In a forest of his country lived two giants, who caused great mischief with their robbing, murdering, ravaging and burning, and no one could approach them without putting himself in danger of death. If the tailor conquered and killed these two giants, he would give him his only daughter to wife, and half of his kingdom as a dowry, likewise one hundred horsemen should go with him to assist him. "That would indeed be a fine thing for a man like me!" thought the little tailor. "One is not offered a beautiful princess and half a kingdom every day of one's life!"

"Oh, yes," he replied, "I will soon subdue the giants, and do not require the help of the hundred horsemen to do it; he who can hit seven with one blow has no need to be afraid of two."

The little tailor went forth, and the hundred horsemen followed him. When he came to the outskirts of the forest, he said to his followers: "Just stay waiting here, I alone will soon finish off the giants." Then he bounded into the forest and looked about right and left.

After a while he perceived both giants. They lay sleeping under a tree, and snored so that the branches waved up and down. The little tailor, not idle, gathered two pocketfuls of stones, and with these climbed up the tree. When he was halfway up, he slipped down by a branch until he sat just above the sleepers, and then let one stone after another fall on the breast of one of the giants. For a long time the giant felt nothing, but at last he awoke, pushed his comrade, and said: "Why are you knocking me?"

"You must be dreaming," said the other. "I am not knocking you."

They laid themselves down to sleep again, and then the tailor threw a stone down on to the second. "What is the meaning of this?" cried the other. "Why are you pelting me?"

"I am not pelting you," answered the first, growling. They disputed about it for a time, but as they were weary they let the matter rest, and their eyes closed once more.

The little tailor began his game again, picked out the biggest stone, and threw it with all his might on the breast of the first giant.

"That is too bad!" cried he, and springing up like a madman, he pushed his companion against the tree until it shook. The other paid him back in the same coin, and they got into such a rage that they tore up trees and belaboured each other so long that at last they both fell down dead on the ground at the same time.

Then the little tailor leapt down. "It is a lucky thing," said he, "that they did not tear up the tree on which I was sitting, or I should have had to sprint on to another like a squirrel; but we tailors are nimble."

He drew out his sword and gave each of them a couple of thrusts in the breast, and then went out to the horsemen and said: "The work is done; I have finished both of them off, but it was hard work! They tore up trees in their sore need, and defended themselves with them, but all that is to no purpose against a man like myself, who can kill seven at one blow."

"But are you not wounded?" asked the horsemen.

"You need not concern yourself about that," answered the tailor, "they have not bent one hair of mine." The horsemen would not believe him, and rode into the forest; there they found the giants swimming in their blood, and all round about lay the torn-up trees.

The little tailor demanded of the king the promised reward; he, however, repented of his promise, and again bethought himself how he could get rid of the hero. "Before you receive my daughter, and half of my kingdom," said he, "you must perform one more heroic deed. In the forest roams a unicorn which does great harm, and you must catch it first."

"I fear one unicorn still less than two giants. Seven at one blow is my kind of affair."

He took a rope and an axe with him, went forth into the forest, and again bade those who were sent with him to wait outside. He had not long to seek. The unicorn soon came towards him, and rushed directly on the tailor, as if it would gore him with its horn without more ado. "Softly, softly; it can't be done as quickly as that," said he, and stood still and waited until the animal was quite close, and then sprang nimbly behind the tree.

The unicorn ran against the tree with all its force and stuck its horn so fast in the trunk that it had not strength enough to draw it out again, and thus it was caught. "Now, I have got the bird," said the tailor, and came out from behind the tree and put the rope round its neck, and then with his axe he hewed the horn out of the tree, and when all was ready he led the beast away and took it to the king.

The king still would not give him the promised reward, and made a third demand. Before the wedding the tailor was to catch him a wild boar that made great havoc in the forest, and the huntsmen should give him their help.

"Willingly," said the tailor, "that is child's play!" He did not take the huntsmen with him into the forest, and they were well pleased that he did not, for the wild boar had several times received them in such a manner that they had no inclination to lie in wait for him.

When the boar perceived the tailor, it ran on him with foaming mouth and whetted tusks,

and was about to throw him to the ground, but the hero fled into a chapel which was near and in one bound sprang out again by the window. The boar ran after him, but the tailor ran round outside and shut the door behind it, and then the raging beast, which was much too heavy and awkward to leap out of the window, was caught.

The little tailor called the huntsmen thither that they might see the prisoner with their own eyes. The hero, however, went to the king, who was now, whether he liked it or not, obliged to keep his promise and give him his daughter and half his kingdom. Had he known that it was no warlike hero but a little tailor who was standing before him, it would have grieved him still more than it did. The wedding was held with great magnificence and small joy, and out of a tailor a king was made.

After some time the young queen heard her husband say in his dreams at night: "Boy, make me the doublet, and patch the pantaloons, or else I will rap the yard-measure over your ears." Then she discovered in what state of life the young lord had been born, and next morning complained of her wrongs to her father, and begged him to help her to get rid of her husband, who was nothing else but a tailor.

The king comforted her and said: "Leave your bedroom door open this night, and my servants shall stand outside, and when he has fallen asleep shall go in, bind him, and take him on board a ship which shall carry him into the wide world." The woman was satisfied with this; but the king's armour-bearer, who had heard all, was friendly with the young lord, and informed him of the whole plot. "I'll put a screw into that business," said the little tailor.

At night he went to bed with his wife at the usual time, and when she thought that he had fallen asleep, she got up, opened the door, and then lay down again. The little tailor, who was only pretending to be asleep, began to cry out in a clear voice: "Boy, make me the doublet and patch me the pantaloons, or I will rap the yard-measure over your ears. I smote seven at one blow. I killed two giants, I brought away one unicorn and caught a wild boar, and am I to fear those who are standing outside the room." When these men heard the tailor speaking thus, they were overcome by a great dread, and ran as if the wild huntsman were behind them, and none of them would venture anything further against him. So the little tailor was and remained a king to the end of his life.

HANSEL AND GRETEL

HARD BY A great forest dwelt a poor woodcutter with his wife and the two children of his former marriage. The boy was called Hansel and the girl Gretel. He earned very little, and once when a great famine fell on the land, he could no longer procure even daily bread. Now, when he thought over this by night in his bed, and tossed about in his anxiety, he groaned and said to his wife: "What is to become of us? How are we to feed our poor children when we no longer have anything even for ourselves?"

"I'll tell you what, husband," answered the woman, "early tomorrow morning we will take the children out into the forest to where it is the thickest; there we will light a fire for them, and give each of them one last piece of bread, and then we will go to our work and

Hansel and Gretel. (Hermann Kalbach)

263

leave them alone. They will not find the way home again, and we shall be rid of them."

"No, wife," said the man, "I will not do that; how can I bear to leave my children alone in the forest? The wild animals would soon come and tear them to pieces."

"Oh, you fool!" said she; "then we must all four die of hunger; you may as well plane the planks for our coffins," and she left him no peace until he consented.

"But I feel very sorry for the poor children, all the same," said the man.

The two children had also not been able to sleep for hunger and had heard what their stepmother had said to their father. Gretel wept bitter tears, and said to Hansel: "Now all is over with us."

"Be quiet, Gretel," said Hansel, "do not distress yourself, I will soon find a way to help us." And when the old folk had fallen asleep, he got up, put on his little coat, opened the door below and crept outside.

The moon shone brightly, and the white pebbles which lay in front of the house glittered like real silver pennies. Hansel stooped and stuffed the little pocket of his coat with as many as he could get in. Then he went back and said to Gretel: "Be comforted, dear little sister, and sleep in peace, God will not forsake us," and he lay down again in his bed.

When day dawned, but before the sun had risen, the woman came and awoke the two children, saying: "Get up, you sluggards! we are going into the forest to fetch wood." She gave each a little piece of bread, and said: "There is something for your dinner, but do not eat it up before then, for you will get nothing else."

Gretel took the bread under her apron, as Hansel had the pebbles in his pocket. Then they all set out together on the way to the forest. When they had walked a short time, Hansel stood still and peeped back at the house, and did so again and again. His father said: "Hansel, what are you looking at there and staying behind for? Pay attention, and do not forget how to use your legs."

"Ah, father," said Hansel, "I am looking at my little white cat; she is sitting up on the roof, and wants to say goodbye to me."

The wife said: "Fool, that is not your little cat, that is the morning sun which is shining on the chimneys."

Hansel, however, had not been looking back at the cat, but had been constantly throwing one of the white pebble-stones out of his pocket on the road.

When they had reached the middle of the forest, the father said: "Now, children, pile up some wood, and I will light a fire that you may not be cold."

Hansel and Gretel gathered brushwood together, as high as a little hill. The brushwood was lighted, and when the flames were burning very high, the woman said: "Now, children, lay yourselves down by the fire and rest; we will go into the forest and cut some wood. When we have done, we will come back and fetch you away."

Hansel and Gretel sat by the fire, and when noon came, each ate a little piece of bread, and as they heard the strokes of the wood-axe they believed that their father was near. It was not the axe, however, but a branch which he had fastened to a withered tree which the wind was blowing backwards and forwards. And as they had been sitting such a long time, their eyes closed with fatigue, and they fell fast asleep. When at last they awoke, it was already dark night.

Gretel began to cry and said: "How are we to get out of the forest now?"

But Hansel comforted her and said: "Just wait a little, until the moon has risen, and then we will soon find the way."

And when the full moon had risen, Hansel took his little sister by the hand, and followed the pebbles which shone like newly-coined silver pieces, and showed them the way.

They walked the whole night long, and by break of day came once more to their father's house. They knocked at the door, and when the woman opened it and saw that it was Hansel and Gretel, she said: "You naughty children, why have you slept so long in the forest? We thought you were never coming back at all!" The father, however, rejoiced, for it had cut him to the heart to leave them behind alone.

Not long afterwards, there was once more great dearth throughout the land, and the children heard their mother saying at night to their father: "Everything is eaten again, we have one half-loaf left, and that is the end. The children must go, we will take them farther into the wood, so that they will not find their way out again; there is no other means of saving ourselves!" The man's heart was heavy, and he thought: "It would be better for me to share the last mouthful with my children." The woman, however, would listen to nothing that he had to say, but scolded and reproached him. He who says A must say B, likewise, and as he had yielded the first time, he had to do so a second time also.

The children, however, were still awake and had heard the conversation. When the old folk were asleep, Hansel again got up, and wanted to go out and pick up pebbles as he had done before, but the woman had locked the door, and Hansel could not get out. Nevertheless he comforted his little sister, and said: "Do not cry, Gretel, go to sleep quietly, the good God will help us."

Early in the morning came the woman, and took the children out of their beds. Their piece of bread was given to them, but it was still smaller than the time before. On the way into the forest Hansel crumbled his in his pocket, and often stood still and threw a morsel on the ground.

"Hansel, why do you stop and look round?" said the father. "Come on, do."

"I am looking back at my little pigeon which is sitting on the roof and wants to say goodbye to me," answered Hansel.

"Fool!" said the woman, "that is not your little pigeon, that is the morning sun that is shining on the chimney."

Hansel, however, little by little, threw all the crumbs on the path.

The woman led the children still deeper into the forest, where they had never in their lives been before. Then a great fire was again made, and the mother said: "Just sit there, you children, and when you are tired you may sleep a little; we are going into the forest to cut wood, and in the evening when we are done, we will come and fetch you away."

When it was noon, Gretel shared her piece of bread with Hansel, who had scattered his by the way. Then they fell asleep and evening passed, but no one came to the poor children. They did not awake until it was dark night, and Hansel comforted his little sister and said: "Just wait, Gretel, until the moon rises, and then we shall see the crumbs of bread which I have strewn about; they will show us our way home again."

When the moon came they set out, but they found no crumbs, for the many thousands of birds which fly about in the woods and fields had picked them all up. Hansel said to Gretel: "We shall soon find the way," but they did not find it. They walked the whole night and all the next day too, from morning till evening, but they did not get out of the forest, and they were very hungry for they had had nothing to eat but two or three berries which grew on the ground. And as they were so weary that their legs would carry them no longer, they lay down beneath a tree and fell asleep.

It was now three mornings since they had left their father's house. They began to walk again, but they always came deeper into the forest, and if help did not come soon, they must die of hunger and weariness. When it was midday, they saw a beautiful snow-white bird sitting on

Suddenly the door opened, and a woman as old as the hills, who supported herself on crutches, came hobbling out. (Warren Chappell)

a bough, which sang so delightfully that they stood still and listened to it. And when its song was over, it spread its wings and flew away before them, and they followed it until they reached a little house, on the roof of which it alighted; and when they approached the little house they saw that it was built of bread and covered with cakes, but that the windows were of clear sugar. "We will set to work on that," said Hansel, "and have a good meal. I will eat a bit of the roof, and you Gretel, can eat some of the window, it will taste sweet." Hansel reached up and broke off a little of the roof to try how it tasted, and Gretel leant against the window and nibbled at the panes. Then a soft voice cried from the parlour: "Nibble, nibble, gnaw. Who is nibbling at my little house?"

The children answered: "The wind, the wind, the heaven-born wind," and went on eating without disturbing themselves. Hansel, who liked the taste of the roof, tore down a great piece of it, and Gretel pushed out the whole of one round windowpane and sat down on the ground to enjoy it.

Suddenly the door opened, and a woman as old as the hills, who supported herself on crutches, came hobbling out. Hansel and Gretel were so terribly frightened that they let fall what they had in their hands. The old woman, however, nodded her head, and said: "Oh, you dear children, who has brought you here? Do come in, and stay with me. No harm shall happen to you."

She took them both by the hand, and led them into her little house. Then good food was set before them, milk and pancakes, with sugar, apples and nuts. Afterwards two pretty little beds were covered with clean white linen, and Hansel and Gretel lay down in them, and thought they were in heaven.

The old woman had only pretended to be so kind; she was in reality a wicked witch, who lay in wait for children, and had only built the little house of bread in order to entice them there. When a child fell into her power, she killed it, cooked and ate it, and that was a feast day with her. Witches have red eyes, and cannot see far, but they have a keen sense of smell like the beasts, and are aware when human beings draw near. When Hansel and Gretel came into her neighbourhood, she laughed with malice, and said mockingly: "I have them, they shall not escape me!"

Early in the morning before the children were awake, she was already up, and when she saw both of them sleeping and looking so pretty, with their plump and rosy cheeks, she muttered to herself: "That will be a dainty mouthful!" Then she seized Hansel with her shrivelled hand, carried him into a little stable, and locked him in behind a grated door. Scream as he might, it would not help him. Then she went to Gretel, shook her till she awoke, and cried: "Get up, lazy thing, fetch some water, and cook something good for your brother; he is in the stable outside, and is to be made fat. When he is fat, I will eat him." Gretel began to weep bitterly, but it was all in vain, for she was forced to do what the wicked witch commanded.

And now the best food was cooked for poor Hansel, but Gretel got nothing but crab-shells. Every morning the woman crept to the little stable, and cried: "Hansel, stretch out your finger that I may feel if you will soon be fat." Hansel, however, stretched out a little bone to her, and the old woman, who had dim eyes, could not see it, and thought it was Hansel's finger, and was astonished that there was no way of fattening him.

When four weeks had gone by, and Hansel still remained thin, she was seized with impatience and would not wait any longer. "Now, then, Gretel," she cried to the girl, "stir yourself, and bring some water. Let Hansel be fat or lean, tomorrow I will kill him, and cook him."

Ah, how the poor little sister did lament when she had to fetch the water, and how her tears did flow down her cheeks! "Dear God, do help us," she cried. "If the wild beasts in the forest had but devoured us, we should at any rate have died together."

"Just keep your noise to yourself," said the old woman, "it won't help you at all."

Early in the morning, Gretel had to go out and hang up the cauldron with the water, and light the fire. "We will bake first," said the old woman, "I have already heated the oven, and kneaded the dough." She pushed poor Gretel out to the oven, from which flames of fire were already darting. "Creep in," said the witch, "and see if it is properly heated, so that we can put the bread in."

Once Gretel was inside, she intended to shut the oven and let her bake in it, and then she would eat her, too. But Gretel saw what she had in mind, and said: "I do not know how I am to do it; how do I get in?"

"Silly goose," said the old woman. "The door is big enough; just look, I can get in myself!" and she crept up and thrust her head into the oven. Then Gretel gave her a push that drove her far into it, and shut the iron door, and fastened the bolt. Oh! Then she began to howl quite horribly, but Gretel ran away and the wicked witch was miserably burnt to death.

Gretel, however, ran like lightning to Hansel, opened his little stable, and cried: "Hansel, we are saved! The old witch is dead!" Then Hansel sprang like a bird from its cage when the door is opened. How they did rejoice and embrace each other, and dance about and kiss each other! And as they had no longer any need to fear her, they went into the witch's house, and in every corner there stood chests full of pearls and jewels. "These are far better than pebbles!" said Hansel, and thrust into his pocket whatever could be got in, and Gretel said: "I, too, will take something home with me," and filled her pinafore full. "But now we must be off," said Hansel, "that we may get out of the witch's forest." When they had walked for two hours, they came to a great stretch of water. "We cannot cross," said Hansel, "I see no foot-plank, and no bridge."

"And there is alas no ferry," answered Gretel; "but a white duck is swimming there: if I ask her, she will help us over." Then she cried:

"Little duck, little duck, dost thou see,
Hansel and Gretel are waiting for thee?
There's never a plank or bridge in sight,
Take us across on thy back so white."

The duck came to them, and Hansel seated himself on its back, and told his sister to sit by him. "No," replied Gretel, "that will be too heavy for the little duck; she shall take us across one after the other." The good little duck did so, and when they were once safely across and had walked for a short time, the forest seemed to be more and more familiar to them, and at length they saw from afar their father's house.

Then they began to run, rushed into the parlour and threw themselves round their father's neck. The man had not known one happy hour since he had left the children in the forest; and the woman, who had been so cruel, was dead.

Gretel emptied her pinafore so that quantities of pearls and precious stones ran about the room, and Hansel threw one handful after another out of his pocket to add to them. Then all anxiety was at an end, and they lived together in perfect happiness.

MOTHER HOLLE

ONCE UPON A time there was a widow who had two daughters; one of them was beautiful and industrious, the other ugly and lazy. The mother, however, loved the ugly and lazy one best, because she was her own daughter, and so the other, who was only her stepdaughter, was made to do all the work of the house, and was quite the Cinderella of the family. Her stepmother sent her out every day to sit by the well in the high road, there to spin until she made her fingers bleed. Now it chanced one day that some blood fell on to the spindle, and as the girl stooped over the well to wash it off, the spindle suddenly sprang out of her hand and fell into the well. She ran home, crying, to tell of her misfortune, but her stepmother spoke harshly to her, and after giving her a violent scolding, said unkindly, "As you have let the spindle fall into the well you may go yourself and fetch it out."

The girl went back to the well not knowing what to do, and at last in her distress she jumped into the water after the spindle.

She remembered nothing more until she awoke and found herself in a beautiful meadow, full of sunshine, and with countless flowers blooming in every direction.

She walked over the meadow, and presently she came upon a baker's oven full of bread, and the loaves cried out to her, "Take us out, take us out, or alas! we shall be burnt to a cinder; we were baked through long ago." So she took the bread-shovel and drew them all out.

She went on a little farther, till she came to a tree full of apples. "Shake me, shake me, I pray," cried the tree; "my apples, one and all, are ripe." So she shook the tree, and the apples came falling down upon her like rain; but she continued shaking until there was not a single apple left upon it. Then she carefully gathered the apples together in a heap and walked on again.

The next thing she came to was a little house, and there she saw an old woman looking out. She had such large teeth that the girl was terrified, and turned to run away. But the old woman called after her, "What are you afraid of, dear child? Stay with me; if you will do the work of my house properly for me, I will make you very happy. You must be very careful, however, to make my bed in the right way, for I wish you always to shake it thoroughly, so that the feathers fly about; then they say, down there in the world, that it is snowing; for I am Mother Holle." The old woman spoke so kindly, that the girl summoned up courage and agreed to enter into her service.

She took care to do everything according to the old woman's bidding and every time she made the bed she shook it with all her might, so that the feathers flew about like so many snowflakes. The old woman was as good as her word: she never spoke angrily to her, and gave her roast and boiled meats every day.

So she stayed on with Mother Holle for some time, but then she began to grow unhappy. She could not at first tell why she felt sad, but she became conscious at last of great longing to go home; then she knew she was homesick, although she was a thousand times better off with Mother Holle than with her mother and sister. After waiting awhile, she went to Mother Holle and said, "I am so homesick that I cannot stay with you any longer, for although I am so happy here, I must return to my own people."

Then Mother Holle said, "I am pleased that you should want to go back to your own people, and as you have served me so well and faithfully, I will take you home myself."

Thereupon she led the girl by the hand up to a broad gateway. The gate was opened, and as the girl passed through, a shower of gold fell

"You must be very careful, however, to make my bed in the right way, for I wish you always to shake it thoroughly, so that the feathers fly about."

upon her, and the gold clung to her, so that she was covered with it from head to foot.

"That is a reward for your industry," said Mother Holle, and as she spoke she handed her the spindle which she had dropped into the well.

The gate was then closed, and the girl found herself back in the old world close to her stepmother's house. As she entered the courtyard, the cock who was perched on the well called out: "Cock-a-doodle-doo! Your golden daughter's come back to you."

Then she went in to her mother and sister, and as she was so richly covered with gold, they gave her a warm welcome. She related to them all that had happened, and when the mother heard how she had come by her great riches, she thought she should like her ugly, lazy daughter to go and try her fortune. So she made the sister go and sit by the well and spin; and the girl thrust her hand into a thorn bush and pricked her finger, so that she might drop some blood on to the spindle; then she threw it into the well and jumped in herself.

Like her sister she awoke in the beautiful meadow, and walked over it till she came to the oven. "Take us out, take us out, or alas! we shall be burnt to a cinder; we were baked through long ago," cried the loaves as before.

But the lazy girl answered, "Do you think I am going to dirty my hands for you?" and walked on.

Presently she came to the apple tree. "Shake me, shake me, I pray; my apples, one and all, are ripe," it cried.

But she only answered, "A nice thing to ask me to do, one of the apples might fall on my head," and she passed on.

At last she came to Mother Holle's house, and as she had heard all about the large teeth from her sister, she was not afraid of them, and engaged herself without delay to the old woman.

The first day she was very obedient and industrious, and exerted herself to please Mother Holle, for she thought of the gold she should get in return. The next day, however, she began to dawdle over her work, and the third day she was more idle still; then she began to lie in bed in the mornings and refused to get up. Worse still, she neglected to make the old woman's bed properly, and forgot to shake it so that the feathers might fly about. So Mother Holle very soon got tired of her, and told her she might go.

The lazy girl was delighted at this, and thought to herself, "The gold will soon be mine." Mother Holle led her, as she had led her sister, to the broad gateway; but as she was passing through, instead of the shower of gold, a great bucketful of pitch came pouring over her.

"That is in return for your services," said the old woman, and she shut the gate.

So the lazy girl had to go home covered with pitch, and the cock on the well called out: "Cock-a-doodle-doo! Your dirty daughter's come back to you."

And, try as she would, she could not get the pitch off and it stuck to her as long as she lived.

LITTLE RED RIDING HOOD

ONCE UPON A time there was a dear little girl who was loved by everyone who looked at her, but most of all by her grandmother, and there was nothing that she would not have given to the child. Once she gave her a little cap of red velvet, which suited her so well that she would never wear anything else; so she was always called "Little Red Riding Hood".

One day her mother said to her: "Come, Little Red Riding Hood, here is a piece of cake and a bottle of wine; take them to your grandmother, for she is ill and weak and they will do her good. Set out before it gets hot, and when you are going, walk nicely and quietly and do not run off the path, or you may fall and break the bottle, and then your grandmother will get nothing; and when you go into her room, don't forget to say, 'Good-morning', and don't peep into every corner before you do it."

"I will take great care," said Little Red Riding Hood to her mother, and gave her hand on it.

The grandmother lived out in the wood, half a league from the village, and just as Little Red Riding Hood entered the wood, a wolf met her. Little Red Riding Hood did not know what a wicked creature he was, and was not at all afraid of him.

"Good-day, Little Red Riding Hood," said he.

"Thank you kindly, wolf."

"Whither away so early, Little Red Riding Hood?"

"To my grandmother's."

"What have you got in your apron?"

"Cake and wine; yesterday was baking-day, so poor sick grandmother is to have something good, to make her stronger."

"Where does your grandmother live, Little Red Riding Hood?"

"A good quarter of a league farther on in the wood; her house stands under the three large oak trees, the nut trees are just below; you surely must know it," replied Little Red Riding Hood.

The wolf thought to himself: "What a tender young creature! What a nice plump mouthful – she will be better to eat than the old woman. I must act craftily, so as to catch both." So he walked for a short time by the side of Little Red Riding Hood, and then he said: "Little Red Riding Hood, how pretty the flowers are about here – why do you not look round? I believe, too, that you do not hear how sweetly the little birds are singing; you walk gravely along as if you were going to school, while everything else out here in the wood is merry."

Little Red Riding Hood raised her eyes, and when she saw the sunbeams dancing here and there through the trees, and pretty flowers growing everywhere, she thought: "Suppose I take grandmother a fresh nosegay; that would please her too. It is so early in the day that I shall still get there in good time;" and so she ran from the path into the wood to look for flowers. And whenever she had picked one, she fancied that she saw a still prettier one farther on, and ran after it, and so got deeper and deeper into the wood.

Meanwhile the wolf ran straight to the grandmother's house and knocked at the door.

"Who is there?"

The wolf thought to himself: "What a tender young creature!" (Richard Hermann Escke)

271

"Little Red Riding Hood," replied the wolf. "I have brought cake and wine; open the door."

"Lift the latch," called out the grandmother. "I am too weak, and cannot get up."

The wolf lifted the latch, the door sprang open, and without saying a word he went straight to the grandmother's bed and devoured her. Then he put on her clothes, dressed himself in her cap, laid himself in bed and drew the curtains.

Little Red Riding Hood, however, had been running about picking flowers, and when she had gathered so many that she could carry no more, she remembered her grandmother, and set out on the way to her.

She was surprised to find the cottage-door standing open, and when she went into the room she had such a strange feeling that she said to herself: "Oh dear! How uneasy I feel today, and at other times I like being with grandmother so much." She called out: "Good-morning," but received no answer; so she went to the bed and drew back the curtains. There lay her grandmother wearing her cap all askew and looking very strange.

"Oh, grandmother," she said, "what big ears you have!"

"The better to hear you with, my child," was the reply.

"But, grandmother, what big eyes you have!" she said.

"The better to see you with, my dear."

"But, grandmother, what large hands you have!"

"The better to hug you with."

"Oh but, grandmother, what a terrible big mouth you have!"

"The better to eat you with!"

And scarcely had the wolf said this, than with one bound he was out of bed and had swallowed up Little Red Riding Hood.

When the wolf had appeased his appetite, he lay down again in the bed, fell asleep and

Little Red Riding Hood.
(Gabriel Joseph Marie Augustin Ferrier)

began to snore very loud. The huntsman was just passing the house, and thought to himself: "How the old woman is snoring! I must just see if she wants anything." So he went into the room, and when he came to the bed, he saw that the wolf was lying in it. "Do I find you here, you old sinner!" said he. "I have long sought you!" Then just as he was going to fire at him, it occurred to him that the wolf might have devoured the grandmother, and that she might still be saved, so he did not fire, but took a pair of scissors, and began to cut open the stomach of the sleeping wolf. When he had made two snips, he saw the little red riding hood shining, and then he made two snips more, and the little girl sprang out, crying: "Ah, how frightened I have been! How dark it was inside the wolf!" After that the aged grandmother came out alive also, but scarcely able to breathe. Little Red Riding Hood, however, quickly fetched great stones with which they filled the wolf's belly, and when he awoke, he wanted to run away, but the stones were so heavy that he collapsed at once, and fell dead.

Then all three were delighted. The huntsman drew off the wolf's skin and went home with it; the grandmother ate the cake and drank the wine which Little Red Riding Hood had brought and was greatly revived; and Little Red Riding Hood thought to herself: "As long as I live, I will never by myself leave the path, to run into the wood, when my mother has forbidden me to do so."

And so it happened that when Little Red Riding Hood was again taking cakes to the old grandmother, and another wolf spoke to her, and tried to entice her from the path, Little Red Riding Hood was on her guard, and went straight forward on her way, and told her grandmother that she had met the wolf, and that he had said "good-morning" to her, but with such a wicked look in his eyes that if they had not been on the public road she was certain he would have eaten her up.

"Well," said the grandmother, "we will shut the door, that he may not come in."

Soon afterwards the wolf knocked, and cried: "Open the door, grandmother, I am Little Red Riding Hood, and am bringing you some cakes."

But they did not speak, or open the door, so the grey-beard crept twice or thrice round the house, and at last jumped on the roof, intending to wait until Little Red Riding Hood went home in the evening, and then to steal after her and devour her in the darkness.

But the grandmother saw what was in his thoughts. In front of the house was a great stone trough, so she said to the child: "Take the pail, Little Red Riding Hood; I made some sausages yesterday, so carry the water in which I boiled them to the trough." Little Red Riding Hood made sure the great trough was quite full. Then the smell of the sausages reached the wolf, and he sniffed and peeped down, and at last stretched out his neck so far that he could no longer keep his footing and began to slip, and slipped down from the roof straight into the great trough and was drowned. So Little Red Riding Hood went joyously home, and no one ever did anything to harm her again.

THE ROBBER BRIDEGROOM

THERE WAS ONCE a miller who had one beautiful daughter, and as she was grown up, he was anxious that she should be well married and provided for. He said to himself, "I will give her to the first suitable man who comes and asks for her hand." Not long after a suitor appeared, and as he appeared to be very rich and the miller could see nothing in him with which to find fault, he betrothed his daughter to him. But the girl did not care for the man as a girl ought to care for her betrothed husband. She did not feel that she could trust him, and she could not look at him nor think of him without an inward shudder.

One day he said to her, "You have not yet paid me a visit, although we have been betrothed for some time."

"I do not know where your house is," she answered.

"My house is out there in the dark forest," he said.

She tried to excuse herself by saying that she would not be able to find the way thither.

Her betrothed only replied, "You must come and see me next Sunday; I have already invited guests for that day, and that you may not mistake the way, I will strew ashes along the path."

When Sunday came, and it was time for the girl to start, a feeling of dread came over her which she could not explain, and that she might be able to find her path again, she filled her pockets with peas and lentils to sprinkle on the ground as she went along. On reaching the entrance to the forest she found the path strewn with ashes, and these she followed, throwing down some peas on either side of her at every step she took.

She walked the whole day until she came to the deepest, darkest part of the forest. There she saw a lonely house, looking so grim and mysterious that it did not please her at all. She stepped inside, but not a soul was to be seen, and a great silence reigned throughout.

Suddenly a voice cried:

"Turn back, turn back, young maiden fair,
Linger not in this murderer's lair."

The girl looked up and saw that the voice came from a bird hanging in a cage on the wall. Again it cried:

"Turn back, turn back, young maiden fair,
Linger not in this murderer's lair."

The girl passed on, going from room to room of the house, but they were all empty and still she saw no one. At last she came to the cellar, and there sat a very, very old woman, who could not keep her head from shaking. "Can you tell me," asked the girl, "if my betrothed husband lives here?"

"Ah, you poor child," answered the old woman, "what a place for you to come to! This is a murderer's den. You think yourself a promised bride, and that your marriage will soon take place, but it is with death that you will keep your marriage feast. Look, do you see that large cauldron of water which I am obliged to keep on the fire? As soon as they have you in their power they will kill you without mercy, and cook and eat you, for they are eaters of men. If I did not take pity on you and save you, you would be lost."

Thereupon the old woman led her behind a large cask, which quite hid her from view. "Keep as still as a mouse," she said; "do not move or speak, or it will be all over with you. Tonight, when the robbers are all asleep, we will flee together. I have long been waiting for an opportunity to escape."

The words were hardly out of her mouth when the murderous crew returned, dragging another young girl along with them. They were all drunk, and paid no heed to her cries and lamentations. They gave her wine to drink, three glasses full, one of white wine, one of red and one of yellow, and with that her heart gave way and she died. Then they tore of her dainty clothing, laid her on a table, and cut her beautiful body into pieces, and sprinkled salt upon it.

The poor betrothed girl crouched trembling and shuddering behind the cask, for she saw what a terrible fate had been intended for her by the robbers. One of them now noticed a gold ring still remaining on the little finger of the murdered girl, and as he could not draw it off easily, he took a hatchet and cut off the finger; but the finger sprang into the air, and fell behind the cask into the lap of the girl who was hiding there. The robber took a light and began looking for it, but he could not find it.

"Have you looked behind the large cask?" said one of the others.

But the old woman called out, "Come and eat your supper, and let the thing be till tomorrow; the finger won't run away."

"The old woman is right," said the robbers, and they ceased looking for the finger and sat down.

The old woman then mixed a sleeping draught with their wine, and before long they were all lying on the floor of the cellar, fast asleep and snoring. As soon as the girl was assured of this, she came from behind the cask. She was obliged to step over the bodies of the sleepers, who were lying close together, and every moment she was filled with renewed dread lest she should awaken them. But God helped her, so that she passed safely over them, and then she and the old woman went upstairs, opened the door, and hastened as fast as they could from the murderer's den. They found the ashes scattered by the wind, but the peas and lentils had sprouted and grown sufficiently above the ground to guide them in the moonlight along the path. All night long they walked, and it was morning before they reached the mill. There the girl told her father all that had happened.

The day came that had been fixed for the marriage. The bridegroom arrived and also a large company of guests, for the miller had taken care to invite all his friends and relations. As they sat at the feast, each guest in turn was asked to tell a tale; the bride sat still and did not say a word.

"And you, my love," said the bridegroom, turning to her, "is there no tale you know? Tell us something."

"I will tell you a dream, then," said the bride. "I went alone through a forest and came at last to a house; not a soul could I find within, but a bird that was hanging in a cage on the wall cried:

"Turn back, turn back, young maiden fair,
Linger not in this murderer's lair."

and again a second time it said these words."

"My darling, this is only a dream."

"I went on through the house from room to room, but they were all empty, and everything was so grim and mysterious. At last I went down to the cellar, and there sat a very, very old woman, who could not keep her head still. I asked her if my betrothed lived here, and she answered, "Ah, you poor child, you are come to a murderer's den; your betrothed does indeed live here, but he will kill you without mercy and afterwards cook and eat you."

"My darling, this is only a dream."

"The old woman hid me behind a large cask, and scarcely had she done this when the robbers returned home, dragging a young girl along with them. They gave her three kinds of wine to drink, white, red and yellow, and with that she died."

"My darling, this is only a dream."

"Then they tore off her dainty clothing and cut her beautiful body into pieces and sprinkled salt upon it."

"My darling, this is only a dream."

"And one of the robbers saw that there was a gold ring still left on her finger, and as it was difficult to draw off, he took a hatchet and cut off her finger; but the finger sprang into the air and fell behind the great cask into my lap. And here is the finger with the ring." And with these words the bride drew forth the finger and showed it to the assembled guests.

The bridegroom, who during this recital had grown deadly pale, up and tried to escape, but the guests seized him and held him fast. They delivered him up to justice, and he and all his murderous band were condemned to death for their wicked deeds.

TOM THUMB

A POOR WOODMAN SAT in his cottage one night, smoking his pipe by the fireside, while his wife sat by his side spinning. "How lonely it is, wife," said he, as he puffed out a long curl of smoke, "for you and me to sit here by ourselves, without any children to play about and amuse us, while other people seem so happy and merry with their children!"

"What you say is very true," said the wife, sighing, and turning round her wheel; "how happy should I be if I had but one child! If it were ever so small – nay, if it were no bigger than my thumb – I should be very happy, and love it dearly." Now – odd as you may think it – it came to pass that this good woman's wish was fulfilled, just in the very way she had wished it; for, not long afterwards, she had a little boy, who was quite healthy and strong, but was not much bigger than my thumb. So they said, "Well, we cannot say we have not got what we wished for, and, little as he is, we will love him dearly." And they called him Thomas Thumb.

They gave him plenty of food, yet for all they could do he never grew bigger, but kept just the same size as he had been when he was born. Still, his eyes were sharp and sparkling, and he soon showed himself to be a clever little fellow, who always knew well what he was about.

One day, as the woodman was getting ready to go into the wood to cut fuel, he said, "I wish I had someone to bring the cart after me, for I want to make haste."

"Oh, father," cried Tom, "I will take care of that; the cart shall be in the wood by the time you want it."

Then the woodman laughed, and said, "How can that be? You cannot reach up to the horse's bridle."

"Never mind that, father," said Tom; "if my mother will only harness the horse, I will get into his ear and tell him which way to go."

"Well," said the father, "we will try for once."

When the time came the mother harnessed the horse to the cart, and put Tom into his ear; and as he sat there the little man told the beast how to go, crying out, "Go on!" and "Stop!" as he wanted, and thus the horse went on just as well as if the woodman had driven it himself into the wood.

It happened that as the horse was going a little too fast, and Tom was calling out, "Gently! Gently!" two strangers came up.

"What an odd thing that is!" said one. "There is a cart going along, and I hear a carter talking to the horse, but yet I can see no one."

"That is queer, indeed," said the other; "let us follow the cart, and see where it goes."

So they went on into the wood, till at last they came to the place where the woodman was. Then Tom Thumb, seeing his father, cried out, "See, father, here I am with the cart, all safe and sound! Now take me down!" So his father took hold of the horse with one hand, and with the other took his son out of the horse's ear, and put him down upon a straw, where he sat as merry as you please.

The two strangers were all this time looking on, and did not know what to say for wonder. At last one took the other aside, and said, "That little urchin will make our fortune, if we can get him and carry him about from town to town as a show; we must buy him." So they went up to the woodman and asked him what he would take for the little man.

"He will be better off," said they, "with us than with you."

"I won't sell him at all," said the father; "my own flesh and blood is dearer to me than all the silver and gold in the world."

But Tom, hearing of the bargain they wanted to make, crept up his father's coat to

Tom Thumb.
(Alexander Zick)

his shoulder and whispered in his ear, "Take the money, father, and let them have me; I'll soon come back to you."

So the woodman at last said he would sell Tom to the strangers for a large piece of gold, and they paid the price.

"Where would you like to sit?" said one of them.

"Oh, put me on the rim of your hat; that will be a nice gallery for me; I can walk about there and see the country as we go along."

So they did as he wished; and when Tom had taken leave of his father they took him away with them.

They journeyed on till it began to be dusk, and then the little man said, "Let me get down, I'm tired."

So the man took off his hat, and put him down on a clod of earth in a ploughed field by the side of the road. But Tom ran about among the furrows, and at last slipped into an old mouse-hole. "Good-night, my masters!" said he, "I'm off! Mind and look sharp after me the next time."

Then they ran at once to the place, and poked the ends of their sticks into the mouse-hole, but all in vain; Tom only crawled farther and farther in; and at last it became quite dark, so that they were forced to go their way without their prize, as sulky as could be.

When Tom found they were gone, he came out of his hiding-place. "What dangerous walking it is," said he, "in this ploughed field! If I were to fall from one of these great clods, I should undoubtedly break my neck." At last, by good luck, he found a large empty snail-shell. "This is lucky," said he, "I can sleep here very well;" and in he crept.

Just as he was falling asleep, he heard two men passing by, chatting together; and one said to the other, "How can we rob that rich parson's house of his silver and gold?"

"I'll tell you!" cried Tom.

"What noise was that?" said the thief, frightened; "I'm sure I heard someone speak."

They stood still listening, and Tom said, "Take me with you, and I'll soon show you how to get the parson's money."

"But where are you?" said they.

"Look about on the ground," answered he, "and listen where the sound comes from."

At last the thieves found him out, and lifted him up in their hands. "You little urchin!" they said, "what can you do for us?"

"Why, I can get between the iron window-bars of the parson's house, and throw you out whatever you want."

"That's a good thought," said the thieves; "come along, we shall see what you can do."

When they came to the parson's house, Tom slipped through the window-bars into the room, and then called out as loud as he could bawl, "Will you have all that is here?"

At this the thieves were frightened, and said, "Softly, softly! Speak low, that you may not awaken anybody."

But Tom seemed as if he did not understand them, and bawled out again, "How much will you have? Shall I throw it all out?"

Now the cook lay in the next room; and hearing a noise she raised herself up in her bed and listened.

Meantime the thieves were frightened, and ran off a little way; but at last they plucked up their hearts, and said, "The little urchin is only trying to make fools of us." So they came back and whispered softly to him, saying, "Now let us have no more of your roguish jokes; but throw us out some of the money."

Then Tom called out as loud as he could, "Very well! Hold your hands! Here it comes."

The cook heard this quite plain, so she sprang out of bed, and ran to open the door. The thieves ran off as if a wolf was at their tails, while the cook, having groped about and found nothing, went away for a light. By the time she came back, Tom had slipped off into the barn; and when she had looked about and searched every hole and corner, and found nobody, she went to bed, thinking she must have been dreaming with her eyes open.

The little man crawled about in the hayloft, and at last found a snug place to finish his night's rest in; so he laid himself down, meaning to sleep till daylight and then find his way home to his father and mother. But alas! how woefully he was undone! What crosses and sorrows happen to us all in this world! The cook got up early, before daybreak, to feed the cows; and going straight to the hayloft, carried away a large bundle of hay, with the little man in the middle of it, fast asleep. He still, however, slept on, and did not awake till he found himself in the mouth of the cow; for the cook had put the hay into

the cow's rick, and the cow had taken Tom up in a mouthful of it.

"Good lack-a-day!" said he, "how came I to tumble into the mill?" But he soon found out where he really was; and was forced to have all his wits about him, that he might not get between the cow's teeth, and so be crushed to death. At last down he went into her stomach. "It is rather dark," said he; "they forgot to build windows in this room to let the sun in; a candle would be no bad thing." Though he made the best of his bad luck, he did not like his quarters at all; and the worst of it was that more and more hay was always coming down, and the space left for him became smaller and smaller. At last he cried out as loud as he could, "Don't bring me any more hay! Don't bring me any more hay!"

The cook happened to be just then milking the cow; and hearing someone speak, but seeing nobody, and yet being quite sure it was the same voice that she had heard in the night, she was so frightened that she fell off her stool, and overset the milk-pail. As soon as she could pick herself up out of the dirt, she ran off as fast as she could to her master the parson, and said, "Sir, sir, the cow is talking!"

But the parson said, "Woman, you are surely mad!" However, he went with her into the cow-house, to try and see what was the matter.

Scarcely had they set foot on the threshold, when Tom called out, "Don't bring me any more hay!"

Then the parson himself was frightened, and thinking the cow was surely bewitched, told his man to kill her on the spot. So the cow was killed, and cut up; and the stomach, in which Tom lay, was thrown out upon a dunghill.

Tom soon set himself to work to get out, which was not a very easy task; but at last, just as he had made room to get his head out, fresh ill-luck befell him. A hungry wolf sprang out, and swallowed up the whole stomach, with Tom in it, at one gulp, and ran away.

Tom, however, was still not disheartened; and thinking the wolf would not dislike having some chat with him as he was going along, he called out, "My good friend, I can show you a famous treat."

"Where's that?" said the wolf.

"In such and such a house," said Tom, describing his own father's house. "You can crawl through the drain into the kitchen and then into the pantry, and there you will find cakes, ham, beef, cold chicken, roast pig, apple-dumplings, and everything that your heart can desire."

The wolf did not need to be asked twice; so that very night he went to the house and crawled through the drain into the kitchen, and then into the pantry, and ate and drank there to his heart's content. As soon as he had had enough he wanted to get away; but he had eaten so much that he could not go out by the same way he came in. This was just what Tom had reckoned upon; and now he began to set up a great shout, making all the noise he could.

"Will you be easy?" said the wolf; "you'll awaken everybody in the house if you make such a clatter."

"What's that to me?" said the little man. "You have had your frolic, now I've a mind to be merry myself;" and he began, singing and shouting as loud as he could.

The woodman and his wife, being awakened by the noise, peeped through a crack in the door; but when they saw a wolf was there, you may well suppose that they were sadly frightened; and the woodman ran for his axe, and gave his wife a scythe. "Do you stand behind me," said the woodman, "and when I have knocked him on the head you must rip him up with the scythe."

Tom heard all this, and cried out, "Father, father! I am here, the wolf has swallowed me."

And his father said, "Heaven be praised! We have found our dear child again;" and he told his wife not to use the scythe for fear she should hurt him. Then he aimed a great blow, and struck the wolf on the head, and killed him on the spot! And when he was dead they cut open his body and set Tommy free. "Ah!" said the father, "what fears we have had for you!"

"Yes, father," answered he; "I have travelled all over the world, I think, in one way or other, since we parted; and now I am very glad to come home and get fresh air again."

"Why, where have you been?" said his father. "I have been in a mouse-hole – and in a snail-shell – and down a cow's throat – and in the wolf's belly; and yet here I am again, safe and sound."

"Well," said they, "you are come back, and we will not sell you again for all the riches in the world."

Then they hugged and kissed their dear little son, and gave him plenty to eat and drink, for he was very hungry; and then they fetched new clothes for him, for his old ones had been quite spoiled on his journey. So Master Thumb stayed at home with his father and mother, in peace; for though he had been so great a traveller, and had done and seen so many fine things, and was fond enough of telling the whole story, he always agreed that, after all, there's no place like home!

RUMPELSTILTSKIN

B Y THE SIDE of a wood, in a country a long way off, ran a fine stream of water; and upon the stream there stood a mill. The miller's house was close by, and the miller, you must know, had a very beautiful daughter. She was, moreover, very shrewd and clever; and the miller was so proud of her that he one day told the king of the land, who used to come and hunt in the wood, that his daughter could spin gold out of straw.

Now this king was very fond of money; and when he heard the miller's boast his greediness was aroused, and he sent for the girl to be brought before him. Then he led her to a chamber in his palace where there was a great heap of straw, and gave her a spinning-wheel, and said, "All this must be spun into gold before morning, if you love your life." It was in vain that the poor maiden said that it was only a silly boast of her father's, and that she could do no such thing as spin straw into gold; the chamber door was locked, and she was left alone.

She had sat down in one corner of the room and begun to bewail her hard fate, when on a sudden the door opened and a droll-looking little man hobbled in and said, "Good-morrow to you, my good lass; what are you weeping for?"

"Alas!" said she, "I must spin this straw into gold, and I know not how."

"What will you give me," said the hobgoblin, "to do it for you?"

"My necklace," replied the maiden.

He took her at her word, and sat himself down to the wheel, and whistled and sang:

> *"Round about, round about,*
> *Lo and behold!*
> *Reel away, reel away,*
> *Straw into gold!"*

And round about the wheel went merrily, the work was quickly done, and the straw was all spun into gold.

When the king came and saw this, he was greatly astonished and pleased; but his heart grew still more greedy of gain, and he shut up the poor miller's daughter again with a fresh task. Then she knew not what to do, and sat down once more to weep; but the dwarf soon opened the door, and said, "What will you give me to do your task?"

"The ring on my finger," said she. So her little friend took the ring, and began to work at the wheel again, and whistled and sang:

Rumpelstiltskin. (Ann Anderson)

> *"Round about, round about,*
> *Lo and behold!*
> *Reel away, reel away,*
> *Straw into gold!"*

till, long before morning, all was done again.

The king was greatly delighted to see all this glittering treasure; but still he had not enough: so he took the miller's daughter to a yet larger heap, and said, "All this must be spun tonight; and if it is, you shall be my queen."

As soon as she was alone the dwarf came in and said, "What will you give me to spin gold for you this third time?"

"I have nothing left," said she.

"Then say you will give me," said the little man, "the first child that you may have when you are queen."

"That may never be," thought the miller's daughter; and as she knew no other way to get her task done, she said she would do what he asked.

Round went the wheel again to the old song, and the manikin once more spun the heap into gold. The king came in the morning, and, finding all he wanted, was forced to keep his word; so he married the miller's daughter, and she really became queen.

At the birth of her first little child she was very glad, and forgot the dwarf, and what she had said. But one day he came into her room, where she was sitting playing with her baby, and put her in mind of it. Then she grieved sorely at her misfortune, and said she would give him all the wealth of the kingdom if he would let her off, but in vain; yet at last her tears softened him, and he said, "I will give you three days" grace, and if during that time you tell me my name, you shall keep your child."

Now the queen lay awake all night, thinking of all the odd names that she had ever heard; and she sent messengers all over the land to find out new ones. The next day the little man came, and she began with timothy, ichabod, benjamin, jeremiah, and all the names she could remember; but to all and each of them he said, "Madam, that is not my name."

"*Rumpelstiltskin is my name!*"
(*Noel Pocock, above; Paul Hey, left*)

The second day she began with all the comical names she could think of: bandylegs, hunchback, crookshanks, and so on; but the little gentleman still said to every one of them, "Madam, that is not my name."

The third day one of the messengers came back, and said, "I have travelled two days without hearing of any other names; but yesterday, as I was climbing a high hill among the trees of the forest, where the fox and the hare bid each other good-night, I saw a little hut; and before the hut burnt a fire; and round about the fire a funny little dwarf was dancing upon one leg, and singing:

> "*Merrily the feast I'll make.*
> *Today I'll brew, tomorrow bake;*
> *Merrily I'll dance and sing,*
> *For next day will a stranger bring.*
> *Little does my lady dream*
> *Rumpelstiltskin is my name!*"

When the queen heard this she jumped for joy, and as soon as her little friend came she sat down upon her throne, and called all her court round to enjoy the fun; and the nurse stood by her side with the baby in her arms, as if it was quite ready to be given up. Then the little man began to chuckle at the thought of having the poor child to take home with him to his hut in the woods; and he cried out, "Now, lady, what is my name?"

"Is it John?" asked she.

"No, madam!"

"Is it Tom?"

"No, madam!"

"Is it Jemmy?"

"It is not."

"Can your name be Rumpelstiltskin?" asked the lady slyly.

"Some witch told you that – some witch told you that!" cried the little man, and dashed his right foot in a rage so deep into the floor that he was forced to lay hold of it with both hands to pull it out.

Then he made off as best he could, while the nurse laughed and the baby crowed; and all the court jeered at him for having had so much trouble for nothing, and said, "We wish you a very good-morning, and a merry feast, Mr Rumpelstiltskin!"

CLEVER GRETEL

THERE WAS ONCE a cook named Gretel, who wore shoes with red heels, and when she walked out with them on, she turned herself this way and that, was quite happy and thought: "You certainly are a pretty girl!" And when she came home she drank, in her gladness of heart, a draught of wine, and as wine excites a desire to eat, she tasted the best of whatever she was cooking until she was satisfied, and said: "The cook must know what the food is like."

It came to pass that the master one day said to her: "Gretel, there is a guest coming this evening; prepare me two fowls very daintily."

"I will see to it, master," answered Gretel. She killed two fowls, scalded them, plucked them, put them on the spit, and towards evening set them before the fire, that they might roast. The fowls began to turn brown, and were nearly ready, but the guest had not yet arrived. Then Gretel called out to her master: "If the guest does not come, I must take the fowls away from the fire, but it will be a sin and a shame if they are not eaten the moment they are at their juiciest."

The master said: "I will run myself, and fetch the guest."

When the master had turned his back, Gretel laid the spit with the fowls on one side, and thought: "Standing so long by the fire there, makes one sweaty and thirsty; who knows when they will come? Meanwhile, I will run into the cellar, and take a drink."

She ran down, filled a flagon, said: "God bless it for you, Gretel," and took a good drink; then thinking that wine should flow on, and should not be interrupted, she took yet another hearty draught.

Then she went and put the fowls over the fire again, basted them, and drove the spit merrily round. But as the roast meat smelt so good, Gretel thought: "Something might be wrong, it ought to be tasted!" She touched it with her finger, and said: "Ah! how good fowls are! It certainly is a sin and a shame that they are not eaten at the right time!" She ran to the window, to see if the master was coming with his guest, but she saw no one, and went back to the fowls and thought: "One of the wings is burning! I had better take it off and eat it." So she cut it off, ate it, and enjoyed it, and when she had done, she thought: "The other must go down too, or else master will observe that something is missing."

When the two wings were eaten, she went and looked for her master, and did not see him. It suddenly occurred to her: "Who knows? They are perhaps not coming at all, and have turned in somewhere." Then she said: "Well, Gretel, enjoy yourself; one fowl has been cut into, take another drink, and eat it up entirely; when it is eaten you will have some peace; why should God's good gifts be spoilt?" So she ran into the cellar again and took an enormous drink then ate up the one chicken in great glee. When one of the chickens was swallowed down, and still her master did not come, Gretel looked at the other and said: "What one is, the other should be likewise, the two go together; what's right for the one is right for the other; I think if I were to take another draught it would do me no harm." So she took another hearty drink, and let the second chicken follow the first.

While she was making the most of it, her master came and cried: "Hurry up, Gretel, the guest is coming directly after me!"

"Yes, sir, I will soon serve up," answered Gretel.

Meantime the master looked to see that the table was properly laid, and took the great knife, wherewith he was going to carve the chickens, and sharpened it on the steps.

Presently the guest came, and knocked politely and courteously at the house-door.

Gretel ran, and looked to see who was there, and when she saw the guest, she put her finger to her lips and said: "Hush! Hush! Go away as quickly as you can; if my master catches you it will be the worse for you; he certainly did ask you to supper, but his intention is to cut off your two ears. Just listen how he is sharpening the knife for it!" The guest heard the sharpening, and hurried down the steps again as fast as he could.

Gretel was not idle; she ran screaming to her master, and cried: "You have invited a fine guest!"

"Why, Gretel? What do you mean by that?"

"Yes," said she, "he has taken the chickens, which I was just going to serve up, off the dish, and has run away with them!"

"That's a nice trick!" said her master, and lamented the fine chickens. "If he had but left me one, so that something remained for me to eat." He called to him to stop, but the guest pretended not to hear. Then he ran after him with the knife still in his hand, crying: "Just one, just one," meaning that the guest should leave him just one chicken, and not take both. The guest, however, thought no otherwise than that he was to give up one of his ears, and ran as if fire were burning under him, in order to take them both with him.

THE LITTLE PEASANT

THERE WAS A certain village wherein no one lived but really rich peasants, and just one poor one, whom they called the little peasant. He had not even so much as a cow, and still less money to buy one, and yet he and his wife did so wish to have one. One day he said to her: "Listen, I have a good idea: let us get our old friend the carpenter to make us a wooden calf and paint it brown, so that it looks like any other, and in time it will certainly get big and be a cow." The woman liked the idea, and their friend the carpenter cut and planed the calf, and painted it as it ought to be, and made it with its head hanging down as if it were eating.

Next morning when the cows were being driven out, the little peasant called the cowherd over and said: "Look, I have a little calf there, but it is still small and has to be carried."

The cowherd said: "All right," and took it in his arms and carried it to the pasture, and set it among the grass. The little calf always remained standing as if it were eating, and the cowherd said: "It will soon run by itself, just look how it eats already!" At night when he was going to drive the herd home again, he said to the calf: "If you can stand there and eat your fill, you can also walk on your four legs; I don't care to drag you home again in my arms."

The little peasant stood at his door, and waited for his little calf, and when the cowherd drove the cows through the village, and the calf was missing, he enquired where it was.

The cowherd answered: "It is still standing out there eating. It would not stop and come with us."

But the little peasant said: "Oh, but I must have my beast back again." Then they returned to the meadow together, but someone had stolen the calf, and it was gone.

The cowherd said: "It must have run away."

The peasant, however, said: "Don't tell me that," and led the cowherd before the mayor, who for his carelessness condemned him to give the peasant a cow for the calf which had run away.

And now the little peasant and his wife had the cow for which they had so long wished, and they were heartily glad, but they had no food for it, and could give it nothing to eat, so it soon had to be killed. They salted the flesh, and the peasant went into the town in order to sell the skin there, so that he might buy a new calf with the proceeds. On the way he passed by a mill, and there sat a raven with broken wings, and out of pity he took him and wrapped him in the skin. But as the weather grew so bad and there was a storm of rain and wind, he could go no farther, and turned back to the mill and begged for shelter.

The miller's wife was alone in the house, and said to the peasant: "Lay yourself on the straw there," and gave him a slice of bread and cheese. The peasant ate it, and lay down with his skin beside him, and the woman thought: "He is tired and has gone to sleep." In the meantime came the parson; the miller's wife received him well, and said: "My husband is out, so we will have a feast." The peasant listened, and when he heard them talk about feasting he was vexed that he had been forced to make shift with a slice of bread and cheese. Then the woman served up four different things, roast meat, salad, cakes, and wine. Just as they were about to sit down and eat, there was a knocking outside. The woman said: "Oh, heavens! It is my husband!" she quickly hid the roast meat inside the tiled stove, the wine under the pillow, the salad on the bed, the cakes under it, and the parson in the closet on the porch. Then she opened the door for her husband, and said: "Thank heaven, you are back again! There is such a storm, it looks as if the world were coming to an end."

The miller saw the peasant lying on the straw, and asked, "What is that fellow doing there?"

"Ah," said the wife, "the poor knave came in the storm and rain and begged for shelter, so I gave him a bit of bread and cheese and showed him where the straw was."

The man said: "I have no objection, but be quick and get me something to eat."

The woman said: "But I have nothing but bread and cheese."

"I am contented with anything," replied the husband; "so far as I am concerned, bread and cheese will do." He looked at the peasant and said: "Come and eat some more with me." The peasant did not require to be invited twice, but got up and ate. After this the miller saw the skin in which the raven was, lying on the ground, and asked: "What have you there?"

The peasant answered: "I have a soothsayer inside it."

"Can he foretell anything to me?" said the miller.

"Why not?" answered the peasant; "but he only says four things, and the fifth he keeps to himself."

The miller was curious, and said: "Let me hear one of his prophesies."

Then the peasant pinched the raven's head, so that he croaked and made a noise like *krr, krr.*

The miller said: "What did he say?"

The peasant answered: "In the first place, he says that there is some wine hidden under the pillow."

"Bless me!" cried the miller, and went there and found the wine. "Now go on," said he.

The peasant made the raven croak again, and said: "In the second place, he says that there is some roast meat in the tiled stove."

"Upon my word!" cried the miller, and went thither, and found the roast meat. The peasant made the raven prophesy still more, and said: "Thirdly, he says that there is some salad on the bed."

"That would be a fine thing!" cried the miller, and went there and found the salad.

At last the peasant pinched the raven once more till he croaked, and said: "Fourthly, he says that there are some cakes under the bed."

"That would be a fine thing!" cried the miller, and looked there, and found the cakes.

And now the two sat down to the table together, but the miller's wife was frightened to death, and went to bed and took all the keys with her. The miller would have liked much to know the fifth, but the little peasant said: "First, we will quickly eat the four things, for the fifth is something bad." So they ate, and after that they bargained how much the miller was to give for the fifth prophecy, until they agreed on three hundred thalers.

Then the peasant once more pinched the raven's head till he croaked loudly.

The miller asked: "What did he say?"

The peasant replied: "He says that the Devil is hiding outside there in the closet on the porch."

The miller said: "The Devil must go out," and opened the house-door; then the woman was forced to give up the keys, and the peasant unlocked the closet. The parson ran out as fast as he could, and the miller said: "It was true; I saw the black rascal with my own eyes."

The peasant, however, made off next morning by daybreak with the three hundred thalers.

At home the small peasant gradually launched out; he built a beautiful house, and the peasants said: "The small peasant has certainly been to the place where golden snow falls, and people carry the gold home in shovels." Then the small peasant was brought before the mayor, and bidden to say from whence his wealth came. He answered: "I sold my cow's skin in the town for three hundred thalers."

When the peasants heard that, they too wished to enjoy this great profit, and ran home, killed all their cows and stripped off their skins in order to sell them in the town to the greatest advantage. The mayor, however, said: "But my servant must go first." When she came to the merchant in the town, he did not give her more than two thalers for a skin, and when the others came, he did not give them so much, and said: "What can I do with all these skins?"

Then the peasants, vexed that the small peasant should have thus outwitted them, wanted to take vengeance on him, and accused him of this treachery before the major. The innocent little peasant was unanimously sentenced to death, and was to be rolled into the water, in a barrel pierced full of holes. He was led forth, and a priest was brought who was to say a mass for his soul. The others were all obliged to retire to a distance. When the peasant looked at the priest, he recognised the man who had been with the miller's wife. He said to him: "I set you free from the closet, set me free from the barrel."

At this same moment up came, with a flock of sheep, the very shepherd who the peasant knew had long been wishing to be mayor, so he cried with all his might: "No, I will not do it; if the whole world insists on it, I will not do it!"

The shepherd, hearing that, came up to him, and asked: "What are you about? What is it that you will not do?"

The peasant said: "They want to make me mayor, if I will but put myself in the barrel, but I will not do it."

The shepherd said: "If nothing more than that is needful in order to be mayor, I would get into the barrel at once."

The peasant said: "If you will get in, you will be mayor."

The shepherd was willing, and got in, and the peasant shut the top down on him; then he took the shepherd's flock for himself, and drove it away. The parson went to the crowd, and declared that the mass had been said. Then they came and rolled the barrel towards the water. When the barrel began to roll, the shepherd cried: "I am quite willing to be mayor." They believed no otherwise than that it was the peasant who was saying this, and answered: "That is what we intend, but first you shall look about you a little down below there," and they rolled the barrel down into the water.

After that the peasants went home, and as they were entering the village, the small peasant also came quietly in, driving a flock of sheep and looking quite contented. Then the peasants were astonished, and said: "Peasant, from whence do you come? Have you come out of the water?"

"Yes, truly," replied the peasant. "I sank deep, deep down, until at last I got to the bottom; I pushed the bottom out of the barrel, and crept out, and there were pretty meadows on which a number of lambs were feeding, and from thence I brought this flock away with me."

Said the peasants: "Are there any more there?"

"Oh, yes," said he, "more than I could want."

Then the peasants made up their minds that they too would fetch some sheep for themselves, a flock apiece, but the mayor said: "I come first." So they went to the water together, and just then there were some of the small fleecy clouds in the blue sky, which are called little lambs, and they were reflected in the water, whereupon the peasants cried: "We already see the sheep down below!" The mayor pressed forward and said: "I will go down first, and look about me, and if things promise well I'll call you."

So he jumped in. Splash! went the water; it sounded as if he were calling them, and the whole crowd plunged in after him as one man. Then the entire village was dead, and the small peasant, as sole heir, became a rich man.

FREDERICK AND CATHERINE

THERE WAS ONCE a man called Frederick: he had a wife whose name was Catherine, and they had not long been married. One day Frederick said. "Kate! I am going to work in the fields; when I come back I shall be hungry so let me have something nice cooked, and a good draught of ale."

"Very well," said she, "it shall all be ready." When dinner-time drew nigh, Catherine took a nice steak, which was all the meat she had, and put it on the fire to fry. The steak soon began to look brown, and to crackle in the pan; and Catherine stood by with a fork and turned it; then she said to herself, "The steak is almost ready, I may as well go to the cellar for the ale."

So she left the pan on the fire and took a large jug and went into the cellar and tapped the ale cask. The beer ran into the jug and Catherine stood looking on. At last it popped into her head, "The dog is not shut up – he may be running away with the steak; that's well thought of." So up she ran from the cellar; and sure enough the rascally cur had got the steak in his mouth, and was making off with it.

Away ran Catherine, and away ran the dog across the field; but he ran faster than she, and stuck close to the steak. "It's all gone, and what can't be cured must be endured," said Catherine. So she turned round; and as she had run a good way and was tired, she walked home leisurely to cool herself.

Now all this time the ale was running too, for Catherine had not turned off the tap; and when the jug was full the liquor ran upon the floor till the cask was empty. When she got to the cellar stairs she saw what had happened. "My stars!" said she, "what shall I do to keep Frederick from seeing all this slopping about?" So she thought a while; and at last remembered that there was a sack of fine meal bought at the last fair, and that if she sprinkled this over the floor it would suck up the ale nicely. "What a lucky thing," said she, "that we kept that meal! We have now a good use for it." So away she went for it: but she managed to set it down just upon the great jug full of beer, and upset it; and thus all the ale that had been saved was set swimming on the floor also. "Ah! well," said she, "when one goes another may as well follow." Then she strewed the meal all about the cellar, and was quite pleased with her cleverness, and said, "How very neat and clean it looks!"

At noon Frederick came home. "Now, wife," cried he, "what have you for dinner?"

"Oh, Frederick!" answered she. "I was cooking you a steak; but while I went down to draw the ale, the dog ran away with it; and while I ran after him, the ale ran out; and when I went to dry up the ale with the sack of meal that we got at the fair, I upset the jug; but the cellar is now quite dry, and looks so clean!"

"Kate, Kate," said he, "how could you do all this? Why did you leave the steak to fry, and the ale to run, and then spoil all the meal?"

"Why, Frederick," said she, "I did not know I was doing wrong; you should have told me before."

The husband thought to himself, "If my wife manages matters thus, I must look sharp myself." Now he had a good deal of gold in the house, so he said to Catherine, "What pretty yellow buttons these are! I shall put them into a box and bury them in the garden; but take care that you never go near or meddle with them."

"No, Frederick," said she, "that I never will." As soon as he was gone, there came by some pedlars with earthenware plates and dishes, and they asked her whether she would buy. "Oh dear me, I should like to buy very much, but I have no money; if you had any use for yellow buttons, I might deal with you."

"Yellow buttons!" said they; "let us have a look at them."

"Go into the garden and dig where I tell you, and you will find the yellow buttons. I dare not go myself."

So the rogues went and when they found what these yellow buttons were, they took them all away, and left her plenty of plates and dishes. Then she set them all about the house for a show, and when Frederick came back, he cried out, "Kate, what have you been doing?"

"See," said she, "I have bought all these with your yellow buttons; but I did not touch them myself: the pedlars went themselves and dug them up."

"Wife, wife," said Frederick, "what a pretty piece of work you have made! Those yellow buttons were all my money; how came you to do such a thing?"

"Why," answered she, "I did not know there was any harm in it; you should have told me."

Catherine stood musing for a while, and at last said to her husband, "Hark ye, Frederick, we will soon get the gold back: let us run after the thieves."

"Well, we will try," answered he; "but take some butter and cheese with you, that we may have something to eat by the way."

Frederick and Catherine. (Noel Pocock)

"Very well," said she, and they set out; and as Frederick walked the fastest, he left his wife some way behind. "It does not matter," thought she; "when we turn back, I shall be so much nearer home than he."

Presently she came to the top of a hill, down the side of which there was a road so narrow that the cart wheels always chafed the trees on each side as they passed. "Ah, see now," said she, "how they have bruised and wounded those poor trees; they will never get well." So she took pity on them, and made use of the butter to grease them all, so that the wheels might not hurt them so much. While she was doing this kind office, one of her cheeses fell out of the basket and rolled down the hill. Catherine looked, but could not see where it had gone; so she said, "Well, I suppose the other will go the same way and find you; he has younger legs than I have." Then she rolled the other cheese after it; and away it went, nobody knows where, down the hill. But she said she supposed that they knew the road, and would follow her, and she could not stay there all day waiting for them.

At last she overtook Frederick, who desired her to give him something to eat. Then she gave him the dry bread.

"Where are the butter and cheese?" said he.

"Oh!" answered she, "I used the butter to grease those poor trees that the wheels chafed so; and one of the cheeses ran away so I sent the other after it to find it, and I suppose they are both on the road together somewhere."

"What a goose you are to do such silly things!" said the husband.

"How can you say so?" said she; "I am sure you never told me not."

They ate the dry bread together; and Frederick said, "Kate, I hope you locked the door safe when you came away."

"No," answered she, "you did not tell me."

"Then go home, and do it now before we go any farther," said Frederick, "and bring with you something to eat."

Catherine did as he told her, and thought to herself by the way, "Frederick wants something to eat; but I don't think he is very fond of butter and cheese. I'll bring him a bag of fine nuts, and the vinegar, for I have often seen him take some."

When she reached home, she bolted the back door, but the front door she took off its hinges, and said, "Frederick told me to lock the door, but surely it can nowhere be so safe as if I take it with me." So she took her time by the way; and when she overtook her husband she cried out, "There, Frederick, there is the door itself, you may watch it as carefully as you please."

"Alas! alas!" said he, "what a clever wife I have! I sent you to make the house fast, and you take the door away, so that everybody may go in and out as they please – however, as you have brought the door, you shall carry it about with you for your pains."

"Very well," answered she, "I'll carry the door; but I'll not carry the nuts and vinegar bottle also – that would be too much of a load; so, if you please, I'll fasten them to the door."

Frederick of course made no objection to that plan, and they set off into the wood to look for the thieves; but they could not find them, and when it grew dark, they climbed up into a tree to spend the night there. Scarcely were they up, than who should come by but the very rogues they were looking for. They were in truth great rascals, and belonged to that class of people who find things before they are lost; they were tired, so they sat down and made a fire under the very tree where Frederick and Catherine were. Frederick slipped down on the other side, and picked up some stones. Then he climbed up again, and tried to hit the thieves on the head with them: but they only said, "It must be near morning, for the wind shakes the fir-cones down."

Catherine, who had the door on her shoulder, began to be very tired; but she thought it was the nuts upon it that were so heavy; so she said softly, "Frederick, I must let the nuts go."

"No," answered he, "not now; they will discover us."

"I can't help that: they must go."

"Well, then, make haste and throw them down, if you will."

Then away rattled the nuts down among the boughs and one of the thieves cried, "Bless me, it is hailing."

A little while after, Catherine thought the door was still very heavy; so she whispered to Frederick, "I must throw the vinegar down."

"Pray don't," answered he; "they will discover us."

"I can't help that," said she, "go it must."

So she poured all the vinegar down; and the thieves said, "What a heavy dew there is!"

At last it popped into Catherine's head that it was the door itself that was so heavy all the time; so she whispered, "Frederick, I must throw the door down soon." But he begged and prayed her not to do so, for he was sure it would betray them. "Here goes, however," said she: and down went the door with such a clatter upon the thieves, that they cried out "Murder!" and not knowing what was coming next, ran away as fast as they could, and left all the gold. So when Frederick and Catherine came down, there they found all their money safe and sound.

SWEETHEART ROLAND

THERE WAS ONCE upon a time a woman who was a real witch and had two daughters, one ugly and wicked, and this one she loved because she was her own daughter, and one beautiful and good, and this one she hated, because she was her stepdaughter. The stepdaughter once had a pretty apron, which the other fancied so much that she became envious, and told her mother that she must and would have that apron. "Be quiet, my child," said the old woman, "and you shall have it. Your stepsister has long deserved death; tonight when she is asleep I will come and cut her head off. Only be careful that you are at the far side of the bed, and push her well to the front." It would have been all over with the poor girl if she had not just then been standing in a corner, and heard everything. All day long she dared not go out of doors, and when bedtime had come, the witch's daughter got into bed first, so as to lie at the far side, but when she was asleep, the other pushed her gently to the front, and took for herself the place at the back, close by the wall. In the night, the old woman came creeping in, she held an axe in her right hand, and felt with her left to see if anyone were lying at the outside, and then she grasped the axe with both hands, and cut her own child's head off.

When she had gone away, the girl got up and went to her sweetheart, who was called Roland, and knocked at his door. When he came out, she said to him: "Listen, dearest Roland, we must fly in all haste; my stepmother wanted to kill me, but has struck her own child in error. When daylight comes, and she sees what she has done, we shall be lost."

"But," said Roland, "I counsel you first to take away her magic wand, or we cannot escape if she pursues us." The maiden fetched the magic wand, and she took the dead girl's head and dropped three drops of blood on the ground, one in front of the bed, one in the kitchen, and one on the stairs. Then she hurried away with her lover.

When the old witch got up next morning, she called her daughter, and wanted to give her the apron, but she did not come. Then the witch cried: "Where are you?"

"Here, on the stairs, I am sweeping," answered the first drop of blood.

The old woman went out, but saw no one on the stairs, and cried again: "Where are you?"

"Here in the kitchen, I am warming myself," cried the second drop of blood.

She went into the kitchen, but found no one. Then she cried again: "Where are you?"

"Ah, here in the bed, I am sleeping," cried the third drop of blood.

She went into the room to the bed. What did she see there? Her own child, whose head she had cut off, bathed in her blood. The witch fell into a passion, sprang to the window, and, as she could look forth quite far into the world, she perceived her step-daughter hurrying away with her sweetheart Roland. "That shall not help you," cried she, "even if you have got a long way off, you shall still not escape me."

She put on her many-league boots, in which she covered an hour's walk at every step, and it was not long before she overtook them. The girl, however, when she saw the old woman striding towards her, changed, with her magic wand, her sweetheart Roland into a lake, and herself into a duck swimming in the middle of it. The witch placed herself on the shore, threw breadcrumbs in, and went to endless trouble to entice the duck; but the duck did not let herself be enticed, and the old woman had to go home at night as she had come.

At this the girl and her sweetheart Roland resumed their natural shapes again, and they walked on the whole night until daybreak. Then the maiden changed herself into a beautiful flower which stood in the midst of a briar hedge, and her sweetheart Roland into a fiddler. It was not long before the witch came striding up towards them, and said to the musician: "Dear musician, please may I pluck that beautiful flower for myself?"

"Oh, yes," he replied, "I will play to you while you do it."

The thorns tore her clothes from her body and pricked her and wounded her till she bled.
(Arthur Rackham)

As she was hastily creeping into the hedge and was just going to pluck the flower, knowing perfectly well who the flower was, he began to play, and whether she would or not, she was forced to dance, for it was a magical dance. The faster he played, the more violent springs was she forced to make, and the thorns tore her clothes from her body and pricked her and wounded her till she bled, and as he did not stop, she had to dance till she lay dead on the ground.

As they were now set free, Roland said: "Now I will go to my father and arrange for the wedding."

"Then in the meantime I will stay here and wait for you," said the girl, "and that no one may recognise me, I will change myself into a red stone landmark."

Then Roland went away, and the girl stood like a red landmark in the field and waited for her beloved. But when Roland got home, he fell into the snares of another, who so fascinated him that he forgot the maiden. The poor girl remained there a long time, but at length, as he did not return at all, she was sad, and changed herself into a flower, and thought: "Someone will surely come this way, and trample me down."

It befell, however, that a shepherd kept his sheep in the field and saw the flower, and as it was so pretty, plucked it, took it with him, and laid it away in his chest. From that time forth, strange things happened in the shepherd's house. When he arose in the morning, all the work was already done: the room was swept, the table and benches cleaned, the fire in the hearth was lit and the water was fetched, and at noon, when he came home, the table was laid, and a good dinner served. He could not conceive how this came to pass, for he never saw a human being in his house, and no one could have concealed himself in it.

He was certainly pleased with this good attendance, but still at last he was so afraid that he went to a wise woman and asked for her advice.

The wise woman said: "There is some enchantment behind it, listen very early some morning if anything is moving in the room, and if you see anything, no matter what it is, throw a white cloth over it, and then the magic will be stopped."

The shepherd did as she bade him, and next morning, just as day dawned, he saw the chest open and the flower come out. Swiftly he sprang towards it, and threw a white cloth over it. Instantly the transformation came to an end, and a beautiful girl stood before him, who admitted to him that she had been the flower, and that up to this time she had attended to his housekeeping. She told him her story, and as she pleased him he asked her if she would marry him, but she answered no, for she wanted to remain faithful to her sweetheart Roland, although he had deserted her. Nevertheless, she promised not to go away, but to continue keeping house for the shepherd.

And now the time drew near when Roland's wedding was to be celebrated, and then, according to an old custom in the country, it was announced that all the girls were to be present at it, and sing in honour of the bridal pair. When the faithful maiden heard of this, she grew so sad that she thought her heart would break, and she would not go thither, but the other girls came and took her. When it came to her turn to sing, she stepped back, until at last she was the only one left, and then she could not refuse. But when she began her song, and it reached Roland's ears, he sprang up and cried: "I know the voice, that is my true bride. I will have no other!" Everything he had forgotten, and everything that had vanished from his mind, suddenly come home again to his heart. Then the faithful maiden held her wedding with her sweetheart Roland, and grief came to an end and joy began.

SNOW WHITE

IT WAS THE middle of winter, when the broad flakes of snow were falling around, that the queen of a country many thousand miles off sat working at her window, the frame of which was made of fine black ebony; and as she sat looking out upon the snow, she pricked her finger and three drops of blood fell upon it. Then she gazed thoughtfully upon the red drops that sprinkled the white snow, and said, "Would that my little daughter may be as white as that snow, as red as that blood and as black as this ebony windowframe!" And so it was that the little girl really did grow up – her skin was as white as snow, her cheeks as rosy as

"Take Snow White away into the wide wood, that I may never see her any more." (Franz Jüttner)

the blood and her hair as black as ebony; and she was called Snow White.

But this queen died; and the king soon married another wife, who became queen, and was very beautiful, but so vain that she could not bear to think that anyone could be handsomer than she was. She had a fairy looking-glass, and she would gaze upon herself in it and say:

> *"Tell me, glass, tell me true!*
> *Of all the ladies in the land,*
> *Who is fairest, tell me, who?"*

And the glass had always answered: "Thou, queen, art the fairest in all the land."

But Snow White grew more and more beautiful; and when she was seven years old

she was as bright as the day, and fairer than the queen herself. Then the glass one day answered the queen, when she went to look in it as usual:

> *"Thou, queen, art fair, and beauteous to*
> * see,*
> *But Snow White is lovelier far than thee!"*

When she heard this she turned pale with rage and envy, and called to one of her servants, and said, "Take Snow White away into the wide wood, that I may never see her any more."

Then the servant led her away; but his heart melted when Snow White begged him to spare her life, and he said, "I will not hurt you, thou pretty child." So he left her by herself;

and though he thought it most likely that the wild beasts would tear her in pieces, he felt as if a great weight were taken off his heart when he had made up his mind not to kill her but to leave her to her fate, with the chance of someone finding and saving her.

Then poor Snow White wandered along through the wood in great fear; and the wild beasts roared about her, but none did her any harm. In the evening she came to a cottage among the hills, and went in to rest, for her little feet would carry her no farther. Everything was spruce and neat in the cottage: on the table was spread a white cloth, and there were seven little plates, seven little loaves and seven little glasses with wine in them; and seven knives and forks laid in order; and by the wall stood seven little beds. As she was very hungry, she picked a little piece of each loaf and drank a very little wine out of each glass;

and after that she thought she would lie down and rest. So she tried all the little beds; but one was too long, and another was too short, and only the seventh suited her: so there she laid herself down and went to sleep.

By and by in came the masters of the cottage. Now they were seven little dwarfs that lived among the mountains and dug and searched for gold. They lit up their seven little lamps, and saw at once that all was not right.

The first said, "Who has been sitting on my stool?"

The second, "Who has been eating off my plate?"

The third, "Who has been picking my bread?"

The fourth, "Who has been meddling with my spoon?"

The fifth, "Who has been handling my fork?"

The sixth, "Who has been cutting with my knife?"

In the morning Snow White told them all her story. (Warwick Goble)

The seventh, "Who has been drinking my wine?"

Then the first looked round and said, "Who has been lying on my bed?" And the rest came running to him, and everyone cried out that somebody had been upon his bed. But the seventh saw Snow White, and called all his brethren to come and see her; and they cried out with wonder and astonishment and brought their lamps to look at her, and said, "Good heavens! What a lovely child she is!" And they were very glad to see her, and took care not to wake her; and the seventh dwarf slept an hour with each of the other dwarfs in turn, till the night was gone.

In the morning Snow White told them all her story; and they pitied her, and said if she would keep all things in order, and cook and wash and knit and spin for them, she might stay where she was, and they would take good care of her. Then they went out all day long to their work, seeking for gold and silver in the mountains, and Snow White was left at home; but they warned her, and said, "The queen will soon find out where you are, so take care to let no one in."

But the queen, now that she thought Snow White was dead, believed that she must be the handsomest lady in the land; and she went to her glass and said:

"Tell me, glass, tell me true!
Of all the ladies in the land,
Who is fairest, tell me, who?"

And the glass answered:

"Thou, queen, art the fairest in all this
*   land:*
But over the hills, in the greenwood shade,
Where the seven dwarfs their dwelling
*   have made,*
There Snow White is hiding her head;
*   and she*
Is lovelier far, O queen! than thee."

Then the queen was very much frightened; for she knew that the glass always spoke the truth, and was sure that the servant had betrayed her. And she could not bear to think that anyone lived who was more beautiful than she was; so she dressed herself up as an old pedlar, and went her way over the hills, to the place where the dwarfs dwelt. Then she knocked at the door, and cried, "Fine wares to sell!"

Snow White looked out of the window, and said, "Good-day, good woman! What have you to sell?"

"Good wares, fine wares," said she; "laces and bobbins of all colours."

"I will let the old lady in; she seems to be a very good sort of body," thought Snow White, as she ran down and unbolted the door.

"Bless me!" said the old woman, "how badly your stays are laced! Let me lace them up with one of my nice new laces."

Snow White did not dream of any mischief, so she stood before the old woman; but she set to work so nimbly, and pulled the lace so tight, that Snow White's breath was stopped, and she fell down as if she were dead.

"There's an end to all thy beauty," said the spiteful queen, and went away home.

In the evening the seven dwarfs came home; and I need not say how grieved they were to see their faithful Snow White stretched out upon the ground, as if she was quite dead. However, they lifted her up, and when they found what ailed her, they cut the lace; and in a little time she began to breathe, and very soon came back to life again. Then they said, "The old woman was the queen herself; take care another time, and let no one in when we are away."

When the queen got home, she went straight to her glass and spoke to it as before; but to her great grief it still said:

"Thou, queen, art the fairest in all this land.
But over the hills, in the greenwood shade,
Where the seven dwarfs their dwelling
*   have made,*

*There Snow White is hiding her head;
    and she
Is lovelier far, O queen! than thee."*

Then the blood ran cold in her heart with spite and malice to see that Snow White still lived; and she dressed herself up again, but in quite another dress from the one she wore before, and took with her a poisoned comb. When she reached the dwarfs' cottage, she knocked at the door, and cried, "Fine wares to sell!"

But Snow White said, "I dare not let anyone in."

Then the queen said, "Only look at my beautiful combs!" and gave her the poisoned one. And it looked so pretty, that she took it up and put it into her hair to try it; but the moment it touched her head, the poison was so powerful that she fell down senseless.

"There you may lie," said the queen, and went her way.

But by good luck the dwarfs came in very early that evening; and when they saw Snow White lying on the ground, they guessed what had happened, and soon found the poisoned comb. And when they took it away she got well, and told them all that had passed; and they warned her once more not to open the door to anyone.

Meantime the queen went home to her glass, and shook with rage when she read the very same answer as before; and she said, "Snow White shall die, if it cost me my life."

So she went by herself into her chamber, and got ready a poisoned apple: the outside looked very rosy and tempting, but whoever tasted it was sure to die. Then she dressed herself up as a peasant's wife, and travelled over the hills to the dwarfs' cottage, and knocked at the door; but Snow White put her head out of the window and said, "I dare not let anyone in, for the dwarfs have told me not to."

"Do as you please," said the old woman, "but at any rate take this pretty apple; I will give it you."

"No," said Snow White, "I dare not take it."

"You silly girl!" answered the other, "what are you afraid of? Do you think it is poisoned? Come! Do you eat one part, and I will eat the other." Now the apple was made up so that one side was good while the other side was poisoned. Then Snow White was much tempted to taste, for the apple looked so very nice; and when she saw the old woman eat, she could wait no longer. But she had scarcely put the piece into her mouth, when she fell down dead upon the ground.

"This time nothing will save thee," said the queen; and she went home to her glass, and at last it said: "Thou, queen, art the fairest of all the fair."

And then her wicked heart was glad, and as happy as such a heart could be.

When evening came, and the dwarfs arrived home, they found Snow White lying on the ground: no breath came from her lips, and they were afraid that she was quite dead. They lifted her up, and combed her hair, and washed her face with wine and water; but all was in vain, for the little girl seemed quite dead. So they laid her down upon a bier, and all seven watched and bewailed her three whole days; and then they thought they would bury her: but her cheeks were still rosy, and her face looked just as it did while she was alive; so they said, "We will never bury her in the cold ground." And they made a coffin of glass, so that they might still look at her, and wrote upon it in golden letters what her name was, and that she was a king's daughter. And the coffin was set beside the cottage among the hills, and one of the dwarfs always sat by it and watched. And the birds of the air came too, and bemoaned Snow White; and first of all came an owl, and then a raven, and at last a dove, and sat by her side.

And thus Snow White lay for a long, long time, and still only looked as though she was asleep; for she was even now as white as snow, and as red as blood, and as black as ebony.

At last a prince came and called at the dwarfs' house; and he saw Snow White, and read what was written in golden letters.

Then he offered the dwarfs money, and prayed and besought them to let him take her away; but they said, "We will not part with her for all the gold in the world."

At last, however, they had pity on him, and gave him the coffin; but the moment he lifted it up to carry it home with him, the piece of apple fell from between her lips, and Snow White awoke, and said, "Where am I?"

And the prince said, "Thou art quite safe with me."

Then he told her all that had happened, and said, "I love you far better than all the world; so come with me to my father's palace, and you shall be my wife." And Snow White consented, and went home with the prince; and everything was got ready with great pomp and splendour for their wedding.

To the feast was asked, among the rest, Snow White's old enemy the queen; and as she was dressing herself in fine rich clothes, she looked in the glass and said:

> *"Tell me, glass, tell me true!*
> *Of all the ladies in the land,*
> *Who is fairest, tell me, who?"*

And the glass answered:

> *"Thou, lady, art loveliest here, I ween;*
> *But lovelier far is the new-made queen."*

When she heard this she started with rage; but her envy and curiosity were so great, that she could not help setting out to see the bride. And when she got there, and saw that it was no other than Snow White, who she thought had been dead a long while, she choked with rage and fell down and died; but Snow White and the prince lived and reigned happily over that land many, many years; and sometimes they went up into the mountains, and paid a visit to the little dwarfs, who had been so kind to Snow White in her time of need.

THE PINK

THERE WAS ONCE upon a time a queen to whom God had given no children. Every morning she went into the garden and prayed to God in heaven to bestow on her a son or a daughter. Then an angel from heaven came to her and said: "Be at rest, you shall have a son with the power of wishing, so that whatsoever in the world he wishes for, that shall he have." Then she went to the king, and told him the joyful tidings, and when the time was come she gave birth to a son, and the king was filled with gladness.

Every morning she went with the child to the garden where the wild beasts were kept, and washed herself there in a clear stream. It happened once, when the child was a little older, that it was lying in her arms and she fell asleep. Then came the old cook, who knew that the child had the power of wishing, and stole it away, and he took a hen, and cut it in pieces, and dropped some of its blood on the queen's apron and on her dress. Then he carried the child away to a secret place, where a nurse was obliged to suckle it, and he ran to the king and accused the queen of having allowed her child to be taken from her by the wild beasts.

When the king saw the blood on her apron, he believed this, and fell into such a passion that he ordered a high tower to be built, from which neither sun nor moon could be seen, and had his wife put into it, and walled her up. Here she was to stay for seven years without meat or drink so that she would die of hunger. But God sent two angels from heaven in the shape of white doves, which flew to her with food twice a day until the seven years were over.

The cook, however, thought to himself: "If the child has the power of wishing, and I am here, he might very easily get me into trouble." So he left the palace and went to the boy, who was already big enough to speak, and said to him: "Wish for a beautiful palace for yourself with a garden, and all else that pertains to it." Scarcely were the words out of the boy's mouth than everything was there that he had wished for. After a while the cook said to him: "It is not well for you to be so alone, wish for a pretty girl as a companion." Then the king's son wished for one, and she immediately stood before him, and was more beautiful than any painter could have painted her. The two played together, and loved each other with all their hearts, and the old cook went out hunting like a nobleman.

The thought occurred to him, however, that the king's son might someday wish to be with his father, and thus bring him into great peril. So he went out and took the maiden aside, and said: "Tonight when the boy is asleep, go to his bed and plunge this knife into his heart, and bring me his heart and tongue, and if you do not do it, you shall lose your life."

Thereupon he went away, and when he returned next day she had not done it, and said: "Why should I shed the blood of an innocent boy who has never harmed anyone?"

The cook once more said: "If you do not do it, it shall cost you your own life."

When he had gone away, she had a little hind brought to her, and ordered her to be killed, and took her heart and tongue, and laid them on a plate, and when she saw the old man coming, she said to the boy: "Lie down in your bed, and draw the clothes over you."

Then the wicked wretch came in and said: "Where are the boy's heart and tongue?"

The girl reached the plate to him, but the king's son threw off the quilt, and said: "You

old sinner, why did you want to kill me? Now will I pronounce thy sentence. You shall become a black poodle and have a gold collar round your neck, and shall eat burning coals, till the flames burst forth from your throat."

And when he had spoken these words, the old man was changed into a poodle dog, and had a gold collar round his neck, and the cooks were ordered to bring up some live coals, and these he ate, until the flames broke forth from his throat.

The king's son remained there a short while longer, and he thought of his mother, and wondered if she were still alive. At length he said to the maiden: "I will go home to my own country; if you will go with me, I will provide for you."

"Ah," she replied, "the way is so long, and what shall I do in a strange land where I am unknown?" As she did not seem quite willing, and as they could not be parted from each other, he wished that she might be changed into a beautiful pink, and took her with him. Then he went away to his own country, and the poodle had to run after him.

He went to the tower in which his mother was confined, and as it was so high, he wished for a ladder which would reach up to the very top. Then he mounted up and looked inside, and cried: "Beloved mother, lady queen, are you still alive, or are you dead?"

She answered: "I have just eaten, and am still satisfied," for she thought the angels were there.

Said he: "I am your dear son, whom the wild beasts were said to have torn from your arms; but I am alive still, and will soon set you free."

Then he descended again, and went to his father, and caused himself to be announced as a strange huntsman, and asked if he could offer him service. The king said yes, if he was skilful and could get game for him, he should come to him, but that deer had never taken up their quarters in any part of the country. Then the huntsman promised to procure as much game for him as he could possibly use at the royal table. So he summoned all the huntsmen together, and bade them go out into the forest with him. And he went with them and made them form a great circle, open at one end where he stationed himself, and began to wish. Two hundred deer and more came running inside the circle at once, and the huntsmen shot them. Then they were all placed on sixty country carts, and driven home to the king, and for once he was able to deck his table with game, after having had none at all for years.

Now the king felt great joy at this, and commanded that his entire household should eat with him next day, and made a great feast. When they were all assembled together, he said to the huntsman: "As you are so clever, you shall sit by me."

He replied: "Lord king, your majesty must excuse me, I am a poor huntsman."

But the king insisted: "You shall sit by me."

While he was sitting there, he thought of his dearest mother, and wished that one of the king's principal servants would begin to speak of her, and would ask how it was faring with the queen in the tower, and if she were alive still, or had perished.

Hardly had he formed the wish than the marshal began, and said: "Your majesty, we live joyously here, but how is the queen living in the tower? Is she still alive, or has she died?"

But the king replied: "She let my dear son be torn to pieces by wild beasts; I will not have her named."

Then the huntsman arose and said: "Gracious lord father, she is alive still, and I am her son, and I was not carried away by wild beasts, but by that wretch the old cook, who tore me from her arms when she was asleep, and sprinkled her apron with the blood of a chicken." Thereupon he took the dog with the golden collar, and said: "That is the wretch!" and caused live coals to be brought, and these

the dog was compelled to devour before the sight of all, until flames burst forth from its throat. On this the huntsman asked the king if he would like to see the dog in his true shape, and wished him back into the form of the cook, in the which he stood immediately, with his white apron, and his knife by his side. When the king saw him he fell into a passion, and ordered him to be cast into the deepest dungeon. Then the huntsman spoke further and said: "Father, will you see the maiden who brought me up so tenderly and who was afterwards to murder me, but did not do it, though her own life depended on it?"

The king replied: "Yes, I would like to see her."

The son said: "Most gracious father, I will show her to you in the form of a beautiful flower," and he thrust his hand into his pocket and brought forth the pink, and placed it on the royal table, and it was so beautiful that the king had never seen one to equal it. Then the son said: "Now will I show her to you in her own form," and wished that she might become a maiden, and she stood there looking so beautiful that no painter could have made her look more so.

And the king sent two waiting-maids and two attendants to the tower, to fetch the queen and bring her to the royal table. But when she was led in she ate nothing, and said: "The gracious and merciful God who has supported me in the tower, will soon set me free." She lived three days more, and then died happily, and when she was buried, the two white doves which had brought her food to the tower, and were angels of heaven, followed her body and seated themselves on her grave.

The aged king ordered the cook to be torn in four pieces, but grief consumed the king's own heart, and he soon died. His son married the beautiful maiden whom he had brought with him as a flower in his pocket, and whether they are still alive or not is known to God.

CLEVER ELSIE

THERE WAS ONCE a man who had a daughter who was called Clever Elsie. And when she had grown up her father said: "We will get her married."

"Yes," said the mother, "if only someone would come who would have her."

At length a man who was called Hans came from a distance and wooed her, but he stipulated that Clever Elsie should be really smart.

"Oh," said the father, "she has plenty of good sense;" and the mother said: "Oh, she can see the wind coming up the street, and hear the flies coughing."

"Well," said Hans, "if she is not really smart, I won't have her."

When they were sitting at dinner and had eaten, the mother said: "Elsie, go into the cellar and fetch some beer."

Then Clever Elsie took the pitcher from the wall, went into the cellar, and tapped the lid briskly as she went, so that the time might not appear long. When she was below she fetched herself a chair, and set it before the barrel, so that she had no need to stoop and thus hurt her back or do herself any unexpected injury. Then she placed the can before her, and turned the tap, and while the beer was running, rather than let her eyes be idle, she looked up at the wall, and after much peering here and there, saw a pickaxe exactly above her, which the masons had accidentally left there.

Then Clever Elsie began to weep and said: "If I get Hans, and we have a child, and he grows big, and we send him into the cellar here to draw beer, then the pickaxe will fall on his head and kill him."

Then she sat and wept and screamed, with all the strength of her body, over the misfortune which lay before her. Those upstairs waited for the drink, but Clever Elsie still did not come.

Then the woman said to the servant: "Just go down into the cellar and see where Elsie is."

The maid went and found her sitting in front of the barrel, screaming loudly. "Elsie why do you weep?" asked the maid.

"Ah," she answered, "have I not reason to weep? If I get Hans, and we have a child, and he grows big, and has to draw beer here, the pickaxe will perhaps fall on his head, and kill him."

Then said the maid: "What a clever Elsie we have!" and sat down beside her and began loudly to weep over the misfortune.

After a while, as the maid did not come back, and those upstairs were thirsty for the beer, the man said to the boy: "Just go down into the cellar and see where Elsie and the girl are."

The boy went down, and there sat Clever Elsie and the girl both weeping together.

Then he asked: "Why are you weeping?"

"Ah," said Elsie, "have I not reason to weep? If I get Hans, and we have a child, and he grows big, and has to draw beer here, the pickaxe will fall on his head and kill him."

Then said the boy: "What a clever Elsie we have!" and sat down by her, and likewise began to howl loudly.

Upstairs they waited for the boy, but as he still did not return, the man said to the woman: "Just go down into the cellar and see where Elsie is!"

The woman went down, and found all three in the midst of their lamentations, and enquired what was the cause; then Elsie told her also that her future child was to be killed by the pickaxe when it grew big and had to draw beer and the pickaxe fell down.

Then said the mother likewise: "What a clever Elsie we have!" and sat down and wept with them.

The man upstairs waited a short time, but as his wife did not come back and his thirst grew ever greater, he said: "I must go into the cellar myself and see where Elsie is."

But when he got into the cellar, and they were all sitting together crying, and he heard the reason – that Elsie's child was the cause, the one that Elsie might perhaps bring into the world someday, who might be killed by the pickaxe, if he should happen to be sitting beneath it drawing beer just at the very time when it fell down – he cried: "Oh, what a clever Elsie!" and sat down, and likewise wept with them.

The bridegroom stayed upstairs alone for a long time; then as no one would come back he thought: "They must be waiting for me below – I too must go there and see what they are about."

When he got down, the five of them were sitting screaming and lamenting quite piteously, each outdoing the other.

"What misfortune has happened then?" asked he.

"Ah, dear Hans," said Elsie, "if we marry each other and have a child, and he is big, and we perhaps send him here to draw something to drink, then the pickaxe which has been left up there might dash his brains out if it were to fall down, so have we not reason to weep?"

"Come," said Hans, "more understanding than that is not needed for my household; as you are such a clever Elsie, I will have you," and seized her hand, took her upstairs with him, and married her.

After Hans had had her some time, he said: "Wife, I am going out to work to earn some money for us; go into the field and cut the corn that we may have some bread."

"Yes, dear Hans, I will do that."

After Hans had gone away, she cooked herself some good broth and took it into the field with her. When she came to the field she said to herself: "What shall I do; shall I cut first, or shall I eat first? Oh, I will eat first."

Then she drank her cup of broth and when she was fully satisfied, she once more said: "What shall I do? Shall I cut first, or shall I sleep first? I will sleep first." Then she lay down among the corn and fell asleep.

Hans had been at home for a long time, but Elsie did not come; then said he: "What a clever Elsie I have; she is so industrious that she does not even come home to eat." But when evening came and she still stayed away, Hans went out to see what she had cut; but nothing was cut, and she was lying among the corn asleep.

Then Hans hastened home and brought a fowler's net with little bells and hung it round about her, and she still went on sleeping. Then he ran home, shut the house-door, and sat down in his chair and worked. At length, when it was quite dark, Clever Elsie awoke and when she got up there was a jingling all round about her, and the bells rang at each step she took.

Then she was alarmed, and became uncertain whether she really was Clever Elsie or not, and said: "Is it I, or is it not I?" But she knew not what answer to make to this, and stood for a time in doubt; at length she thought: "I will go home and ask if it be I, or if it be not I, they will be sure to know."

She ran to the door of her own house, but it was shut; then she knocked at the window and cried: "Hans, is Elsie within?"

"Yes," answered Hans, "she is within."

Hereupon she was terrified, and said: "Ah, heavens! Then it is not I," and went to another door; but when the people heard the jingling of the bells they would not open it, and she could get in nowhere. Then she ran out of the village, and no one has seen her since.

ASHPUTTEL

THE WIFE OF a rich man fell sick; and when she felt that her end drew nigh, she called her only daughter to her bedside, and said, "Always be a good girl, and I will look down from heaven and watch over you."

Soon afterwards she shut her eyes and died, and was buried in the garden; and the little girl went every day to her grave and wept, and was always good and kind to all about her. And the snow fell and spread a beautiful white covering over the grave; but by the time the spring came, and the sun had melted it away again, her father had married another wife. This new wife had two daughters of her own that she brought home with her; they were fair in face but foul at heart, and it was now a sorry time for the poor little girl.

"What does the good-for-nothing want in the parlour?" said they; "they who would eat bread should first earn it; away with the kitchen-maid!"

Then they took away her fine clothes, and gave her an old grey frock to put on, and laughed at her, and turned her into the kitchen. There she was forced to do hard work; to rise early before daylight, to bring the water, to make the fire, to cook and to wash. Besides that, the sisters plagued her in all sorts of ways, and laughed at her. In the evening when she was tired, she had no bed to lie down on, but was made to lie by the hearth among the ashes; and as this, of course, made her always dusty and dirty, they called her Ashputtel.

It happened one day that the father was going to the fair, and he asked his wife's daughters what he should bring them.

"Fine clothes," said the first;

"Pearls and diamonds," cried the second.

"Now, child," said he to his own daughter, "what will you have?"

"The first twig, dear father, that brushes against your hat when you turn your face to come homewards," said she.

Then he bought for the first two the fine clothes and pearls and diamonds they had asked for; and on his way home, as he rode through a green copse, a hazel twig brushed against him, and almost pushed off his hat: so he broke it off and brought it away; and when he got home he gave it to his daughter. Then she took it, and went to her mother's grave and planted it there; and cried so much that it was watered with her tears; and there it grew and became a fine tree. Three times every day she went to it and cried; and soon a little bird came and built its nest upon the tree, and talked with her, and watched over her, and brought her whatever she wished for.

Now it happened that the king of that land held a feast, which was to last three days; and out of those who came to it his son was to choose a bride for himself. Ashputtel's two sisters were asked to come, so they called her up, and said, "Now, comb our hair, brush our shoes and tie our sashes for us, for we are going to dance at the king's feast."

Then she did as she was told; but when all was done she could not help crying, for she should so have liked to have gone with them to the ball; and at last she begged her mother very hard to let her go.

"You, Ashputtel!" said she; "you who have nothing to wear, no clothes at all, and who cannot even dance – you want to go to the ball?" And when the girl kept on begging, she said at last, to get rid of her, "I will throw this dishful of peas into the ash-heap, and if in two hours' time you have picked them all out, you shall go to the feast too."

Then she threw the peas down among the ashes, but the little maiden ran out at the back door into the garden, and cried out:

Ashputtle. (Alexander Zick)

"Hither, hither, through the sky,
Turtle-doves and linnets, fly!
Blackbird, thrush and chaffinch gay,
Hither, hither, haste away!
One and all come help me, quick!
Haste ye, haste ye – pick, pick, pick!"

Then first came two white doves, flying in at the kitchen window; next came two turtle-doves; and after them came all the little birds under heaven, chirping and fluttering in, and they flew down into the ashes. And the little doves stooped their heads down and set to work, pick, pick, pick; and then the others began to pick, pick, pick; and among them all they soon picked out all the peas and put them into the dish, but left the ashes. Long before the end of the hour the work was quite done, and all flew out again at the windows.

Then Ashputtel brought the dish to her mother, overjoyed at the thought that now she should go to the ball. But the mother said, "No, no! You slut, you have no clothes, and cannot dance; you shall not go." And when Ashputtel begged very hard to go, she said, "If you can in one hour's time pick two of those dishes of peas out of the ashes, you shall go." And thus she thought she should at least get rid of her. So she shook two dishes of peas into the ashes.

But the little maiden went out into the garden at the back of the house, and cried out as before:

"Hither, hither, through the sky,
Turtle-doves and linnets, fly!
Blackbird, thrush and chaffinch gay,
Hither, hither, haste away!
One and all come help me, quick!
Haste ye, haste ye – pick, pick, pick!"

Then first came two white doves in at the kitchen window; next came two turtle-doves; and after them came all the little birds under heaven, chirping and hopping about. And they flew down into the ashes; and the little doves put their heads down and set to work, pick, pick, pick; and then the others began pick, pick, pick; and they put all the peas into the dishes, and left all the ashes. Before half an hour's time all was done, and out they flew again. And then Ashputtel took the dishes to her mother, rejoicing to think that she should now go to the ball. But her mother said, "It is all of no use, you cannot go; you have no clothes, and cannot dance, and you would only put us to shame" – and off she went with her two daughters to the ball.

Now when all were gone, and nobody left at home, Ashputtel went sorrowfully and sat down under the hazel tree and cried out:

"Shake, shake, hazel tree,
Gold and silver over me!"

Then her friend the bird flew out of the tree, and brought a gold and silver dress for her, and slippers of spangled silk; and she put them on, and followed her sisters to the feast. But they did not know her, and thought it must be some strange princess, she looked so fine and beautiful in her rich clothes; and they never once thought of Ashputtel, taking it for granted that she was safe at home in the dirt.

The king's son soon came up to her, and took her by the hand and danced with her, and no one else; and he never left her side, and when anyone else came to ask her to dance, he said, "This lady is dancing with me."

Thus they danced till a late hour of the night, and then she wanted to go home; and the king's son said, "I shall go and take care of you to your home;" for he wanted to see where the beautiful maiden lived. But she slipped away from him, unawares, and ran off towards home; and as the prince followed her, she jumped up into the pigeon-house and shut the door. Then he waited till her father came home, and told him that the unknown maiden, who had been at the feast, had hid herself in the pigeon-house. But when they had broken open the door they found no one within; and as they came back into the house, Ashputtel was lying, as she always did, in her dirty frock by the ashes, and her dim little lamp was burning in the chimney. For she had run as quickly as she could through the pigeon-house and on to the hazel tree, and had there taken off her beautiful clothes, and put them beneath the tree, that the bird might carry them away, and had lain down again amid the ashes in her little grey frock.

The next day when the feast was again held, and her father, mother, and sisters were gone, Ashputtel went to the hazel tree and said:

"Shake, shake, hazel tree,
Gold and silver over me!"

And the bird came and brought a still finer dress than the one she had worn the day before.

And when she came in it to the ball, everyone wondered at her beauty; and the king's son, who was waiting for her, took her by the hand, and danced with her; and when anyone asked her to dance, he said as before, "This lady is dancing with me."

When night came she wanted to go home, and the king's son followed here as before, that he might see into what house she went; but she sprang away from him all at once into the garden behind her father's house. In this garden stood a fine large pear tree full of ripe fruit; and Ashputtel, not knowing where to hide herself, jumped up into it without being seen. Then the king's son lost sight of her, and could not find out where she was gone, but waited till her father came home, and said to him, "The unknown lady who danced with me has slipped away, and I think she must have sprung into the pear tree." The father thought to himself, "Can it be Ashputtel?" So he had an axe brought; and they cut down the tree, but found no one upon it. And when they came back into the kitchen, there lay Ashputtel among the ashes; for she had slipped down on the other side of the tree, and carried her beautiful clothes back to the bird at the hazel tree, and then put on her little grey frock.

The third day, when her father and mother and sisters were gone, she went again into the garden and said:

"Shake, shake, hazel tree,
Gold and silver over me!"

Then her kind friend the bird brought a dress still finer than the former one, and slippers which were all of gold, so that when she came to the feast no one knew what to say for wonder at her beauty; and the king's son danced with nobody but her; and when anyone else asked her to dance, he said, "This lady is my partner, sir."

When night came she wanted to go home; and the king's son would go with her, and said to himself, "I will not lose her this time;" but, somehow, she again slipped away from him, though in such a hurry that she dropped her left golden slipper upon the stairs.

The prince took the shoe, and went the next day to the king his father, and said, "I will take for my wife the lady that this golden slipper fits."

Then both the sisters were overjoyed to hear it; for they had beautiful feet, and had no doubt that they could wear the golden slipper. The eldest went first into the room where the slipper was, and wanted to try it on, and the mother stood by. But her great toe could not go into it, and the shoe was altogether much too small for her. Then the mother gave her a knife, and said, "Never mind, cut it off; when you are queen you will not care about toes; you will not want to walk." So the silly girl cut off her great toe, and thus squeezed on the shoe, and went to the king's son. Then he took her for his bride, and set her beside him on his horse, and rode away with her homewards.

But on their way home they had to pass by the hazel tree that Ashputtel had planted; and on the branch sat a little dove singing:

"Back again! back again! Look to the shoe!
The shoe is too small, and not made for you!
Prince! Prince! Look again for thy bride,
For she's not the true one that sits by thy
side."

Then the prince got down and looked at her foot; and he saw, by the blood that streamed from it, what a trick she had played him. So he turned his horse round, and brought the false bride back to her home, and said, "This is not the right bride; let the other sister try and put on the slipper." Then she went into the room and got her foot into the shoe, all but the heel, which was too large. But her mother squeezed it in till the blood came, and took her to the king's son, and he

set her as his bride by his side on his horse, and rode away with her.

But when they came to the hazel tree the little dove sat there still, and sang:

"Back again! back again! Look to the shoe!
The shoe is too small, and not made for you!
Prince! Prince! Look again for thy bride,
For she's not the true one that sits by thy
side."

Then he looked down, and saw that the blood streamed so much from the shoe, that her white stockings were quite red. So he turned his horse and brought her also back again. "This is not the true bride," said he to the father; "have you no other daughters?"

"No," said he; "there is only a little dirty Ashputtel here, the child of my first wife; I am sure she cannot be the bride." The prince told him to send her. But the mother said, "No, no, she is much too dirty; she will not dare to show herself."

However, the prince would have her come; and she first washed her face and hands, and then went in and curtsied to him, and he reached her the golden slipper. Then she took her clumsy shoe off her left foot, and put on the golden slipper; and it fitted her as if it had been made for her. And when he drew near and looked at her face he knew her, and said, "This is the right bride."

But the mother and both the sisters were frightened, and turned pale with anger as he took Ashputtel on his horse, and rode away with her. And when they came to the hazel tree, the white dove sang:

"Home! home! Look at the shoe!
Princess! The shoe was made for you!
Prince! Prince! Take home thy bride,
For she is the true one that sits by thy side!"

And when the dove had done its song, it came flying, and perched upon her right shoulder, and so went home with her.

THE WHITE SNAKE

A LONG TIME AGO there lived a king who was famed for his wisdom through all the land. Nothing was hidden from him, and it seemed as if news of the most secret things was brought to him through the air. But he had a strange custom; every day after dinner, when the table was cleared, and no one else was present, a trusty servant had to bring him one more dish. It was covered, however, and even the servant did not know what was in it, neither did anyone know, for the king never took off the cover to eat of it until he was quite alone.

This had gone on for a long time, when one day the servant, who took away the dish, was overcome with such curiosity that he could not help carrying the dish into his room. When he had carefully locked the door, he lifted up the cover, and saw a white snake lying on the dish. But when he saw it he could not deny himself the pleasure of tasting it, so he cut of a little bit and put it into his mouth. No sooner had it touched his tongue than he heard a strange whispering of little voices outside his window. He went and listened, and then noticed that it was the sparrows who were chattering together, and telling one another of all kinds of things which they had seen in the fields and woods. Eating the snake had given him the power of understanding the language of animals.

Now it so happened that on this very day the queen lost her most beautiful ring, and suspicion of having stolen it fell upon this trusty servant, who was allowed to go everywhere. The king ordered the man to be brought before him, and threatened with angry words that unless he could before the morrow point out the thief, he himself should be looked upon as guilty and executed. In vain he declared his innocence; he was dismissed with no better answer.

In his trouble and fear he went down into the courtyard and took thought how to help himself out of his trouble. Now some ducks were sitting together quietly by a brook and taking their rest; and, while they were making their feathers smooth with their bills, they were having a confidential conversation together. The servant stood by and listened. They were telling one another of all the places where they had been waddling about all the morning, and what good food they had found; and one said in a pitiful tone: "Something lies heavy on my stomach; as I was eating in haste I swallowed a ring which lay under the queen's window." The servant at once seized her by the neck, carried her to the kitchen, and said to the cook: "Here is a fine duck; pray, kill her."

"Yes," said the cook, and weighed her in his hand; "she has spared no trouble to fatten herself, and has been waiting to be roasted long enough." So he cut off her head, and as she was being dressed for the spit, the queen's ring was found inside her.

The servant could now easily prove his innocence; and the king, to make amends for the wrong, allowed him to ask a favour, and promised him the best place in the court that he could wish for. The servant refused everything, and only asked for a horse and some money for travelling, as he had a mind to see the world and go about a little. When his request was granted, he set out on his way, and one day came to a pond, where he saw three fishes caught in the reeds and gasping for water. Now, though it is said that fishes are dumb, he heard them lamenting that they must perish so miserably, and, as he had a kind heart, he got off his horse and put the three prisoners back into the water. They leapt with delight, put out their heads, and cried to him: "We will remember you and repay you for saving us!"

He rode on, and after a while it seemed to him that he heard a voice in the sand at his feet. He listened, and heard an ant-king complain: "Why cannot folks, with their clumsy beasts, keep off our bodies? That stupid horse, with his heavy hoofs, has been treading down my people without mercy!" So he turned on to a side path and the ant-king cried out to him: "We will remember you – one good turn deserves another!"

The path led him into a wood, and there he saw two old ravens standing by their nest, and throwing out their young ones. "Out with you, you idle, good-for-nothing creatures!" cried they; "we cannot find food for you any longer; you are big enough, and can provide for yourselves." But the poor young ravens lay upon the ground, flapping their wings, and crying: "Oh, what helpless chicks we are! We must shift for ourselves, and yet we cannot fly! What can we do, but lie here and starve?" So the good young fellow alighted and killed his horse with his sword, and gave it to them for food. Then they came hopping up to it, satisfied their hunger, and cried: "We will remember you – one good turn deserves another!"

And now he had to use his own legs, and when he had walked a long way, he came to a large city. There was a great noise and crowd in the streets, and a man rode up on horseback, crying aloud: "The king's daughter wants a husband; but whoever seeks her hand must perform a hard task, and if he does not succeed he will forfeit his life." Many had already made the attempt, but in vain; nevertheless when the youth saw the king's daughter he was so overcome by her great beauty that he forgot all danger, went before the king and declared himself a suitor.

So he was led out to the sea, and a gold ring was thrown into it, before his eyes; then the king ordered him to fetch this ring up from the bottom of the sea, and added: "If you come up again without it you will be thrown in again and again until you perish amid the waves." All the

The one in the middle held a mussel in its mouth, which it laid on the shore at the youth's feet. (Rie Cramer)

people grieved for the handsome youth; then they went away, leaving him alone by the sea.

He stood on the shore and considered what he should do; suddenly he saw three fishes come swimming towards him, and they were the very fishes whose lives he had saved. The one in the middle held a mussel in its mouth, which it laid on the shore at the youth's feet, and when he had taken it up and opened it, there lay the gold ring in the shell. Full of joy he took it to the king and expected that he would grant him the promised reward.

But when the proud princess perceived that he was not her equal in birth, she scorned him, and required him first to perform another task. She went down into the garden and strewed with her own hands ten sackfuls of millet-seed on the grass; then she said: "Tomorrow

307

morning before sunrise these must be picked up, and not a single grain be wanting."

The youth sat down in the garden and considered how it might be possible to perform this task, but he could think of nothing, and there he sat sorrowfully awaiting the break of day, when he should be led to his death. But as soon as the first rays of the sun shone into the garden he saw all the ten sacks standing side by side, quite full, and not a single grain was missing. The ant-king had come in the night with thousands and thousands of ants, and the grateful creatures had by great industry picked up all the millet-seeds and gathered them into the sacks.

Presently the king's daughter herself came down into the garden, and was amazed to see that the young man had done the task she had given him. But she could not yet conquer her proud heart, and said: "Although he has performed both the tasks, he shall not be my husband until he has brought me the Golden Apple from the Tree of Life."

The youth did not know where the Tree of Life stood, but he set out, and would have gone on for ever, as long as his legs would carry him, though he had no hope of finding it. After he had wandered through three kingdoms, he came one evening to a wood, and lay down under a tree to sleep. But he heard a rustling in the branches, and a golden apple fell into his hand. At the same time three ravens flew down to him, perched themselves upon his knee, and said: "We are the three young ravens whom you saved from starving; when we had grown big, and heard that you were seeking the Golden Apple, we flew over the sea to the end of the world, where the Tree of Life stands, and have brought you the apple."

The youth, full of joy, set out homewards, and took the Golden Apple to the king's beautiful daughter, who had now no more excuses left to make. They cut the Apple of Life in two and ate it together; and then her heart became full of love for him, and they lived in undisturbed happiness to a great age.

THE GOLDEN GOOSE

THERE WAS A man who had three sons, the youngest of whom was called Simpleton and was despised, mocked and sneered at on every occasion.

It happened that the eldest wanted to go into the forest to hew wood, and before he went his mother gave him a beautiful sweet cake and a bottle of wine in order that he might not suffer from hunger or thirst.

When he entered the forest he met a little grey-haired old man who bade him good day, and said: "Do give me a piece of cake out of your pocket, and let me have a draught of your wine; I am so hungry and thirsty."

But the clever son answered: "If I give you my cake and wine, I shall have none for myself; be off with you," and he left the little man standing and went on.

But when he began to hew down a tree, it was not long before he made a false stroke, and the axe cut him in the arm, so that he had to go home and have it bound up. And this was the little grey man's doing.

After this the second son went into the forest, and his mother gave him, like the eldest, a cake and a bottle of wine.

The little old grey man met him likewise, and asked him for a piece of cake and a drink of wine. But the second son, too, said sensibly enough: "What I give you will be taken away from myself; be off!" and he left the little man standing and went on.

His punishment, however, was not delayed; when he had made a few blows at the tree he struck himself in the leg, so that he had to be carried home.

Then Simpleton said: "Father, do let me go and cut wood."

The father answered: "Your brothers have hurt themselves with it; leave it alone, you do not understand anything about it."

But Simpleton begged so long that at last he said: "Just go then, you will get wiser by hurting yourself." His mother gave him a cake made with water and baked in the cinders, and with it a bottle of sour beer.

When he came to the forest the little old grey man met him likewise, and greeting him, said: "Give me a piece of your cake and a drink out of your bottle; I am so hungry and thirsty."

Simpleton answered: "I have only cinder-cake and sour beer; if that pleases you, we will sit down and eat."

So they sat down, and when Simpleton pulled out his cinder-cake, it was a fine sweet cake, and the sour beer had become good wine.

So they ate and drank, and after that the little man said: "Since you have a good heart, and are willing to divide what you have, I will give you good luck. There stands an old tree; cut it down, and you will find something at the roots." Then the little man took leave of him.

Simpleton went and cut down the tree, and when it fell there was a goose sitting in the roots with feathers of pure gold. He lifted her up, and taking her with him, went to an inn where he thought he would stay the night.

Now the host had three daughters, who saw the goose and were curious to know what such a wonderful bird might be, and would have liked to have one of its golden feathers.

The eldest thought: "I shall soon find an opportunity of pulling out a feather," and as soon as Simpleton had gone out she seized the goose by the wing, but her hand remained sticking fast to it.

The second came soon afterwards, thinking only of how she might get a feather for herself, but she had scarcely touched her sister than she was held fast.

The next morning Simpleton took the goose under his arm and set out, without troubling himself about the three girls who were hanging on to it. (Leslie Brooke)

At last the third also came with the like intent, and the others screamed out: "Keep away; for goodness' sake, keep away!"

But she did not understand why she was to keep away. "The others are there," she thought, "I may as well be there too," and ran to them; but as soon as she had touched her sister, she remained sticking fast to her. So they had to spend the night with the goose.

The next morning Simpleton took the goose under his arm and set out, without troubling himself about the three girls who were hanging on to it. They were obliged to run after him continually, now left, now right, wherever his legs took him.

In the middle of the fields the parson met them, and when he saw the procession he said: "For shame, you good-for-nothing girls, why are you running across the fields after this young man? Is that seemly?"

At the same time he seized the youngest by the hand in order to pull her away, but as soon as he touched her he likewise stuck fast, and was himself obliged to run behind.

Before long the sexton came by and saw his master, the parson, running behind three girls. He was astonished at this and called out: "Hi! Your reverence, whither away so quickly? Do not forget that we have a christening today!" and running after him he took him by the sleeve, but was also held fast to it.

While the five were trotting thus, one behind the other, two labourers came with their hoes from the fields; the parson called out to them and begged that they would set him and the sexton free. But they had scarcely touched the sexton when they were held fast, and now there were seven of them running behind Simpleton and the goose.

Soon afterwards he came to a city, where a king ruled who had a daughter who was so serious that no one could make her laugh. So her father had put forth a decree that whosoever should be able to make her laugh should marry her.

When Simpleton heard this, he went with his goose and all her train before the king's daughter, and as soon as she saw the seven people running on and on, one behind the other, she began to laugh quite loudly and as if she would never stop. Thereupon Simpleton asked to have her for his wife; but the king did not want him for a son-in-law, and made all manner of excuses and said he must first produce a man who could drink a cellarful of wine.

Simpleton thought of the little grey man, who could certainly help him; so he went into the forest, and in the same place where he had felled the tree, he saw a man sitting, who had a very sorrowful face.

Simpleton asked him what he was taking to heart so sorely, and he answered: "I have

such a great thirst and cannot quench it; cold water I cannot stand, a barrel of wine I have just emptied, but that to me is like a drop on a hot stone!"

"There I can help you," said Simpleton, "just come with me and you shall be satisfied."

He led him into the king's cellar, and the man bent over the huge barrels and drank till his loins hurt, and before the day was out he had emptied all the barrels.

Then Simpleton asked once more for his bride, but the king was vexed that such an ugly fellow, whom everyone called Simpleton, should take away his daughter, and he made a new condition; he must first find a man who could eat a whole mountain of bread.

Simpleton did not think long, but went straight into the forest, where in the same place there sat a man who was tying up his body with a strap, and making an awful face, and saying: "I have eaten a whole ovenful of rolls, but what good is that when one has such a hunger as I? My stomach remains empty, and I must tie myself up if I am not to die of hunger."

At this Simpleton was glad, and said: "Get up and come with me; you shall eat yourself full."

He led him to the king's palace where all the flour in the whole kingdom was collected, and from it he caused a huge mountain of bread to be baked.

The man from the forest stood before it, began to eat, and by the end of one day the whole mountain had vanished.

Then Simpleton for the third time asked for his bride; but the king again sought a way out, and ordered him to find a ship which could sail on land and on water.

"As soon as you come sailing back in it," said he, "you shall have my daughter for wife."

Simpleton went straight into the forest, and there sat the little grey man to whom he had given his cake.

*Simpleton went straight into the forest, and there sat the little grey man
to whom he had given his cake. (Noel Pocock)*

When he heard what Simpleton wanted, he said: "Since you have given me to eat and to drink, I will give you the ship; and I do all this because you once were kind to me."

Then he gave him the ship which could sail on land and water, and when the king saw that, he could no longer prevent him from having his daughter.

The wedding was celebrated, and after the king's death, Simpleton inherited his kingdom and lived for a long time contentedly with his wife.

THE WATER OF LIFE

LONG BEFORE YOU or I were born, there reigned, in a country a great way off, a king who had three sons. This king one day fell very ill – so ill that nobody thought he could live.

His sons were very much grieved at their father's sickness; and as they were walking together very mournfully in the garden of the palace, a little old man met them and asked what was the matter.

They told him that their father was very ill, and that they were afraid nothing could save him.

"I know what would," said the little old man; "it is the Water of Life. If he could have a draught of it he would be well again; but it is very hard to get."

Then the eldest son said, "I will soon find it," and he went to the sick king and begged that he might go in search of the Water of Life, as it was the only thing that could save him.

"No," said the king. "I had rather die than place you in such great danger as you must meet with in your journey."

But he begged so hard that the king let him go; and the prince thought to himself, "If I bring my father this water, he will make me sole heir to his kingdom."

Then he set out: and when he had gone on his way some time he came to a deep valley, overhung with rocks and woods; and as he looked around, he saw standing above him on one of the rocks a little ugly dwarf, with a sugarloaf cap and a scarlet cloak; and the dwarf called to him and said, "Prince, whither so fast?"

"What is that to thee, you ugly imp?" said the prince haughtily, and rode on.

But the dwarf was enraged at his behaviour, and laid a fairy spell of ill-luck upon him; so that as he rode on the mountain pass became narrower and narrower, and at last the way was so straitened that he could not go a step farther; and when he thought to have turned his horse round to go back the way he had come, he heard a loud laugh ringing round him, and found that the path was closed behind him, so that he was shut in all round.

He next tried to get off his horse and make his way on foot, but again the laugh rang in his ears, and he found himself unable to move a step, and thus he was forced to abide spellbound.

Meantime, the old king was lingering on in daily hope of his son's return, till at last the second son said, "Father, I will go in search of the Water of Life."

For he thought to himself, "My brother is surely dead, and the kingdom will fall to me if I find the water."

The king was at first very unwilling to let him go, but at last yielded to his wish. So he set out and followed the same road which his brother had done, and met with the same elf, who stopped him at the same spot in the mountains, saying, as before, "Prince, prince, whither so fast?"

"Mind your own affairs, busybody!" said the prince scornfully, and rode on.

But the dwarf put the same spell upon him as he put on his elder brother, and he, too, was

*He saw standing above him on one of the rocks
a little ugly dwarf. (Arthur Rackham)*

at last obliged to take up his abode in the heart of the mountains.

Thus it is with proud silly people, who think themselves above everyone else, and are too proud to ask or take advice.

When the second prince had thus been gone a long time, the youngest son said he would go and search for the Water of Life, and trusted he should soon be able to make his father well again.

So he set out, and the dwarf met him too at the same spot in the valley, among the mountains, and said, "Prince, whither so fast?"

And the prince said, "I am going in search of the Water of Life, because my father is ill, and like to die; can you help me? Pray be kind, and aid me if you can!"

"Do you know where it is to be found?" asked the dwarf.

"No," said the prince, "I do not. Pray tell me if you know."

"Then as you have spoken to me kindly, and are wise enough to seek for advice, I will tell you how and where to go. The water you seek springs from a well in an enchanted castle; and, that you may be able to reach it in safety, I will give you an iron wand and two little loaves of bread; strike the iron door of the castle three times with the wand, and it will open; two hungry lions will be lying down inside gaping for their prey, but if you throw them the bread they will let you pass; then hasten on to the well, and take some of the Water of Life before the clock strikes twelve; for if you tarry longer the door will shut upon you for ever."

Then the prince thanked his little friend with the scarlet cloak for his friendly aid, and took the wand and the bread, and went travelling on and on, over sea and over land, till he came to his journey's end, and found everything to be as the dwarf had told him. The door flew open at the third stroke of the wand, and when the lions were quieted he went on through the castle and came at length to a beautiful hall. Around it he saw several knights sitting in a trance; then he pulled off their rings and put them on his own fingers. In another room he saw on a table a sword and a loaf of bread, which he also took.

Farther on he came to a room where a beautiful young lady sat upon a couch; and she welcomed him joyfully, and said if he would set her free from the spell that bound her, the kingdom should be his, if he would come back in a year and marry her.

Then she told him that the well that held the Water of Life was in the palace gardens; and bade him make haste, and draw what he wanted before the clock struck twelve.

He walked on; and as he walked through beautiful gardens he came to a delightful shady

How the sister fetched the Water of Life. (H. J. Ford)

spot in which stood a couch; and he thought to himself, as he felt tired, that he would rest himself for a while and gaze on the lovely scenes around him.

So he laid himself down, and sleep fell upon him unawares, so that he did not wake up till the clock was striking a quarter to twelve. Then he sprang from the couch dreadfully frightened, ran to the well, filled a cup that was standing by him full of water, and hastened to get away in time.

Just as he was going out of the iron door it struck twelve, and the door fell so quickly upon him that it snapped off a piece of his heel.

When he found himself safe, he was overjoyed to think that he had got the Water of Life; and as he was going on his way homewards, he passed by the little dwarf, who, when he saw the sword and the loaf, said, "You have made a noble prize; with the sword you can at a blow slay whole armies, and the bread will never fail you."

Then the prince thought to himself, "I cannot go home to my father without my brothers" – so he said, "My dear friend, can you tell me where my two brothers are, who set out in search of the Water of Life before me and never came back?"

"I have shut them up by a charm between two mountains," said the dwarf, "because they were proud and ill-behaved, and scorned to ask advice."

The prince begged so hard for his brothers that the dwarf at last set them free, though unwillingly, saying, "Beware of them, for they have bad hearts."

Their brother, however, was greatly rejoiced to see them, and told them all that had happened to him; how he had found the Water of Life, and had taken a cup full of it; and how he had set a beautiful princess free from a spell that bound her; and how she had engaged to wait a whole year, and then to marry him, and to give him the kingdom.

Then they all three rode on together, and on their way home came to a country that was laid waste by war and a dreadful famine, so that it was feared all must die for want. But the prince gave the king of the land the bread, and all his kingdom ate of it. And he lent the king the wonderful sword, and he slew the enemy's army with it; and thus the kingdom was once more in peace and plenty. In the same manner he befriended two other countries through which they passed on their way.

When they came to the sea, they got into a ship and during their voyage the two eldest said to themselves, "Our brother has got the water which we could not find, therefore our father will forsake us and give him the kingdom, which is our right;" so they were full of envy and revenge, and agreed together how they could ruin him.

Then they waited till he was fast asleep, and poured the Water of Life out of the cup, and took it for themselves, giving him bitter sea-water instead.

When they came to their journey's end, the youngest son brought his cup to the sick king, that he might drink and be healed.

Scarcely, however, had he tasted the bitter sea-water than he became worse even than he was before; and then both the elder sons came in, and blamed the youngest for what they had done; and said that he wanted to poison their father, but that they had found the Water of Life, and had brought it with them. He no sooner began to drink of what they brought him, than he felt his sickness leave him, and was as strong and well as in his younger days.

Then they went to their brother, and laughed at him, and said, "Well, brother, you found the Water of Life, did you? You have had the trouble and we shall have the reward. Pray, with all your cleverness, why did not you manage to keep your eyes open?

"Next year one of us will take away your beautiful princess, if you do not take care. You had better say nothing about this to our father, for he does not believe a word you say; and if you tell tales, you shall lose your life into the bargain; but be quiet, and we will let you off."

The old king was still very angry with his youngest son, and thought that he really meant to have taken away his life; so he called his court together, and asked what should be done, and all agreed that he ought to be put to death.

The prince knew nothing of what was going on, till one day, when the king's chief huntsmen went a-hunting with him, and they were alone in the wood together, the huntsman looked so sorrowful that the prince said, "My friend, what is the matter with you?"

"I cannot and dare not tell you," said he.

But the prince begged very hard, and said, "Only tell me what it is, and do not think I shall be angry, for I will forgive you."

"Alas!" said the huntsman; "the king has ordered me to shoot you."

The prince started at this, and said, "Let me live, and I will change dresses with you; you shall take my royal coat to show to my father, and do you give me your shabby one."

"With all my heart," said the huntsman; "I am sure I shall be glad to save you, for I could not have shot you."

Then he took the prince's coat, and gave him the shabby one, and went away through the wood.

Some time after, three grand embassies came to the old king's court, with rich gifts of gold and precious stones for his youngest son; now all these were sent from the three kings to whom he had lent his sword and loaf of bread, in order to rid them of their enemy and feed their people.

This touched the old king's heart, and he thought his son might still be guiltless, and said to his court, "Oh that my son were still alive! How it grieves me that I had him killed!"

"He is still alive," said the huntsman; "and I am glad that I had pity on him, but let him go in peace, and brought home his royal coat."

At this the king was overwhelmed with joy, and made it known throughout all his kingdom that if his son would come back to his court he would forgive him.

Meanwhile the princess was eagerly waiting till her deliverer should come back; and had a road made leading up to her palace all of shining gold; and told her courtiers that whoever came on horseback, and rode straight up to the gate upon it, was her true lover, and they must let him in; but whoever rode on one side of it, they must be sure was not the right one, and they must send him away at once.

The time soon came when the eldest brother thought that he would make haste to go to the princess and say that he was the one who had set her free, and that he should have her for his wife, and the kingdom with her.

As he came before the palace and saw the golden road, he stopped to look at it, and he thought to himself, "It is a pity to ride upon this beautiful road;" so he turned aside and rode on the right-hand side of it. But when he came to the gate, the guards, who had seen the road he took, said to him that he could not be who he said he was, and must go about his business.

The second prince set out soon afterwards on the same errand; and when he came to the golden road, and his horse had set one foot upon it, he stopped to look at it, and thought it very beautiful, and said to himself, "What a pity it is that anything should tread here!" Then he too turned aside and rode on the left side of it. But when he came to the gate the guards said he was not the true prince, and that he too must go away about his business; and away he went.

Now when the full year was come round, the third brother left the forest in which he had lain hid for fear of his father's anger, and set out in search of his betrothed bride.

So he journeyed on, thinking of her all the way, and rode so quickly that he did not even see what the road was made of, but went with his horse straight over it; and as he came to the gate it flew open, and the princess welcomed him with joy, and said he was her deliverer, and he should now be her husband and lord of the kingdom. When the first joy at their meeting was over, the princess told him she had heard of his father having forgiven him, and of his wish to have him home again; so, before his wedding with the princess, he went to visit his father, taking her with him.

Then he told him everything – how his brothers had cheated and robbed him, and yet that he had borne all those wrongs for the love of his father. And the old king was very angry, and wanted to punish his wicked sons; but they made their escape, and got into a ship and sailed away over the wide sea, and where they went to nobody knew and nobody cared.

And now the old king gathered together his court, and asked all his kingdom to come and celebrate the wedding of his son and the princess.

And young and old, noble and squire, gentle and simple, came at once on the summons; and among the rest came the friendly dwarf, with the sugarloaf hat, and a new scarlet cloak.

And the wedding was held, and the merry bells rung, and all the good people they danced and they sang, and feasted and frolick'd I can't tell how long.

THE TWELVE HUNTSMEN

THERE WAS ONCE a king's son who had a bride whom he loved very much. And when he was sitting beside her and very happy, news came that his father lay sick unto death, and desired to see him once again before his end.

Then he said to his beloved: "I must now go and leave you. I give you a ring as a remembrance of me. When I am king, I will return and fetch you."

So he rode away, and when he reached his father, the latter was dangerously ill, and near his death. He said to him: "Dear son, I wished to see you once again before my end to have your promise you will marry as I wish," and he named a certain king's daughter who was to be his wife.

The son was in such distress that he did not think what he was doing, and said: "Yes, dear father, your will shall be done," and thereupon the king shut his eyes, and died.

When therefore the son had been proclaimed king, and the time of mourning was over, he was forced to keep the promise which he had given his father, and caused the king's daughter to be asked in marriage, and she was promised to him. His first betrothed heard of this, and fretted so much about his faithfulness that she nearly died.

Then her father said to her: "Dearest child, why are you so sad? You shall have whatsoever you will."

She thought for a moment and said: "Dear father, I wish for eleven girls exactly like myself in face, figure and size."

The father said: "If it be possible, your desire shall be fulfilled," and he caused a search to be made in his whole kingdom, until eleven young maidens were found who exactly resembled his daughter in face, figure and size.

When they came to the king's daughter, she had twelve suits of huntsmen's clothes made, all alike, and the eleven maidens had to put on the huntsmen's clothes, and she herself put on the twelfth suit. Thereupon she took her leave of her father, and rode away with them, and rode to the court of her former betrothed, whom she loved so dearly.

Then she asked if he required any huntsmen, and if he would take all of them into his service. The king looked at her and did not know her, but as they were such handsome fellows, he said he would willingly take them, and so they became the king's twelve huntsmen.

The king, however, had a lion which was a wondrous animal, for he knew all concealed and secret things. It came to pass that one evening he said to the king: "You think you have twelve huntsmen?"

"Yes," said the king, "they are twelve huntsmen."

The lion continued: "You are mistaken, they are twelve girls."

The king said: "That cannot be true! How will you prove that to me?"

"Oh, just let some peas be strewn in the ante-chamber," answered the lion, "and then you will soon see. Men have a firm step, and when they walk over peas none of them stir, but girls trip and skip and drag their feet and the peas roll about."

The king was well pleased with the counsel, and caused the peas to be strewn.

There was, however, a servant of the king's who favoured the huntsmen, and when he heard that they were going to be put to this test he went to them and repeated everything, and said: "The lion wants to make the king believe that you are girls."

Then the king's daughter thanked him, and said to her maidens: "Show some strength, and step firmly on the peas."

So next morning when the king had the twelve huntsmen called before him, and they came into the ante-chamber where the peas were lying, they stepped so firmly on them, and had such a strong, sure walk, that not one of the peas either rolled or stirred.

Then they went away again, and the king said to the lion: "You have lied to me, they walk just like men."

The lion said: "They had been informed that they were going to be put to the test, and they assumed some strength. Just let twelve spinning-wheels be brought into the ante-chamber, and they will go to them and be pleased with them, and that is what no man would do."

The king liked the advice, and had the spinning-wheels placed in the ante-chamber.

But the servant, who was well disposed to the huntsmen, went to them, and disclosed the project. So when they were alone the king's daughter said to her eleven girls: "Show some constraint, and do not look round at the spinning-wheels."

And next morning when the king had his twelve huntsmen summoned, they went through the ante-chamber, and never once looked at the spinning-wheels.

Then the king again said to the lion: "You have deceived me, they are men, for they have not looked at the spinning-wheels."

The lion replied: "They have restrained themselves." The king, however, would no longer believe him.

The twelve huntsmen always followed the king to the chase, and his liking for them continually increased.

Now it came to pass that one day, when they were out hunting, news came that the king's bride was approaching. When the true bride heard that, it hurt her so much that her heart was almost broken, and she fell fainting to the ground.

The king thought something had happened to his dear huntsman, ran up to him, wanted to help him, and drew his glove off. Then he saw the ring which he had given to his first bride, and when he looked in her face he recognised her. Then his heart was so touched that he kissed her, and when she opened her eyes he said: "You are mine, and I am yours, and no one in the world can alter that."

He sent a messenger to the other bride, and entreated her to return to her own kingdom, for he had a wife already, and someone who had just found an old key did not require a new one. Thereupon the wedding was celebrated, and the lion was again taken into favour, because, after all, he had told the truth.

THE SEVEN RAVENS

THERE WAS ONCE a man who had seven sons, and last of all one daughter. Although the little girl was very pretty, she was so weak and small that they thought she could not live and they said she should at once be christened.

So the father sent one of his sons in haste to the spring to get some water, but the other six ran with him. Each wanted to be first at drawing the water, and so they were in such a hurry that all let their pitchers fall into the well, and they stood very foolishly looking at one another, and did not know what to do, for none dared go home.

In the meantime the father was uneasy, and could not tell what made the young men stay so long. "Surely," said he, "the whole seven must have forgotten themselves over some game of play" – and when he had waited still longer and they yet did not come, he flew into a rage and wished them all turned into ravens.

Scarcely had he spoken these words when he heard a croaking over his head, and looked up and saw seven ravens as black as coal flying round and round. Sorry as he was to see his wish so fulfilled, he did not know how what was done could be undone, and comforted himself as well as he could for the loss of his seven sons with his dear little daughter, who soon became stronger and every day more beautiful.

For a long time she did not know that she had ever had any brothers, for her father and mother took care not to speak of them before her; but one day by chance she heard the people about her speak of them.

"Yes," said they, "she is beautiful indeed, but still 'tis a pity that her brothers should have been lost for her sake."

Then she was much grieved, and went to her father and mother, and asked if she had had any brothers, and what had become of them. So they dared no longer hide the truth from her, but said it was the will of heaven, and that her birth was only the innocent cause of it; but the little girl mourned sadly about it every day, and thought herself bound to do all she could to bring her brothers back; and she had

The seven ravens. (Rie Cramer)

neither rest nor ease, till at length one day she stole away, and set out into the wide world to find her brothers, wherever they might be, and free them, whatever it might cost her.

She took nothing with her but a little ring which her father and mother had given her, a loaf of bread in case she should be hungry, a little pitcher of water in case she should be thirsty, and a little stool to rest upon when she should be weary.

Thus she went on and on, and journeyed till she came to the world's end; then she came to the sun, but the sun looked much too hot and fiery; so she ran away quickly to the moon, but the moon was cold and chilly, and said, "I smell flesh and blood this way!" So she took herself away in a hurry and came to the stars, and the stars were friendly and kind to her, and each star sat upon his own little stool; but the morning star rose up and gave her a little piece of wood, and said, "If you have not this little piece of wood, you cannot unlock the castle that stands on the glass mountain; it is there your brothers live."

The little girl took the piece of wood, rolled it up in a little cloth, and went on again until she came to the glass mountain, and found the door to the castle shut. Then she felt for the little piece of wood; but when she unwrapped the cloth it was not there, and she saw she had lost the gift of the good stars.

What was to be done? She wanted to save her brothers but had no key to the castle of the glass mountain; so this faithful little sister took a knife out of her pocket and cut off her little finger, that was just the size of the piece of wood she had lost, and put it in the door and opened it.

As she went in, a little dwarf came up to her, and said, "What are you seeking for?"

"I seek for my brothers, the seven ravens," answered she.

Then the dwarf said, "My masters are not at home; but if you will wait till they come, pray step in."

Now the little dwarf was getting their dinner ready, and he brought their food upon seven little plates, and their drink in seven little glasses, and set them upon the table, and out of each little plate their sister ate a small piece, and out of each little glass she drank a small drop; but she let the ring that she had brought with her fall into the last glass.

All of a sudden she heard a fluttering and croaking in the air, and the dwarf said, "Here come my masters."

When they came in, they wanted to eat and drink, and looked for their little plates and glasses.

Then said one after the other, "Who has eaten from my little plate? And who has been drinking out of my little glass? Caw! Caw! Well I ween mortal lips have this way been."

When the seventh came to the bottom of his glass, and found there the ring, he looked at it, and knew that it was his father's and mother's, and said, "Oh that our little sister would but come! Then we should be free."

When the little girl heard this (for she stood behind the door all the time and listened), she ran forward, and in an instant all the ravens took their right form again; and all hugged and kissed each other, and went merrily home.